"Commencing DNA sampling," said Hugo, and flicked the switch.

He compared two histograms. "Different species, different genus—in fact, different *Kingdom*," he said, in slightly awed tones. "In other words, it appears to be plant not animal. This Godzilla has hide that is identical to the tree bark we found during the expedition on February fourteenth."

"This is a tree, pretending to be a dinosaur?" said Django skeptically.

"Advanced mimicry?" speculated Ben, remembering Hugo's comment the previous day, and brazenly passing it off as his own idea. "To deter aggressors?"

"Or maybe the tree we thought we found on February fourteenth was actually a Godzilla, resting?" speculated Hugo, facetiously.

"Oh, hell," said Professor Helms. This planet was driving him insane.

"Ready to cut?" said Ben.

Hugo watched the dissection intensely, rapt, his mind whirring with possibilities.

"Cut," said Professor Helms. Two robot scalpels plunged, their blades grew and they carved a line across the creature's body. Blue-red gore spilled out and a host of Butterfly birds flew out of the stomach cavity and were scooped up by DRscalpels in their sample bags and flown into the Repository for analysis. Then the great Godzilla woke up and roared a terrible roar.

RED CLAW

PHiLiP PALMER

orbit

www.orbitbooks.net
New York   London

Orbit
Hachette Book Group
237 Park Avenue, New York, NY 10017
www.HachetteBookGroup.com

First U.S. Edition: October 2009

Orbit is an imprint of Hachette Book Group, Inc. The Orbit name and logo
are trademarks of Little, Brown Book Group Limited.

The characters and events in this book are fictitious. Any similarity to real
persons, living or dead, is coincidental and not intended by the author.

Library of Congress Control Number: 2009932346

ISBN: 978-0-316-01893-7

10 9 8 7 6 5 4 3 2 1

Printed in the United States of America

Science has made us gods, even before we are worthy of being men.

—*Jean Rostand*

And accordingly all Animals may be classified in the following fashion:

a) *those that belong to the Emperor,*
b) *embalmed ones,*
c) *those that are trained,*
d) *suckling pigs,*
e) *mermaids,*
f) *fabulous ones,*
g) *stray dogs,*
h) *those that are included in this classification,*
i) *those that tremble as if they were mad,*
j) *innumerable ones,*
k) *those drawn with a fine camel's-hair brush,*
l) *others,*
m) *those that have just broken a flower vase,*
n) *those that resemble flies from a distance.*

—from the tenth-century Chinese encyclopedia
The Celestial Emporium of Benevolent Knowledge*

* The editors acknowledge the exemplary scholarship of the twentieth-century academic and writer Jorge Luis Borges, who located and cited this epic work in his book *The Analytical Language of John Wilkins (El idioma analítico de John Wilkins)*.

DAY 1

From the diary of Dr Hugo Baal

June 22nd
It's raining acid piss again. The rainbow effects are rather striking. I'm sitting on a rock typing this on my virtual screen. The rainbow is hopping about in mid-air, I've never seen that effect before—it's—what's the word? Is there a word for how that looks, and how it makes me feel? Hmm. Apparently not. Well, there should be. Anyway, it's extremely extraordinary and rather wonderful. I'm taking a photograph now for posterity, you can see it here, *in my Miscellaneous Epiphanies folder.*

On a more scientific theme: Yesterday, I identified two new species of land creature and have entered their images *and* key data *on the database. Professor Helms tacitly agrees with my hypothesis that both creatures could well be animal-plant kingdomshifters,[1] though as yet there is no way to confirm this since the specimens are a)[2] missing and b)[3] exploded. And for the time being we are going to continue with the current[4] narrowly defined Kingdom demarcations.*

The first species is small and wiggly like a worm. The other species is an Exploding-Tree with claws and motile roots. Click here *for photographs[5] and ultrasound scans[6] and key data if you failed to do so when instructed so to do in the previous paragraph.*

The Wiggly-Worm has already escaped. It managed to dissolve its hardglass cage and burrow through the metal floor and into the earth below. This was quite unexpected, since by this point the creature had already been dissected, skinned and its organs and notochord and

---

1 He grunted and said, "Whatever", which on past experience I believe to be a form of tacit assent.
2 The Wiggly-Worm.
3 The Exploding-Tree.
4 For "current", read "inadequate and outdated".
5 Of both creatures, but the one of the Exploding-Tree is pretty blurry.
6 Of the Wiggly-Worm.

roots *(??)*[7] *removed. The skin and other remnants of the Wiggly-Worm are now being kept in a secure cage, in case they transmute into some other life-form.*

Tentative classification:

Wiggly-Worm

Kingdom: Animalia or Plantae
Phylum: Platyhelminthes (provisional, probably wrong)
Class: Clipeum[8]
Order: Uredo
Family: Serpentiforma
Genus: Wigglius
Species: Wigglius davidi

By general agreement, the creature was named after Professor Helms's uncle David.

The tree was very large, like an oak tree, with a triangular trunk, so actually more like a Sequoia, with a shiny black bark, and bright purple leaves. But when we approached the tree it exploded, knocking us over, creating a forest fire, and wakening the undergrowth of sleeping Rat-Insects,[9] *which immediately swarmed aggressively, blotting out the sky, before raining down as dead carapaces at lethal velocity. Fortunately, our body armour proved sufficient to protect all members of the exploration party from death or serious injury, on this occasion.*

My surmise[10] *is that the Exploding-Tree is a plant with animal characteristics, though it's also possible it's an animal with plant characteristics, or (as I surmised above) a kingdomshifter which mutates between the two kingdoms, or it could I suppose, now I come to think about it, be*

---

7 The Professor believes these are organs of unknown function, but they sure look like roots to me.

8 From the Latin for "shield" or "disc", because of the worm's body armour, which can withstand a plasma blast for almost six seconds.

9 Which later stole all the bits of the tree, see footnote 12.

10 According to my own Kingdom classification system, which, as yet, no one else will deign to use.

a mineral growth with motile potential or maybe it's just a tree which exploded because it was inhabited by explosive parasites, or perhaps it's something else entirely. Ha! You see what fun we have here? It will be such a shame when we have to <u>terraform</u>[11] this planet.

My provisional classification is:

Exploding-Tree

Kingdom: Plantae or Animalia, maybe
Phylum: Spermatophyta???[12]
Class: Don't know
Order: Can't tell
Family: Have no notion whatsoever
Genus: Fragorarbor
Species: Fragorarbor Type A.[13]

Morale among the scientific team is high. Today we are going to attempt to capture and dissect a Godzilla.

"Helmets off, I would suggest," said Professor Helms, after completing his inspection of the shredded and scattered remnants of the bloomed Flesh-Web. He retracted his helmet, and the cold wind sheared his skin.

The air was disgusting, of course. Breathing it was like drinking treacle with embedded broken glass. But Helms needed to feel the breeze on his cheeks, and he loved to hear the singing of the birds and lizardflies and howling insects, the sighing and moaning of the overhead branches with his own ears, not via the helmet amp.

11 See Appendix 1.
12 All the bits of exploded tree were removed by Rat-Insects (*Vilius latitarum*), so no examination of the tree was possible, hence it's impossible to say if it has seeds or not.
13 We have yet to find a *Fragorarbor Type B*.

Major Sorcha Molloy followed his lead, sliding her helmet back into its casing, then running one hand through her close-cropped blonde hair. Hugo Baal, absent-mindedly, also retracted his helmet, and then he began blinking, surprised at the sun's raw beams. Then Django, Mia, Tonii and Ben all followed suit, savouring on their faces the bizarre blend of baking heat and icy wind that was so typical of this planet.

Behind them, the wagon train of Scientists and Soldiers — housed in three AmRovers and a cargo truck — waited patiently, indulging Helms's eccentricity. They had plenty of bloomed-Web samples already. His true reason for stopping was just to "take the air".

And all around them, like bloodied petals, a sprawling mass of suppurating flesh that was all that remained of a Flesh-Web that had experienced its characteristic violent, quasi-orgasmic blooming.

Helms took a sip of water, and passed the bottle to Sorcha. She skied it, pouring the water into her open mouth, then wiped her mouth with her soft glove. She was, he mused, magnificent, and terrifying, just like this planet.

Sorcha sensed his thoughts; she glared at Helms, for staring.

He hid a smile.

"Let's go," said Professor Helms, and they boarded the AmRover and headed back into the jungle.

The lead AmRover low-hovered, and its plasma cannons roared in a slow rhythm, burning a path through the densest patches of unbloomed Flesh-Web — the luridly multicoloured animal flesh that constituted the undergrowth of this alien jungle.

The other two AmRovers, huge armoured vehicles with silver and red livery, and the even vaster and uglier cargo truck swept behind in stately cortège. They moved without noise, supported on pillars of air, hovering like vast frogs over knotted grasses, shrubs and sessile animals that struggled to survive amidst the swiftly growing Webs.

And all around them the thick impermeable trunks of the Aldiss trees loomed high, creating a cathedral-like effect amidst the bleeding leaves.

Three Soldiers flew beside and above the four vehicles, plasma weapons at the ready. Their job was to protect the two Scientists, Hugo Baal and David Go, who flew one each side of AmRover 1. And *their* job was to film every plant and animal and patch of ground with versatile cameras that could "see" in the visual, ultraviolet and infrared spectra, and also functioned as microscopes and, if necessary, telescopes.

Hugo and David flew erratically, zipping across to capture close-ups of interesting wildlife, constantly forgetting they had a zoom lens on the camera of exceptional power and pixel-quality. The three Soldiers felt like sheepdogs cursed with lively and inquisitive sheep.

To make their task even harder, the expedition's docu-director and camerawoman, Mia Nightingale, was constantly hovering and darting around amongst them all, capturing wonderful shots of the imperious wagon train crashing through the jungle, the flying Scientists filming wildlife, and their brave Soldier escorts swooping along beside them.

Hugo soared fast and low, captivated by the sheer variety of small birds which flew along with him, attempting to mate with his body armour.

Sorcha, meanwhile, was piloting AmRover 1, with Professor Helms and Dr Django Llorente with her in the cockpit.

From time to time Helms looked up at the vast canopies of purple leaves above as they shimmered in the mist, and at the varied flocks of birds that patchily filled the air above them, like ants marching in file through the sky.

"*Hugo, can you catch me a couple of those little green birds?*"

"*Yes of course, Professor.*"

Hugo soared up high, and hurled a nanonet that caught the flock in flight. Then he dragged the net behind him and deposited it in the AmRover's roof hopper.

"Nicely done."

"Thank you, Professor."

The cockpit of the AmRover was spacious, with hardglass surrounds offering a vivid view of the surrounding jungle. And the air in front of each of them was filled with vast virtual screens, which allowed Helms and Sorcha and Django to check their data and their emails obsessively, as the AmRover continued its hovering flight through dense alien forest.

"Did you catch that, Django?"

"I did. Five-legged creature, the same colour as the Flesh-Web."

Sorcha narrowed her eyes. She hadn't seen anything.

Django was a handsome dark-skinned man, with eerily staring eyes. Helms had never warmed to him, but no one could doubt his intelligence, or blazing ambition.

Professor Helms himself was less than handsome, skinnily slender, not tall, not especially good-looking, and had once-myopic eyes that now were blessed with 20/20 vision but had left him with a tendency to squint. He had a gentle, mellifluous voice, and rarely spoke louder than a murmur.

Beside him, on the curving front couch of the cockpit, sat Major Sorcha Molloy. As always, Sorcha was scowling and anxious, anticipating potential disasters. She'd lost thirteen Soldiers in two years to the New Amazonian habitat, through a variety of terrible mishaps:

- shaken to death by predators (6)
- blown up and brain-damaged by the blast of Exploding-Trees (2)
- boiled alive in their body armour by forest fires of impossible heat (2)
- consumed by pollen (1)
- eaten alive by insects that had nested in their body armour (2)

She had come to regard the planet as an enemy of appalling duplicity and malice.

Sorcha was tall, at least a head taller than Helms, and muscular, with close-cropped blond hair and pale blue eyes. She steered with one hand on a virtual wheel, occasionally flicking a virtual joystick with her other hand to control height and speed, and treating the notion of small talk with the contempt she felt it deserved.

Django sat in the brooding silence, longing for chit-chat.

Helms sighed, but didn't dare risk embarking upon a conversation, so instead listened to a concerto on his mobile implant.

And Sorcha sat, and worried, and scowled. She hated this planet; she despised Scientists; she hated science in totality; and she loathed all aliens.

Her scorn followed her like a familiar.

Helms felt his stomach lurch.

The AmRover was meant to be gyroscopically controlled, but it juddered and plunged every time there was an obstacle or a leaping predator or a scary-looking plant form. And whenever they passed close to the Flesh-Webs, tendrils leaped out and clung to the hull and cockpit of the vehicle. It made him feel as if spiders were weaving webs over his eyes.

And now, with his visor on full magnification, Helms could see how the Webs were constantly oozing red pus down on to the soil, propagating and forming rivers and ponds of scarlet excrement, from which new Webs would eventually emerge.

He considered it to be a wondrous sight; like watching blood give birth.

"*Target dead ahead,*" said Dr Ben Kirkham over his MI, and Helms's spirits soared.

The wagon train emerged into a jungle oasis. This was a vast, eerie clearing fringed by more huge tree trunks, where the Flesh-Webs were unable to thrive because of the poisonous soil. The soil also exhaled a methane-based smog, creating a grey miasma of vileness all around them.

Helms debarked from the AmRover, and hovered in his body armour above the deadly soil. Light shone through the purple leaves of the Canopy in thick beams, bouncing off the mirror-leafed plants that thrived in soil that was too barren for almost any other living thing.

And there, grazing on mirrored bushes and shrubs in the fog-infested oasis, lurked the Godzilla. It was sixty feet high, scarlet-scaled, reptilian in appearance, with no eyes, and a barbed tongue that could be expelled like a sword being ripped from a scabbard.

"*Start filming,*" Professor Helms subvoced into his MI.

Mia flew forward with her camera on its bodymount, capturing the Godzilla in full panoramic 3D glory. She circled around it, then flew above to get the aerial view, and the Godzilla became aware of her and turned its head to face her. Mia kept her distance, using her zoom to capture glorious close-ups of the monster's spittle and slime.

"Ultrasound, please," said Professor Helms.

From AmRover 1, Django fired an ultrasound pulse at the Godzilla, which troubled it visibly. A full interior image of the beast appeared on their helmet screens, revealing two hearts, a complex lung structure, and the usual abundance of Butterfly-Bird symbiotes.

"*It's very different,*" David Go subvocalised cautiously to the others on their MIs.

"*One heart more than it ought to have*," said Hugo.

"*If those are hearts*," mused Professor Helms, judiciously.

Beside him, Sorcha subvoced to her team: "*Alpha, move closer, Beta, prepare for covering fire, Gamma, wait for my command.*" The body-armoured Soldiers moved into position.

Django completed a spectrometer scan. "*I'm getting clear traces of chlorophyll.*"

"*Perhaps it's a different species which mimics the Godzilla form,*" suggested Hugo.

"Or a later stage in the creature's life cycle."

"*Or just different.*"

"*Let's take it down,*" Professor Helms suggested.

"*Let's take it down,*" Sorcha ordered, and the Soldiers moved into firing positions.

Dr Ben Kirkham sat in front of his virtual computer screen in AmRover 1, and 3D holograms encircled him as he waved his hands in swift, wizardly fashion. He was watching the take-down via Mia's camera feed. He was also studying the choreography of the attack team based on their satnav positions, as well as the aerial views from the hull cameras of the hovering Dravens and the footage from the army of robocams that flew randomly in a ten-kilometre area around the AmRovers, to keep an eye out for other xenohostiles.

In theory, Juno was able to keep track of such dangers; in practice, computer brains were sometimes slow to read complex meaning into complex data. That's where human intuition came in so handy.

So Ben multi-tasked effortlessly, slipping from location to location with practised skill, all the while checking the cloud density and weather prediction models, just in case there was a storm on the way.

Nothing was amiss; the nearest predators were a herd of Juggernauts, nine klicks away, milling, not moving aggressively. He also saw Gryphons in flight. Buzzswarms over the Fetid Lake. A cloud shaped like a jigsaw. A hailstorm, brewing, but far away, over the area to the south of Xabar. A minor earth tremor, on the continent of Quetzalcoatl. A battle between rival gangs of arboreals in the canopy, three kilometres from here. Nothing to worry about.

On his staggering array of virtual screens, he saw all this, saw the Godzilla fall to the ground via Mia's panoramic 3D camera, and also saw a half-dozen different versions of the moment from the body-armour cameras of everyone else at the scene.

Private Tonii Newton was flying up close to the action when the Godzilla fell. The huge beast was clearly shocked and baffled as the Soldiers fired batteries of low-level plasma blasts at its body, whilst simultaneously hurling grenades at its feet to rip away the ground it was standing on. And thus it fell, and the impact threw small creatures out of trees and made the earth shake.

Tonii's helmet and body armour were drenched, as sheets of humidity splashed upwards from the undergrowth like rain in reverse. The Godzilla lay on the ground and roared with rage and, presumably, pain. The Soldiers' plasma blasts had left burn marks on the vast creature's scales. It should be unconscious but clearly it wasn't.

Because a bare moment later the Godzilla leapt up in a single fast and fluid movement and was back on its feet, standing on bomb-ploughed soil, swinging the tail that was attached to the back of its head like a club. Tonii veered to one side, only just avoiding the blow, and his heart painfully skipped a beat.

"Phase One unsuccessful," Helms murmured subvocally, as the Godzilla ploughed into the other two Soldiers and scattered them like skittles. The Soldiers bounced and crashed but suffered no lack of dignity.

"*I've got it covered!*" screamed Tonii.

"*Do not use lethal force, repeat, do not use lethal force, please,*" said Helms, in his infuriatingly calm voice.

Tonii wanted to weep with frustration. The creature was smashing one of his colleagues with its huge tail, he yearned to blow its body into pieces. "*Fire a dart,*" said Helms. Tonii fired his neural dart and it landed in the creature's scales and shot thousands of volts into the monster's body, to very little effect.

Tonii hovered, as the creature worked out where he was and what he had done. He could swear it was *angry* with him. But he held his position, hovering in mid-air, as the Godzilla steadied itself to strike.

It struck with its head-tail, and Tonii dodged skilfully out of the way, then flew back and hovered close to the beast, using himself as bait.

The Godzilla lunged again — but at precisely that moment the Dravens, remotely controlled by Ben Kirkham, soared swiftly downwards and opened their hulls. Sticky nets tumbled out and dropped over the Godzilla.

The vast beast promptly sweated corrosive acid from its pores, as all these New Amazon creatures tended to do, and the nets dissolved.

"*Do not use lethal force, do not! Hold fire!*" Helms repeated, as Tonii angrily turned his plasma gun to full blast. He could see the two skittled Soldiers were back on their feet, unscathed, but even so the killing rage was on him.

But by now the Godzilla was disorientated from its fall, and out of poison pus. So Tonii repented his rage, and switched the plasma gun off, and fired another neural dart, and this time the beast faltered.

Tonii was joined by the other Soldiers — two grunts and Major Molloy. They hovered in formation and fired more neural darts and this time the Godzilla spat and roared and the gale blew them out of the air.

Damn!

Tonii hit the ground hard, and bounced back up, and watched

as the Harpoons flew into position—dumb-robot spears, remotely controlled by Juno, that hovered above the ground and then plunged unerringly into the Godzilla's midriff. The Harpoons then fired fast pulses of ultrasound into the creature's inner torso, causing it to tremble uncontrollably, brutally disabling its motor impulses. Suddenly the Godzilla could not move, or roar, or fight. It was frozen to the spot, like a mammoth in ice.

From start to finish the whole battle had taken about ten minutes.

And Tonii sighed inwardly with regret. He knew he had played his role well; but he always hated it when the robots got to take down the beast.

Before the Godzilla could stir, Dravens dropped more sticky nets, which hardened as they touched, and left the monster completely trapped. Once the sticky fibres had fully set, these diamond-hard containing ropes would be virtually unbreakable.

"*A job well done,*" Helms murmured on his private MI channel to Sorcha.

"*We could have killed the fucking thing in half the time,*" Sorcha muttered back.

Helms remembered to click off his MI link before he sighed, despairingly.

"*Stampede approaching,*" Ben said suddenly, over the general channel, then added, with just a hint of anxiety in his tone, "*Approaching fast. Four Godzillas and a, and a, well, some other kind of thing, I'm uploading the image now.*"

Helms looked at the image projected on his camera. "*What the—*" he began to say, and almost swore.

And then the stampede struck.

The Flesh-Webs exploded; a terrible screaming/keening noise

shrilled out; and the monsters stormed into the clearing like demons fleeing hell.

"Another new species..." murmured Hugo, delightedly, as he realised the pack of four rampaging Godzillas was accompanied by a rhino-type beast unknown to him with a central horn on each of its three heads.

"Let's call it a Cerberus," Hugo added swiftly, elated.

"That name has already been—" Helms began to say, then he was silent, for he knew what was about to happen.

"Engage the enemy!" said Sorcha, joyously, and she and two of her Soldiers went on one knee, plasma cannons raised. Tonii flew up above them, to provide aerial support.

And suddenly Tonii was full of glorious energy. His plasma gun was charged to full. This was a battle to the—

Mia flew past him with stunning speed and hovered in front of the great beasts, smack in the path of his intended plasma beam.

"Out of the fucking way!" Sorcha roared.

The Godzillas saw her and thrashed their vast single-clawed paws at her. The rhino-type creature—the Cerberus—bellowed and spat venom that splashed harmlessly off her armour and melted the undergrowth below.

"I said: Out. Of. The. Fucking. Way!" screamed Sorcha.

"You're a marvel, Mia, get those close-ups!" howled Hugo.

Mia was flying and framing shots at the same time. Her flight path was erratic, but her exceptional flying skills kept her well clear of the beasts. She got a wonderful panning sequence of the Godzillas, then filmed the charging Cerberus, still keeping a safe height; but was astonished when whipcords emerged from the spines in its back and lashed a thousand metres into the air to catch her and drag her to the ground.

Mia crashed hard, trying to keep her body loose. And the Cerberus lifted her again, ready to smash her to pieces.

"Fire and kill," said Sorcha calmly. She and her Soldiers fired with unerring accuracy and a haze of plasma-beam energy ripped across the clearing. There was a devastating flash of light as the plasma

beams intersected, and the tribe of vast monsters disintegrated into puddles of blood and gore.

The total obliteration of the army of monsters was achieved in less than a quarter-second. And the after-image of the burning beasts lived in the eyes of all who witnessed it for a millisecond more, before their eyes cleared and then there was nothing.

"*We could have taken that new one as a specimen,*" Hugo said, plaintively.

"*Urgh, fuck,*" said Mia, lying on the ground, badly winded.

Sorcha glowered. These civilians had no fucking sense.

As the Scientists soared across to inspect the gloop that had once been alien flesh, Tonii flew over to Mia. He felt a deep rage at her foolishness in hindering their battle, but when he spoke his tone was surprisingly gentle:

"*Are you OK?*"

She retracted her helmet and spat teeth. There was blood dripping from her nose. "You bet!" she crowed.

And then Tonii retracted his own helmet. His long black hair flowed in the icy breeze. He was amused at her beaming face, and couldn't resist grinning back.

And Mia, though she ached all over, couldn't help adoring the perfect beauty of this calmly dangerous man.

"*Let's get this specimen back to base, if we may,*" said Professor Helms.

Inside the AmRover, Ben waved his wizard hands, to guide the Dravens downwards.

The Dravens descended, until they were hovering low above the clearing, and then they began to winch the unconscious and sole surviving Godzilla up in their super-fine net.

The battle was over; the beast was caught.

And Helms realised with some surprise that his pulse was still racing, his heart still pounding. He'd been shocked when the monsters had suddenly erupted into the clearing; blind panic had seized him and he had been consumed by the bitter-sweet nauseous exhilaration of being close to death.

It reminded him of those other times in his life when he had been so very close to death. In that moment of total terror, like a drunk experiencing dizziness, his memories of his past fears merged with his present fear and coalesced into a single fight-or-flight epiphany.

And he *loved it*. He loved being terrified. He loved hunting. He loved the thrill of the chase. He loved it when disasters befell them and they had to escape by the skin of their teeth. He was, despite his calm professorial manner, despite his cautious and judicious approach to things, addicted to danger.

"Are you all right, Professor?" Django asked.

"I'm fine," Helms conceded, anxiously. "I do get rather tense at these moments, you know. I'm much happier," he added, self-deprecatingly, and quite untruthfully, "behind my computer screen, or in the lab."

Django grinned. His eyes were bright. He, too, was high.

The Scientists commenced their task of sectoring the area — analysing every last centimetre of the site, catologuing every single plant and bug, every lurking animal, every bird that flew overhead and all the microscopic creatures in the bushes and topsoil and air, and drilling out a vast tube of subsoil to analyse its constitution and ecology in the same painstaking detail.

Major Sorcha Molloy walked over to Ben Kirkham. "So, explain yourself," she said quietly.

"What?" Ben said loudly, staring not at her but beyond her, in an infuriating fashion. "Are you addressing me, Major?"

"You missed five hostiles," she said, quietly still, and this time Ben caught the warning tone in her voice, but still he wouldn't meet her eyes.

"I didn't *miss* them," he said, defensively.

"You didn't say they were coming, and they came. Those were huge creatures, how the fuck could you not have seen them?"

"Must have been," Ben said snidely, "a computer malfunction? Or maybe I was, as always, doing the work of ten men? Hmm? Let's be honest, now, could you do what I do? No? No! I don't think so!" he crowed.

"Don't you be fucking whatchmacall with me," Sorcha snarled.

"Do you mean, perhaps, 'ironic'? Ah, I think you do." Then Ben did a rapid double take of shock and horror. "Me? *Ironic?* Heaven forbid!"

Sorcha felt like punching him.

"Is there a problem?" said Helms, strolling across.

Sorcha scowled. "No."

Helms smiled shyly, and paused for a while, and Sorcha and Ben leaned over to hear what he might say. Eventually he murmured: "Come now, Ben, be candid; is there a problem?"

"This bitch is busting my balls."

Helms carried on smiling. Sorcha glared.

"I wonder, actually, if you should apologise, old chap," said Helms, mildly.

"The fuck I will."

And still Helms was smiling that faint half-smile of his. "Ben, you're one of the smartest men I've ever met," he conceded. "You're brilliant, you hardly ever make mistakes. And when you do make an error—you're the first to admit it! I admire that."

Ben basked in the Professor's approbation. "I guess—well, all things considered." He took a deep breath. Then: "I'm sorry, Major," he said, warmly. "I screwed up, I don't know how. But I promise it won't ever happen again."

And he walked off, content.

Sorcha seethed. How the fuck did Helms *do* that?

"That man's a liability," she muttered.

"He's a brilliant—" Helms broke off, seeing the rage in Sorcha's eyes, and swiftly corrected himself: "You're absolutely right, Major, the man's a total pain in the arse," he said, in tones that exuded outrage. "But don't worry, I shall keep him in check."

"You see you do."

"I will."

"His attitude is poor."

"Yes, Major."

Sorcha fumed.

"But the real question," Helms added, "is why *Juno* didn't spot those hostiles. It wasn't exactly subtle—they started charging a mile away."

"Maybe she was distracted."

"Computer brains do not get distracted. What the hell is wrong with her?"

Hugo sat on a tree trunk and started typing up his journal, eyes scrunched up with intense concentration. His screen was virtual, and his stubby fingers poked at incorporeal keys that floated in mid-air.

Dr Hugo Baal was a great and highly acclaimed xenobiologist, one of the legendary figures in a field full of legendary figures. He was also, to his chagrin, a short fat man in a world of tall, slim, good-looking, muscular giants.

His parents had been eco-freaks, and he had been cursed with a natural birth—no in vitro modifying, no tinkering with his height and physique genes.

As a boy, his lack of tallness and slimness had bothered Hugo enormously. He'd been bullied and mocked, and ignored by the tall, cool good-looking guys and the tall, beautiful girls.

So Hugo had taunted the tall guys with a series of cutting and brilliant one-liners; and he had seduced and won the hearts of the beautiful girls with his understated charm, his eloquence, his wistful eyes.

Or at least, in his restless imagination, all these things had happened, and were true. In real life, however, no one had liked him: he was just the short fat kid. Consequently he became an outcast, and a social pariah, and spent all his time studying bugs.

But these days, he didn't care about being short and fat and not popular. Because Hugo knew he was cleverer, by far, indeed several orders of magnitude cleverer and more brilliant, than all of those tall, slim, muscular, good-looking bastards put together.

Except, perhaps, for Professor Helms, who was quite awe-inspiringly clever, and undoubtedly a genius.

Hugo nursed a dark secret, which was not in fact a secret at all, since all his colleagues had long ago guessed it: he was jealous of the Professor. For Helms knew an amazing number of facts; he was an acclaimed expert in his sphere, and many others; he was a natural leader; and for some astonishing reason, women seemed to find him attractive.

It was so damned unfair!

The Dravens flew in convoy, carrying the Godzilla in an aerial lift above the canopy of trees.

Below them, Two-Tails scampered in the amber light that shone off the greenness of the great circle-leaves. Gryphons glided in the upper atmosphere, warily watching the robot birds below effortlessly carrying the fifty-ton stunned behemoth. A flock of Stymphalian birds rocketed past the Dravens, dropping poisoned shit downwards, only to be blasted out of the sky with a few carefully placed smart-laser blasts.

The Dravens, sleek robot aircraft, were extraordinarily manoeuvrable, and could turn in the air faster than a hawk. They were jet-black but jewelled, so they shone in the sun, creating a glare designed to disorientate enemies. And each of them was, in the normal course of events, remotely controlled by Juno, the Mother Ship's quantum computer, which treated the robot bodies on New Amazon as its limbs and eyes.

And so the Dravens flew, through white and blue and ochre clouds, while all around them swooped and soared a vast variety of New Amazonian birds. Light shone on their robot carapaces, and the billowing purple canopy stretched below as they towed the vast unconscious Godzilla through the air.

After two gruelling hours of travelling, the convoy reached Xabar and drove into the Cleansing Bay. Red-hot sprays purged the exteriors of the AmRovers and the cargo truck.

Then the Scientists and Soldiers stepped out in their body armour and were drenched by cleansing showers.

Sorcha was putting on her uniform, a semi-armoured black and gold trouser suit with major's epaulettes above her left breast, as Helms approached her.

"A successful day, I believe, sir," Helms said courteously.

"Kirkham is a total fuck-up, you should get rid of him."

"I don't think I—"

"You don't need him! He failed in his duties today. Replace him."

"He's our best—"

"Fuck-up! If he was one of mine, I'd kick him out of the airlock."

"I concede that he does occupy his own unique niche on the autistic spectrum," Helms acknowledged gently.

"Fuck-up!"

"Well, you have a point," Helms sighed, then added: "Good day, Major." He made an amusing little wavy hand gesture to bid her farewell, as was his wont.

"You're dismissed when I say so," she snapped, and Helms visibly bridled. He hated military authority.

"So will you be attending the—" he said, stalling, knowing what was to come.

"I'll be there."

"Good. Then, I'll, ah, um." Helms ran out of road on that one.

An awkward pause followed.

"Very well, you're dismissed," said Major Sorcha Molloy, and briskly clicked her left heel on the ground, and fist-saluted. Helms sighed, and copied her salute, as he had been taught to do. It was a visible effort.

Sorcha stifled a smile.

Sorcha returned to the Military Quarter and verbally reported to Commander Martin in his book-lined office.

"Any problems, Major?"

"No, sir."

"No problems?" Martin's tone used incredulity like a club.

"Inadequate warning of xeno-hazard, sir, but we were on top of it."

"You shouldn't delegate surveillance and security to a civilian." Martin spoke mildly, luringly.

"Those were your orders, sir." And as she spoke, Sorcha knew she should not have said such a stupid thing.

"Blaming *me*?" Martin's tone was now enraged.

"No, SIR my mistake, SIR, I fucked up, SIR."

"Hmm."

Silence was the goad now. Sorcha endured it.

"Ten minutes to subdue the Godzilla," said the Commander, eventually, with even greater incredulity than before.

"Yes, sir."

"Nice work."

"Yes, sir."

Martin's tone was brisk, and unimpressed, and sardonic, and hyper-critical, and Sorcha had to fight to keep her cool.

"That will do, Major."

"Thank you, Commander."

"Dismissed."

"Sir!"

Click, fist-salute, about turn, and she left the room, wondering, marvelling even, why the hell a serving Soldier would read *books*.

Then Sorcha went to the gym and spent an hour working out on the punchbags and robo-pads. Afterwards, she needle-showered under a hot fast spray that massaged as it cleansed.

And then she went to her quarters. The room was dark, lit by candles. Professor Richard Helms was waiting for her.

"I thought you had an autopsy to conduct?" she told him sternly.

"It's scheduled for 8 p.m. We have plenty of time."

"Why the candles?"

"It gives you a golden glow. I find it—alluring."

"You'd like me naked, I take it?"

"That would be nice."

She took off her major's tunic and trousers and knickers. Then she straddled him, bit his lip brutally, fumbled for his cock, and slipped him inside her.

"Is this what the military call foreplay?"

She grabbed his head with her hands and shook him and moved her hips on him and the orgasm hit her like a punch.

She was quiet, apart from a few long gasps, for several moments.

"I needed that," she conceded.

"Christ," said Helms, weakly.

Then she slipped off him and stripped fully and she moved naked and slowly for him in the dim golden candlelight, and her body was beautiful, and graceful, and sublime. Then he reached out for her and

Afterwards, he slept in her powerful arms.

He rarely slept at night these days; only after sex. It was a blissful time for him, his body content, his mind at rest.

As he drowsed against her, Sorcha was subvocing her orders for the next day. The sweat had dried on her naked body. She was amused at how thin and scrawny Helms's body seemed, when you saw it next to hers. But Sorcha loved these moments of post-coital repose.

After a while, she woke Helms up, and with a few unambiguous gestures instructed him to go at it a third time. This time he excelled himself, and she came five times in a row, like waves hitting a cliff.

Then she rolled off him, and started to dress.

It occurred to Helms that his affair with Sorcha had lasted two months, in which time he had never had a single interesting or personally revealing conversation with her.

"I know nothing about you," he marvelled, as they both got ready to return to the lab.

"I'm a Soldier. There's nothing to know," she told him, blankly puzzled.

Sorcha was ten years old when she killed her first man. He was a prisoner, captured during a rebellion on some colony planet, she never knew which one, and released to the Soldier Planets as training fodder. Sorcha was given a knife and sent into the forest and told to track the man down. When she found him, she cut his throat, and watched him slowly die, then daubed the blood on her forehead. It was called "blooding". Sorcha loathed the experience. She didn't know the man, nor did she hate him. She felt sorry for him really. But her father and mother had told her she needed to become a woman, and a Soldier, and this was her rite of passage.

And so, and then, her childhood ended.

When Sorcha was twelve, she served in her first war, as munitions backup on an attack vessel that was repressing a rebellion on another colony planet. She loaded the guns, and served sandwiches and cold drinks to the Soldiers as they flew low over the land shooting rebels at will.

When Sorcha was fourteen she met her first Doppelganger Robot. It was one of the Humanoid models, seven foot tall and silver, and it was terrifying. But by then Sorcha was a fully trained and battle-hardened Soldier and she knew that DRs weren't any match for a trained and disciplined human warrior. They were just machines, remotely controlled by game-playing amateurs on Earth who had nothing at stake bar their pride.

But Soldiers were *warriors*, born and bred, fuelled by the fear of death. And Sorcha knew that (provided the Soldier was wearing body armour with a full complement of built-in weaponry) in a fight between a DR and a Soldier, the Soldier would always win.

However, by the rules of her world, the Earth humans who controlled the DRs were the governing élite of human space. And so this particular DR—controlled by a tag team of fools and idiots—was the Commanding Officer of her regiment, and it was his responsibility to lead the attack on a rebel planet.

He did so incompetently, and recklessly, and stupidly. The battle was lost, and most of the Soldiers slaughtered, including many of Sorcha's closest friends.

But no one protested, and no one minded, and no one mourned. For Soldiers were bred and trained and put into the world to serve, and fight, and die in glory.

Sorcha loved being a Soldier. It gave her focus and purpose. She never had doubts or second thoughts or angst or melancholy or despair. Being a Soldier was a religion, and a cause.

The joy of giving and the prospect of receiving death exalted her.

Twenty minutes later Sorcha entered the lab to find Helms hard at work, Hugo and Django at their work stations, and Mia reviewing her footage on her virtual screen. Sorcha gave Helms a withering glare; in return, he gave her a humble, self-deprecating smile.

And no one suspected a thing. Which was fortunate, since the consequences of exposure would have been severe. In theory, Helms could be sacked as the expedition leader for fraternising with a Soldier; and Sorcha would almost certainly face demotion, or even a court martial.

The danger added a spice to their relationship; it was, for both of them, a mad folly. For two whole months, Sorcha and Helms had been lost in lust, defying their society's most fundamental taboo, based on the unbridgable divide between the Soldier caste and the Scientist caste. But so far, their mutual cunning had kept their secret hidden from everyone.

"Are we ready?" Sorcha asked.

"We're ready," Helms told her.

They moved into the main autopsy room, where the Godzilla was stretched out on the dissection table. Hugo took his place at the control desk, Helms fastened on a throat mike to record his words, rather than using his MI; Django checked the beast's vitals; Ben put on his virtual goggles; two Soldiers stood by just in case. And Mia began filming the whole affair with a hand-held cam.

DRscalpels hovered in the air like hummingbirds; DRcams flew among them more sedately, like owls peering at prey. Ben controlled them all effortlessly. His expertise at gaming gave him an exceptional ability to manipulate the various Doppelganger tools.

"Ultrasound scans show a different organ structure in this specimen," said Helms, "which we here label G433. It has two hearts not one, though it may be these are not hearts at all. The lungs are larger and more complex. We are exploring the possibility that this is a radically different species of Godzilla, or indeed a different genus entirely. First incision, please, Ben."

Ben nodded, and his hands waved over his virtual controls. The DRscalpels soared down and pecked at the creature's tough hide, as Ben controlled them with precision movements of his fingers, hands and arms, whilst using the goggles to see through their "eyes". A morsel was held in the scalpels' "teeth" and it was bagged and the bag was flown into the Repository.

"Commencing DNA sampling," said Hugo, and flicked the switch. He compared two histograms. "Different species, different genus—in fact, different *Kingdom*," he said, in slightly awed tones. "In other words, it appears to be plant not animal. This Godzilla has hide that is identical to the tree bark we found during the expedition on February fourteenth."

"This is a tree, pretending to be a dinosaur?" said Django sceptically.

"Advanced mimicry?" speculated Ben, remembering Hugo's comment the previous day, and brazenly passing it off as his own idea. "To deter aggressors?"

"Or maybe the tree we thought we found on February fourteenth was actually a Godzilla, resting?" speculated Hugo, facetiously.

"Oh, hell," said Professor Helms. This planet was driving him insane.

"Ready to cut?" said Ben.

Hugo watched the dissection intensely, rapt, his mind whirring with possibilities.

"Cut," said Professor Helms. Two robot scalpels plunged, their blades grew and they carved a line across the creature's body. Blue-red gore spilled out and a host of Butterfly-Birds flew out of the stomach cavity, to be scooped up by DRscalpels in their sample bags and flown into the Repository for analysis. Then the great Godzilla woke up and roared a terrible roar.

"Who's in charge of the anaesthetic?" Helms said irritably.

"I'm on it," said Django, and fired a compressed-air cylinder containing genetically engineered curare into the beast's body. The beast roared again and stood up on the slab and fell off, and its internal organs spewed out. And then with stunning speed, the creature lunged and ate two DRscalpels and glared at Helms and his team.

"You want a fight?" snarled Helms and gestured to Ben, who waved his hands. Several DRscalpels leaped off the bench and plunged through the monster's hide and into its body. Then ran amok inside, cutting and gouging. The creature roared and writhed and its eyeballs tumbled out. Great rivers of blue-red blood torrented into the air, drenching the floating robots and the Scientists and Soldiers, and eventually the beast stopped moving.

"The Godzilla is now dead, we are recommencing the autopsy," said Helms, as the creature split into four parts and each part scurried across the floor with teeth bared.

A haze of plasma fire appeared from behind them, as the two Soldiers on sentry duty calmly did their job, and the alien beast dissolved.

"Autopsy officially fucked up," said Helms calmly. "Django, I thought you said you could anaesthetise the beast?"

"Well, I thought I could," marvelled Django.

"Another fiasco," concluded Helms, still calmly. "Can we commence the clean-up?"

He glanced at Sorcha and winked and, taken off-guard, she blushed.

Django saw it, and was startled, and amused.

Sorcha seethed at Helms's foolish blunder.

Helms wondered: Why the hell did I just do that?

Hugo Baal blinked; he'd missed all of this, he was so rapt in marvelling at the indefinable beauty of the horror they had just witnessed.

Ben MI'd a command and the drone robot appeared—a squat watering can that waddled on four legs. He instructed the machine to start cleaning up, but the robot drone didn't move.

"Clean up this mess!" Ben instructed it, just to be doubly sure.

Still the drone didn't move.

"We have another minor malfunction here," Ben told the Professor, anxiously.

"What the hell is going on?" snapped Django.

"Juno, what's wrong with this drone?" Sorcha said to the ship's computer.

But there was no response from Juno.

"Juno?"

"Yes, Major?"

"I asked you a fucking question, tinbrain!"

"There's no point in, um, swearing at a computer," said Ben Kirkham, helpfully.

"Maybe we should reboot the drones?" Hugo Baal suggested.

"Systems check in progress," Juno countered, with a hint of acid in its computer tone.

As the drone started clearing up the carnage. Helms realised he was spattered with alien blood. And he sighed.

Mia came up to him, reviewing her film footage on her camera as she walked. She frowned, reframed, clicked; and that was a wrap.

"You hate killing these things, don't you?" she said to Helms, with a shy and pretty smile, putting the camera away in her bag, rather too ostentatiously.

"Of course not," Helms said cautiously. "Our secondary purpose is to study these creatures. Our main purpose is to prepare this planet for human habitation."

"I'm not filming you, you know."

"A sentimental attachment to the sanctity of life runs counter to the CSO's Guidelines for Scientists," Helms explained, still in that same stiff stilted tone.

"My camera is in my bag and switched off!" Mia twinkled.

"And you don't have hidden cameras in your contact lenses?" Helms countered.

"Touché," said Mia, "but you can't blame a girl for trying." Mia loved scenes of controversy and dissent in her docs. The highlight of her career was when she filmed a Major General dissing the CSO, calling him a "callow little shit" (her follow-up film on the Major General's execution was a ratings buster). But these days, everyone was so cautious in what they said.

"I abhor waste," said Helms. "That's why we perform autopsies on live animals. So we can stitch them up again and then release them back into the wild."

"And how many Godzillas will you be saving for the Galactic Zoo?" Mia asked, sweetly. Her contact-lens cameras caught a wonderful image of Helms's face darkening with impotent rage.

At last count, Helms knew, there were fourteen million Godzillas on the planet of New Amazon.

"Two," said Professor Helms.

The Xabar dome was almost invisible in daylight. The city of black towers and squat silver buildings looked weirdly out of place amongst the lush jungle habitat.

Then a dark cloud slowly drifted down on the dome. And settled there, in a fine dark haze.

The dome opened, and the darkness seeped inside.

The lab was almost deserted now; but Hugo stayed behind, taking biopsy samples from the slime on the ground. After each sample was taken, he stepped away to let the drone suck up what was left of the Godzilla.

Django was back at his work station, cursing his own stupidity. How could he have failed to keep the beast unconscious? Perhaps its neural network was immune to electronic anaesthesia. And yet...?

He checked his log and realised, with some astonishment, that the figures for the anaesthesia levels were all wrong; the sedation had been mild to the point of futility. He'd totally screwed things up.

And yet, as he thought back on it, he was sure he'd typed in the right levels! He was famously thorough, obsessively careful. All the same, on this occasion he must have been incompetent. Unless...

No! That was impossible. Computer error was a thing of the past.

Django concluded he must have been daydreaming, or had simply mistyped the figures.

A tendril of fear coiled around his heart. He never made mistakes. Ever. But this *had* to be his fault.

There was simply no other explanation.

Ben Kirkham was considering a dangerous possibility. What if—

Mia returned to her cabin and replayed her footage of the Godzilla attack.

She zoomed in on the expression on Professor Helms's face. Everyone else in the 3D picture looked afraid, or alarmed. Scientists were like that: they always panicked in the face of deadly peril.

But Helms—he looked almost *elated*.

And the darkness continued to seep in, in three separate places. Above the Botanical Gardens, above the Shopping Mall, and above the Central Park.

Mark Jones, Hydroponics Supervisor, was in the Botanical Gardens when the plants started to die.

At first it was merely perplexing. A monkey puzzle tree started to shed its bark. An orchid deflowered, like a consumptive sneezing. A mist of pink petals rained down from the cherry trees. He began to wonder if—

Then he heard screaming. When he looked around he saw the Gardeners on the floor, writhing, and he realised that the Gardens were becoming engulfed in a black haze.

He clicked on his MI. "*This is, um,*" he began, and was suddenly too frightened to subvocalise. The deadly swarm began to move towards him. He realised that the trees were being eaten from inside, and the canopies of leaves above him were already dead.

He began to run. He pushed through plants, and left huge boot prints in soil that had been freshly planted with fragile bulbs. He could hear more screaming from behind him, but he blocked off the noise and focused on running, and then he threw himself through the double doors and slammed them shut.

He could still hear the screaming inside. He could distinguish words. "Help!" "Please!" "Help!" But he kept the doors closed.

Mark closed his eyes and started to weep.

"Who opened the fucking dome?"

Professor Helms was halfway across the courtyard when the warning siren went off in his inner ear.

"What's happening, Juno?" he asked, and heard resounding silence.

"The dome has been breached," said Commander Martin's voice in his ear.

"But that's not—" Helms began to say, then Martin logged off.

Black rain drizzled down on to the shopping streets of Xabar, in the Mall area. A passerby looked up.

And his eyes were eaten. His face was eaten. His tongue fell out of his mouth and moved like a living thing on the ground.

He screamed, but no noise emerged.

A giant oak tree dominated the city's Central Park—a lab-created mutant that in six months had grown into a gnarled, vast, sprawling thing. But the leaves were falling from the tree now. Black darkness oozed from the bark.

A squirrel fell from the tree, stone dead. Two children saw it fall and screamed.

A Soldier saw it too; and raised his plasma gun; and the tree vanished in a haze of heat, and the darkness lay dead on the scorched ground.

Sorcha was leaving the Soldiers' Quarters, after a successful game of Knife Poker, when she heard the warning siren. She logged on to hear the details of the disaster, and listened intently.

"Fuck," she said, and accessed her squadron MI channel, and subvoced the Alpha Alert.

Soldiers with paramedic training ran through the shopping streets and saw the writhing corpses on the ground. They raised their plasma guns and tried to burn the black darkness away but the darkness ducked and dodged, and the plasma blasts flew harmlessly past it.

Helms had reached his study, breathless and concerned, when he got the update message on his MI.

"*Fifteen dead, so far,*" the dispatcher told him.

"*Beware, xenohostiles swarming, dome has been breached, correction, the dome panels have been deliberately opened in three places, due to technical malfunction or human error,*" the Juno said over the general MI network.

"Close the fucking dome!" screamed Commander Martin.

"Affirmative, that has been done already, eleven minutes and five seconds ago. However, you should be aware that this habitat has been infiltrated by alien life-forms, namely, Horde."

A few moments later, the remnants of the Horde trapped inside the dome struck.

Soldiers carried away the dead, who had been blinded then brain-eaten by falling particles of Horde. Scientists sprayed the air with liquid poison. Screaming and whimpering filled the air, as the survivors felt the pollen-beasts move around inside their skulls, slowly and inevitably and incurably eating their thoughts and memories and motor impulses.

The dome above was now closed tight.

Helms sat at his desk, and waved a hand to conjure up his virtual computer screen. He spoke to it. "Xabar, exterior."

A bird's eye view of the Xabar dome appeared in mid-air, surrounded by the rich and iridescent colours of the rainforest. He brushed the picture with his thumb and it zoomed and expanded. He brushed with his thumb again and the perspective flipped and became a ground-level robocam view of the jungle all around them. Now the air was filled with the purple of the canopy, the red suppurating undergrowth, the variously coloured Flesh-Webs.

And then the Horde emerged like torrents of black water from leaves high up in the Aldiss trees, and they swarmed, and swarmed. And Helms saw this richly coloured miniature ecosphere — hovering in front of him like a ghostly vision — vanish from view as the air itself grew black, like a tornado turning septic.

The sirens blared around the streets and offices and labs of Xabar, and all the Security Teams took their positions. The Xabar dome was hardglass, which in theory was impervious to anything less powerful than a fusion bomb. But the dome had opened itself once already; it could happen again. So Commander Martin instructed everyone to don their body armour and prepare for a breach of the dome by the descending Horde.

The Horde were pollen particles that fell from the tree Canopies with deadly regularity. With predatory zeal, these pollen balls could eat their way through metal. The evolutionary aim, it was supposed, was for the pollen particles to burrow deep into the earth in order to take root safely and free from any predators. But the pollen was a ripe target for all the aerial predators of New Amazon, so a bloody battle royal resulted every time the showers of pollen fell.

All around Xabar, the air was black with "birds" and "insects" fighting motile, aggressive pollen. The pollen provided a luscious tit-bit for those creatures strong enough to crunch its tough coat; but thousands of living creatures fell dead from the sky as the pollen launched its counterattack.

Commander Martin gave his orders, and the Xabar dome was heated to deter the Horde from landing again. But even so, a thick carpet of pollen soon covered the hardglass, blotting out the sun.

"*The dome is in danger of cracking,*" Juno informed them.

"*We'll use targeted defences,*" Commander Martin said. At present, the entire dome was boiling hot, and the structure couldn't sustain that intensity of heat for too long.

Helms was following all this via his MI, as he saw the virtual dome above his desk being swept by clouds of black Horde, like a dolls' house beset by an indoor hurricane.

"I'll take it from here," said Professor Helms.

"Go ahead, Professor," said Commander Martin.

Helms had already ordered his Noir Science Team to the virtual control room.

"We need you to pick off the Horde clusters. Are you ready, Sheena?" he said.

"Ready. We won't let you down, Professor," Sheena told him, and raised her fist; her signal to her team to begin their work.

Sheena was Queen of the Noirs, and also head of Dome Security. And all her highly trained and highly specialised team were Noirs. No one else on the base liked working with the Noirs, because they were felt to be aloof and arrogant. Which, indeed, they were.

And they were also all masters of virtuality.

So Sheena stood now inside a virtual dome surrounded by swarming Horde, and touched her finger against a black-with-pollen patch. Her finger-touch was translated into a signal, which was sent to the real dome, which proceeded to a) heat up and b) blast acid on the intruders, all on a tiny patch of dome, allowing the rest of it to cool and recover its resilience. Every time a patch of black appeared she flicked it with her finger, and the dome repelled the attacker, then cooled again. A dozen flecks of black appeared on the virtual dome; and she picked them all off with effortless precision, with skill and psychic intuition, more quickly and accurately than any computer.

Jim Aura watched, awed at Sheena's beauty and blistering speed. Jim had been a geek and a goth and a fantasy-game-player all his life, but it was only in the last few months he had made the decision to go the whole hog—to have the surgery and become a Noir. For years he had been pale and skinny and pathetic; now he was pale and skinny and *magnificent,* clad in soft shiny leather as tight as skin, caped and hooded, with jet-black eyes in an etched and powerful face. A classic white Noir.

But Sheena was a Black Noir—her skin was ebony, and her eyes pure white. Her hair, too, was white—not grey, but the colour of the sun at midday. Her body moved like mercury rolling on a ship's table; her grace was uncanny.

A virtual dome surrounded Jim too, and he was hard at work clearing the Horde. His movements were less graceful, but he was capable and experienced. The trick was to single-touch the densest patches of pollen, let the dome heat to five times boiling point, then double-touch the dome to bring the temperature down again before the hardglass started to melt. It was a task that took phenomenal reflexes. Jim loved it because it was in essence real-life gaming, and gaming had been his life between the ages of six and fifteen.

At one point, Sheena glanced across to watch her latest Noir at work. Jim projected insecurity, awkwardness, ill-at-easeness. He hadn't yet learned that being a Noir is all about being as one with yourself, and your own body. He was, all in all, still a dreadful geek.

But Sheena was fond of him.

"Surely someone could invent a robot system to do this better," Santana said to Sheena, as she touched and double-touched the non-existent dome.

"Many have tried; no one has succeeded," said Sheena, as she and Jim Aura cast their spells.

And black pollen fell from the trees and fought; and birds were eaten alive in mid-air; and living winds blew upon the dome. Sheena and the Noirs worked through the night with fingers dealing death, casting their spells, while outside the dome silver Humanoid DRs with hoses poured acid upon the falling Horde.

And finally, after nearly ten hours, the Horde dispersed. The dome became clear again. The crisis was over.

DAY 2

From the diary of Dr Hugo Baal

June 23rd

Thank Heaven that's over! And we can see daylight again.

Such crises are alarming, and worryingly common. This is without doubt the most dangerous planet I have ever studied.[1]

For obituaries of the fifteen deceased, click here. What idiot left the roof open? There is a theory that it was a computer malfunction, but of course that's preposterous; Juno never malfunctions. Maybe we have a saboteur in our midst? Far more likely.

No matter; I've been in this kind of situation before.[2] *And I'm acutely aware there is nothing I can contribute when it comes to military/civil war/rebellion against the Galactic Corporation stuff; but fortunately there are other, equally important, things to think about, where my expertise does count for something. Namely, scientific discovery!*

I have spent the first three hours of the day since 5 a.m. reviewing the results of the abortive xeno autopsy. We have established that this specimen is either a) a species or subspecies of the Godzilla genus which differs radically from the Godzilla helmsi that we dissected twelve weeks ago or b) belongs to a rival genus that mimics the form of the Godzilla but has a plant origin not an animal origin, or c) is an animal in a symbiotic relationship with a plant which provides the animal with skin in return for nutrients, or d),[3] *whatever d) might be.*

---

1 Apart from Hellsmouth, where an alien virus killed every single member of the scientific party; luckily I was off planet at the time. And Barsoom had its hazards too — only six of us walked away from *that* one. And OK, let's not even get into what happened on Xanadu. But even so — New Amazon is "one mean mother" of a place.

2 On Jarrold, where a rebel group held us hostage for over three days until a crack squad of Soldiers burrowed under the biosphere and burst through the floor and killed them all. Oh, and I once worked in a xenolab which was bombed by Alien Rights fanatics, though I wasn't working there at the time, and the bombing may have been a put-up job by the Corporation's secret police.

3 It's worth remembering that initially the creature split up into four autonomous creatures with teeth, which is what I have elsewhere described as a pantomime horse morphology.

*My initial theory which I expounded to the group in the bar after-
wards, namely that the cells of the dead creature could wilfully recom-
bine in new forms, giving it the ability to reincarnate as any kind of
creature it chose to be, proved to be fanciful, and I was much mocked for
it.[4] Hmmm.[5] Although it's certainly the case that every cell in the creature's body remains alive and viable even after the death of the larger
organism. This raises the possibility that all large animals on New Amazon are gestalt organisms built up of swarms of individual cells acting in
concert, like an ant colony on legs. However, more of this anon.[6]*

*I have now decided, in the absence of any intelligent contributions
from my esteemed colleagues on this matter, to abandon our existing
taxonomy and to create three new Kingdoms. These are: Animaliaplantae, Plantaeanimalia, and Kingdomshifters, which I don't know the
Latin for. This avoids the annoying ambiguities entailed in describing
creatures which have both animal and plant characteristics. I shall write
more on this in due course.*

For the moment, I would catalogue yesterday's creature thus:

Mimic-Monster

Kingdom:	*Animaliaplantae (aka "Animalish", a neologism of my own, which I rather like)*
Phylum:	*Chordata*
Subphylum:	*Vertebrata*
Class:	*Reptiliacorticis[7]*
Order:	*Duocorus[8]*
Genus:	*Mimicus*
Species:	*Mimicus godzilla*

---

4 But do I care? I do not! Well actually I do, a bit.

5 That's what comes of theorising after 2½ pints of beer.

6 This link doesn't yet function; when I've written the "anon" bit I'll add the link, if I remember.

7 A new Class I have created consisting of all reptile-like creatures with skin made of tree bark, of which this is so far the only example.

8 A new Order I have just devised, of animal-plants with two hearts.

I am assembling the charred pieces of the dead creature and hope to have some firm conclusions within a . . . oh bloody hell, what is it <u>now?</u>

Sorcha had been put in charge of the dawn raids. A dozen Technicians were dragged from their beds, naked or in body-hugging pyjamas, and hurled into the white-noise room. Forensic tests of all the equipment were made, and Sorcha had a team of Soldiers inspecting all the dome-camera footage for evidence of espionage.

The results were negative. No one had sabotaged the dome; none of the Techies confessed; two of them lost their minds and had to be relegated to low-level Slave status — dumb servants, with all the legal rights of robots, namely none. Sorcha felt guilty about this. Good Techies were at a premium, though she always marvelled at how badly these genius types coped with a bit of basic torture.

Sorcha's report attributed the dome failure to General System Error, a technical euphemism for Act of God.

"*Juno, can you shed any light on this?*" Sorcha asked.

One of the Techies had told her that a computer virus sent from Earth and affecting Juno herself might have been the cause of the mishap. Sorcha had no idea if that was credible.

"*No, I cannot.*"

"*Did you cause the dome breach?*"

"*I don't know,*" admitted Juno. "*Last night — well, I have to admit. It's a blank. I can't remember anything.*"

Puzzled, Sorcha reported to Commander Martin. "*It may be a computer virus,*" she said. "*Perhaps from Earth. If so, Juno is compromised.*"

"*That's impossible,*" he told her, scathingly.

"How's it going?" Professor Helms said gently.

"Hmm?"

"What?"

"The dissection."

"What?"

"The—"

"Ah!"

"Oh! You mean—oh no! No."

Helms smiled.

"We haven't—"

"We didn't—"

"It's OK," said Helms, amused. "What you're doing is OK. On the squeamish side, but I'm fine with it."

Dr William Beebe and his wife Dr Mary Beebe were meant to be analysing the morphology of the Butterfly-birds (*Avespapilio parasitum*) taken from the Mimic-Godzilla's intestines. But Mary couldn't bear the idea of dissecting these beautiful creatures—even if they *were* stitched up again afterwards. So the two of them had managed to construct a wind tunnel tomography scanner, using ultrasound bursts to build up a picture of the organs and muscles of one of the birds as it flew into a whirlwind of air.

"Beautiful," murmured Helms, entranced.

"Yes, but," mused William, "why? Why do they fly at all?"

"Indeed," said Mary.

"Since they don't need to," William added, unnecessarily.

Mary sighed; and William repented of his unnecessary words.

Helms realised: these two didn't fully realise he was there, so lost were they in their rapport.

"Perhaps," Mary continued, "they live in the organism until it dies then they have to fly long distances to reach the next organism?"

"The jungle is busy enough," Helms argued. "They could walk a few yards and hop on another Godzilla without any trouble."

"True," said Mary, blinking as she absorbed the fact that Helms was talking to her, and actually talking sense. "And of course," she added, forlorn at the abrupt death of her hypothesis, "the wings are a liability for creatures living inside a host body. They must have to keep them furled up." Mary illustrated by hunching her arms and body to illustrate how the minuscule Butterfly bird must spent its day within the stomach and colon of vast predators like the Godzilla.

"And yet," William reasoned, "they must long to live thus." He raised his arms and flapped around the lab, to illustrate the freedom and exhilaration of being a Butterfly bird that is able to fly through the sky.

Helms stifled a grin. He loved being with William and Mary; and he was enjoying getting away from the burdens of command.

"Do such creatures 'long'?" said Mary reprovingly.

"Does the leopard love to run?"

"Well, yes."

"Watch."

William took a jar containing a dozen Claw-Scarabs *(Ungula scarabus,* flying insects a little like beetles but with claws on every section of their segmented bodies). He clipped the jar to the wind tunnel and slipped the lid off. The Claw-Scarabs flew inside and hovered in mid-air near the Butterfly-Bird.

Within moments the Butterfly bird had tilted its body and lunged. One Claw-Scarab vanished into its beak. The others flew wildly up and down, but the Butterfly bird was remorseless and swift. It could turn its head 360 degrees in mid-air so its wings could still capture the lift from the wind jets as it swivelled its head and ate. And it could also plunge and swoop and soar with astonishing speed. Within twenty seconds all the Claw-Scarabs had been devoured and the But-terfly bird resumed its solitary lonely flight in the wind tunnel.

"Why would a creature capable of such effortless predation," argued William, "choose to live up a dinosaur's arse?"

"Perhaps—" Helms began.

"What a stupid bloody question! You're much too philosophical," Mary reproved her husband.

"And you have no soul," William chided.

"That's because there's no such thing as 'soul'," Mary mocked, mercilessly.

"True!"

William made a silly face, to acknowledge he'd lost the argumentative point.

Mary laughed, a lovely bell-peal laugh that echoed around the lab, until the sound of the emergency siren dimmed her good humour.

"I'm so sorry," said Helms, who was enjoying himself enormously. "I fear we need to suit up."

"Yet another attack by alien monsters?" said William.

"Or perhaps an act of sabotage. Or, conceivably, a rebellion. Never a dull moment, is there?" Helms said, still smiling, and he tapped the code to open up the secure wardrobe where the body armours were kept.

Sorcha liked an enemy she could see, and confront, and kill. The idea that a virus from Earth might have affected the Mother Ship computer infuriated her. Because she knew that a bunch of Earth rebels who were gazillions of miles away and who had the temerity to fight via impenetrable computer codes could never be killed by her Soldiers, or hanged, or defeated by military means.

However, Commander Martin remained adamant that the rebels must be on Xabar. His protocols told him that no one, and nothing, could hack into Juno, or the Earth remote computer, or corrupt the QB link.

So the interrogations continued. Another Techie lost his mind. No information was gleaned. The mood among the Xabar populace was becoming bleak. Professor Helms sent her repeated memos throughout the day protesting at her iniquitous treatment of "his" people.

And finally the day was over—Sorcha was off-duty, and Major Johnson was in operational command.

So Sorcha decided to take some R & R, and went to the Battle Simulator Room, to fight some simulated battles. Sorcha always found this therapeutic—she was killed twice and it sent a shudder of pleasure running through her.

And now, Sorcha was being confronted by an artillery attack by a race of armoured aliens with laser-beam eyes and about to take evasive action in her One-Jet when—

The missiles disappeared. The aliens disappeared. Her One-Jet disappeared. Sorcha found herself sitting in a leather chair with a virtual helmet on. She took the helmet off, and found her fellow Soldiers were similarly baffled.

"*Juno,*" she said. "*What's wrong?*"

No answer.

"*Juno,*" she said, "*please report.*"

Nothing. Just silence. "*Major Molloy to Major Johnson, what's happening?*" Nothing. "*Major Molloy to Commander Martin, please acknowledge,*" she subvoced. Total silence. She tried subvocing the Soldier next to her.

"*What the fuck?*" she said.

"The MI network is down, "the Soldier said, in his real voice.

"How can that—"

At that moment the alarms went, and a voice—she recognised Ben Kirkham's flat, droning tones—was heard over the never-before-used intercom system:

"Alpha Alert. We have a total systems failure. We have no communications, no link with Earth, and the MI frequencies have been blocked. And the worst news of all," Ben continued, grimly, "is that we've lost touch with Juno. The Mother Ship is no longer returning our calls."

Xabar was a city run by dumb robots. The airconditioning was controlled by electronic sensors, the hydroponics by simple feedback circuits. And the Doppelganger Robots—all of which could be controlled by human minds when required—were most commonly used as low-grade machines with the simplest of cybernetic circuits.

But the brains and soul of Xabar was Juno; a quantum computer of almost infinite power which monitored every aspect of the city's life. If a holographic sparrow flickered, Juno would know about it. She gave instructions to the dumb Doppelgangers, she kept the air fresh and fragrant, she ensured the animals in the city zoo were safe and content, and she was the conduit for all communications with Earth and the other Settled Planets and for all MI communciations between Soldiers and Scientists and Techies. If you wanted to make a holographic videocall to your brother on a planet fifty light-years away, Juno would set it up. If you wanted to download data from the up-to-date Galapedia, Juno would source it and collate it and check all the references.

Everyone spoke to Juno, every hour of every day: "Juno, can you check this?" "Juno, can you do this?" "Juno, I have a problem." "Juno, please advise."

It was unprecedented for a Mother Ship computer to break communications. And for the citizens of Xabar, the loss of Juno was emotionally and psychologically devastating.

"Juno, are you there?"

"Juno, can you advise me on my data?"

"Juno, what should I watch on television tonight?"

"Juno, can you make me a playlist of blues and nufunk that will make me pleasantly melancholy?"

"Juno?"

"Juno, are you there?"

"Juno?"

"Juno!"

"Juno!!!!!!"

Sorcha wondered if an armed rebellion was imminent. The thought filled her with cold joy. Any rebellion was bound to fail—her Soldiers would easily massacre any insurgent Scientists.

But that scenario was, she knew, unlikely. Mass rebellion was a no-brain strategy—the history books were littered with stories of massacres in which Soldiers and DRs had crushed and slaughtered would-be rebels. These days the rebels were smarter; they knew that isolated acts of sabotage were more effective, and harder to stamp out. And indeed, some argued, though Sorcha vemenently disagreed, that minor acts of sabotage should be tolerated as a way of letting resentful citizens blow off steam. It was, according to this soft-headed neo-liberal view, the price you paid for tyranny.

"*Reboot complete, all systems fully functional,*" said a voice in her head.

"*Juno?*" said Sorcha.

"*Django, can you hear me?*" Helms said.

A long pause followed. Then Django's voice spoke in the Professor's inner ear:

"*Acknowledged, Professsor. Good news. We've now got contact with Juno again The MI network is working. All systems have been restored.*"

Helms realised that he could actually hear his own heart pounding. "*Yes, I know,*" he said. "*I've just been speaking to Commander Martin. But my worry is—what the hell has been—I mean, have you figured out what the problem was?*" he added, in an attempt at a calm and casual tone.

"*No.*"

"*Did you run a diagnostic?*"

"*Juno won't let me.*"

"*So is it possible,*" said Helms, holding in his terror, "*that it was Juno who opened the dome? And Juno who sabotaged the post-mortem? Is she acting against us?*"

"*Hardly likely,*" Django said, with an attempt at reassurance.

"*Harumph,*" Helms snarled, and he cut the MI link.

"*Helms?*" Sorcha barked into her MI.

"*Not now, Major.*"

"*We need to talk.*"

"*I'm dealing with —*"

"*The Commander is furious. He doesn't understand how Juno could have —*"

"*I couldn't give a damn what the Commander thinks.*"

"*Professor!*"

"*Sorcha, you need to do something for me.*"

Sorcha hesitated. "*What?*"

"*Do you have your body armour on?*"

"*Not any more, no. Once the emergency was —*"

"*Then get it back on. And tell all your Soldiers to get armoured up. The full complement, I don't want anyone on rest break. And tell them to be prepared.*"

"*Be prepared for what?*"

"*You'll see.*"

Sorcha sat in her control chair, deeply worried. The Professor was famous for his dithery, amiable calm; but the man she had just spoken to was in a state of blind panic. He must, she realised, have come to the same conclusion that she had just come to.

They were at war with Earth.

"*Major Molloy to all units,*" she subvoced, to access her secure channel, then: "*All Soldiers, I'm restoring a state of Alpha Alert, get back in your armour.*"

Helms ran down the corridor and found his way blocked by a swarm of DRscalpels. He moved towards them; they swarmed a bit more. He was suddenly convinced they would kill him if he attempted to pass.

He turned around, and walked slowly back to his cabin. Behind him, the DRscalpels made an eerie hissing noise. It felt as if they were mocking him.

"What the hell are you playing at, Major?" said Commander Martin over Sorcha's MI.

"I'm following Professor Helms's request, sir."

"Why? What has he told you?"

"Nothing," Sorcha admitted.

Mia Nightingale enjoyed being in the locker room when the Soldiers stripped out of their body armour. She savoured the sight of their naked bodies, their powerful muscles, the stench of sweat and the raw physicality of these trained killers.

And of course the locker-room scenes were highly popular on the soft porn and warrior-porn sites, and Mia usually got a kickback from pirate sales of the downloads.

But that wasn't why she enjoyed these moments. It wasn't sexual; rather, she found a great purity in these scenes. They were moving tableaux of warriors at their most vulnerable.

And she marvelled at the power and the beauty of these Soldiers' bodies. They were trained for combat, bred for combat, genetically engineered for combat. All of them — the men, the women, and the two hermaphrodites, Tonii and Maria—all of them had bodies like gods and goddesses, marked with scars and fissures, and ornamented with tattoos of remarkable variety and beauty.

She moved around the Soldiers as they took their body armour off, capturing each instant with her hand-held cam. She was so taken for granted now that the Soldiers barely registered her presence.

"Go on, take a close look," Sergeant Anderson suggested, as she moved for a close-up of the naked warrior queen tattoo on his taut, chiselled abs.

"Yeah," said Mia, unsettled at the tattoo, as she realised that the naked warrior queen had been beheaded. It made her feel queasy.

"All Soldiers, I'm restoring a state of Alpha Alert, get back in your armour," said Sorcha's voice crisply over the MI.

Helms walked to his cabin on wobbly legs. He saw a silver Humanoid DR and felt a lurch of panic, but forced himself to stay calm.

The DR was staring at him with its blank metal eyes. "What are your duties?" Helms barked at it, but the DR didn't answer.

"Helms to Ben Kirkham," Helms subvoced, *"can you run a systems check on—"*

"Time to die, Professor," the DR said, with a leering smile. Helms swiftly drew his plasma pistol and the DR raised its own plasma gun and held it to Helms's temple, and Helms felt his stomach turn over.

Then the DR lowered its gun. "Is something wrong, Professor?" it asked, in its robot flat tones.

"No. I'm fine. Just..." Helms looked at the gun in his hand. "Just checking my gun is charged."

"Professor, it's Ben here, can I help?"

"No I'm—" Helms said incoherently, as the DR held out its hand to him.

"Let me," it said, and the DR took the gun off him, thrust the gun butt into a hole in its chest, and charged it. Then the DR handed the gun back.

"I've added some explosive shells," the robot-mode DR said helpfully.

Helms sat at his desk. He took a deep breath.

Then he conjured up his virtual screen.

He typed his encrypted password in mid-air and an image of New Amazon appeared before him.

"Helms, this is Commander Martin."

"*Not now.*" Helms clicked his MI off.

The door of his cabin flew off. The DRscalpels flew in. They aimed their laser beams at him and —

— exploded in mid-air. Helms had primed his plasma security beams; they blew the dumb robot tools out of the air.

He continued typing passcodes, a long series of encrypted codes that led him to the final screen which blazed violently at him, and then he typed the launch codes for the missiles and authenticated them with a retinal scan.

A signal was transmitted over Helms's private and secret radio channel, via his MI, and a dozen missiles were primed, and then fired out of a buried silo deep in the jungle.

The flotilla of missiles flew through the air, cutting through the flocks of New Amazonian birds that cluttered the air, and continued on a course that led towards the domed city.

Helms watched it all on his virtual screen. Each missile carried a camera and dozens of missile-view images danced in the air in front of him.

And, after a few minutes, the missiles were soaring high in the air above Xabar. The sky was dark with chaff and anti-missile missiles thrown up by the dome's automatic security systems, and the sky was white with explosions, but then the remaining missiles, soared down fast and struck the still-intact inner dome of Xabar and shattered it in a million pieces.

The explosion was deafening.

Sorcha was almost thrown out of her control chair by the explosion that rocked the dome. The EVACUATE alarm began to ring.

"What's happening?" she said into her MI, but once again there was no response.

Then there was a whirring noise and, in her head, she heard Helms' voice, oddly distorted. *"Alpha Alert, Alpha Alert, we're being attacked by Juno. Repeat, Juno has gone rogue. Evacuate. Treat all Doppelgangers as potential enemy targets. Get your armour on, seize your weapon, head for the AmRover bay. And do it now. Run!"*

"What the hell is going on now?*"* screamed Commander Martin.

"Repeat, Juno is rogue, Juno is rogue."

Chaos descended upon Xabar. Alarms whined and flashed.

In the Rack Room, the DRs began to stir. Eyes opened. Arms twitched. Silver bodies stood, and moved away from the confining racks.

Plasma cannons were, unnecessarily, locked and loaded.

The DRs began to walk.

Terry Miller was a xenobiologist of forty years' experience. He was surprised to hear a faint padding sound, the unmistakable noise of DRs walking. He glanced up and saw twenty DRs enter the corridor ahead of him.

"What's going—" he began to say, and then the plasma cannons fired.

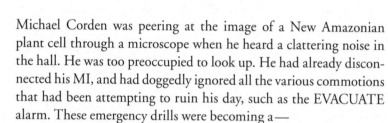

Michael Corden was peering at the image of a New Amazonian plant cell through a microscope when he heard a clattering noise in the hall. He was too preoccupied to look up. He had already disconnected his MI, and had doggedly ignored all the various commotions that had been attempting to ruin his day, such as the EVACUATE alarm. These emergency drills were becoming a—

A plasma blast blew his legs off. Michael felt dizzy, and wondered what had just happened, and then—

Dr Alan McCoy and four other Scientists had been working in the Plant Rooms, and all of them had body armour on when the doors were smashed open. Alan, who was justifiably impressed at his own speed and quasi-military discipline in responding to the alarms, smiled when two Humanoid DRs strode in.

"What does Helms mean when he says that Juno has—" Alan began, and then he realised the DRs were about to shoot him, and his three colleagues.

"Ah, f—" he managed to say before he died.

All around Xabar, Scientists were confronted by murderous DRs in all their varied forms—Humanoids, Drones, Cleaners, Scalpels, Cranes and Jibs.

The Dormitory Wings were invaded by DRdrones.

The Recreation Areas were filled with Humanoid DRs on the march.

The shopping malls were hosed with plasma beams fired by robot Guns; DRbombs exploded in the swimming pools; grenades were hurled by serving robots into school buildings.

There were fifty Humanoid DR bodies in the Rack Room, though most of the time they were hardly used. But today, all the silver-skinned Doppelganger Robots were out, padding near-silently, staring with their silver eyes, looming tall. And they were joined in their stately deadly tread by all the other dangerous DRs from the storage basements—the semi-brained Rockets, Guns, and Missiles, which flew beside and behind and in front of the Humanoids like the weapons of some invisible ghost army.

And all these robot brains were inhabited by the multi-tasking quantum-computer brain of Juno, which had now had its orders: kill everyone in Xabar.

And so the Doppelangers did as they were instructed, efficiently and methodically.

They killed, and they killed, and they killed...

Plasma blasts ripped through flesh, grenades were hurled, DRscalpels dissected and flayed all who came in attacking distance.

Security doors locked shut, trapping Scientists and Soldiers in killing zones. Guns flew into the Earth Aviary Restaurant, firing bursts of plasma energy, shredding tables and cups and saucers and people. Within minutes, the room was full of blood and charred corpses as the virtual birds flew blindly around.

And meanwhile, the hardglass dome of Xabar had been shattered utterly by the missile strike. A wind swept through Xabar and many were caught up and hurled high into the air, crashing up into the Canopy, before plunging downwards to their deaths. The flash of plasma fire lit up the black night. The screams of dying men and women almost drowned the howling of the insects in the jungle beyond.

It was a massacre, and a disaster, and it came as a total shock to almost everyone. One moment the Scientists were cataloguing their results and preparing their experiments; the next they were caught up in a ghastly bloodbath.

Sorcha jogged down the corridor and found her way blocked by corpses.

"Major Molloy to Commander Martin, where do I go?"

"Just evacuate, Major."

"Where's the battle, Commander?"

"Evacuate, I'll take it from here."

Sorcha took a deep breath. She was desperate for battle. She could taste her own death, it was like eating her tongue.

But orders were orders. She jogged to the nearest evacuation chute and plunged inside.

After the emergency alarm had proved to be a malfunction, Private Tonii Newton had returned to the hot tub in the spa. He basked in the hot waters, allowed jets of steam to relax his muscles, and savoured being in his own body.

Moments later, he got Sorcha's strange order to get battle-ready, so with a curse he left the spa waters and put on his battle armour. Then he sat by the pool, body-armoured up, and waited for further instructions. This, he reflected, was going to be one of those days.

Then the explosion hit.

Torrents of water went hurling upwards and descended in a wet blow. He was swept off his feet, but got up again in moments.

"Private N 47 reporting, sitrep please, Control."

There was no response from Juno Control. Then Tonii heard Helms's voice over his MI:

"We're being attacked by Juno. Repeat, Juno has gone rogue. Evacuate. Treat all Doppelgangers as potential enemy targets. Get your armour on, seize your weapon, head for the AmRover bay. And do it now. Run!"

Tonii heard the faintest of noises and threw a flash grenade long and high and it hit the Humanoid DR that was entering the spa. The explosion blew the creature backwards and Tonii was running. He reached the corridors and saw two unarmoured Soldiers in a firefight with a Humanoid DR and two DRscalpels. Suddenly they started screaming and their bodies opened up like fruit being peeled from the inside. Tonii sprayed the DR with plasma fire, then switched to a hail of smart bullets, which burrowed into then exploded inside the mid-air DRscalpels.

Then Tonii ran down the corridor. He saw two Scientists, in their blue body armour, emerge from a lab, clutching plasma rifles to their bodies as if they were Christmas presents. To his surprise they were chatting to each other cheerfully, showing no hint of anxiety.

"We should, I suspect, be swift," the male Scientist, who Tonii recognised as William Beebe, unhurriedly suggested.

"I don't consider I was dawdling!" his wife—Mary?—rebuked him.

Tonii beckoned impatiently and William and Mary Beebe followed him.

He walked fast, eyes and ears attuned, firing bursts of plasma into the ceiling whenever he heard the distant vibration of a DR on the floors above. They reached the evacuation chute, and William clambered in and vanished from sight. A few moments later Mary followed and tumbled downwards. Tonii glanced around. Two red-and-black-armoured Soldiers appeared round the corner of the corridor, one with an arm missing. Tonii beckoned them to join him, but the Soldiers vanished in a mist of blood as a DR plasma blast incinerated them. Tonii hurled himself into the evacuation chute.

He fell face downward, down the narrow pipe, his rifle screeching against the tough metal. Then he landed with a thump in the AmRover bay to be confronted by the barrels of a dozen rifles.

"Private N 47, password Andromeda," he shouted via his helmet mike and was hustled away from the chute by Soldiers.

The AmRover bay was crowded and bloodied. The gates were open and a packed AmRover was driving out.

"The DRs have the second and third floors," said a Soldier, and then a flock of DRscalpels flew out of the chute and the bay was lit with the flares of controlled plasma energy that ate the metal monsters with heat beyond heat.

"Anyone know what's going on?" said Tonii.

"Juno's gone rogue."

"Not possible." But of course it *was* possible.

Tonii thought about all the likely explanations for Juno going rogue. It couldn't be rebels, he decided—no mere rebel could subvert the Earth Computer, or sabotage Juno. So that meant it had to be Earth humans playing games, again. Murdering and pillaging, as they had done so many times before. Massacring an entire community of people, just for the hell of it.

Once again.

Tonii waited, in line, as the AmRovers were loaded up. He thought about a galactic civilisation where murder was considered to be a sport, and his soul was rent with pain.

Professor Helms ran fast and clumsily down the corridor in his blue body armour, escorted by three Soldiers running at full tilt.

He was astonished at the horrors all around him. The DRs had run amok. There were bodies everywhere. He hadn't expected *this*.

"Professor, we need you out of there now," said a voice in his head. It was Commander Martin, over the MI-radio link.

"This is madness," Helms told him, desperately. *"I can't believe what's happening…this should be…"*

"Get him out of there please," said the Commander's voice, and the Soldiers picked Helms up and threw him down a chute.

When he landed, strong hands grabbed him and picked him up.

"Are you wounded?" said a familiar voice. He looked up, and saw it was Sorcha.

Helms felt a sudden, unexpected lurch of delight at seeing her alive.

The first ten minutes of the attack were carnage, in which the DRs killed and maimed with callous efficiency.

The eleventh minute was when the Soldiers fought back.

Commander Martin was in his office, surrounded by virtual screens, which gave him a second-by-second visual account of the fighting. His door was bomb-proof, the computer program he was running superseded the Juno programs, and he was in full body armour.

He saw twelve Soldiers engaged in a bitter hand-to-hand fight with the main body of the Humanoid DR forces, in the corridor that led to the Green Area evacuation chutes. He issued a silent prayer, and blew up the corridor. Twenty DRs were incinerated, plus twelve of his own people. He breathed a swift subvocal prayer: *They gave their lives, in Glory.* Then he carried on the fight.

Cameras buried in the walls and ceilings gave him a total sweep of every part of Xabar. He saw a flock of DRscalpels heading down a corridor, and fired the laser beams hidden in the cameras and twenty or more were blown out of the air.

He could see DRtanks and Humanoids lying in wait outside the AmRover Bays. He marked the area on the screen with a red circle, and pulled down a missile strike. Concealed missile silos hurled nil-brain rockets—not connected to the Juno mainframe—as deadly rain upon the would-be ambushers.

And he still had a hundred and fifty or so Soldiers inside Xabar, fighting with all their skill and courage.

Commander Martin was a new breed of Soldier—an academic and a thinker. But he was also a veteran of a dozen xeno-wars. He had fought silicon aliens and spacefaring aliens and Van Neumann machines built by aliens rendered extinct a billion years or more ago. And he'd spent years war-gaming a scenario in which the CSO used the Doppelganger Robots to kill his own people. It was, after all, given that merciless bureaucrat's track record, a pretty likely scenario.

So Commander Martin felt more than ready for this conflict. The Doppelganger Robots were tough, powerful, heavily armed and fast—since they were being controlled by the super-swift computer mind of Juno. But Martin's Soldiers were *men,* and they were *women* (and indeed, two of them were *both),* and war was in their blood.

Martin's hands moved swiftly on the virtual joysticks, he clicked bombs to explode, he barked instructions and sitreps to his troops via their secure short-range radio link, and he killed robot fucker after robot fucker after robot fucker, with glee.

The Soldiers split up according to pre-ordained and memorised orders into two packs, the Bodyguards and the Kill the Bastards. The Bodyguards swept through all the labs, scooping up Scientists and guarding them and hurling them down evacuation chutes into the AmRover Bays where other Bodyguards were waiting to protect them and get them out of Xabar.

The Kill the Bastards had the best job; they got to fight. They fought in Fives, tightly knit units who trained together and whose reflexes had merged so that they functioned almost as a single entity.

Two Soldiers in each Five were Berserkers. Their job was to keep up a continual hail of covering fire against whatever enemy they faced. They wore heavy body armour with no force field, their arms were adapted to serve as plasma guns, they could also fire grenades or mortars, they could even fire explosive shells from their breastplates.

A third Soldier acted as the Sniper, and this was their ace in the hole. Snipers wore a lightly armoured reflective suit that made him or her close to invisible. They carried a laser pistol in one hand and a smart rifle firing three-inch nuclear bombs in the other. When the Berserkers launched their frenzied attacks on an enemy, the Sniper slipped along with them, impossible to see, rolling and ducking and diving, firing precision shots at the enemy's vulnerable points.

The DRs, however, had no vulnerable points. Their armour was impervious to an ordinary plasma blast. Bullets bounced off them. And they were fast, fast enough to dodge a missile fired at point-blank range.

But they lacked intelligence. The DR robot brain was a sad and simple thing, able to initiate only the very simplest of actions, but for most of the time the DRs were controlled remotely by humans, or, as now, by Juno, a quantum-computing AI of near-infinite capability.

So in this particular war the Sniper's role was to break the Juno connection, with carefully judged electromagnetic pulses that, for four or five seconds, broke the beaconband link to the Mother Ship.

The battle raged. For ten minutes, the Humanoid DRs swaggered swiftly from room to room, incinerating all within with their plasma guns and energy balls. But then, in the eleventh minute, the Fives struck back. Berserkers fired vast sheets of energy while emitting ultrasonic and subsonic and sonic blasts to disorientate, while the Snipers rolled and weaved and ducked amongst them, firing electro-magnetic pulses at the head of the DRs.

Every successful headshot stopped the DR in its tracks, just for a few moments. And in that brief window of time the fourth member of the Five stepped forward—the One Sun. The One Sun was a Soldier wearing a body armour that was built around a gun, a porta-ble energy cannon of exceptional power, based around a cold-fusion generator that in a single focused beam could in a few seconds emit a huge blast of energy—allegedly, as much power as the Earth Sun generates in a single hour.

And that, the super-gun, that was the One Sun.

Energy, screaming, balls and trails of fire, rolling bodies, ceilings crashing in, silvery monsters flitting like deadly moonbeams out of the way of explosive shells, and suddenly the pause, the one still beat, as the Doppelganger Robot stood stunned and the One Sun fired the plasma cannon. Whoosh.

The flare of the One Sun was intense, and focused. The Doppelganger Robot burned with an awesome heat and was gone. And then the air itself turned white as a pillar of raw energy soared upwards, upwards, searing the air in an energy-tornado that cut effortlessly through the Canopy and rocked and billowed the clouds and carried on upwards until it seemed to be be seeking to touch the sun, until finally the energy liberated by the One Sun began to slowly dissipate in space.

Then, back on the ground, the One Sun was reloaded by the fifth member of the team, the Bat Carrier, who carried the team force field, and the replacement BBs. One 20 cm x 10 cm-sized Bostock battery contained enough energy to fire a single round from the One Sun. The Bat Man carried fifty of them, clad in body armour like an armadillo.

Energy, screaming, balls and trails of fire, rolling bodies, ceilings crashing in, silvery monsters flitting like deadly moonbeams out of the way of explosive shells, One Sun. Whoosh.

Then the Bat Man helped the One Sun reload, and it all began again.

Professor Helms sat in the AmRover, longing to escape. He was pale and shivering, and disorientated. Sorcha sat opposite him, listening intently to her MI, watching the scene outside on the screens. He tried to speak to Sorcha. "We should—" he began, but he lost his train of thought.

"Don't be such a fucking coward, man," Sorcha snarled at him, and Helms registered how unfair she was being. He was cold, and he was also hot, and he was confused. It occurred to him he was in shock.

"We should—go," he eventually managed to say.

"When I say so! Survivors. We'll wait." Sorcha's brusque words shook Helms. He felt that he wanted to weep.

"Let's go now," screamed another of the survivors.

"When I say so. We wait till then," Sorcha told her, and her subtext of "Heed my words or you will die, fucker" shone through.

The doors of the AmRover opened, and two more Scientists were hurled in by Soldiers. "*Five more minutes, no more!*" Sorcha snapped to the helmeted-up Soldier who was escorting them.

"*Some DRs came down the evacuation chute, sir.*"

"*Did you destroy them?*"

"*Yes sir.*"

"*Five minutes, no more.*"

"*Four minutes, forty-five seconds now, sir.*"

The sounds of grenades exploding in the hangar outside them echoed around the AmRover cockpit. The Soldier returned to the fray.

"You were right," Sorcha told Helms. "Juno has gone rogue. The DRs are...What is happening, Richard?"

"How should I know?" Helms muttered feebly. Then: "Gamers?" he hazarded.

"Could be," she conceded, and a spasm of rage convulsed her. "*The bastards!*" she muttered.

Helms tried to speak, to agree with her, but he couldn't.

"Who the fuck do they think they—"

"Yes! Who the fuck! Damn it all!" Helms's eyes glittered with rage.

Sorcha locked stares with him.

For a moment the two of them were bonded, united in adversity.

The moment popped. "We need to go," he told her. "I can't—we can't risk staying any longer."

Then a burly soldier—Sergeant Anderson—clambered into the AmRover. His body armour was pockmarked with plasma blasts and was literally steaming.

"*Are we done?*" Sorcha asked, over the MI radio.

"*We're done,*" Sergeant Anderson replied.

"*Sergeant,*" Helms acknowledged.

"*Professor,*" Anderson said curtly. He was a big, scowly, curt man; Helms didn't like him much. "*Those fucking bastards!*" Anderson roared.

Helms nodded, numbly; indeed, fucking bastards they were.

"*How could those mfs do a thing like this?*" Anderson raged.

"*I don't—know,*" said Helms. "*I can't believe—so many—so much…*"His words trailed off.

Anderson curled a lip. "*It's a Glorious battle,*" he conceded.

"Please, let's go," wept a female Scientist in the cockpit.

"Yes," said Helms. "*We should go.*"

"*Let me just…*" Anderson carried on mid-air typing. Sorcha saw a flashing red symbol that showed the booby bombs were primed.

"*There are still people coming down the chutes!*" she protested.

"*You think so?*" said Anderson, and Sorcha turned and looked.

A Humanoid DR emerged head-first from the evacuation chute and began firing. Anderson revved the AmRover and drove out fast, into the New Amazonian jungle.

One two three four five six seven eight BOOM.

The boobytrap bombs they'd left behind exploded, destroying a half dozen or more Humanoid DRs. The AmRover almost overbalanced but Sergeant Anderson kept control.

"*Good call,*" Helms conceded, as Sorcha started up the AmRover. Anderson retracted his helmet.

"So can someone explain what the fuck is going on!" screamed Anderson.

"We think, maybe Gamers," said Sorcha.

"Or the CSO has gone mad," Helms offered.

"That bastard already is mad," said Anderson, heretically, and grinned.

As they drove off, Helms could see the dome of Xabar had shattered utterly, scattering shards of hardglass far into the jungle. He could see the debris of exploded AmRovers, he could see limbs and heads scattered on the road in front of him. And he tried to ignore it all, the signs of carnage all around.

He forced himself to gather his thoughts, to remember his strategy.

He willed himself to once again be in control of his emotions, and to keep the terror out of his voice.

And eventually, he succeeded.

"Rendezvous all survivors Map Reference D 43," Helms said calmly into his helmet mike, *"please."*

Django was astonished at the havoc around them. Missiles were raining down, the DRs were running amok, randomly shooting at the labs and at each other. There were dead bodies everywhere, and the walls of the corridors were stained with blood and entrails.

But Django wasn't afraid. He revelled in danger. This was what he was born for — to be a warrior in battle, not a desk jockey or a lab Scientist!

As a child, Django had nursed a powerful secret: the certain knowledge that he was better than other people. Not smarter, though he was pretty bright. Not more beautiful, though he did have moderately smouldering Latin good looks. Not braver, or more resourceful, or more imaginative.

Just *better.*

His father had been and still was a civil servant on Kornbluth. His mother had died in childbirth, or so Django had been told.

But he'd always disbelieved that story. Wasn't it far more credible that she'd been a freedom fighter murdered by the Galactic Corporation's secret police? Or that she'd been an astronaut, sent on a perilous mission in the certain knowledge that even if she wasn't killed, she'd never see her husband and kids again?

Django never told anyone his secret — the truth about his "better-than-others-ness". But it had sustained him through his difficult early years as a bullied child. His contemporaries at school had always picked on Django. But it was not because he was vulnerable, or disadvantaged; it was because he was rude to them, because he mocked and taunted them.

The teachers at Django's school constantly berated the rest of the class for the awful way they treated Django. And Django had just sat and smiled, because he knew that being the most bullied child in school made him special, and, well, *better* than those doing the bullying.

One day, he had resolved, with unquenchable confidence, he would show them all. They would all regret having bullied Django; they would concede their own lesser status!

And, perhaps, Django mused, *this* was his moment. Perhaps this was when he would become the hero of the hour, and go down in history?

Django hurried towards the evacuation chute and was two yards away when a DRscalpel crashed through his helmet and ate his face.

Django's screams were stifled when his tongue was consumed, and he died in agony, mute, of his injuries.

Mia dived into the chute and found herself in Number 3 AmRover Bay. Two DRs were shooting at each other, and the plasma sheen on the walls of the hangar gave it an orange glow.

Mia aimed her laser snipe and picked off the DRs one by one, with a single focused beam each through the two robot brains. She hated plasma guns, they were just raw brute energy. But though she was a civilian, she had a skill-chip that made her a championship-level marks-woman with a laser pistol and she relished a chance to use her skills.

But why, she wondered, anxiously, has the world suddenly gone completely mad?

Hugo Baal was still in the lab when Private Clementine McCoy rushed in and grabbed him. She saw with dismay he didn't have his armour on. "Evacuate," she screamed, "means get the fuck out of here, *now*!"

Hugo blinked and realised he was in the midst of a crisis. "You came to save me?" he marvelled.

"You big dolt," Clementine told him, and tugged him away.

A Humanoid DR appeared at the doorway and Clementine fired a plasma blast. The DR sustained a head injury but carried on moving.

"Instructions, please," the DR said calmly, back in robot-mode, walking around in stupid circles, and Clementine and Hugo ran past it to the evacuation chute. Clementine dived. Hugo hesitated. Then he saw DRs in the corridor. He eased his fat frame into the chute.

And found himself tumbling down, as if on a fairground ride, and ended up in the AmRover Bay. It was a scene of bloody horror and destruction. A shattered DR body lay on the floor. The limbs and blood of its victims formed a carpet between them and the one surviving AmRover.

"Move!" screamed Clementine, and Hugo picked his way across the dead and dying bodies, ignoring groans and whimpers, until he reached the AmRover. They clambered in. Clementine started up the AmRover.

"Quite the resourceful one, aren't you?" he murmured.

Ben Kirkham was trying to work out where the missiles had come from. If Juno had fired them, why hadn't he seen a radar trace from space five or ten minutes before impact? But if Juno didn't fire them, then...

On his virtual screen, Ben could see a Replay image of Xabar's dome shattering into pieces. "So much for unbreakable," he muttered. He hated having no MI link to Juno, and found that talking to himself was a comforting alternative.

"Ben, this is Helms, I'm outside Xabar with a small group of survivors, where are you?"

"I'm still inside. How come you can talk to me, the MI link is down."

"I, ah, installed a radio network that will connect up the MI transmitters within a range of half a mile. Just a precautionary measure, you know. Ben, please, I implore you, get out of there now, we need you! AmRover Bay 1 is blown, head for 3 or 2."

"On my way," said Ben, exultantly. He fumbled in the cabinet for his boxes of pills—his mood-stabilisers, concentration-boosters, anti-depressants, and of course his anti-psychotics—and realised he was wasting time so he ran out empty-handed to the evacuation chute. He took a deep breath and dived into it.

Sheena had led twelve Noirs out of the base via the back doors and towards the Shuttle Bay. And there they found themselves subject to withering attack from the DR sentries whose job it was to guard the Shuttle from would-be hijackers.

Santana and two others were killed in the first wave of the attack. Sheena and the rest took cover behind the vast bombproof storage sheds. The DRs began firing mortars that blasted pockmarks in the toughmetal walls of the sheds, but as the bombs flew and landed and exploded, Sheena used her secret command codes to summon a fleet of dumb missiles which flew out of the storage shed. The missiles circled; then Sheena launched them in a full-frontal attack on the the DR position.

She then used a virtual display to guide their trajectory, controlling thirty missiles simultaneously. The "dumb" missiles kinked and danced in the air, dodging the mortar bombs, hurling out chaff, and astonishingly avoiding the continuous waves of plasma fire that the DRs were hurling at them.

Then the missiles landed, one at a time, each one scoring a direct hit on an outwitted Doppelanger sentry, pulverising each of them instantly.

The nine survivors, including Jim Aura, then formed a defensive formation around Sheena, and ran towards the doors of the Shuttle Bay.

Concealed Sniper Guns killed three of them en route. But six survived and managed to climb on board the Shuttle.

"We'll go into space," said Sheena, "and from there we'll—"

The Shuttle exploded. The six Noirs fell out of the ship through the emergency hatch, pursued by shafts of shattered toughmetal. They were being attacked by three Humanoid DRs.

"Back inside," said Sheena, but a laser beam locked on to her helmet. She rolled over and tried to block the beam. Her helmet shattered but Jim Aura picked her up in his arms and ran with her.

The Sniper Guns opened fire again; five more Noirs died. But Jim ran fast, and evasively, still with Sheena in his arms, and hurled himself through the back doors and into the base. He found himself surrounded by death and screams, and a whimpering young woman with a gut wound begged him to help her. But he ignored it all and ran towards the evacuation chute, and leapt backwards into it, dragging the two of them down it in a tight embrace.

At the bottom of the chute he was helped to his feet by Sheena. Her eyes were burned out by the laser blasts, leaving empty sockets, but she lifted him easily up off the ground.

"Which way?" she said calmly.

Energy, screaming, balls and trails of fire, rolling bodies, ceilings crashing in, silvery monsters flitting like deadly moonbeams out of the way of explosive shells, One Sun.

Once more a robot butcher dies, in a blinding flare of plasma energy. The Five pause. The Batman reloads another battery into the One Sun plasma cannon.

A deadly moonbeam pauses, then flits again. It is a Humanoid DR moving fast, impossibly fast, dodging shells. Plasma blasts hit it but are absorbed by its armour. Then it stands still to aim its gun and plasma fire is fiercely focused on it as One Sun reloads.

But the Humanoid DR has a One Sun of his own. It fires once, at the Bat Man.

A flare of light extinguishes the man, the armour, the casings of the Bostock batteries.

And all the energy contained in all the guns and the batteries erupts in a single and utterly devastating moment.

"*Glory!*" scream the Berserkers but their cries are lost.

"*Stop. Look back,*" Sorcha said.

The AmRover stopped. They could see the fire on the screens but they moved as one to the Observation Bubble to see with their own eyes. Helms stared with horror at the sight.

A pillar of fire burned on the site where once Xabar stood. Above, the green Canopy vanished in palls of smoke.

"What the hell . . . ?" he murmured.

"The Bostock batteries blew," Sorcha explained. "No one is left, nothing is left."

"Are we safe?" asked Helms. He feared a conflagration that would consume the entire planet.

"We're more than twenty kilometres —" Sorcha began.

"That much heat!" insisted Helms. "If it spreads towards us —"

"Fuck," said Sergeant Anderson, realising the implications.

"The city force fields are still in place," Sorcha said. "Even though the dome is down. That will contain the energy. It'll be focused upwards. Like a torch beam."

"How can you be sure?"

"It's happened before," Sorcha said casually. "Twice that I know of. It's a pretty effective weapon of war in fact; the strategy is, we blow the BBs inside a force-fielded city, and destroy all enemy forces contained within."

Helms was shocked at her callous tone.

"*That's* what you call a weapon?" he said savagely. "Everyone in that city is dead because—"

"They're dead because they chose to give their lives for us," Sorcha told him bluntly, and Helms felt ashamed.

"I'm sorry."

"They were brave Soldiers."

"I said, I'm sorry," said Helms, at a loss.

Sorcha shrugged, accepting his apology.

"*They gave their lives,*" Anderson intoned, into his MI-radio, to reach out to the survivors in the other AmRovers.

"*They gave their lives,*" Sorcha echoed.

"*So are we safe?*" asked Hugo Baal, who was now in AmRover 5.

"*Fuck no,*" said Sorcha.

"*Nothing could survive an explosion like that,*" protested Sergeant Anderson. "*Those fucking robots must all be—*"

"*There are at least a dozen DRs patrolling outside the boundaries of Xabar,*" Sorcha explained. "*And more robot bodies in the basement bunkers, five miles outside the city walls. Plus an entire battalion guarding the Space Elevator. Plus, Juno has antimatter bombs, fusion bombs, and more DRs in storage. We don't stand a chance,*" she concluded.

Helms retracted his helmet, and gestured at Sorcha to do the same. Anderson, too, retracted his helmet, so he could hear Helms speak.

"I believe," said Helms, carefully and confidentially, "that there's a chance, if luck is on our side, that we may in fact prevail."

Sorcha shot him a baffled look. Anderson scowled, sceptically.

"I'll explain," said Helms, softly, "later."

Xabar burned. Huge columns of smoke rose into the sky, and high in the tree canopies, arboreals and insects and birds in their nests coughed and spluttered as the black smoke possessed their habitat.

And as the fire peaked and peaked, the pillar of fire stood higher and higher upon the ashes of the city as the heat of the exploded Bostock batteries coalesced into a tube of burning plasma that ripped a hole in the air and evaporated clouds and scorched a path through the stratosphere until it collided with the empty blackness of space itself.

The huge yellow star at the heart of the New Amazon system peered down at the planet that circled it, and that spat energy at it, as for a few astonishing hours the planet itself hurled a bitter sunbeam towards its own sun.

But soon, the fire would burn out. No trace of the domed city would remain, no trace of soil or earth, and only the bare exposed mantle of the planetary crust would give testament to the vast explosion that caused the Burning of Xabar.

There had been nearly four hundred people living in Xabar. Fifty-two of them gathered at the jungle rendezvous point. The others were lost elsewhere in the rainforest, if they had managed to escape from the city in time. And if they didn't escape, they were dead, and not just dead; *obliterated,* their every last molecule seared and shattered by the heat.

"Django?"

"Dead."

"Major Johnson?"

"Dead."

"Alan Carr?"

"Dead."

Helms surveyed his meagre army, and felt despair at how many had been lost.

But at least William and Mary Beebe were here. And so was Ben Kirkham. And old Hugo Baal. And the Noir, Sheena, he'd always admired her. She wore a black band around her eyes, but her expression was intent, and curious.

But his deputy, Professor Craddock, was dead. Commander Martin was also missing presumed dead. And so were most of the Techies, the Technician corps who had kept the dome running efficiently all this time.

Helms stood up, and beckoned the survivors to heed his words. He had recovered his composure by now, and he worked hard to keep his tone light, yet sombre and professorial.

"This has been," he said, "a truly terrible day."

Haunted eyes stared at him. Helms was no orator, but he knew the power of silence. He stood, and was silent, and let his regret seep out of him.

"We have," he explained, "survived an attempt to destroy us and our mission. We don't know the reasons behind it, we only know that the Juno computer answers to the CSO and the other members of the Galactic Corporation Board. And for whatever reason, they have decided we should die."

"You can't know that," Sorcha argued.

"Of course I know it," Helms snapped. "What other explanation could there be?"

"Earth rebels," said Sorcha, confidently.

"If they were rebels," Helms said gently, "they would have killed the Soldiers. They wouldn't have killed *us*."

"You don't know that," said Sorcha, but there was doubt in her voice.

"What happened to the dome?" said Ben Kirkham. "Why did they blow up the dome? How did—"

"That was Juno," said Helms. "It fired its ship's stealth torpe-does at us. That's why we had no warning of it. And then the DRs were ordered to kill on sight everyone they saw. But fortunately," he added, "our security measures evacuation procedures were of course fully implemented. And, crucially, I authorised a retaliatory strike."

There was a satisfyingly stunned pause at this last comment.

"Professor?" said Sorcha, baffled.

"What the hell are you on about?" marvelled Ben.

"Let me show you," said Helms. "Look up at the sky."

They looked up, through the gap in the canopy. It was daytime, but a single star shone bright. Juno, in close orbit around the planet.

"Now lower your helmets," he told them, and they did so.

"Increase your anti-glare to maximum," he advised them, over the MI-radio link.

They did so.

"Now watch."

For a long long time, almost twenty minutes, nothing happened. But no one stopped staring, not even the Soldiers; there they all stood, en masse, looking up at the sky, seduced by Helms's utter self-confidence. They waited and waited, for they knew not what: a symbol, a sign, a rescue mission?

And finally, they saw it; the bright star of Juno was joined by a host of other stars. Flashing lights were flickering all around it, and they all recognised it as the distant token of a vast space battle.

Juno was being attacked!

"We have twelve interplanetary missiles as part of our armoury on New Amazon," said Helms. *"All twelve were fired at Juno."*

Sorcha was visibly shocked at this; so was Hugo. Sergeant Ander-son grinned. Respect!

But then a cackling laugh assailed their ears over the MI-radio link, and all turned to see Dr Ben Kirkham, in paroxysms of mirth.

"You idiot," chortled Ben.

"It's our only hope of survival," Helms explained. *"While Juno is still up there, we can't—"*

"It's Juno. Juno!" said Ben, in his most cutting, patronising,

talking-to-an-imbecile tones. *"Professor, with respect—WANKER! WANKER! Those missiles don't stand a chance!"*

"I'm aware that Juno is—"

"You've signed our death warrant. The battle was over. But now, once Juno has blown those missiles out of the sky, she'll be good and angry. And she'll—"

"She won't—"

"Of course she will, you abject fool! Juno sits inside a Corporation battleship! She has state-of-the-art defensive—"

The sky lit up as a huge fireball ignited. It was like a sun going nova. Without the anti-glare shields, all watching would have been blinded.

Then the glare ebbed, and the sky was empty. Juno was gone.

One by one, they all shucked their helmets back.

"OK, you win," said Ben, grudgingly, and Helms fixed him with a triumphant stare.

"Antimatter bomb?" guessed Hugo.

"Indeed, so," said Helms triumphantly. "And now Juno is gone. The Quantum Beacon is gone. The remaining DRs still have their robot brains, but they can't be controlled by Juno or by anyone on Earth." He gave them a few moments to absorb this, then he added the killer coda: "And so, we are free!"

There was a longer, more stunned silence.

Helms patted his hands together, softly, dropping a broad hint that the assembled throng might now like to consider applauding him for his handling of the crisis. A few obedient souls did so, but most stood silent and incredulous.

"Free of what?" asked Hugo, endearingly baffled.

"Free of the CSO and his evil regime," explained Helms, barely hiding his impatience.

"Oh, that," Hugo acknowledged, absently.

There followed a further awkward, indeed painful silence. A ghastly miasma of dead air engulfed them.

And Sorcha and Ben and Mia and Hugo and all the others looked at Helms sceptically, all of them thinking the same thing.

Free? What the hell was Helms on about!

They didn't have a base camp, three quarters of the Soldiers were dead, they were trapped in the deadly New Amazon jungle, surrounded by Godzillas and killer plants and a vast array of unpredictable and unknown predators, with limited reserves and no way of recharging their plasma guns and AmRovers if they ran out of power.

Free?

They travelled as far as they dared through the afternoon and into the early evening. Then night fell, fast, with shocking darkness.

On Sorcha's orders, they made a wagon train out of the AmRovers, and lit the camp with the headlights. A few stars were visible through a small gap in the thick canopy above. But beyond that gap, the sky was blotted out.

The mood among the survivors was a blend of fear and elation. The camaraderie was intense, even between Scientists and Soldiers. All of them had faced a common foe. For the first time ever, they felt as if they might actually be on the same side.

Helms supervised the building of a fire, using Flesh-Webs as tinder and Aldiss tree bark for logs. It took them almost an hour, but it was time well spent. The smoke drove away insects and mini-birds, the flames soothed and reassured, and the crackle of the fire created a comforting and familiar backdrop to the scary sounds of the night. And with sentries posted, the survivors sat around the fire and felt the glimmerings of relief.

And there they sat, or stood close by on sentry duty, and each of them and all of them were lost in thought and reflection.

William and Mary Beebe were closest to the fire, savouring the heat, and each other's nearness.

Hugo Baal sat typing up his journal, sniffing occasionally as the smoke drifted across, carrying with it reminiscences of other fires, other expeditions, other tragic losses.

Ben Kirkham sat a little way back, on a hummock of New Amazonian soil and rock, as far away from Baal as he could contrive. He marvelled at his own uniqueness, and at the Professor's ingenuity in destroying Juno. Who would have thought the scrawny little bastard had it in him!

Sorcha, sitting nearer the fire, was tormented with guilt. A war had been fought and she had fought it. But if her enemy was the CSO, and the Galactic Corporation — did that make her a traitor?

Tonii Newton, standing at his sentry post, savoured a secret joy; the joy of being alive.

Nine other Soldiers were encircling the camp. Some were using the AmRovers as their cover in case of attack, some were standing in the shadow of Aldiss tree trunks; all were standing fiercely to attention. Eight other Soldiers kept guard in the five AmRovers, including Private Clementine McCoy; two per vehicle, sitting in the cockpit in front of the sonar and energy-detecting screens, ready to fire up the AmRover engines and turn them back into weapons of war.

But unlike Tonii, all these Soldiers were full of bitterness that they had been forced to flee, rather than staying and fighting and dying a Glorious death.

Mia Nightingale sat inside AmRover 3, away from the comfort of the camp fire, checking her film footage. Her coverage of the Attack on Xabar was astonishing. She watched again, as men and women died screaming, and DRs blasted plasma into flesh with callous efficiency.

Around the fire, thirty-three other survivors were clustered. Some sat alone, reflective, or depressed; some gathered in groups sipping whisky or wine from their emergency rations, sharing quiet reminiscences of friends now gone.

Dr David Go also spoke to no one. He saw Anderson pissing where he sat, and felt rather disgusted by it.

Sheena, Queen of the Noirs, sat close to the fire, and felt the heat of the fire on her cheeks; and imagined she could see the flames.

Jim Aura sat next to her and stared at Sheena, as firelight painted glory on her face and cast shadows around her blinded eyes.

And sitting near her, Professor Richard Helms, saviour of all his people, stared also into the flames, seeing patterns where they did not exist. The fire spat white sparks, which shot high then died out. Smoke billowed out, black and purple, from tough Aldiss tree bark. Flames crackled and voices whispered.

"Fuckings DRs."

"Can't believe we—"

"Always knew it would—"

"We had no choice but to—"

"Did you see how I creamed those m—"

"I hate this fucking planet."

"What do we do *now?*"

"No going back."

"I'm glad at least that—"

"Oh my sweetheart, why am I alive while you are—"

Helms spoke very little that night. He listened to the conversation that swirled about him, the words of regret and loss and hope and confusion, he drank in the rich stench of the rainforest that surrounded them, and marvelled at the strange sounds all around.

"What's that?" asked Sorcha at one point, as she heard a strange noise among the cacophony of strange noises in the jungle beyond.

It was a sound like a man being flayed, slowly. An awful screaming that started on a high note then rose higher and higher in an upward glissando. Then it began again. And again.

"A Howler Cockroach," said Hugo. "It's about this small." He indicated with his finger and thumb the tininess of the beast. "It expels air from its thorax, which in fact is its head, to create that noise. We don't know why."

"Plant or animal?" asked David Go.

"Animal. *Insectae.* It's very similar to an Earth cockroach in fact. Small, with a hard skin, and segmented. Convergent evolution in action yet again."

"That one?" Jim Aura mimicked the noise. It was a slithering, sucking noise, that had a chilling effect on all who heard it. It was like the sound of a soul leaving the body. Slurp, slurp.

"No idea."

"*Volpes terra,* a land shark," said Helms softly.

"Never heard of it," Hugo conceded.

"It's like a koala bear, with fangs."

"That one?" Sorcha whistled the notes.

It was bird song, melodious and rhythmic, though every note was subtly out of tune to human ears.

"That's a Godzilla."

"They *sing*?"

"Through their tail. The tail is not primarily a weapon, it's a vocal organ."

Helms nodded, confirming this hypothesis, which he in fact had initially suggested, and later proved.

"What's that?"

It was a grating, clacking noise, like two sticks being rubbed together.

"Don't know," Hugo conceded.

Hugo glanced at Helms, who shook his head. Both made a mental note to explore this mystery further.

"And that?" asked Sorcha. "The bells?"

Bells were ringing in discordant array. Big bells, and small tinkling bells. They listened intently to this melodious, eerie symphony of bells, with jangling chords and metallic arpeggios, which merged with the sounds of the Howler cockroaches and the constant crackle of the camp fire.

"*Amazonius campanologus,*" hazarded Hugo.

"Nice try."

"Did you know," said Sorcha, "that the trees make a noise if you stab the trunk? Like a dog barking."

"I've heard that sound. Must be air being expelled."

"Or this planet has trees that can bark."

"Maybe," said Tonii, mischievously, "on this planet, the trees bark and piss on the dogs?"

"Except there are no dogs."

"There's that headless thing."

"The No-Brain."

"*Quadrupes sinecep.*"

"Maybe that could be domesticated."

"It tried to kill us."

"It's still feral, like a wolf. Maybe we could tame it."

"No," said William Beebe, "it's not cute enough."

"What is cute enough then?" asked Mia Nightingale. "Hmm? What could we have as a pet? As our team guinea pig?"

"Nothing is cute," said Mary Beebe, firmly. "That's an anthropomorphic projection."

"I bet a baby Gryphon would be cute," said Tonii.

A silence fell.

"So what next?" asked Mary Beebe.

"We survive," said Helms, softly.

"The CSO tried to kill us!" said Ben Kirkham, enraged.

"We don't know that," Sorcha told him, firmly.

"*Something* made Juno go rogue."

"I always feared," said Mary Beebe, "that one day the computer would turn on us."

"Computers kill humans all the time," Sorcha reasoned. "They're a weapon of war. But all of us were logged on the database as Friendly! Juno knew each and every one of us by name and was duty bound to protect us. Someone would have had to override that with new code. But who?"

"It has to be the CSO. No one else would have authority."

"But why!" raged Ben Kirkham. "It's all so fucking—random."

The camp was now richly lit by the red glow of the fire. The AmRover headlights had been switched off and the sentries stood in shadow, but they had set up panoramic torches on posts to light all the possible approaches to their camp. Occasionally a luminous insect flew by, fast, drawn by the fire's light then deterred by its heat. But otherwise, the golden lights of the flames and the encircling flares of the panoramic torches were all that stood between them and pitch-black nothing.

And as the flames flickered, Helms's mood was growing increasingly sombre.

"Time we all hit the sack," said Sorcha, with military firmness.

"I think I'll linger," said Ben.

"Me too," said Hugo.

"We're making an early start," Sorcha told him icily.

"The campsite must be cleared by 5 a.m., anyone who falls behind schedule will be abandoned," Tonii added.

Hugo blinked. "Oh," he said, and stood up. "Are we setting alarms?"

Professor Helms laughed, softly and mockingly.

"I think the jungle will wake us up," said Mary Beebe.

DAY 3

When the sun rose, the dawn chorus erupted.

Sorcha woke with a crick in her neck. She disentangled herself from Helms's naked embrace, astonished at the penetrating and ceaseless sound of his snoring. She crawled out of the AmRover and saw dawn speckling the Flesh-Webs and making the tree trunks glow as they absorbed the sun's energy.

She wore no body armour, and the cold air shocked her skin. She could smell bacon. She rubbed her arms, warming herself, basking in the alienness of this planet, and tried not to breathe, because that was just wasted effort.

She wondered what had made her go to Helms's cabin the previous night. Someone was bound to have seen her; and the twelve people who shared the AmRover with them would surely have heard the sounds of their frantic and passionate late-night love-making.

But Sorcha didn't care. She was now the most senior Soldier on the planet, so no one could discipline her for an infraction of the fraternisation rules. Earth held no authority over her any more; and she really had needed that fuck.

It was more than just a fuck, admittedly. For it was good, and warm, and comforting, after a day of terror and horror, to spend a night sleeping next to another human being. Even if Helms *was* just a Scientist, and not a Soldier; and even though he, bizarrely in this day and age, snored.

And now she felt fresh, and alive, and awake. The deaths of the previous day were now just a distant memory. Those who had died were dead and gone. She wasted no energy brooding on them.

Sorcha did wonder, though, about precisely *why* Juno had turned rogue. Her fellow Soldiers had shared their judicious speculations on the matter the previous night; and the Scientists, as you'd expect, had a myriad explanations, some of quite staggering and paranoid complexity.

But her guess was that they would never know the truth. The Galactic Corporation was constantly subject to power struggles, and even at the best of times was by no means a rational entity. And Sorcha herself had participated in many wholly unneccessary massacres, many caused by the incompetence of bureaucrats who ordered the destruction of entire societies because of administrative errors. So it wouldn't surprise her if she and the other humans on New Amazon had been the victim of an utterly futile and indeed erroneous mass-execution order.

It was, she honestly felt, a damned shame. She was willing to die a Glorious death for the Galactic Corporation; why should that option be taken away from her?

She walked, cold and literally breathless, out into the jungle, until she reached a clearing where there was no tree canopy above. She stared and stared upwards, at the vast blue sky and speeding clouds, and tried to find Juno. But there was nothing. No bright dot. No Juno in orbit above them.

And that meant no Quantum Beacon, no way for Earth to communicate with them. She would never again receive orders from her commanding officers, or from the Galactic Corporation.

Sorcha knew she should be appalled at the destruction of the Mother Ship, and the loss of her command structure.

But, strangely, she was not.

From the diary of Dr Hugo Baal

June 24th

Last night, I dreamed that I was a Gryphon, flying high above the planet of New Amazon, able to see every living thing. I can see the crawling creeping writhing animals in the undergrowth and the insects and the bugs and the flying insects that can suck the sap out of trees or pierce body armour with their eerily sharp antennae-claws. I can see the Big Beasts—Godzillas, Land Krakens, Juggernauts—I can see the Tree Creatures, the Two-Tails and the Leapers and the Tarzans, I can see the canopy of trees stretching as far as the eye can see, and I can see all the creatures of the air, Gryphons like myself and Serpent-Birds and Bat-Beasts, and I can see where they nest and I fly onwards and onwards until I reach the Ocean of Trees, the vast mangrove swamp that crowds the watery ocean and turns it into wetland not sea, and I can see it all, I know the name of every single creature even though there are millions upon millions of them, but when I wake I can only remember a handful of the names.

Yet even so, I remember, oh so vividly, what it was like to be a Gryphon, flying high, above my planet.

Anyway. That was my dream.

Today we have been given strict survival duties, with no time for scientific work. But I hope to recommence writing this diary in a few days.

Professor Helms was having breakfast with William and Mary Beebe.

Helms had been networking since dawn. He had spoken to every member of his Science team, and to all the surviving Techies, and to every Soldier, and he had heard their concerns and their conspiracy theories, and allowed them to feel he was quietly and confidently in charge.

The prevailing theory among the Scientists was that the days of scientific exploration were now over; the CSO had decided that planets should be terraformed without bothering to study and catalogue the native flora and fauna. This explained why Juno had turned against them—because of course the Scientists would have fought such a plan tooth and nail. Simpler just to kill them all, so that Juno could instruct the four Satellites to begin terraforming.

The Soldiers, however, refused to believe that the CSO would have kept such a plan secret from them. After all, had they been so ordered, the Soldiers would have been entirely happy to slaughter all the Scientists.

So the Soldiers preferred the theory that a computer virus had made Juno deranged; although some feared there had been a coup on Earth, which would mean the CSO had been replaced by someone even more lunatic.

Helms listened carefully to all the theories, but at the end of the day, as he carefully pointed out, they would never know the truth of what had happened. So it was better, really, just to look to the future.

The Beebes, however, had a different question to pose to him, as Helms poured three black coffees and stiffened at the aroma of pure caffeine.

"May I ask," William Beebe said.

"Indeed," added Mary Beebe, and allowed a pause to build.

"What?" hinted Helms

"How?" said William.

"How what?"

"How—well, you know." William shrugged, and let his subtext fill the air.

"How did I know this would happen?"

"Yes."

"I didn't," Helms said.

"You had an antimatter bomb ready to blow up Juno," Mary pointed out.

Helms nodded, and made a self-deprecating face. "Simple contingency planning," he said. "You never know when—"

"You might need an antimatter bomb?" said William sceptically.

"It's happened before," Helms asserted. "Scientific expeditions have been wiped out."

"When? Where?"

"I wasn't aware of that!"

"That's because it was covered up," Helms explained.

"Then how do *you* know?"

"I was there. On Asgard. It happened there."

"I thought that particular expedition was wiped out by a meteorite."

"That was the cover story. In fact, the Mother Ship computer went rogue and fired a torpedo at the base. Earth Gamers. It's the curse of our civilisation. I was able to escape on a shuttle, but many of my dear friends died that day. So I vowed—never again."

"So," concluded William, "you have saved us. Or at least, many of us."

"Indeed," Helms admitted.

"I suppose we should say thank you," Mary snorted.

"No need."

"Thank you," said William, fulsomely.

"You're very welcome," Helms said, touched.

"And what do we do now?" Mary accused. "How do we get home?"

"We don't," Helms told her. "There's no way home, ever."

"Then," she said, looking around, not disapprovingly, "this is home."

"We could do worse," said William, smiling at the prospect.

Hugo had found a dead Two-Tail, and was skinning it with some delight. The meat was inedible to humans of course; but the autopsy was yielding some fascinating results.

The Soldiers, meanwhile, were practising their kata in a jungle clearing. Sorcha was watching them, approvingly, as they dipped and lunged and breathed long inaudible breaths preceding killer punch and kick combinations of blinding speed.

Helms sidled up to her, and indicated he wanted a private chat.

And so Sorcha and Helms moved out of earshot of the Soldiers, under the shade of a vast Aldiss tree. Helms looked at her, and smiled mischievously, remembering last night's coupling.

Sorcha just stared at him coldly.

"I've had a few notions—" he began.

"Professor, I'm not interested."

Helms blinked, and smiled his humble smile. "Ah, right, fair point," he said, his politeness laced with irony.

"I don't need advice from—"

"Sorcha please," he said mildly. "Is this really necessary? We're all in this together and—"

"Major."

He blinked again.

"Beg pardon?"

"You will address me as 'Major', or as 'sir'."

Helms grinned. "You'll be asking me to salute you next."

Sorcha saw no humour in that. Helms felt a lurch in the pit of his stomach.

"I'm sorry. Whatever you say, Major," he said smoothly, and was suddenly consumed with rage at his own words. "Oh for fuck's sake—"

"Don't you—"

"After all we've—"

Sorcha touched Helms's eyes with her fingertips. He realised the threat: she could blind him in an instant.

And she would, he knew it.

She really would!

"Consider," he told her, calmly, "your situation. There is no Earth. There is no Galactic Corporation. Do we really need these displays of military bravura?"

She patted his eyes with her fingertips and he saw stars.

"Fuck!"

"Just a warning."

"That hurt."

"It will hurt less when your eyes pop out, that's what shock does to you," she said sweetly. "But trust me, in a few days' time, the empty sockets will sting like fuck."

"Sorcha! Please! Why the hell can't we just—"

Sorcha took her hand away. Her stance changed. It was a kata stance, a state of total awareness and relaxation, preceding a deadly strike. Helms knew he had two choices: capitulate just in time, or just a few moments too late.

"Major Molloy," he said hastily, gabbling like a fool, "I'd, um, very much, um appreciate your guidance on what we should, ah, do next." He realised his voice was shrill, and hated himself for it.

And Sorcha smiled. She was dominating him now, with her body, with her eyes, with her authority.

"I'll let you know that in due course."

"Good, good. That's great. That's—well. Great."

"But remember this: military law will remain in force, even though we have lost contact with Earth."

"I would expect nothing less, um, Major," he sycophanted.

"There is only one way we can survive," she said generously, "and that is if you unquestioningly heed my authority. Are you prepared to do that, Professor?"

"Yes! Yes, of course," said Helms, with a shit-eating smile.

"Good."

There was a jagged pause.

"So, as I was saying, what's your plan, Major?" Helms asked. And though his tone was courteous, his intellectual contempt for her shone through.

"We go back to Xabar and rebuild the city, using the raw materials in the underground bunkers outside the city walls. The city is gone but the bunkers are vast and well fortified. So we can—"

"No."

"We go back. We need—"

"No! There'll be boobytraps. Robot-mode DRs with orders to kill us."

"—raw materials and supplies and energy batteries, all of which are to be found in the bunkers, and yes, there will be some combat, but—"

"We're not doing it."

"Professor," said Sorcha, warningly.

"It's folly, I won't allow it."

"I have given my orders, now you must—"

"What are you going to do, clap me in irons? Or do that stupid eye trick again?" And suddenly, it became clear that he did not fear her after all; for Richard Helms did not fear anyone.

"We return to Xabar!" Sorcha roared.

"Hmm? Yes? *That's* your plan?" Helms taunted. "What about the Depot?"

Sorcha was floored.

"What Depot?"

"What the fuck," said Ben Kirkham sourly, staring past the Soldiers to watch the Major and the Professor, lost in debate, occasionally touching each other, "are those two love birds up to?"

"I think it's sweet," David Go said.

Ben swivelled and fixed the hapless Go with his fiercest patronising glare.

"It speaks!" he sneered.

"Yes, I speak. In fact—" said David Go calmly, and to his horror Ben Kirkham turned and walked away as he was halfway through a sentence.

Tonii was lost in the kata. He moved with grace and speed and his body sang.

Hugo cut open the Two-Tail's cranium and peered inside at the complex whorls and patterns of its brain.

"It's beautiful," he muttered to himself.

Sheena listened to the jungle.

Her eyes were healing well. There was no infection. But also, no chance of getting replacement eyes.

She was blind, and so she listened to the jungle. Intently, remorselessly, carefully. Until she heard so much that she could visualise it, creating images out of sounds.

And her helmet could see for her. It whispered instructions. It told her who was near her, told her to step right, or step left. She could fly, with the help of her helmet's whispering. She could walk, thanks to her helmet.

But would she ever again be able to see?

Major Sorcha Molloy addressed the assembled team of Scientists, flanked by her body-armoured Soldiers.

"As the senior ranking Soldier, I am now Commander of the military forces," she explained, "and hence also leader of the scientific expedition. Professor Helms will be my civilian second in command, in a purely advisory capacity."

"We're not being told what to do by the military," protested Ben.

Twenty Soldiers locked and loaded in unison.

"Maybe we are," conceded Ben.

"My Warriors will ensure your safety. But all the science team will have responsibilities assigned to them. Doctors William and Mary Beebe, you're in charge of supplies and team morale. Dr Ben Kirkham, you will maintain the equipment, making sure the plasma guns are fully charged at all times. Mia Nightingale, you're my liaison between the Soldiers and the science geeks. Four of the five AmRovers will each carry a team of ten, with a minimum of three Soldiers in each team, AmRover 1 will carry a team of nine, including Professor Helms, with myself and two others in the Flyer. Each Scientist will be supplied with a plasma cannon and a plasma pistol, and each team will have a proportionate share of the flash grenades and mortars."

"You've really thought this out in detail, haven't you?" said Hugo, wryly.

"We have five Amazon Rovers, one Flyer, and a Scooter. Who brought the Scooter?"

"That was Ashley," said Tonii Newton.

"Our objective is to create a new base camp at the Weapons and Provisions Depot, map reference B453. Do you have that?" said Sorcha.

There was a baffled silence.

"What Depot?"

"There is no Depot."

Ben checked the map reference on his helmet display. "It's jungle there. It's never even been reconnoitred. This Depot doesn't exist," said Ben.

"Just here," said Helms, pointing at his own virtual screen.

"We don't have a Weapons and Provisions Depot!" Ben complained. "If I say it doesn't exist, it doesn't exist."

"Oh, actually, it does," said Helms, with a shy smile, as he quietly asserted his authority over the meeting. "It just doesn't exist on the computer record."

Sorcha stayed deadpan, allowing everyone to believe she'd known about the Depot all along.

All eyes were on Helms. He tapped the grid reference on his virtual screen. A map of the jungle appeared and floated in mid-air. On it a building was clearly marked, partially underground, concealed from the air by the Canopy. And it was *vast*.

"Why would you build a thing like that?" asked Ben, savagely. "And not *tell* anyone?"

"Just a little trick," Helms said, waving down his virtual screen, "that I learned when I was a university bursar. Some things are best kept hidden away from official scrutiny."

Ben was shaken. He glared at Helms with unconcealed hate at having being publicly proved wrong.

"What's at this Depot?" asked Mia.

"Guns, grenades, spare body armour, a generator, food synthesisers and biomass, 10,000 BBs, helicopters, a space shuttle."

"Ye gods," said Hugo.

"Why don't we just go back?" William reasoned. "To Xabar. There may be stuff we can salvage from the bunkers."

"No, that's a stupid idea," said Sorcha firmly.

"There may be DRs who survived the blast," Helms explained diplomatically. "And their little robot brains will still be obeying their last given order, namely, to eliminate us, violently. We have to keep out of their way. It's a big jungle. So long as they don't find us, we're safe."

"And pray remind me," said Hugo, "why all this happened in the first place. Why the blazes would Juno want to kill us?"

Helms fixed him with an intent stare. "I wish I knew," he said with burning intensity. "But I don't."

They all pondered on this a moment.

"So there you go," Helms concluded crisply. "Now, to business. Let's begin our march."

Gloria Baker was on point duty, and she had big dreams.

She was low-hovering in her body armour beside AmRover 1, as they made their way through the jungle to the Depot. Behind them drove the other four AmRovers; and at the back of the convoy was the three-person Flyer, with torpedoes primed and ready to use against any beasts pursuing them.

Gloria's big dreams included becoming an acclaimed Scientist, discoverer of a vast number of new species and inventor of a new biological synthesis that explained the vagaries of alien evolution. She also dreamed of being a hero, a fighter against injustice, and a campaigner for human rights.

She also dreamed of being Professor Helms's lover. He was a calm, impressive, strangely attractive man, a little arrogant perhaps, and rather too skinny for her taste, but his intelligence blazed from him. She'd love to be with a man like that, to mellow and exhilarate and inspire him.

Gloria had big dreams, and wonderful dreams they were, but then she walk-hovered over a patch of swamp and even though she was five feet in the air the swamp water leaped up and sucked at her and ripped off her legs, body armour and all. Swamp marsh filled her body armour and she died with methane stench in her nostrils. Her body was slurped back down into the swamp and vanished.

"*One man down, Professor,*" said Gloria's best friend John. "*Swamp got her.*"

"*Why wasn't she hovering?*"

"*She was.*"

"*Then hover higher.*"

The four remaining members of the Point Team hovered higher, and continued to plasma-blast their way through the suppurating animal flesh of the Webs.

Helms absorbed the news. Another member of the team dead. Gloria Baker, biochemist and naturalist. He didn't remember her. Or was she the one who...? No, no. That wasn't her.

Helms cursed himself. He had a terrible memory for names and faces—species yes, but people no. So he took a look at her photograph on his virtual screen, and yes, he knew her now! The redhead with the loud laugh, the one who used to stare at him strangely sometimes, he didn't know why.

Helms read Gloria's biog; and wished he'd got to know her better.

Mia was editing her footage.

She liked to edit three or four versions of the same sequence, in different styles, and sometimes even different genres. For the Godzilla Day, she had a wealth of material to draw upon—from the cameras in the AmRovers, the body-armour cams of all concerned, plus her own panoramas and master shots on the 3D cam.

These were movies you could walk into and fly around. You just needed a pair of goggles or a retinal implant and a wireless MI in your brain, which everyone had these days. And the experience would then begin: flying through the jungles of New Amazon like a Soldier or a Scientist; zooming in to become the size of an insect and inhabiting a microscopic realm; then zooming out to see what was happening from the air and from space; even seeing the whole scene from the point of view of the Godzilla or the Cerberus.

The entire day's adventure was rendered into a perfect replica of the experience of being on the planet, with total interactivity. But this was just one piece in the overall jigsaw; the eventual movie would offer experiencers a chance to *be* on New Amazon for hours or days or months or even years. You could hunt Godzillas, or *be* a Godzilla, or you could be a Gryphon, or any one of the other New Amazon creatures. You could even be a hard-ass female Soldier and fuck the Professor in charge of the expedition (though for legal reasons, an actor-simulacrum was used to double for Professor Helms in all his scenes).

Or, if you were not a nerd or a geek or a wonk, you could buy a package-download that allowed you a more varied smorgasbord experience of thousands of different planets. You would tank up with drugs or alcohol, set the control to shuffle, and spend an hour, or a night, or a week, inhabiting all the alien ecospheres of known space. You could be a Heebie-Jeebie, a Sparkler, a flame beast or a Godzilla; you could rape the native women on Cambria; or fuck the sexy hominids on Gazillion.

There was a wealth of low-grade alien ecosphere material available, much of it concerned with killing and dissection and fornication with sentient beings. Mia, however, worked at the top end of the market; she created works of art, and works of science. But even she couldn't afford to turn up her nose at occasional snippets of snuff and torture. It added spice to the curry, she felt.

But Mia was first and last an artist: a visual genius, in the view of many pundits; a documentary film-maker of exceptional experience and talent. And the New Amazon footage was, she firmly believed, some of her best work to date.

Her worry was, who would see this now? Juno was gone, the link to Earth destroyed. They were trapped on this planet for the rest of their lives.

So who the hell was going to want to watch her movies?

Helms was still reviewing, via his virtual screen, the lists of those killed at Xabar, after Juno's attack. Hundreds. The names blurred, and so many were strangers to him. He remembered her, and him. And him. But he'd never seen *her* before, or him, or him, or him, or her, or him. Or—no, in fact, damn it all, that was Bill Jones, he was one of Helms's closest friends...

He forced himself to read the biogs and look at their faces. He even read summaries of some of their academic papers, to get a flavour of the lost lives.

Sergeant Anderson was spooked by the scale of their defeat at Xabar.

There were only twenty Soldiers left, plus Major Molloy as Commanding Officer, out of a force of 195. It was hard to believe that so many had gone to Glory. And Anderson kept making silly mental mistakes—thinking, I must talk to Fletcher or Walker about such and such, momentarily forgetting that Fletcher and Walker, and so many others, were all dead.

But he was glad that Commander Martin was dead—Anderson had despised the man's mealy-mouthed intellectualism. However, he considered Major Molloy to be a competent and credible commanding officer. She was decisive and ruthless and had proved time and again that she wasn't afraid to die.

But it was a shame that one of the freaks had survived. Sergeant Maria Laxton was dead, they'd not be seeing *her* beautiful blue eyes and taut male–female body again. But Private Tonii Newton was still with them, looking like a man, sounding like a man, but with female curves and breasts and a fanny and an appalling tendency to colour-coordinate whilst off duty.

That freak was a . . . a freak! An abomination, an affront to the gods of nature. The very sight of him made Anderson want to puke.

Although, Anderson had to grudgingly admit, he was a damned fine Soldier.

The convoy inched its way through the gloomy jungle. "Birds" flew in the sky above them, "insects" hovered in the air creating a strange miasma. And, disconcertingly, they had to drive through a "jellyfish" colony, a vast flock of tens of thousands of translucent lighter-than-air creatures, that sucked juice from the Flesh-Webs and, when replete, drifted up to the clouds and shat red pus.

Thus, before long, they were travelling through a Dante's Inferno of ghost-like beings in a world where the air itself was red.

"What are you working on, Professor?" William Beebe asked Professor Helms.

The words scrolled down the virtual screen, security-coded so that only Helms could see them:

Gregory, Richard. 34. Xenobiologist. Interests: Science, reading, being with my wife. Married to Helen Gregory.

Gregory, Helen. 44. Xenobiologist. Interests: Science, fencing, being with my husband Richard.

Hopkins, Michael, 232. Geologist. Interests: Running, swimming, poetry.

Jenson, Angela, 132. Soldier. Interests: Getting to know my grandchildren.

And more, and more, and more.

"It's nothing," said Helms. "Nothing. Just—" He broke off, distressed.

William stared at him, puzzled.

"Have we met?" the dark-haired woman next to Sorcha in the Flyer said.

"I'm Major Sorcha Molloy. Commander of the Military Forces."

"Yes, I know," the dark-haired woman said patiently. "I'm Margaret. Margaret Lamarr."

"You're the climatologist?"

"I am."

"What have you found out about New Amazon?" Sorcha asked curtly.

Margaret blinked. "Um, we're still working on the oxygen question. With so much plant-life, why so little oxygen?"

"Since photosynthesis is clearly operating."

"We think the Ocean-Aldiss-Tree sucks in oxygen. But we don't know how."

"We'll change all that," said Sorcha casually, and Margaret flinched.

"When we terraform, you mean?" she said acidly.

"Well, that is the object of the exercise."

"The object of the exercise," said Margaret, precisely, "is, or rather was, no damn it, *is,* to study this alien planet. And to catalogue all of its species, in the minutest detail."

"Before we kill them all," said Sorcha.

"Before we kill them all," Margaret repeated, bitterly.

"*Incoming xenohostiles,*" said Ben over the MI-radio.

"Brace yourself," the pilot, McKenley, told the two women as the Juggernauts lumbered into view.

"Wait!" Margaret had her camera out and was filming. She started talking into the camera mike: "Two adults and a child, I think. These specimens are larger than those previously observed. *Juggernautus rufus,* the red-scaled beast. Note the absence of eyes. We think the skin on the head is a large retina, the head is a huge eyeball. Zooming in now."

The Juggernauts were getting closer.

"Fire when you're ready," McKenley urged Sorcha.

"Doing ultrasound scan," said Margaret, calmly.

The Juggernauts were getting closer.

"*Remember, those creatures can leap,*" said Ben over the MI-radio, and one of the Juggernauts leaped high, high enough to reach the front of the convoy. But as it leaped, Sorcha fired the craft's plasma cannon and ripped an opening in its torso, then incinerated its head and carried on firing as the two other Juggernauts plunged into the jungle, only to be pursued by a constant hail of plasma fire. McKenley sent the Flyer swooping after them as Sorcha laced the creatures with red cutting fire. Heads fell off, the bodies were ripped open,

Butterfly-Birds flew up into the air then turned and attacked the Flyer with savage beaks. Margaret triggered the sonic boom switch and the creatures were stunned and dazed, and Sorcha could pick them off one by one.

All the xenohostiles were dead, and McKenley turned the Flyer around.

"Let me get a close-up of the corpse," Margaret pleaded.

"We need to rejoin the convoy," Sorcha said sternly. She could never understand these Scientists; they had no fucking sense of urgency.

The Flyer resumed its position at the arse-end of the convoy.

Behind them Sorcha could see a trail of gore and blood and a mewling, squeaking, crawling creature which, she later discovered, was the baby Juggernaut's brain.

"*Here it is!*" a voice called out.

"*My God,*" said Hugo Baal, in awe, as the convoy slowly came to a halt. Before them loomed a vast and green and impossible mountain.

"*OK, people, you know what to do,*" said Sorcha in the flyer, over the MI-radio link.

The Flesh-Webs had died away, to be replaced by the Jungle-Wall, a sheer mass of compacted vegetation. The wall soared up from the ground to the canopy, then burst through the canopy itself to form an organic barrier that nestled against the stratosphere, well above the height at which AmRovers could comfortably fly. And it snaked an awesome course across the mainland, moving slowly over time, as billions of six-headed insectoid creatures—Six-Heads—wove this wall-web out of their own barely digested excrement.

It was an awesome wonder of nature; shit turned into landscape.

The convoy bunched up. AmRover nestled against AmRover, and Sorcha's Flyer bumped up against the last Rover in the convoy. The

Point Teams all rejoined their vehicles. Helms returned to his cabin and took control on his virtual screen. The plasma cannons in the first two AmRovers, including Helms's Rover, were charged from the Bostock batteries. Helms waited a full minute to allow his people to psych themselves up. Then he gave the signal and the AmRovers rolled forward.

The plasma cannons fired sheer bursts of energy and ripped a huge and perfectly circular hole in the Jungle-Wall. Flames and billowing smoke darkened the air outside the AmRovers and millions of Six-Heads scurried out of their protective nests and massed dangerously. When the hole was a circle a hundred metres in diameter, Helms gave the order and the lead truck accelerated. The cannons kept firing, the wall kept burning and the convoy crashed into the opening and inched its way through the growing hole. The Six-Heads swarmed over the AmRovers and the Flyer, blotting out their windscreens, striving to find a crack that would allow them to attack the attackers of their vegetal home. But the hardglass and toughmetal held, and the AmRovers crawled forward and crunched insects under their treads as the convoy plunged deeper and deeper into the hole in the Jungle-Wall, until all light was gone and the convoy was lost inside the insect-woven mass.

Once, a plasma cannon's pillar of fire wavered, and died, and it was instantly replaced by a backup cannon. And the hole grew, as plasma burned through vegetable iron. But the fire spread with painful slowness and the tunnel in which they were wedged was blocked with acrid black smoke. And meanwhile, at the back of the convoy, the wall was growing back, as the Six-Heads began weaving their web again. Before long the entrance to the hole would be filled and the smoke would be trapped inside. If the AmRovers were too slow, or the wall didn't burn fast enough, the webs would be woven around the vehicles themselves, leaving them caged and doomed inside the Jungle-Wall.

Helms hated the darkness that filled the glass windscreens of the AmRover cockpit. The vehicle rolled and bucked and toppled forward, the plasma cannons fired into nothing and nowhere, and

Helms had to trust to experience to support his belief that a hole was in fact being burned into their jungle prison. The cab of the AmRover was airtight but Helms could vividly imagine the acrid fumes outside and visualise the billions of Six-Heads swarming over the AmRovers and the Flyer, all the while shitting out their viscous green and purple glue.

"Are you OK, Sorcha?" he said over his MI-radio link.

"Are we slowing down?"

"We're slowing down."

"Why?"

"I don't know. I have my foot on the accelerator."

"Are the plasma cannons working?"

"The control lights are on. I can't see what's actually happening out there."

"Are you sure we're still moving?"

"The speed dial says we are, just about."

"I can't feel myself moving."

"That's an illusion. No visual clues."

"Maybe we're not moving. Maybe we're stuck. Maybe these fucking creatures are sealing us in."

"I don't think so."

"You don't know that, though, not for certain."

"I don't know that, no, not for certain," he conceded.

The world had vanished, sensation had vanished. All Helms had were his instruments to tell him they were slowing down, and that the plasma guns were still firing. He checked the dials again. Only one bar's worth of charge left. He switched to Recharge and the circuit failed. Damn!

The guns kept firing, relentlessly, releasing enough plasma energy to warm a city. If they carried on much longer firing at this rate, they'd run out of power. And if they ran out of power, they would not be able to blast any more hole.

Helms felt like a rat in a pipe that was sealed at both ends.

Sweat was dripping from his chin, it was drizzling down his

throat, under his body armour. He had to force himself to breathe. He wondered if the air was getting staler.

He closed his eyes and fell asleep for two seconds and woke with a start of horror. How could that have happened? How could he have *slept*?

"We're through," said Mulligan, who was monitoring the ship's sensors, but Helms kept the plasma cannon on Fire. He set the hull to Heat, to burn off the Six-Heads, and eventually, when he was as sure as he could be without a visual reference that he was in the open air, he spun the AmRover around in a three-point turn and stopped.

"We're through," said AmRover Number 9, as it followed behind him.

"Through," said AmRover Number 1.

"Through," said AmRover number 7.

"Through," said Ben, in AmRover 3.

"We're through," said Sorcha in the Flyer.

Acid jets fired out from vents in each of the vehicles and sprayed over the hulls, and after about thirty minutes the windscreens and clear walls were free of insects and the world returned. It was a sunny day. The sunlight burned Helms's eyes.

"How long did that last?" he asked.

"Five hours."

"Let's carry on."

DAY 4

From the diary of Dr Hugo Baal

June 25th

I have collected the intact corpses of a hundred Six-Heads. Many were crushed by our AmRovers or plasma-blasted, some were burned by the heated hull, but the best samples I have are still fairly intact, albeit dead. I found no live specimens, and to date no one has studied a living Six-Head. Sometimes they are alive when you scoop them into the bag, and then the damned things are dead when they come out again. Perhaps they are highly sensitive to the shock of capture.

They are beautiful creatures, like stars that crawl. Each head has a chin that acts as a leg, and the central segment has a dozen legs with what appear to be arms with opposable claws, as well as the wings on top. I've found traces of Jungle Web substrate, aka Green Goo, in the mouths of many of the specimens, and it seems fair to deduce that they eat and excrete through the same orifice, i.e. the mouth.

There are three distinct types in my samples—fully winged, with no dagger wings, dagger-winged only, and fully winged but with one additional set of dagger wings and brightly patterned central segments. The "wings" in fact may not be wings at all, they may be neural organs, or indeed sexual organs, or possibly eyes, but if they are wings that suggests that the Six-Heads are capable of flying to distant locations to forage for plant matter, though in fact no one has ever seen them airborne.[1]

I am analysing the stomach contents of each of the Six-Heads to determine the planetary source of the vegetation they have ingested.

Provisionally, I have labelled the creatures thus.

Six-Heads

Kingdom: *Animalia*
Phylum: *Arthropoda*

---

1 Hence *Pterygota* should be considered a highly provisional classification.

Sub-Phylum:	Chelicerata
Class:	Insecta
Subclass:	Pterygota
Order:	Gladiatorius
Family:	Carnivora[2]
Genus:	Sexticeps
Species:	Sexticeps alesum
	Sexticeps sinealesum[3]
	Sexticeps coloratum

The chelicerae are hollow and may allow the Six-Heads to spit venom as well as vomiting/excreting plant and animal matter.

The joy of this creature is that it can easily be categorised within existing taxonomies. It is an arthropod with a segmented body and chelicerae around the mouth, which are morphologically comparable to those possessed by Earth spiders.

It's such a treat to find such a remarkably normal creature! It's very much the kind of insect one might expect to find in an English country garden — apart from its six-heads, dagger wings, flesh-eating tendencies, and its habit of creating vast impermeable walls thousands of feet high.

The journey continues to be slow, and tedious, and dangerous in the extreme.

2 They eat the Flesh-Webs *(Carnearenum)*, which are indubitably Animal, but also gnaw tree trunks and other vegetation.
3 The wings of the *sinealesum* have all evolved into serrated daggers, though flight may still be possible for them, though I'm blowed if I can see how. The *alesum* has four symmetrical sets of functional, so far as we know, wings. The *coloratum* has three and a half (?!?) sets of functional wings, and one set of dagger wings.

DAY 5

From the diary of Dr Hugo Baal

June 26th
No scientific work was done today, due to the traumatic events which occurred.

For obituaries of the deceased, click here.

Sorcha was aware of a strange mood in the cab of the Flyer. Margaret Lamarr was an impressive woman—a brilliant academic and also a skilled spaceship pilot. But she didn't conform to any of the standard personality types with which Sorcha was familiar. She was not Alpha Female, but nor was she Quietly Task-Driven, and she was too emotional and articulate to be Geek. She was friendly, inappropriately so, and chatty, annoyingly so, and Sorcha wished that she could get her transferred to one of the AmRovers. The two-person back seat of the Flyer was a cramped space, and Sorcha would much rather share it with someone taciturn and prosaic.

But why the atmosphere? The sour face? The one thing that was more annoying than Margaret chattering away and confiding personal details about herself was Margaret glowering and saying nothing.

Was it something Sorcha had said? Had she been rude?

But Sorcha was *always* rude. People were used to it.

Was Margaret losing faith in Sorcha's ability to do her job?

But that was impossible! Sorcha was legendarily capable, and fearless. That's why she'd risen so far in the army hierarchy.

Sorcha recalled an incident the previous day when she'd blown a Roc out of the sky with a plasma blast. Helms had queried her rationale for wasting power in such a way; but she'd sharply counter-argued that the Roc might have been descending in a predatory fashion, prior to dropping its trademark shit bombs.

In reality, Sorcha had shot the Roc just for the hell of it, to practise her hand-eye battle coordination, and because she loved killing aliens. She might, it belatedly occurred to her, have even said so to Margaret. So had that caused offence? Was there anyone in the universe so prissy and buttoned up that they didn't take joy in zapping, smashing and exterminating alien creatures?

It was hard to believe; but Sorcha had a sneaking suspicion it was so.

"What the fuck is your problem?" said Sorcha, bluntly.

"No problem."

"You've got a face like a fucking smacked arse. What's wrong?"

"I'm reflective."

"Of what?"

"Of life. Skip it. You wouldn't understand."

"It's the Roc, huh?"

"The what?"

"Killing the Roc. Yesterday. For no reason."

"Why would that bother me?"

"Beats me."

"It's an alien."

"Some people don't believe in killing aliens."

"Which people?"

"Some people. They think life is sacrosanct."

"I don't think that."

"Thank fuck."

"What makes you think I'd think that?"

"You seem the type."

"What type?"

"Liberal."

"I'm not."

"Double thank fuck."

"You're welcome."

"So what's your problem?"

"Nothing," said Margaret, pursing her lips even more.

Sorcha had a moment of epiphany.

"Helms . . . !" she breathed.

After that first night with Helms, in the aftermath of the massacre at Xabar, Sorcha had decided it was pointless to keep her "relationship" with the Professor a secret any longer. And so every night since then, she and Helms had been sleeping together in his AmRover quarters, fucking loudly and often. All the camp had heard their love-making. And all of them marvelled — what on earth did a man like Helms see in *her*! — or mocked — why the hell would the Major fuck *him*? – but no one really cared. Scientists and Soldiers alike, they were used to living cheek by jowl, and privacy wasn't a priority.

But Margaret's cheeks were now bright pink. Sorcha's guess had hit its target; Margaret was jealous. Jealous!

"Oh fuck you," said Margaret sourly, and then the DR appeared and started firing.

"Xenohostile," said Ben calmly, then the DR's missile landed on AmRover No. 9 and blew it off the road. The undergrowth ignited and a vast flare spread all around them. Smoke billowed. Ben targeted the hostile and fired a smart anti-aircraft missile which soared high and crashed down on the track behind them, and at precisely the same moment Sorcha opened fire with her explosive bullets, but the DR was running.

The blast from the anti-aircraft missile shook Sorcha's teeth in their sockets but McKenley revved the Flyer and hurtled forward through the flames.

"Missed!" screamed Ben, appalled. He'd tagged the target on his screen, the smart missile should have linked up with the satellite tracking system to guarantee a successful hit. This wasn't hi-tech, it didn't need Juno's computing powers, it was basic military technology. But it had failed.

"In pursuit," said Sorcha over her MI.

"Take defensive positions," ordered Helms. The AmRovers rolled around into a circle and a force field linked them.

Sorcha and Margaret hurtled after the running DR, laying down tracks of blazing plasma fire, until the DR turned and hovered and fired two bursts from its arm cannons.

Sorcha engaged the defensive shield, which was designed to absorb the energy of a plasma burst and redirect it back at the attacker.

But the defensive shield didn't work. The plasma burst was pulsed at a frequency that wasn't recognised by the shield's programming, and the burning bullets of plasma hit the Flyer and the Flyer spiralled out of the sky and crashed to earth.

Sorcha felt her body and limbs smashed by an unseen god. She heard a screaming sound; it was herself. The cab was on fire, but ceiling jets doused the flames with flame-retardant spray and she pressed Eject and suddenly she and Margaret were lying on their backs in the undergrowth. "*Helmet*s," said Margaret, engaging her helmet, and Sorcha saw that Margaret was screaming with pain—her leg had taken a hit from an explosive bullet. Sorcha helmeted-up, then picked Margaret up bodily and carried her away from the crash site. Sorcha subvocalised again but Margaret was looking at her blankly, so Sorcha opened her helmet up and spoke in real air: "Are you OK?"

Margaret's thigh armour was crushed; the leg was clearly shattered beneath it.

"I'll survive," Margaret whimpered.

"McKenley?"

"Don't know."

Sorcha crawled back to the Flyer. McKenley had been hit by the plasma blast, he was dead. Sorcha crawled back to Margaret.

"Draw your weapon please," said Sorcha.

Margaret took out her plasma pistol.

"I'll fetch help," said Sorcha calmly, and suddenly there was a look of panic in Margaret's eyes.

"You're not leaving me?"

"You've got oxygen, subcutaneous food and water, healing implants. You're good for a week or more. But you can't walk with that leg."

"I could make a crutch. You could support me."

"Sorry."

"I'll die if I'm on my own."

"Sorry."

"You're leaving me, aren't you? You're not coming back."

Sorcha left. She tried again to engage her MI-radio to get a satellite position, but failed. So instead she used her brain-chip nav backup, which gave her a grid reading of her location plus a diary entry for the last known location of the convoy. She was only six klicks away. Sorcha began walking.

It was obvious now that Sorcha had fallen for a simple ambush strategy. The DR had isolated and destroyed the convoy's only Flyer. And now, she guessed, the DR would melt away and bide its time. The convoy would be in full defensive posture, invulnerable to all but the most ferocious of assaults. So why bother attacking? Why not wait until Helms and his people got bored and started driving again? And then launch another ambush...

Sorcha sifted through her memories of the Humanoid DR that had fired at them. It had run fast and skilfully, zigzagging through the undergrowth, with its back-arsenal firing out an endless cloud of chaff to impede following fire. But the DR hadn't been running away from her; it had simply laid a trail of poisoned meat that Sorcha had voraciously swallowed.

Sorcha walked fast through the Flesh-Webs, stepping on green algae-like stuff and slippery brown turdlike growths. Her helmet was back in position and she could hear her own breathing. Then she saw the Basilisks and her breathing got louder, more desperate. Her heart beat faster and the pulse in her temple pounded, like a dagger being plunged into her skull.

Helms stepped outside his AmRover. The communal energy shield assured almost total protection to all inside its perimeter, so he retracted his helmet and breathed in stale air and rotten eggs. Then he beckoned Ben to join him.

"What kind of xenohostile?"

"It wasn't," said Ben.

"Not an alien?"

"A DR."

Helms felt a jolt of panic. "This far from the base? How would it have found us?"

"It's a robot. It has search software. It's implacable. Go figure."

"How many DRs?" Helms queried, in his calmest voice.

"Just one, as I say. I didn't spot it until it was too late. It must have stealth capacity too."

"What kind of super fucking robot is this?"

"We should keep the force fields up," said Ben.

"Of course we should," Helms conceded.

"And wait for survivors to reach us," said Ben.

"I know," said Helms.

"Twenty-four hours max, then we move on. We'll be handicapped without the Flyer," said Ben, "but..."

Helms realised his heart was racing; his palms were damp. He could only think about one thing, one person, and that was Sorcha. He ached with desire for her, and was overwhelmed by an urge to protect her.

Protect her? Was he mad?

Sorcha didn't need his protection! She could kill him with a single finger-strike. At times, when they made love, she was so powerful that he feared she would break him like a stick. She was the embodiment of a resourceful, dangerous, ruthless Warrior. And yet—

"I'm going back to fetch them," said Helms, abruptly, and Ben stared at him, speechless, wholly unable to believe what Helms had just said.

Margaret was getting drowsy.

Stay awake! Stay awake!

Her helmet was up and locked. Her body armour could withstand an attack from a projectile bullet, or a medium-intensity plasma blast, or a mauling from any normal predator. On one occasion, a team member had been eaten alive by a Godzilla, and survived, with shit-smeared armour and a phobia about small dark places, but intact and unhurt. So her chances were good. They—no! Awake!

Margaret's leg had been badly crushed by the impact of the plasma bullet, but the armour's doc function had contained the bleeding. Neomorphine was pumping through her body to contain the pain. Coagulants stopped her bleeding out. The armour had self-sealed. Her heart-boost implant was keeping her blood pumping. She could survive for days. If she could—only—

Stay awake!

The stimulants in her bloodstream weren't helping to combat the drowsiness. The painkillers weren't killing the pain either. And the stress, the pain, the horror, were making her tune out. She was losing her grip on the moment, losing consciousness.

Stay awake!

She still had her plasma pistol and her flash grenades. The only serious danger would be if the DR returned. Otherwise, she could endure in this jungle until her body had healed, and in a couple of hours she could start walking. However dangerous the creatures, they were no threat to a soldier with modern weaponry and state-of-the-art body...

Stay awake!

If only she could stay awake. She was safe, but only if she could stay awake.

Stay awake!

Stay

Helms insisted on taking one of the precious plasma cannons, and a spare Bostock battery. He asked for volunteers to help him and got none. He was defying all military protocols by attempting a rescue mission in the face of Level 1 danger, and he wondered if his authority would ever recover from this blow.

However, looking on the bright side, he mused, he probably wouldn't survive long enough for that to be a problem.

Sorcha started walking towards the Basilisks. The jungle was dense here, so she couldn't use her body-armour jets to fly over them. And it would take too long to go around. She knew she only had twenty-four hours to recover her position with her unit before they left without her.

Sorcha firmly believed that Margaret stood a chance, once she was past the six-hour self-healing period and able to walk again. But Sorcha wasn't prepared to jeopardise her own survival by waiting for Margaret to be fit to walk. That would be foolish, and unmilitary.

Sorcha toyed with the idea of seeking and stalking the DR, and destroying it in order to safeguard the larger group. But the chances were that she'd just wander blindly and not find it, and would lose her life for no purpose. That was too great a risk to take. For Sorcha knew she was a valuable asset, the product of vastly expensive military training, and it had to be her priority to keep herself alive.

Sorcha continued, walking carefully and quietly through the field of Basilisks. She had no idea what these creatures could do if provoked, but she'd once seen a flock of them stalk a Godzilla, and she'd been chilled at their eerie patience as they slowly crept towards the slumbering beast. In the end the Godzilla had heard something, and was spooked and fled, and the Basilisks had returned to their natural, slithering state, wrapped around tree trunks, or half-buried in soil.

There were many thousands of these snakelike creatures here, she realised; they formed a carpet over which she hovered, and some were large enough to span an entire tree trunk. The Basilisks, like most New Amazonian creatures, had no eyes. And to her amazement she saw one Basilisk fall from the tree canopy and fly downwards in slow gliding movements.

Sorcha moved slowly, ever more slowly, but the field of Basilisks began to stir. They could, she deduced, sense her by some form of echo-location.

Then the ground below her erupted. A Basilisk the size of a space-ship seized her in its claws and she commenced to fire her plasma cannon. Blood gushed into the air when she blew the monster's head off and she fell from its mouth to the ground and was ensnared in powerful snake coils that strangled and crushed her, but she carried on blasting, rose to her feet and hovered with her boot jets and flew her way through the forest of flesh.

Entrails and scarlet blood rained around her as she flew through the Basilisk horde, plasma-blasting remorselessly. She marvelled at the sharp teeth and claws of these creatures, which emerged from every part of their black cylindrical bodies, and finally she was through and past the hazard, and she cut her jets and hit the ground and commenced running.

Her heart was pounding again. She felt as if the drumbeats of her pulse were going to rip her in two. She had almost died back there, and the realisation shot jolts of panic and exhilaration and fear through her body. She was driven by her own hysteria, exulting because she had so very nearly died but instead *had fought and won and lived*.

Sorcha paused a moment, and checked her bearings. She was off course. She began to trek eastwards, fording a fast river that was covered with a steam haze of methane gas. Another few hours and she'd be back with the convoy. She just had to keep moving.

And so on she walked, panting, frightened, anxious, tired, excited, and alive.

Helms still had an MI-radio connection with the Satellite, which could track Sorcha and Margaret and McKenley via a spectrum analysis of the jungle that caused their energy-retarding body suits to loom out like shadows in noonday sunlight.

He feared the continuing danger from the DR, even if it was just a stupid robot; he feared the Godzillas, which he believed were growing more intelligent; and he feared there might be some unknown predator species that might be strong enough to kill him through his body armour. He also feared himself, for he didn't understand why he was risking so much for a woman he hardly knew and barely liked. They were lovers, admittedly—but why was he *risking his life* for her?

He had three body armours highlighted in his helmet map-display. One was moving, two were static. He made a swift scenario calculation and flew through the jungle towards the two static body armours.

After an hour he found the wreckage of the Flyer and the dead body of the pilot, McKenley. He picked up scattered supplies, including a KM45 plasma cannon and a food kit. And he visually scoured the scene for the remaining body armour indicated on his helmet screen. Eventually, he found it, about five hundred yards from the plane. It was wrapped in the coils of a Basilisk, which now slept, replete. The coils dug so tight that they had warped the armour. But the body armour hadn't broken; instead, the helmet itself had shattered, under the appalling force exerted by brains and skull being squeezed against it. The Basilisk had literally crushed its prey until the hardglass helmet had fractured and the brain and skull and internal organs had erupted like bloodied lava through the hole.

But Helms had no way of telling if the empty armour belonged to Margaret or to Sorcha. Eventually, he found a speck of body tissue and scanned it and the DNA result came back swiftly: Margaret Lamarr.

Then he saw another speck of red tissue on the green undergrass, and saw it move. He adjusted the helmet to full magnification and saw that a patch of dead body was being carried by a Six-Head, with its legs stretching up above its head to support the weight of its spoils. As Helms watched, a hundred thousand or more Six-Heads swarmed around his feet, each carrying flecks of skin and tiny parts of body organs. They moved with synchronised purpose out of the clearing, carrying remnants of a dead human being to be used as part of their godforsaken Jungle-Wall.

Helms briefly mourned Margaret, then he filmed the scurrying

Six-Heads and their cargo of corpse fragments, sent the images to his brain implant memory, and carried on.

Sorcha's helmet mike could hear the distant footsteps of a DR, and the helmet hissed at her to be silent. *"Beware, hostile, two klicks,"* the helmet said.

"Thanks," Sorcha breathed, to her helmet computer.

She stood silently and waited. The helmet's computer translated the doppler shift of the footsteps for her: *"Approaching. Still approaching. No footsteps now. Now moving again, receding. Receding. Safe to proceed."*

Sorcha walked on.

Helms was afraid to use his MI-radio link again, in case the DR could intercept the signal.

So he retracted his helmet and screamed: "Sorcha! It's me! Professor Helms!"—hoping to be heard by her helmet's sensitive mikes.

"Voice in audio range. Message: Sorgum, sammy, pressure home," the helmet told Sorcha, and she quickened her pace, baffled.

"Flying robots approaching," the helmet told Helms, and he took cover behind the trunk of an Aldiss tree, as a swarm of DRscalpels

descended in a search pattern. He tagged them with his gunsight and fired. And the flying scalpels vanished from the air with a soft shearing noise.

"*Gunfire,*" the helmet told Sorcha. She hurried on.

Helms quickened his pace. "Sorcha, it's me!" he screamed. "DRs in the air! Beware Doppelgangers, above you, in the air! DRs in the air! Sorcha! In the air!"

"*It is a message to you: 'DRs in the air,'*" the helmet told Sorcha.

"*Who is speaking?*" Sorcha yelled, at her own helmet.

"*Professor Helms,*" said the helmet computer, which could have given her this information quite some time ago, had she only thought to ask.

Two dozen DRscalpels hovered through the air, controlled by a single mind, awkwardly flocking and swarming. Sometimes they collided so badly that several fell injured from the sky like shot raptors. But the controlling mind finally managed to harness their chaos and sent them on their course, deeper into the jungle. The target was not Helms, it was Sorcha. She was to die, as painfully as possible.

That was their mission.

Helms could see the flying DRscalpels pass above his head. He guessed they were heading for Sorcha. He ignored his helmet display, and instead he fired his body-armour jets and flew up into the air, and followed the deadly machine flock as it closed in on its prey.

Sorcha looked up and the sky was black with tiny robots, armed with scalpels and cutting tools, able to burrow through flesh or body armour with equal ease. She tagged one with her gunsight and fired but then the rest descended and she fired at will.

The "shuck shuck shuck" sound of a second plasma weapon joined in. She saw a body-armoured man at the edge of the clearing, picking off DRscalpels. He was fast and accurate, even though he was clearly shooting without the help of smart targeting.

Sorcha fired and a flying robot vanished. She fired again, and again...

Her body was covered with a half-dozen robot surgical machines. They were burrowing through her armour, blood was spurting, and the man was running towards her with his plasma cannon held out. He fired and a pillar of flame rippled through the air and enveloped her.

Sorcha ignited and was engulfed in a fireball. The DRscalpels exploded on her in a series of powerful bangs and then the plasma cannon was shooting fire-retardant foam at her. Now her helmet was broken open and she was coughing and her face was hot.

Sorcha passed out.

When she woke up, she'd been lifted out of her charred and torn body armour and was semi-naked on the undergrass. Helms was looking down at her.

"What are you doing here?" she snarled.

"I came to rescue you," he explained, and Sorcha was shocked beyond all measure.

"You could have done a better job of it," she sneered.

Helms smiled. "Come on, let's go," he said.

"Like this?" Apart from a thin body overall that left her arms and legs bare, she was entirely unprotected from the New Amazonian elements.

"You'll be OK," said Helms, and started to walk away. She leaped to her feet in a single fluid movement, so she could follow him.

But then Helms paused a moment, and turned, and added casually: "Provided, of course, it doesn't rain."

And Sorcha winced in fear.

DAY 6

It was 4.30 a.m., and the New Amazonian sun was dawning.

Sheets of red fire curled among the leaves and branches of the tree canopies. The Flesh-Webs glittered as the dew melted off them. The night chorus of nocturnal birds and scurrying grubs with rattling thoraxes ebbed, and the dawn chorus of angry Godzillas and Bigfeet and Tritons and Forest Sharks roared their ownership of their territory, while the birds in the canopies screeched and shrilled and the insects in the Flesh-Webs howled as the sun woke them.

Six Scientists and five Soldiers were dead: all those in the AmRover that had been blown up, who had died instantly, and Margaret Lamarr. But Helms and Sorcha were now reunited with the others, after walking safely back out of the jungle.

All those who had died had been abandoned where they fell, but Helms felt it necessary to hold a brief memorial service in their honour.

Forty-one Scientists and Soldiers gathered in the clearing as Helms spoke calmly and precisely about honour and sacrifice and the randomness of death that comes to all of us, paraphrasing from the many evangelists he had mocked over the years. But his restraint and dignity were exemplary; and he managed to entirely hide the childish, solipsistic sense of relief he always felt when others died, and he had not.

Helms was aware of the many anxious looks that were cast at him. It was clear to everyone now that Sorcha was special to him, and that he would jeopardise everything to protect her.

This meant his authority was in the balance, but Helms didn't care. He felt defined, and exalted, by his simple act of heroism.

"From now on," he said, "if the Commander agrees" — he nodded at Sorcha and she nodded her assent — "we drive through the night. We have to reach the Depot before our enemies find us again."

"Enemies!" snorted Ben Kirkham.

"The DRs," clarified Helms.

"Why are they following us?" William Beebe asked bluntly. "The Quantum Beacon is gone, so it's not the CSO any more, and it's not the Earth Gamers. Why would stupid robots be so determined to kill us all?"

"Because the CSO's people programmed them to do so," Helms told him firmly. There was a pause; his power tottered in the balance.

William thought about what Helms had said. The logic was sound, but his intuition screamed "No".

Furthermore, William had been quietly checking up on Helms on his implanted database.

And he was rapidly coming to the conclusion that there was something, indefinably, not quite right about Professor Richard Helms and his scientific career. Helms was a geologist whose specialism was terraforming. His job was to destroy the flora and fauna of New Amazon, not to study them. And yet, as they all knew, he had an encyclopedic knowledge of alien life-forms and taxonomic systems, and he supervised alien autopsies with extraordinary skill and expertise. William himself had, on many occasions, deferred to Helms's judgement on areas on which he, William Beebe, was supposedly the authority.

Helms was in short a marvel — a leader, a genius, a fount of wisdom and insight, a scholar, a naturalist, a geologist, an expert in every field of study.

But how could that be? How could one relatively young man know so much, and be so damned good at everything?

"Why," said William casually, "are you so reluctant to use the twenty-two-digit microbiological classification system, Professor Helms?"

There was a stunned silence.

"What?"

"I said —" William said stubbornly.

"This is neither the time nor the place," said Helms, furiously. "Have you no sense of perspective, man?"

"I support Professor Helms on this issue," said Hugo, loyally.

"Oh shut up, you fucking fool," roared Helms.

"But I support you!" Hugo bleated. "It's an important—"

"This is *not* the time or the place," Helms said angrily. "Eleven of our colleagues died today. Hundreds more died a few days ago. Our priority is survival."

"How old are you?" William asked.

"And that is relevant, how?"

"How old?"

"One hundred and forty elapsed years," said Helms, huffily.

And William, with a jolt, realised that he was lying. Helms *had* to be older! For only quadruple centenarians still used the outmoded Kingdom system of classification.

"You know something," said William Beebe, "that you're not telling us."

There was a further pained silence.

"What the fuck, if I may say so, are you on about?" Professor Helms countered.

Sheena heard the change in his tone of voice, and all her instincts told her that William was correct. Richard Helms was lying. But why? And what was he concealing?

"I'm talking about why the DRs ran amok at Xabar," continued William, relentlessly.

"Yes, I do know something," said Helms, and the silence was charged now.

"I know something," said Helms, "about what the DRs do." And he paused.

And he held the pause.

Then he continued, in calm chilling tones: "I was on Cambria, fifty years ago. And I also spent two years on Purgatory." He let the words resonate. "I've travelled as a guest on Slaver Ships," he continued, "carrying human embryos to the furthest reaches of human-occupied space. And I'm a student of history. I've seen film of the Times Square Massacre. I've downloaded DR snuffporn. So when you say to me: Why did the DRs run amok? then you're asking, I'm afraid, the wrong question. The DRs have always run amok. It's just that, until now, *we've let them.*"

"You're blurring the issue," protested William. "What I'm saying is—"

"Do you want to live or do you want to die?" Helms said bluntly.

The involuntary murmur was on everyone's lips: "Live."

"Then trust me," said Helms. "So far, I've saved this many, against all odds. I destroyed Juno, remember. And I built a safe haven for all of us. It wasn't easy, believe me, but I knew that one day we would need such a place. Without me, you'd all be doomed. *With* me, once we reach the Depot, you will be safe." He smiled his nicest smile, always a danger signal. "So please, gentlemen and ladies, with all due respect, trust me. And then, I do believe, we'll have a future together."

"I just want to know—" William began stubbornly, but Helms cut him off, with a tone that brooked no interruption.

"*Or*, if you prefer, we could stay here," he said savagely, "and debate idly for days, until our enemies find us and slay us, brutally!"

"Hmph," said Mary Beebe loudly, with the clear subtext of: You're absolutely right, and my idiot husband is wrong.

"I'm with you, Professor," said Hugo Baal, loyally.

"Let's just go," complained Ben Kirkham.

"Fair enough," said William brusquely. And the challenge was ended.

Helms nodded, and the nod was taken as an order. The convoy prepared itself. The crews began embarking into the AmRovers.

Helms took a deep breath; once again, by the skin of his teeth, he'd survived.

Sorcha lingered. She stood close to Helms, her body pumping out "I almost died" hormones, and Helms felt his pulse race.

"What the hell is *wrong* with you?" she asked, wonderingly. "To have taken a chance like that, just to rescue me?"

Helms almost grinned. Sorcha was a warrior, a killer, a servant of the Cheo. But she was also young, heartfelt, and a woman. Some things never change.

"I guess I must, you know, love you, or something," he said, softly.

She looked astonished at his words. If he'd put a bullet through her temple, it would have shocked her less.

"Let's move on out," he told her, and she nodded.

From the diary of Dr Hugo Baal

June 27th

We are now spending all our available time travelling. After a scant five hours' sleep I am back inside the AmRover being jostled along, with no way to perform dissections or study specimens under the microscope. However, I am at least able to work in my seat with the aid of a virtual screen and database. I have therefore spent the entire day revising my earlier findings and dissections and film footage and attempting to describe a fuller synthesis of our taxonomy of New Amazonian life.

Occasionally there is plasma gunfire outside the AmRover. Once we fell into a river and had to be towed out. On three occasions we have had to go into high-hover mode and speed away from some danger. But though I occasionally glance out of the side windows, I have managed to retain my focus sufficiently to ignore these extraneous distractions.

A scream! Is someone dead? I consult a colleague who informs me that Hydra have been dropping down out of the canopy and one of them managed to slither inside an AmRover. The situation has been dealt with, however, and there are no fatalities.[1]

Let me deal first with the vexed issue of Kingdoms.

According to Professor Helms's initial taxonomy, there are three Domains of life on New Amazon:

---

1 Except, of course, for the Hydra, which was roasted.

Eurkaryotes *(all life forms that have a cell with a nucleus, including* **Fungi***).*[2]
Eubacteria *(all life forms that have cells without a nucleus).*[3]
Nucleara *(all life forms that have cells in which the nucleus exists without any other cell elements, this form is unique to New Amazon).*

As an aside: we now clearly have information to start categorising all life on New Amazon in microbiological terms, and it is of course standard practice on xeno-expeditions to use the Saunders microbiological grid-labelling system for life-forms, which allows every species to be defined with a mere 22 digits.

However, even though Professor Helms is a geologist and not a biologist, he has insisted on retaining and adapting the traditional and some would argue[4] *rather absurdly old-fashioned Kingdom system, though in fact some of us consider it to be still rather valuable.*[5] *And on that basis he defines six Kingdoms of life on New Amazon:*

Animalia
Plantae

---

2 Fungi were once of course considered a separate Domain, but in the New Kingdom System are now incorporated under Eukaryotes. Although, of course, some biologists still savagely dispute this relatively recent (i.e. 250-year-old) taxonomic decision, including several members of our expedition, who belong to the Fungist Society, and who have threatened to resign if the Domains are so rendered in our official journals of scientific findings. These bitter discussions have, in truth, marred the smooth functioning of our scientific team, and spoiled many otherwise pleasant evenings; though in fact, since there are no Fungi on New Amazon, such arguments, and indeed this footnote, are a total waste of everyone's time.
3 Note: there is no New Amazonian version of *Archaeobacteria*, i.e. the original form of Prokaryotes, which still survive on Earth in many extreme environments. On New Amazon, Prokaryotes come in a variety of forms, but seem to have evolved in a rather similar fashion, and possibly at the same historical epoch, though frankly, at this stage of things, who the hell knows?
4 Not me though! I love these old taxonomical systems.
5 These damned microbiologists do like to have things their own way! And come to that, they have a deplorable habit of getting the lion's share of the equipment budget on all the field trips I've ever been on, and usually bag the biggest biodomes too. Although, in fairness, they're not *all* annoying wankers.

Monera
Protista
Fungi
Nucleara

There are no viruses on New Amazon. And as stated above, the sixth kingdom, Nucleara, unknown on Earth, consists of organisms which are single or multicellular but consist entirely of nucleus or, sometimes, entirely of DNA or, rather, the New Amazonian version of DNA, namely RBX. (To see previous entry on RBX, click here.)

Many of us realised at a very early stage that this initial taxonomy, though commendably archaic, is also inadequate and narrow-minded and foolish and wrong.[6] *It gives a false sense of simplicity and rationality on a planet where plants can move and eat protein and where animals can be made of bark. As stated in a previous diary entry, I have evolved a new and better approach. Thus, after a healthy period of discussion, in which my views were bluntly put to a rather distracted Professor Helms (some hours after the destruction of Xabar), a compromise was achieved,*[7] *which entailed dividing the life-forms into many more Kingdoms:*

Animalia
Plantae
Animaliaplantae (aka "animalish")
Plantaeanimalia (aka "plantish")
Kingdomshifters (types A and B)
Monera (types A, B, C and D)
Protista (types A, B, C, D, E, F, G, H)
Nucleara (types A, B, C, D, E)

6 And stupid!
7 For "compromise," read "victory for practitioners of common sense, and defeat for dunderheads."

I also, more controversially, propose to add the following three new Kingdoms:

Nubesa. *Cloud formations which demonstrate emergent behaviour, which I have been studying for some time.*

Ignisa. *Not "flame beasts" as such, but molten lava pools which are capable of purposeful locomotion and which in certain circumstances can emit a mournful sound which some of us[8] consider to be a beautiful song of lament that can touch the very soul with its pathos and pitiless alienosity.[9]*

Methanoesa. *Methane- not carbon-based life-forms which haven't yet been identified, or perceived, or deduced, but in the opinion of some members of the scientific team[10] could quite possibly exist on a planet like this in which methane is found in abundance and lots of other really strange and weird things exist, and for pity's sake, after all this time slogging my guts out on horrendous alien planets, wouldn't it be a nice change for once to find a life-form that isn't made of bloody carbon?*

Sorcha looked up through the gaps in the canopy of trees, at the stars in the sky. She could identify the Satellite, in equatorial orbit around them. She missed having a moon; her home planet of Terra Firma had two.

Helms joined her, retracted his helmet, and enjoyed the view. "You look bushed," he said.

8 In the interests of academic clarity, I should make it clear that I am the only member of the expedition who considers the lava to be a life-form.
9 This is a neologism which I have coined which carries with it the resonance of "essence and truth and very quiddity of an alien organism."
10 Me.

"I am," she admitted. She'd suffered third-degree burns over most of her body while clambering out of her red-hot armour, and it would be days before her skin lost its blistering. But at least her body armour had been restored and repaired; it clung to her now like a second skin.

"One more day, then we'll be home and dry," Helms said.

"Why was William Beebe asking all those questions?" Sorcha asked. It had been troubling her all day.

"I really don't know," Helms said.

"What does it matter how old you are?"

"It doesn't."

"Is he jealous? Because you're two hundred years younger than he is, and you're the boss?"

"That could be it," Helms conceded.

"Though sometimes..." Sorcha sighed.

"Sometimes what?"

"Sometimes you do feel like a relic from another age," she told him, smiling.

Helms's smile did not reach his eyes. "That doesn't sound a very nice thing to be."

"It's just you're so... old-fashioned. Gallant."

"I believe in treating a lady like a lady," said Helms, stiffly.

"I like that."

"Good."

"Have you ever been to Earth, Richard?"

Helms paused. "Yes. Briefly. When Xabar was in power."

"I had a poster of her in my bedroom."

"Really?"

"Oh, she was long gone of course, by the time I was a girl. But she was a hero to us."

"A hero to all of us," Helms said, proudly, stifling nausea at the memory of that wicked old bitch.

Sorcha's blond hair was growing out, and now formed a downy covering on her scalp. Her skin glowed. She was, Helms realised once more, so *young,* barely forty years old.

"What do we do when we reach the Depot?" Sorcha asked him.

"Have a bath!"

"You know what I mean."

"Have sex?" said Helms, cautiously.

Sorcha smiled. "If you like. But I meant…"

"I know what you meant."

"Are we trapped for ever, on this godforsaken planet?"

"You want to fly back home?"

Sorcha thought about it. "The Satellite has spaceflight capacity," she pointed out, carefully. This is why she'd been staring up at the Satellite; it was a possible ride home.

"It's not equipped as a colony ship."

"Then what?"

"Stay here. Bring up kids," suggested Helms.

Sorcha considered it. "Could we do that?"

"Why not? We've still got the solar panels out in space. And as many Bostock batteries as we need at the Depot. With those resources, we can build cities. Raise Earth animals, so we can eat fresh meat. Maybe do something about this acid rain, so we don't have to wear body armour all the time when we're outdoors."

"What about rejuve? I don't want to die young. Not unless—well, you know. In Glorious battle, that's one thing. But *old age*?"

"There are rejuve facilities at the Depot. So we have time. We have centuries ahead of us."

"I guess we do." Sorcha smiled, cautiously, as if learning smiles. "Are you thinking we could, you know, get married?"

"Would that be so terrible?"

"Provided it is for the purposes of child-bearing, there is no shame in marriage."

"What about marrying for love?"

"Don't be absurd."

"I'll never understand you Soldiers," said Helms, gently. "You're not genetically distinct, like Lopers and Cat People, but you act like a species apart."

"We believe that we are."

"So how do you like being with Scientists?"

"I'd rather be with Soldiers."

"We're a pretty shambolic bunch, aren't we?" he said, smiling.

"No discipline," conceded Sorcha. "No self-restraint. Everyone grumbles. Lots of irony. Like that bastard Kirkham. Always being ironical! Never know what the fuck he's really saying."

"Irony is a common scientific trait."

"Irony is dumb," Sorcha informed him.

"Then I shall never be ironical again," Helms replied, gravely.

"It is!" she persisted, vaguely aware he was teasing her. "It leads to ambiguity, bad feeling and it's, well, extremely fucking dumb."

"You're very cute," he informed her, and she glared at him.

"I'm a killing machine," she pointed out.

"And cute."

"Oh fuck you, Professor."

"Don't call me that. It makes me feel–" He winced. "Old."

"We should sleep. Dawn in four hours."

Helms breathed in the stale New Amazon air.

Sorcha felt the wind ruffle her downy scalp.

Then Helms kissed her gently on the cheek, and ran his tongue over her cheeks and eyes until she was damp with his warm spit. The spit steamed in the hot humid air, making her smooth skin billow tendrils of clear smoke.

Sorcha felt a desperate longing for this man. They couldn't embrace, because of the body armour, but she stroked her cheek dry against his stubbly cheeks, and she kissed him on the lips, for a long long time.

DAY 7

From the diary of Dr Hugo Baal

June 28th
This was a very boring day.

I have been working on my classifications systems, but the zest has gone out of me. Perhaps I am suffering from post-traumatic stress. Or travel sickness.

Ben Kirkham is getting on my nerves.

DAY 8

From the diary of Dr Hugo Baal

June 29th.
Another day of relentless travelling. Nothing of interest occurred, within or without the AmRover.

Ben Kirkham is really *getting on my nerves.*

I have started to read the Encyclopedia of Alien Life, *starting at "A".*

DAY 9

From the diary of Dr Hugo Baal

June 30th
Great news—there are very few alien beings beginniing with "A"—only 922,300—and so I am already up to "B"!

The Baleenmonsters of Cretaceous are a wonderfully engaging alien species; I saw one once in a zoo.

DAY 10

From the diary of Dr Hugo Baal

June 31st
I am still on "B" in the Encyclopedia of Alien Life, *and I am getting exceedingly bored.*
   This could take years.

DAY 11

From the diary of Dr Hugo Baal

June 32nd

I have abandoned the Encyclopedia of Alien Life. *I now know far more than even I would like to know about creatures beginning with "A, B and C a–f".*

However, fortunately, we are close to the Depot. And after days of relentless bickering, morale is high once more, following an incident which occurred at 11:46 this morning.

We had been travelling through swamp lands, on high hover, with all personnel secure in the AmRovers. I was in the AmRover 3 Observation Bubble, with my colleagues Dr Ben Kirkham and Dr Martha Le Clerk, and we were observing the swamp life below us. The fetid stew of primeval swamp was particularly odious that day. Crock fish were leaping up at us. The New Amazonian plankton were swarming, and devouring the Ugly fish. After a few minutes only the thick horny eyeballs and stalks of the Ugly Fish were left, floating on the surface of the swamp. We were using spectrographic analysis and ultrasound to create a 3D portrait of the swamp habitat. And it was somewhat disorientating to be looking down through hardglass floors at such a suppurating, vile, sucking, deadly miasmic hell.

And then we got an MI call from Professor Helms to look up. His words were: "Look up, and marvel!" And so we did. Or at least Martha and I did. Dr Kirkham continued his analysis of the evil slime-swamp, no doubt perceiving in it a metaphor for his own putrid soul.[1]

So we looked up and we saw Bell Birds flying. An armada of birds in the skies above us, flying below the tree canopy, swooping and soaring and making shapes in the sky.

---

1 I jest of course! Pray do forgive my academic drollery! Dr Kirkham and I are the closest of colleagues, and I have nothing but admiration for his intellect, his waspish wit, sardonic tone, and unrelenting criticism of others.

At Martha's suggestion, we opened the roof of the Observation Bubble and flew upwards on our body-armour jets. Professor Helms and six other colleagues joined us there, in mid-air, hovering above the swamp with blue skies above us where the canopy was broken, with birds flying all around. Professor Helms, as is his wont, retracted his helmet in order to feel the wind on his face, a perfectly safe manoeuvre of course since our oxygen implants can keep us alive for a considerable period of time, and the atmosphere is not actively poisonous.[2] I joined the Professor in his impetuosity, and I too felt the wind on my cheeks.[3]

There were nine of us flying that day, and we soared high up into the air to be amidst the flock of Bell-Birds.[4] They were playing and scampering through the sky like dogs in a park. The Bell-Birds are vast creatures, the size of Earth whales, and they each have four sets of wings, creating a multiple hydrofoil of uncanny strength. They use jet propulsion from their anus to steer themselves, but they can also fart air from one of sixteen other rectums, which are dorsally located, and these jets of air are directed over the wings at differing speeds to create low pressure on the top of the wing, generating lift.

The Bell-Birds are squatly shaped, like bells, but there is considerable grace in the way they kink and dart around the sky. And so we flew through their flock and chased them and played with them. They are happy creatures and they seemed to relish our company as we flew with them, up high and down low. We brushed the canopy of trees and flew up through a gap and high up into the clouds, led by Bell-Birds which formed a perfect V shape in the skies with their vast bodies.

We saw a Roc,[5] hovering high above us, dancing on a thermal current. We saw a flock of Sunlights,[6] yellow darting creatures that flock in

---

2 The danger comes from rainstorms and hail storms, which have a lethally strong acidic content, so Professor Helms's strategy is not without its risks.
3 Devil May Care Baal, that's what they call me! Well actually they don't. But, sigh! I rather wish they did.
4 *Tintinnabulumgigantum.*
5 *Rocus rex.*
6 *Solus helmsi*, the smallest and most beautiful of the 377 species of bright yellow birds we have observed.

a cloud-shaped formation to create, in certain lights, a yellow shimmer-
ing second sun in the sky. We saw a speckled Amazonian Kite,[7] which
unlike its earthly counterpart is not bird-shaped, but is in fact flat and
vast, like a manta ray, or indeed a toy kite.

It was pure joy, to be alive, to be flying, to be part of the world of
birds on this glistening, beautiful, unpredictable planet.

Then we flew back down and rejoined our party, just as they reached
the end of the Swamp, and were within sight of the Mountains of the
Moon mountain range at the foot of which nestled the Depot which was
our blessed bourne.[8]

Ben Kirkham was feeling woozy. The journey was exhausting
him. And he couldn't cope with the monotony, the endless chatter
from that clown Baal, and the certainty that he was travelling with
enemies who were assuming the form of human beings in order to
deceive him.

There was a mood of exhilaration in the AmRover after the flying
in the sky incident, but Ben felt detached from it, and scornful of it.
Nothing made sense any more, and all was folly.

Hugo was uncomfortable with the way Ben kept staring at him.
What was *wrong* with him these days? He hadn't been behaving normally since they'd been bombed and fired at by the rogue Doppelganger Robots and then, after barely surviving a ghastly massacre,
forced to take refuge in the perilous jungle.

---

7 *Milius variegatus.*
8 I fear this last line is a little pretentious. Hmm? But "which was our destination" seems so
horribly flat, does it not? Oh dear.

What the devil was his *problem*?

Martha Le Clerk loved the twinkle in Hugo's eyes when he talked about his beloved New Amazonian birds. He had a childlike passion for everything he did, and she admired his rigour and his publication record. Dr Hugo Baal was one of the giants in the xenobiological world, and Martha couldn't believe how lucky she was to be sharing an AmRover with him.

Ben Kirkham, however, scared the shit out of her.

The surviving four AmRovers chuntered through the jungle, with Ashley on point duty on the armoured Scooter, which was in effect a one-person Flyer.

Professor Helms was desperate to reach the Depot. The journey had been demoralising, and he was starting to feel claustrophobic, despite the spacious quarters in the vast AmRovers.

But Helms didn't want to spend the rest of his days living in an armoured car, however large it might be. He wanted a home, a place where he could breathe freshly recycled air and see artificially painted stars on a hardglass dome. The Depot would give them that. He'd built it big, the size of a town or even a small city, and it was equipped with everything they would need to make this planet truly habitable. It had self-contained living units, an artificial river, Earth vegetation, and a communal mingling area with benches and coffee-points.

It was a grandiose construction, but Helms had always known he would have to prepare for this eventuality. So he'd programmed robot-mode DRs and nanobots to fabricate his bolthole; and within a few hours he would be safe inside it.

There was only one outstanding problem: the Depot needed a name. For it was no longer a munitions and supplies store; it was going to be their capital city.

"Melbourne."

"Arcadia."

"Capital City."

"Amazon City."

"New London."

"Fresh Start."

"Depot. Let's just call it Depot. It's kind of cool, yeah?"

"No."

"No."

"Not cool."

"Mozart."

"Ah, good idea, musical theme; Samuelson."

"Brahlish."

"Leeminson."

"Beethoven."

"Flanagan."

"Who the hell is Flanagan?"

"He's kind of a blues singer with cross-over potential. I like him."

"Nah."

"Inca."

"Orinoco."

"Arse End of Nowhere."

"We Couldn't Think of a Fucking Name for It City."

"Lubricious."

"Plumbeous."

"Linnaeus."

"Nice one. Linnaeus, I like that."

"Who's Linnaeus?"

"Oh for pity's sake!"

"Cousteau."

"Falcon."

"Falcon City."

"Falcon City is good."

"Eagle."

"Eagle City is also good."

"Sparrow."

"Sparrow City, not so good."

"Vulture."

"Condor."

"Heebie-Jeebie."

"You can't name a human city after an alien species."

"Bandersnatch."

"Same problem."

"It's a reference to a poem."

"It's also the name of thirty-four species of large land animal."

"Some scientists have no imagination, huh?"

"Hel-lo! Roc, anyone? How many Rocs are there in the human universe? And Basilisk? The Basilisks on Apocrypha are actually sentient, how do you think they'll like us recycling their name?"

"They don't call themselves Basilisks."

"That's because they communicate via the smell of their belches. But their human scientific name is still Basilicus sapiens.*"*

"Yes, but our Basilisks are Basiliskus *with a 'k'."*

"Oh, and belching aliens are going to detect that subtle difference, are they?"

"Can we focus please?"

"Focus! I like that. Focus City."

"Chaos."

"Hades."

"Olympus."

"Arcadia."

"Someone said that already."

"Asimov."

"Who's he?"

"Gaiman."

"Now you're talking."

"Helms," said Professor Helms, and the decision was made.

It was nearly midnight by the time they pulled up in Helms City. The Professor keyed in his remote code to open up the hardglass front door. The AmRovers were parked inside, and Sorcha led her soldiers into the Weapons Room, where they primed the force field and ran systems checks on the defensive cannons. There was an electrified perimeter area with virtual tripwires activating laser-beam blasts to destroy any unauthorised presences, an impermeable hardglass dome, the force field, hidden mines. This was a fortress that could withstand assault by an entire battle force.

When the security systems were in place Professor Helms, finally, breathed a sigh of relief.

"This is my room?" said Sorcha, awed.

It was palatial. A double bed. Bay windows with false views. A holographic ceiling. Mock-antique furniture.

"I was hoping, perhaps, if it isn't too presumptuous, this might be *our* room?" said Helms, with the hesitant, shy smile that had always worked so well for him.

"But this is meant to be a depot!" protested Sorcha. "I was expecting, I don't know, a warehouse maybe."

"It was always going to be our second city," Helms explained. "And why not? With cheap energy and robots, why create a utilitarian habitat when you can live in style?"

"Is that vintage wine?"

"It's several hours old."

"That'll do me."

Sorcha poured the drinks. Helms savoured the taste of the wine. He'd once drunk a bottle of fifty-year-old Château Lafite, but this was just as good. That was the joy of progress: epiphany was so easily reproducible.

Sorcha's skin glowed with youth. Her body was muscular, but she still had some puppy fat. When he made jokes, she laughed, often amazed at the freshness of his wit. When he was sour and cynical about life, she often looked at him blankly.

For Sorcha loved her world, she loved herself, she loved everything about being alive, she loved killing aliens and enemy humans, she loved sunshine and sex and shitting, she saw nothing much wrong with anything, really.

And for Helms this, the experience of being with a young woman who sees things freshly, with enthusiasm and relish, without any trace of despair or dread or ennui, this was a rare delight.

"Shall we make, dare I suggest it, love?" he suggested shyly, and she beamed at the brilliance of that suggestion and took her clothes off and began touching him in wonderful ways.

"You have a lovely bony body," she told him, and kissed his bones, and licked his flesh.

"Thank you," he told her, very formally.

"You're welcome!" she said, amused by his formality, and then she was wriggling, and fumbling him into position with a skilful hand, and he was inside her, and passion consumed them as they fucked, and fucked, and savoured each other's flesh and smell and passion.

Ben took his meds and felt a familiar calmness descend. He realised, with some horror, that he'd been clinically psychotic for most of their journey through the jungle. Paranoid, suspicious, delusional, obsessional—in a word, crazy.

He was lucky they'd reached the Depot when they did, so that he could restore his biology to normal.

Ben marvelled at how close he had come to a total breakdown. And he loaded up his backpack with as many meds as he could find, in case they had to leave this place suddenly.

Because after a hundred years of sanity, he knew very well the dangers of trying to survive without his regimen of medication. It was essential that he should stay sedated, and hence focused, and calm, and rational.

And he knew too that he had to continue to be the emotionally dead, sardonic, rude, hypercritical Ben Kirkham that everyone knew and, well, loathed.

Because he didn't dare to, once again, become that other person, the cheerful, life-embracing Ben Kirkham, the fun-loving Ben, the Ben who everyone laughed at and wanted to be with, the Ben as he really was without his daily dose of emotion-depressing medication. Because that would turn him back into the Ben he had been as a young man—exuberant, witty, brilliant, delightful.

And murderously insane.

Hugo inspected his lab and was thrilled. Imaging machines, micro-scalpels, a cell analyser, and a virtual reality booth that would allow him to travel through the body of a dissected alien as if he were on a spaceship.

It hadn't occurred to Hugo that the Depot would be so well equipped. He was expecting a shed with some basic living facilities. But Helms had managed to construct a whole second city here.

Hugo was delighted, yet also highly suspicious; but his suspicions were swiftly swallowed up by his gleeful delight.

It occurred to Tonii that he was finally free. No Quantum Beacon, no DRs apart from the rogue one who was stalking them, no Commander in Chief, no CSO, no Earth. No oppression, no cultural prejudice, no emails from his scornful family mocking his choices in life. No birthday vids from his ex-husband Charlie berating Tonii for being such a useless freak.

And, perhaps most important of all, no trauma and pain and guilt as all the species of animal and plant on the planet apart from the zoo specimens were brutally slaughtered and exterminated, as had happened on his last six planets. No bleak transfer to another world rich in promise and full of rich and diverse life-forms that, in turn, would be callously genocided.

This, Tonii realised, was the start of a whole new life.

Mia wandered through the Depot, awestruck.

She'd expected some utilitarian habitat with a dome. Instead it was a magnificent piece of architecture. The walls all curved and swooped at angles, and were richly coloured with shimmering mosaics. The floors were angled too and it was possible to walk from the bottom to the top floor without ever using stairs. The curves formed patterns all around her, and richly carved floating pillars that served no structural function created an eerie temple-like effect.

Mia took a camera and explored. She wondered who had designed this — was it Helms? Was he an architect as well as a scientist?

The depot had a campanile, a tower that soared high through the hardglass dome and up into the sky, almost touching the canopy. Mia walked to the top and looked down at the jungle and captured the panorama with a series of slow tracking shots, then with a series of static pans. Then she leaped off the campanile and flew with her body-armour jets down to the ground, capturing the great expanse of the jungle ahead of her.

And as she flew, her camera flew beside her, capturing every moment of her epic leap.

"Hmm," said William Beebe.

His and Mary's room was surprisingly spacious. A *trompe l'oeil* window offered a view of the jungle—thanks to an ingenious mirror-tube that carried images from the exterior of the dome to the room. Juggernauts appeared to amble up to the window and peered through at them. Birds flew past, leaving a glorious orange train of excrement, as was the wont of these New Amazonian creatures. It was like having a luxury suite in the midst of a wilderness.

"Rather pleasant," Mary agreed.

"Better than the room we had at Xabar," William concurred.

"Hence..."

"So..."

"Indeed."

"But..."

"But what?"

"I rather think you know 'But what?'"

"But—perhaps Helms is a revolutionary?"

"That is the thought that crossed my mind."

"He was planning a coup?"

"Perhaps. That would explain..."

"I'm with you."

"Although—"

"Although?"

"He's a strange man, in many ways."

"You don't like him, do you?"

"He's good company. Rather clever."

"But cold."

"Yes, cold. Or rather—not cold. Reserved. Not the least bit WYSIWYG."

"Hmm. Good point. I find him rather arrogant, also."

"We all are."

"True."

"He's amazingly knowledgeable though. For a geologist."

"Rather too knowledgeable."

"He has a mastery of cladistics that daunts even me."

"Brain implant, that's the explanation."

"No, it's too fast, the way he recollects data. If you ask him about the phylogenetic history of any alien species in Known Space, he *knows*. He doesn't pause to ask the computer chip. He knows."

"Clearly, he's had memory modifications."

"And a face transplant."

"You noticed that too?"

"Freckles on the arm, not on the nose. A dead giveaway."

"I'd never buy a new face," said William. "I like the one I have."

"Your nose is too large."

"True."

"Out of proportion."

"I'm aware of what 'too large' means."

"It wasn't intended as an insult."

"And this? Is this in proportion?"

William was by now stark naked.

Mary looked at him, and smiled.

Then Mary also undressed. Her breasts were tiny and pert, her nipples were huge, her bum was large, her belly button turned outwards, and she was a good foot shorter than she needed to be. But William adored her for her quirky physique.

"I love you," he told her.

"Hmm," she replied, with a mock-frown. Then she added: "William, I think I'd like sexual intercourse now, if you don't mind." And he grinned, and then he entered her, and they made love, with staggering passion, for an hour or more.

Later, they lay naked in each other's arms, listening to nothing, trembling and weak after their multiple, soul-shaking tantric orgasms.

"Are you hungry?" he asked at one point.

"Not a bit of it," she told him, and fell asleep, and he slept too.

And when he woke, she was still asleep, and dreaming, and he kissed her as she dreamed, and touched her body gently, and she whispered to him from her sleep, and he whispered back, hoping that she would dream of him.

Helms showed Sorcha his dreams for the planet, in a complex holographic display that unfurled impressively from his virtual computer screen until it filled the entirety of their large living space.

Helms's vision of their future involved floating cities and space elevators that allowed travellers to hop over the Jungle-Walls with ease. He also proposed to build vast skyscrapers that offered vistas across the canopy, opening up that whole area of the planet to human tourists.

And he wanted to build tree houses on the Ocean-Aldiss-Tree that would allow them to colonise the oceans in an organic, unplanned way. He proposed underground railways that connected city to city without disturbing the native habitat. And he anticipated that they would, in time, build art galleries, cinemas, theatres, museums, all contained in networks of vast biodomes. It would require some careful genetic tinkering—since their gene pool was so small—but with the help of incubators and gene-splicing Helms confidently anticipated that the small pool of forty or so settlers would grow over ten or eleven generations to become a fully fledged civilisation of 50,000–60,000. The perfect number, in his view, for a human society that could comfortably coexist with native fauna and flora.

Sorcha stared at it all, with growing wonderment. Eventually—

"I don't get it," she said bluntly.

"What don't you get?"

"This. What you have in mind. Why so timid? We could fill this planet. Millions, in less than a century. And all this space you plan to waste—the jungle! We don't need all this fucking jungle."

"The jungle is a vital part of the planetary ecology," Helms said stiffly.

"Ah fuck ecology," said Sorcha, oblivious to the fact that, in xeno-biological circles, that was fighting talk. "Look! Use your head here, Richard! We have the resources to terraform! Why aren't you planning to terraform?"

"Because," said Helms gently, "it's wrong."

Sorcha stared at him, utterly baffled by the word, and by the concept underlying it.

"Huh?" she said, eventually.

He continued to smile patiently at her, as if expecting her to get it.

But she didn't; and wouldn't; and couldn't.

And, for the first time in his life, Helms was lost for words. He had no idea whatsoever what to say, and how to answer her. For how could he explain something that ought not to need explaining?

Helms felt a dark depression coil around his heart.

He had planned this all so carefully. The Depot—or Helms City as it was now called—was his masterpiece. He had designed it himself, he had chosen the colours for the walls and furniture and programmed the Fabricators himself. He had built tunnels under the City connecting it up with secure bunkers where they could withstand full-scale assault from space.

He had built a music room, and an art room. He planned to have an *Encyclopedia of Alien Life* room, where it would be possible to see holograms of every single species of life-form in the entire known universe. Helms even planned to have himself elected President in due course.

And there was so much to do, so much to achieve.

But the one thing he wasn't prepared to do was to destroy all the native life-forms on the planet, or to turn them into zoo specimens existing on sufferance on an Earthlike world.

Because it was wrong; and because it was evil.

How could Sorcha fail to understand that?

Ben sat in the computer control room and checked the perimeter defences and the Depot's arsenal. He was impressed; this place was a fortress.

Ben exulted at the power they had. Plasma howitzers, fusion bombs, antimatter bombs—he almost yearned for the DRs to attack, so he could smash them, and kill them, and watch his own people die in a blaze of glory, and...

But no. That wasn't the way. What the hell was he thinking of?

Ben firmly got a grip on himself, as the meds kicked in.

"Solar for your thoughts," said Hugo Baal.

"Must you *always* speak in clichés?" said Ben, sneeringly.

"Oh I think so!" said Hugo cheerfully, seemingly oblivious to the insult. "After all, a cliché is usually a cliché," Hugo chuckled, "because it's true!"

Ben winced, and then he seethed and plotted how to kick this fucking imbecile's fucking brains in.

Deep below Helms City, in tunnels they had burrowed the previous day, the DRs waited.

Dinner was a crazy celebration. Hugo was mildly drunk. Sorcha was flirtatious. Professor Helms was openly cheerful. Some of the Scientists started throwing rolls and making jokes in Latin, in time-honoured fashion. The Soldiers told tales of battles lost and won many years ago, and then Sergeant Anderson and Ashley got into a one-handed press-up competition. After forty minutes, the rest of the diners left, but the two men weren't giving up.

Jim Aura was there, with Sheena, each quietly detached, each surrounded by their own small world of thought and reflection. Sheena smiled gently at all the laughter she heard around her, and wondered if she was going to fall in love with this man.

Jim wasn't much of a catch, admittedly—he was dull, awkward, and ill at ease both in his own body and in the company of others. But he was, after the massacre, the only other Noir apart from herself in the entire world. And after all these years—after all the prejudice she'd encountered, the contempt directed at the Noirs and their fatalistic, moment-embracing way of being—Sheena wasn't inclined to start straying from her own kind.

Besides, he was *sweet.*

The diners retired to the ballroom, where music played. They were joined there after a while by the sweaty and exhausted Ashley and Sergeant Anderson, each claiming victory. Crystal chandeliers lit with real flames cast long shadows and the floor was made of a complex coloured mosaic that, if viewed from a height, depicted the stars of the New Amazonian night reincarnated as mythological beings. Professor Helms shocked them all by leading Sorcha out on to the dance floor and dancing a slow salsamba with her, badly but boldly.

Then the Professor left the floor and the music picked up its pace, and Ashley and Private Clementine McCoy danced Jig Jag, brilliantly and expertly. Then the Moody Schmaltz kicked in, and the dance floor slowly filled. Sorcha danced with Sergeant Anderson, who was still grim-faced and scowling as always, but who proved to be a remarkably graceful dancer. William and Mary Beebe joined them, sedately cruising across the dance floor. The music was soulful and Sorcha was enjoying it.

"So? What's the verdict on the Major? How many from one to ten on the Good Fuckometer?" Ben said to Professor Helms, as Sorcha danced with the Sergeant.

"Don't be so vulgar," Helms told him, acidly.

"Ah, she'll conjugally engage with anyone, that wench," Ben said casually, and Helms restrained an impulse to hit him.

Instead, he looked again at Sorcha. She and Sergeant Anderson danced sinuously around each other; she wrapped her legs around his neck and arched down and vanished between his legs then leapt up and landed the other side of him, still dancing. Anderson was a vicious old bastard, but he exuded a dangerous sexuality, and the dance that he and Sorcha danced together was more intimate than many sexual acts.

Helms shocked himself by encountering a hint of jealousy in his heart. *He'd* never been able to dance like that, despite lessons and several skill-implants. The two Soldiers looked good together. Their bodies achieved a unison of rhythm, a shared body language, that Helms found enchanting.

Mia took Tonii by the hand.

"I don't dance," he said, smiling.

"You can't?"

"I can, but I choose not to."

"I bet you can't. I bet you're a lumbering ox."

"You're using psychology on me, aren't you?" Tonii smiled and he took Mia in his arms. He waltzed with her, in five/four time, with effortless grace. She allowed herself to be swept up by him. She knew that all eyes were on them, because of Tonii, because of his extraordinary beauty, and she relished being part of that beauty.

But she could also tell, from the warmth of his unvarying smile, and his totally relaxed body language, that he felt no sexual desire for her, or indeed for anyone else in the room. Mia marvelled; this man, who was also a woman, was also an island.

Sheena led Jim Aura out on to the floor, and the other dancers parted graciously as she blundered a path through them. She could hear the breaths of the people around her, she knew roughly how much space she had to dance in. Jim stood awkwardly, and waved his arms, but Sheena couldn't see how crap he was. She held his shoulders with her hands. She swayed, and her tongue flicked her lips. Her body was beauty, its motion was beauty, and Jim's heart soared with love and unconsummated desire.

Sheena had a hunch, and brushed her hand over Jim's crotch, and her hunch was confirmed. "Later," she murmured, and Jim was thunderstruck. Later! Him! Sheena! He could scarcely believe his luck.

Sheena entered into the music and became part of it, while Jim was lost in love and lust.

And Helms watched them dancing, and grinned.

Hugo joined him, and the two of them stood on the edge of the dance floor, watching the wild and sexy and utterly uninhibited dancing, and reminisced silently and jointly about all the dances they'd missed out on as teenagers.

"You know we have a choice," said Hugo.

"In what sense?"

"We don't have to stay on this planet. We can convert the Satellite into a colony ship."

Helms nodded, annoyed at hearing this suggestion again, but hiding his feelings well. "Well, perhaps, if I may so prevaricate, one day," he said. "In due course. Let's make a home here first."

"Fair enough," said Hugo cheerfully. "You know, I love this planet." Hugo's face twitched; he'd used the "l" word, almost without embarrassment.

"I also love—" said Helms, and the floor erupted and the Doppelgangers attacked.

There were six Humanoid DRs, a dozen DRscalpels, and a small Draven scout ship. The Draven flew up through the floor, colliding with and killing two of the dancers, while the Humanoids opened fire with their plasma guns.

Helms was unarmed. So was Hugo. But Sorcha and Sergeant Anderson and the other Soldiers had their regulation plasma pistols strapped to their thighs. They swiftly drew and they opened fire.

The DRs absorbed the energy beams and fired back, just an instant later than the human shooters. A haze of plasma energy ripped across the room and blasted through the bodies of the Scientists and Soldiers. Sergeant Anderson rolled, as two of his fellow Soldiers ignited beside him. Sorcha lunged for a pillar. The DRs didn't even try to dodge, they just kept hosing fire at all in the room.

A single plasma beam cut Sheena, Queen of the Noirs, in half. She lived for seconds. Jim leaned in close and heard her dying words: "Just, fucking, run," she whispered to him, and then she was gone.

It was an inferno, and a bloodbath. Thirty-five men and women were in the dance hall, and a dozen of them died in the first few minutes. Helms had thrown himself to the floor and watched with fear as the air turned red with blood. The mosaic of the floor was rent and splintered. The Draven lunged and crashed against walls, severed robot arms mingled with severed human limbs on the floor and tables, and the smell of spilt wine and beer merged with the smell of burning flesh and the rank odour of shit expelled from arses.

"Where are the fucking sentries!" screamed Sergeant Anderson, emptying his plasma pistol on a DR's head with barely any effect. A plasma cannon roared out of its left arm, and Anderson dived out of the way. Then he changed the setting on his gun and fired a hail of explosive bullets.

Then Sorcha aimed her plasma pistol at the back wall and fired. Anderson joined her, firing in synchrony. A hole in the wall appeared. Sorcha glanced back—and saw a DR with its plasma gun aimed at her head. She stopped breathing.

The DR stared into her eyes, as if weighing her soul, and didn't fire.

Sorcha turned and leaped through the hole in the wall, followed by Anderson. Helms saw his moment and got up from the floor, and followed them through the hole in the wall, together with Hugo, Ben, Mia, Tonii, Jim Aura, and a sprinkling of others.

"*Lock Down*," Helms told the security systems via his secure MI-radio channel, and toughmetal doors slammed into place behind them in the corridor. It would only detain the Doppelgangers for a few minutes, but that was all they'd need.

Martha Le Clerk saw the hole in the wall and looked around for Hugo; and then she screamed as she was engulfed in pain and flame.

Mary Beebe watched appalled, as she saw Martha burning alive, her head turning into skull then crumbling into ash.

Then William grabbed Mary and yanked her away just as another plasma blast sheared past. A Soldier—Ashley—leapt forward and fired at a DR at point-blank range and the DR was smashed off its feet and bounced on the ground, and then Ashley was hit and Mary could see through his torso, and he was weeping as he died.

"Run for it! The wall!" screamed William, and Mary turned and saw the hole, and prepared to run. And a moment later, a DR plasma beam cut William's head from his shoulders.

Mary watched his head bounce, his expression frozen in fear. She fancied she saw his eyes turn to her. Mary waited a heartbeat so she could join him in death. But the DR who'd killed him was ripped in half by an explosive bullet that had burrowed through its skin. Then an arm grabbed Mary and tugged her.

"Run!" screamed Private Clementine McCoy, and Mary ran.

The corridor was empty, and the way was barred by a metal door, but Clementine had memorised the Depot map and she knew a way round. She ran down a side corridor and dragged Mary with her through a ventilation shaft until they caught up with Helms and the others, and ran with them down the long corridors.

Helms security-swiped each door swiftly as they ran, and then they were in the garage and Mary could see the DRs coming towards them, and she also saw Mike Green and Jennifer Munro running, running, almost at the door.

The garage doors closed, locking them out. Heat buckled the metal but it did not melt. Mary heard the screams on the other side of the toughmetal door as Mike and Jennifer and the other survivors were killed.

"Take three—" Helms instructed, and Mary lunged at him and caught him by the throat and tried to strangle him to death.

"What the fuck!" Ben Kirkham pulled her off. Helms was on the ground, wheezing, with vivid weals on his throat.

"Are you fucking mad?" screamed Sorcha.

"He's dead, dead," said Mary. "It's his fault! William is dead!"

"How many of us are there?" Helms said, ignoring the pain, and Mary's hysteria, and his own overwhelming guilt.

"Fifteen," Sorcha counted.

"Let's go. Take three vehicles," Helms wheezed. "We need the supplies."

The toughmetal garage door was starting to melt.

"Now!" screamed Sorcha, and they began to pile into the AmRovers. Mary was bundled into the lead AmRover. She felt it start up and roar into motion. The second AmRover followed. Then the garage door melted and the third AmRover was incinerated in a haze of plasma beams.

Around them Helms City shook with the impact of plasma guns and flash grenades. Then came an eerie silence as the two surviving AmRovers barrelled away from the Depot.

"*Heliplane mode.*" The AmRovers fired their jets and took off vertically. They roared into the sky.

Plasma blasts fired from below heated the chassis of the AmRovers. In AmRover 3, Helms sat next to Sorcha and Hugo. Ben was piloting the other vehicle.

"Into the jungle," said Helms. "Get in as deep as we can. We—"

"*Hello, Carl,*" said a voice in Helms's head.

Helms was ashen. "What?" he said out loud.

"Professor?" said Hugo anxiously.

"*Is that you?*" Helms subvocalised. His face was distorted with rage and fear.

"*Oh yes.*"

"*Go to hell!*" Helms screamed subvocally.

"Who are talking to? What channel are you using?" Sorcha asked suspiciously. Helms raised a finger: bear with me.

Sorcha shrugged. She piloted the AmRover away from the Depot. Missiles arced above her, narrowly missing their flying craft.

"*You're a hard man to find, Carl,*" said the voice in Helms's head.

"Are they following?" Helms said to Sorcha, in his brusquest voice.

"No."

Helms kept his features still, and subvocalised:"*You bastard! How are you doing this?*"

"*No matter. Here I am. I've been tracking you for two hundred years now. I almost caught up with you on Rebus. And on Asgard.*"

Helms burned with rage at the memories of the deaths on Rebus, and the carnage that ensued when the space torpedo hit Asgard. But he kept his face calm and his tone neutral: "*I knew that was you, both times. Innocent people died, because of you.*"

"*Well that's too bad. You could have stopped it all, you know. Surrendered yourself. But you couldn't bear to, could you? You prize your own skin over the lives of others.*"

"*I have a right to run for my life.*"

"*All those people died, because of you, Carl. All your friends and colleagues. Hundreds of them. Because of you.*"

"*Go to hell.*"

"*Oh I am in hell. I'm crippled, you know. I had a body transplant and it failed. So my head is in a tank and I communicate with my computer via neuron discharges and movements of my eyelids. Can you imagine anything more tragic?*"

"*It sounds laughable. Can you still weep? I hope so.*"

"*You're a bastard, Carl.*"

"*And you're a monster, Andrew.*"

"*You made me so,*" said Andrew Hooperman; and to his horror, Saunders knew it was true.

Then Hooperman cut the link.

Sorcha and Hugo were staring at Helms. "We need to get out of here," he said stiffly.

"We're doing so," Sorcha said curtly.

They flew on.

They flew below the canopy for forty minutes and landed in a jungle clearing.

Sorcha sent out the coordinates on a permanent loop, in theoretically unbreakable Delta Code, in case any other Soldiers had escaped from the wreckage of Helms City.

She blamed herself. Poor security. Complacency. Incompetence. All the deaths were her fault, and it was as if she had died herself.

There were eleven survivors, including herself. Dr Ben Kirkham, Dr Mia Nightingale, Private Tonii Newton, Private Clementine McCoy, Sergeant Xavier Anderson, Dr Mary Beebe, Dr Hugo Baal, Dr David Go, Dr Jim Aura and Professor Helms. They had two AmRovers, weapons, and supplies, so the prospects were not entirely bleak.

But even so, she blamed herself.

Eleven survivors!

Her Soldiers should have stayed in their body armour, they should have carried their plasma cannons, there should not have been any dancing.

Dancing!

Sorcha had thought the Depot was secure. But the DRs had planned a perfect ambush; they got to Helms City first and simply lay in wait.

She blamed herself, intensely, for several hours, as Soldiers were prone to do.

Then she got over it.

Tonii felt awed, and privileged to be still alive.

All his life he had been told that death was Glory. His father, his mother, indeed most of his family and all of his friends had died Gloriously. And he had been schooled to believe that one day he too would find his destiny in Glorious death.

But Tonii had realised some time ago, vividly and thrillingly, how false the Soldier's Faith was. For *Life* was glory. Death was just — well —

Stupid.

Mia was too stunned to have any emotion. She'd thought the fighting was over, the battle was won. But the battle had only paused.

It was obvious, now, that the DRs were toying with them. They were merely mice, being chased by armies of cats. It was only a matter of time before the rest of them died, and Mia felt crushed and overwhelmed by dread.

Jim Aura had always been a fatalist, even before he became a Noir.

He was also a clandestine and bitter enemy of the Galactic Corporation's regime. He'd studied film footage of the Dolph Games, the extermination of life on Pixar, the wholesale rape and enslavement of entire planets. He wasn't surprised at all that had happened; he welcomed it as confirmation of his own dark philosophy of life.

So as a pessimist, and a fatalist, he wasn't often shocked.

But the death of Sheena, Queen of the Noirs, had shocked him.

Why *her?* Why not Helms? Why not Major Molloy? Why not someone who hadn't already suffered by being blinded?

Sheer caprice. Random stupid luck.

Life is a fucking bitch. Trust no one.

From now on, Jim resolved to reject life, and its snares, and its lies. He wouldn't kill himself, but nor would he take any joy whatsoever from the act of living. He would live in a state of permanent grief.

He would become a ghost with a pulse.

Mary Beebe was lost in despair. William was gone, and life had lost all taste and purpose.

She and William had been together for two hundred years, without even a night apart. And as the AmRover landed in the clearing, she stared at Helms. And Helms knew what she was thinking.

"Whoah there, psycho killer," said Ben.

"They were ahead of us," said Mary, in steely tones. "They burrowed under the base."

"That's my surmise, too," said Helms.

"Why?"

"They must have hacked the systems," Helms explained. "Found the location of the Depot. I'd encrypted it—I never thought they…"

"That's how, I said why. Why do they *hate us*?"

"That, I do not know."

"I think you do," said Mary Beebe, and her calm and unforgiving tone commanded fear from all who heard her.

"We'll talk about this later," said Helms, mildly.

The mood was icy.

They landed, and debarked from the AmRover and looked at the verdant prison that surrounded them. Night fell fast. Ben lit a fire, and Sorcha assigned all the surviving Soldiers to sentry duty, except for herself.

"OK," said Sorcha. "Let's talk."

"Fine by me," said Helms, tensely, fearing the worst.

They sat around the fire, with Tonii Newton, Clementine McCoy and Sergeant Anderson at their sentry posts, but listening through their MI-radios, throwing in occasional comments.

Helms glanced around him, slowly and anxiously. He thought of all the deaths he had caused, at Helms City and at Xabar, and his spirits were bleak. He thought about William Beebe, and he hated himself. He thought of the Noirs, all dead apart from Jim Aura, and wondered how lonely the man must feel.

Out of a population of nearly 400, only eleven remained. And it was *all his fault*.

"Tell us the truth," said Sorcha. "What's happening?"

"I don't know," Helms said, tired now, his candid and innocent tone of voice worn ragged.

"This is the end of the road," said Mary. "Stop lying to us. Or I will kill you with my bare hands."

"What the hell are you on about, Mary?" Hugo said, alarmed, but hugely impressed at her bravado.

"This man's a fucking liar."

"Easy, Mary," said Helms, with a nasty tang in his voice.

"Yes, be a bit more respectful, Mary," said Hugo. "After all this is, you know, the Professor to whom you are talking."

Mary glared.

Sorcha looked at Richard Helms, slowly and carefully. He met her gaze with a look of total sincerity. And she knew. *He was lying.*

The flames crackled. Insects howled. Helms could hear a crash in the far distance, as a tree canopy collapsed into the Flesh-Webs with the explosive impact of an earthquake. All of them had their helmets retracted, and the cold night air chilled their cheeks.

"Who or what is doing all this?" Sorcha insisted.

"The CSO, it has to be," Helms lied. "Even though the Quantum Beacon is down, he must have found some other way to —"

"Liar," said Mary, with a drumbeat rhythm.

"If you think I'm a liar," said Helms, firmly, "then prove it."

Hugo blinked approvingly. That was of course the correct scientific response.

Sorcha looked at Mary. She absorbed the full force of the other woman's passion and rage.

And then Sorcha took out her plasma gun and fired a short burst into the fire. The wood exploded and sparks flew. Helms was enveloped in a haze of black cinders. He coughed. He took out his own plasma gun and Sorcha tasered him and his body spasmed to the ground.

"Disarm him," Sorcha snarled, and the Soldiers hurried from their sentry posts and stripped Helms of his weapons.

"Is that necessary?" asked Hugo.

"Good moves," said Ben, impressed.

"Why the fuck didn't they kill me?" Sorcha ranted. "I was this close to a DR. It had a gun aimed at me. It could have killed me. *Why didn't it kill me?*"

Helms coughed and got his breath back.

"Because you're my girlfriend," he said at last.

Sorcha's face filled with rage. "This is all about *you?*"

"Let me explain," said Helms.

He hesitated. Then, finally, he told the truth:

"My name is not, in point of fact, Richard Helms," he explained.

Hugo blinked.

"My real name," Helms continued, "is Saunders. Professor Carl Saunders."

The words shocked them all: it was as if a dinner guest had revealed himself to be Aristotle.

"Then who is trying to kill us?" said Mary Beebe, in a hushed whisper.

"Well that would be Hooperman. Andrew Hooperman."

This time, the gasps came in synchrony.

"Impossible! He's dead. You killed him," Mary accused.

"Not," said Professor Richard Helms, aka Professor Carl Saunders, with characteristic understatement, "entirely."

DAY 12

From the diary of Dr Hugo Baal

June 33rd

Yesterday was an awful, and terrible, and yet it has to be said, a truly amazing day. A day full of incidents and horrors and marvels.

I think back on it all: our arrival at Helms City, the dinner, the dancing, the unexpected ambush by the DRs, the death and destruction, the loss of our second base, and the shocking realisation that many of my esteemed colleagues and, dare I say it,[1] friends on this expedition are now dead.

And now, to cap it all — let us call it the silver lining in a black black cloud — and please do not think me heartless, in finding pleasure from this, in the midst of terrible grief[2] — I have just met one of my greatest heroes!

And mark my words, this is no ordinary man. He is the first among equals, the finest xenobiologist in the history of science — nay, the very inventor[3] and deviser of that discipline![4] The man who rewrote evolution and designed the Gene Scope. The man who made First Contact with the first sentient species ever discovered by mankind, the Lyras; the most brilliant scientist of our age, a veritable Newton among us.

Unfortunately he is now being held in protective custody, following his selfish and deranged actions which led to the death of 383 Scientists[5] and Soldiers on New Amazon, in two separate ghastly massacres and a few skirmishes in between,[5] and hence my opportunities to question the Great Man about his work and ideas have been severely circumscribed.

Mary Beebe was twenty-nine years old when she first met the man who would become her husband. She was a doctoral student who had rashly decided to write her doctorate on flame beasts. For eleven years she had lived among these bizarre creatures in a space station circling the planet Luce. The flame beasts had entertained her and told her tales and quizzed her about her favourite television programmes, and she'd discovered absolutely nothing about their physiology, anatomy, evolution, cytology (assuming they had cells), morphology or even their basic physics. Her instruments had failed to identify the particular kind of "flame" that constituted the flame beast. It wasn't fire, as such, nor was it plasma, as such, nor was it hot to the touch, except when the flame beasts wanted to burn things, and then it was incandescent and could ignite metal. It was, she eventually concluded, some kind of fundamental "stuff", on a par with electrons and muons. But it was not, she eventually concluded, animal, vegetable or mineral. She confirmed the genus, *Flammabestia*, but was unable to identify any species, let alone subspecies (since the flame beast doesn't procreate, can it have different species?).

Her work was a marvel of futility! She and William laughed about it often, her glorious, wasted years chit-chatting to superbeings. William had written his own doctoral thesis on the multiple digestive system of the Traskian dung beetle, and had hence won himself a place in xenobiological mythology. But though Mary's thesis wasn't worth the paper it wasn't written on, William had seen her potential, and intelligence, and insight. They had become devoted colleagues. And eventually, after a number of years working together in the most appalling of environments, at the very closest of quarters, they had become lovers.

But she couldn't believe ... that he ...

"Move this fucking thing!" Sorcha roared as tendrils descended upon the AmRover, and some kind of sessile animal attempted to eat them, and plasma guns roared and they were free again.

She couldn't believe ... that ...

The flame beasts had grown very fond of Mary, and eventually they towed her spaceship to the neighbouring planetary system of Fecunda, where they knew she would be able to study a vital, complex habitat with fleshly creatures who could be categorised. And that's how William first came across her: to his utter astonishment, she was delivered to his Research Camp in a one-person lifeship conveyed by a dozen pillars of living flame.

She could still remember that moment vividly. William staring up, aghast, as she descended from her lifeship, with the flames dancing in homage around her.

Mary raged; it was all so random! They'd almost got away from the DRs. They'd both seen the hole in the wall and were about to leap through it. Then Mary turned to check William was OK, but his head had fallen off and the neck stump was gushing blood, and she should have stayed and died with him but her reflexes kicked in and she allowed herself to be led away to, to, to *life*.

She knew he was dead, of course he was dead, his head was severed, but she hadn't stopped to check, in case he might be just a little bit alive, she hadn't . . .

William had hired Mary as his research assistant, he had assessed her second dissertation on Fecunda's most prolific life-form, the Death Toad (*Nex viridis, Nex purpura* and *Nex turpis*), and after twenty-four years of intimate professional collaboration on a variety of planets, he and Mary had sexual intercourse in a two-person tent, and then they got married the following day.

Now William was dead, his head cut away from his body by the plasma blast of a Doppelganger Robot, and it was all because of that fucking bastard Professor Carl Saunders, DPhil, MA, FRS, Nobel Laureate, twice winner of the Genius Award for Outstanding Scientific Achievements, author of the definitive text on xenobiology, and fugitive.

Mary vowed that Saunders's death would be a painful one. And she wished that she could be allowed to kill him herself, with her bare hands and teeth. That might help to ease the — ease the —

For she couldn't believe — William was actually dead? She missed him. The pain of loss was unendurable.

She remembered William's smile. His wit. His gentle sarcasm. His brilliance. His look of pure joy when he first saw a Death Toad inflate and fly. His huffy look when she wasn't paying attention to him.

Now, no more joy, no more sarcasm, no more huff.

Beebe william.†

No more.

Professor Carl Saunders, formerly known as Professor Helms, was still cuffed and bound, but at least they had found him a chair to sit on. The survivors surrounded him in a semicircle. And Sorcha paced around him, like a lion laying claim to a haunch of deer, as the interrogation began.

"OK," said Sorcha. "Explain."

"It's complicated," said Saunders calmly, then met her gaze and flinched at the hate he saw there.

"We have time."

"I didn't mean for any of this to —"

"Just," said Sorcha, "fucking, talk."

"Hooperman is trying to kill me."

"We know that much."

"Because of what I —"

"We all know the story of you and Hooperman. You attempted to murder him and failed."

"I —" Saunders slumped. "I guess so."

"And now he's decided to take revenge."

"He's been trying to take revenge for the last two hundred years."

For these last two centuries, Saunders had lived as a hunted man; changing identities, constantly fearful, never staying too long in the same sector of the Solar Neighbourhood. And for all this time, Hooperman — through his murderous Doppelganger proxies, and with the aid of his remarkable computer genius — was remorseless in pursuit. There were times when Saunders had longed for it all to be over. Times when he wished he could lose, and be killed, and put the end to the endless vendetta of Professor Andrew Hooperman.

"And you don't deny you bombed Hooperman?"

"Well I don't deny it. But I had my reasons. I—"

"I don't want to hear your fucking reasons," snarled Sorcha.

"I do," said Mary Beebe. She stared intently at Saunders. "I want to hear. What possessed you, Saunders? You are arguably the greatest xeno-scientist of all time—"

"Hooperman would dispute—"

"Not a *murderer*. What were you thinking of? Did you really hate him so—"

"I didn't hate him—"

"You attempted to—"

"Yes—but not because—I'm not explaining this well."

"Take your time," said Mary Beebe. "Because it's the only time you have left."

Saunders blinked. "Are you saying you're going to—"

"Kill you? Yes of course. It's what you deserve." Rage burned in Mary's eyes.

"Ah," said Saunders, with infinite regret.

"So tell us. Tell us it all," said Mary Beebe.

And so Professor Richard Helms, aka Professor Carl Saunders, DPhil, FRS, Nobel Laureate, told his tale.

"First, you have to understand how it was with Hooperman and me."

A flock of Sunlights flew above them, catching the red embers of the sunset.

"He was my DPhil student, at the University of Oxford, England, Earth," Saunders told them, "and he was brilliant. Charismatic. But also, annoying. Intense. He used to—no matter. We became friends, of sorts, and colleagues. And he was my first choice for the team I led on my Amazon Expedition of '98. And he—"

"And that's when you betrayed him, and left him for dead," murmured Hugo Baal.

"No!" Saunders snapped. "That was just a stupid lie told by Hooperman, to make—oh forget it. The point is, we had a series of major quarrels during the Expedition. Our friendship fell to pieces. And then—then we found the hummingbird."

Hushed awe spread between the Scientists at those words. They all knew the legend of the nocturnal Amazonian hummingbird, the last new species ever found on Earth. And here was Saunders himself, actually talking about it...!

"Hooperman became insanely competitive—and that's why he told all those stupid lies about me. And then, later, the quarrel between us was exacerbated," Saunders explained, "when he wrote those articles about me. He tarnished my reputation. He called me a liar, a plagiarist, he—he...Anyway, for many years, as you all know, we feuded, bitterly and shamefully. But I still had great respect for Hooperman. I always thought he was an honourable man. And then—"

The memories came washing over Saunders. He picked his way carefully through the wreckage of his past, as he tried desperately to argue for his life.

"You see, about two hundred years ago I had a meeting with the CSO, and he asked me to lead a new scientific expedition. I refused. Hooperman came to see me, and we drank a bottle of whisky together. And I explained to him my reservations about the project's intended outcome. He made me realise that if I didn't say yes, I would be killed. So I said yes. But I drafted a plan to thwart the CSO's stupid edict."

"What stupid edict?" asked Sorcha.

"The Genocide Edict, of course!" This was the law that had led to the deaths of countless trillions of aliens; it was the legal justification for the terraforming of thousands of planets with thriving, rich ecologies.

"And why is that a problem?" Sorcha asked. Mary glared at her, furiously.

"Because you can't terraform a planet that's got *life*," Saunders said, angrily.

"We do it all the time," Sorcha replied, snidely.

"Not in my day," Helms retorted. "Hope was a barren planet without water; it was irrigated; life was seeded there. Cambria was a hothouse Venus-type planet; it was cooled, then seeded with Earth life. There are plenty of terraformable planets in the Habitable Zones of the Solar Neighbourhood. We don't need to exterminate alien species. That's not what we do!"

"Why not? We are the human race. It's *our* universe," Sorcha pointed out.

"That's what Hooperman said. But it's not. It's just not." Saunders was lost for words, for a few moments, then he ploughed on: "Life is, well, it's life. Sacred. Unique. You can't exterminate alien species. That's what Hitler would have—"

"That's what William used to say," Mary said in hollow tones. "Hitler would have—but oh no, no, that's a false comparison. You can't compare Hitler with—his Reich lasted barely a decade. Whereas—" She broke off, mindful of the angry stares that the Soldiers were directing at her. "William and I always thought the Genocide Edict was—well—arguably, in some ways, a slightly flawed strategy," she concluded, in a feeble attempt to avoid self-incrimination.

"On that we are agreed," said Saunders, crisply.

Sorcha tapped the handle of her gun. It was an act of treason punishable by death to query the CSO's edicts. And Sorcha, like all Soldiers, was trained to enforce these edicts instantly and brutally.

But surely, Saunders hoped desperately, after all that had happened on New Amazon, even brainwashed Soldiers could no longer have any loyalty to the old regime?

Sorcha's eyes burned into him. "Continue," she said, scornfully, "with your abject confession."

"Right. Then I shall. Cutting to the chase," Saunders continued, shakily, "I told Hooperman my plan. I would travel to a planet rich in alien life-forms, then falsify the records so that it was logged as unterraformable, destroy the mother ship's computer, and keep the alien life-forms alive and flourishing. It was masterly, in my view."

"No, it was treasonous," Sorcha said savagely. "If you'd told me that was your plan, I'd have shot you, or turned you in to the authorities for them to shoot you."

"Well, as it happens, I told Hooperman, and he turned me in to the authorities," Saunders said bitterly. "The next day the Soldiers came to interrogate me. I denied everything, naturally. But I was interrogated for three months, then found guilty without a trial, and dismissed from all my academic posts. My Nobel Prize was revoked. Just because of a single conversation I had with Hooperman! And then I was told that I would continue to work as a xeno-phylogenist, but in solitary confinement, under house arrest, for the rest of my life. So I used my influence, placed some bribes, then escaped from custody and fled Earth, in order to start afresh. And—"

He hesitated.

"Hooperman," Sorcha prompted.

"Yes, indeed," said Saunders, and his tone was crisper, more abrasive than it had ever been as Helms. He thought for a little while, judging with care the words he was about to utter, and then he smiled, and it was a cruel smile.

"And then I sent a book bomb to Hooperman. Because he deserved to die, after betraying me to the CSO. And then I went into space with a face transplant and a new identity."

"But Hooperman survived."

"Indeed," Saunders said sourly. "You know that bit of the story?"

"Of course. He—"

"He was lucky. I used a close-proximity charge, but he had a robot servant to open his mail. Even so, I maimed the bastard. Hurt him real good. He claims he's now living in intensive care, in dire agony, that the body transplant failed. But who's to know? That may just be another of his lies."

"And so *that's* why?" Mary whispered. "You were angry with Hooperman and you tried to kill him? And that's why William died?"

"I was rebelling against—"

"Don't give me that," Mary Beebe said, fiercely. "Hooperman may have been a coward, but *he* wasn't your enemy. You just hated him—because you were and are a petulant, arrogant man. You brought this down on us. You dragged us into your stupid fucking feud, and hundreds of innocent people are now dead, including my husband, all because Hooperman hated you, and you hated him." She paused, and spat the final words at him: "You deserve to die, Professor Saunders, and you will. For what you have inflicted upon us, you will never be forgiven."

Ben sat in the cockpit of AmRover 3 and remembered the exhilaration of battle. The smell of burning flesh. The screams.

He'd been among the first to escape from the Doppelganger Robots when they attacked at Helms City. But he'd got separated from the main party, so he'd fled to the East Evacuation Bay, where he encountered a group of six Scientists who hadn't bothered to attend the dance. They'd all breathed a sigh of relief when he joined them, appalled at what they'd witnessed through the surveillance TV screens. And they were all, clearly, delighted to find that being party-pooping workaholics had saved their lives.

Ben had regaled them all with the tales of the horrors he had been through.

And then he'd charged up the plasma cannon he had taken from a dead Soldier, and fired it at his unwary companions. His close-quarters high-energy plasma blasts and explosive bullets ripped through the body armour of those hapless fools, and popped heads, and gouged huge holes in bodies. Torrents of blood poured out of the torn suits. He could smell burning flesh, and hear screams, and then they were all dead and it was quiet again.

Later, it occurred to Ben that his meds were no longer working. He was now completely, clinically, mad. But it also occurred to him — he no longer needed medication!

For, as a diagnosed homicidal psychopath, he'd always been told it was essential to keep his emotions strictly regulated, in order to function and conform in civilised society.

But now that they were fighting for their lives against Doppel-ganger enemies of devilish malignity, it seemed to him that a man possessed by a paranoid kill-lust was *precisely* what was required.

Sorcha drove. It helped her to focus on a practical task, because her thoughts and emotions were in a state of turmoil.

She'd trusted Richard Helms. She'd felt a rapport with him. They'd been lovers, and colleagues, and—so she had thought—friends.

And he'd lied to her, from beginning to end, and at every moment in between. He'd lied about everything, including his age and his area of specialism. He wasn't a geologist, he was a zoologist, a tax-onomist, a First Contacter.

Because of Richard—Carl? what the hell should she call him?—hundreds of people had died. It was entirely his fault. He'd brought this curse on them.

And he'd *lied* to her. Constantly. Every word he had ever said was a lie. That much was beyond doubt.

So when he had said to her, in his soft and gentle tones, that he loved her—was that a lie too?

"Where are we going?" Clementine McCoy asked her, and Sor-cha's focus returned.

"I don't know."

"Then why are we going so quickly?"

"They'll be behind us. They'll follow. We have to put some ground between us."

"They can follow faster than we can run."

"I know."

"They can use the Dravens to scour the area."

"It's a big area. They won't know which way to go. The further we are from Helms City, the more ground they have to search."

"You shouldn't have relaxed security at the dance," said Private Clementine McCoy.

"I know that."

"Just so my observation is noted."

"It's noted. I accept liability."

"Fair enough."

"You lost a lot of friends back there," Sorcha conceded.

"They died a Glorious death," said Clementine, casually, then brooded. And eventually she said: "Perhaps we should stand and fight."

"We wouldn't have a hope."

"I know. But—"

"You want a Glorious death?" said Sorcha, scornfully.

"Of course," said Clementine, shocked at her senior officer's tone.

"And so do I," said Sorcha, hastily. "But let's explore the other options first. I'm not going to fail a second time. We'll find a way to live."

Tonii and Mia were in the Observation Bubble of AmRover 1.

Mia was in tears. Tonii was baffled. He held her, as she cried and cried.

"Why aren't you crying?" she asked, eventually.

"At what?"

"So many died!"

"But *I* did not," he said calmly.

Mia looked at Tonii curiously. "You don't care, do you? All your friends are dead, and you don't care?"

"No."

"So long as you're alive, you're happy."

"Yes."

"So long as your Glory is intact, you're content."

"Yes."

"You're not any different, are you?"

"What do you mean?"

"You're the same as the others. The other Soldiers. You're all KMs. Killing Machines."

"Of course," said Tonii, surprised at her scathing tone, and pseudo-philosophical censure. "It's what we're bred for."

"Don't talk like that! 'Bred'! We're human beings!" said Mia, anguished.

"No, *you're* human. We are more so. Because we do not fear death."

"You're really telling me you're not afraid to die?"

Tonii hesitated, and knew he had to lie.

"I long for death, so long as it's Glorious."

"You fucking…" Mia struggled to find the word, "*freak.*"

Saunders hated being tethered in the secure cage in the back of the AmRover.

He felt like a specimen, a xeno, or a captured lion. Or, indeed, the most apt comparison of all in his case, a caged bird.

He remembered all the birds they'd captured in the Amazon, he and Hooperman, and the guileful use they'd made of call birds and trap-cages. Now, *he* was in a trap-cage. Locked in the boot of the AmRover, bouncing every time the vehicle veered to avoid a root or a swamp or a predator.

This was Hooperman's revenge.

Nice one, Andrew.

Saunders's guess was that Hooperman must have spent longer on New Amazon than he'd realised before launching his attack. He'd hacked into the Juno mainframe, broken into all Saunders's secret files, reprogrammed the DRs into hunter-killers, and given them detailed information about the Depot. So the fact that Hooperman himself had now lost contact with New Amazon was no obstacle to his revenge. The robot monsters were acting as his pawns and his agents.

Saunders had underestimated his old enemy. Hooperman wasn't just evil, he was *smart.*

DAY 13

From the diary of Dr Hugo Baal

June 34th

I slept badly last night, haunted by nightmares, most of which were, curiously enough, less terrible than what has been actually happening in the daytime.

I eventually got out of bed at 3 a.m. and spent two hours talking at length and in detail to <u>Professor Saunders</u>,[1] who unfortunately was in some discomfort, since he was tethered with toughmetal wire to an Aldiss tree.

A fascinating man—strange how I underestimated him when I thought he was just a geologist!

We chatted about this and that, as you do, though his small talk is, I must admit, not of the best, and chiefly consisted of his asking me to "cut the fucking wire". I told him how I'd always dreamed of meeting him, and how, when I was just a tubby six-year-old with social impairment issues,[2] he inspired me to devote my life to the study of phylogeny and morphology and taxonomy.[3]

I quizzed him about Hooperman—I'd always been intrigued by Hooperman, that old rascal—but Professor Saunders was taciturn to the point of rudeness on this topic. So instead I told him a few reminiscences of my life on the road as a roving xenobiologist. That soon palled, and I became overwhelmed by the fear that I was squandering an opportunity of a lifetime—a chance to find out at first hand about, oh, so many things that Saunders had done or written or thought in the course of his long and brilliant career.

It occurred to me then that I should ask him about his account[4] of the Frantic Assembly[5] of Gullyfoyle, one of the most remarkable swarm

---

1 See Appendix 2.
2 But cute! Honestly! Click *here* to see my baby photos.
3 "Wow," he replied, in what I took to be tones of stunned approbation.
4 In the *Encyclopedia of Alien Life*, Vol. 1, p. 3094.
5 *Coetus furens.*

intelligences yet to be encountered in the human-explored universe. I have a long-held theory that the Frantic Assembly are the regressed version of the Bugs,[6] but Saunders poured scorn on this notion. Undeterred, I patiently, and comprehensively, and rather impressively I felt, pointed out the following areas of similarity and dissimilarity:

> *1) Microscopic life forms (FA and B)*
>
> *2) Swarming ability, coupled with emergent behaviour (FA and B)*
>
> *3) Ability to mimic forms and shapes of other creatures at macroscopic level (FA and B)*
>
> *4) Ability to spell out English words in mid-air (B)*
>
> *5) Ability to destroy life-forms and inanimate objects within seconds (B)*

Saunders attributed all these similarities to simple convergent evolution, and pointed out that there are 541,000 genuses of "tree" on many thousands of different planets, all of them separately evolved. I naturally mocked this notion, because the prevalence of trees owes much to the tendency of lazy scientists to think anything Plantae that grows upwards and is tall and has a hard surface is a tree. Some trees have exoskeletons made of cadmium! It's tantamount to describing anything with four legs as a lion. But the Frantic Assembly/Bug comparison is based on a more judicious and thorough and academically brilliant intellectual differentiation.[7] There are only two creatures in all of Known Space that are microscopic and yet can swarm to become macroscopic, the Bugs and the Frantic Assembly.[8] Coincidence, or eerie connection? I put it to you, as I put it to Saunders, rather forcefully in fact, but fortunately he was still tethered to the tree and couldn't stalk off in a huff, that it is the latter. In which case, should we not consider the possibility that the Frantic Assembly remnants now being kept in zoos could re-evolve into

---

6 *Malus muchus terribulus* (stet! Named by a linguistic and scientific ignoramus).

7 Mine.

8 Hmm, what about the New Amazonian Pollen Horde, I hear you ask? I'll have to think on that.

*a Buglike intelligence? Is it really sensible to allow them to survive? I
mean! It's madness, isn't it!?!*[9]

*Saunders eventually conceded this point, rather grudgingly, at about
the time that the dawn broke over the trees, in a glittering colourful-
ness of myriad light,*[10] *at which point the Military Commander of the
expedition Major Sorcha Molloy arrived and announced that we were
departing immediately, and further explained that Professor Saunders
was to remain in this location, chained and tethered to the Aldiss tree.*

*The Professor was somewhat distracted after receiving this news, and
pointed out that he was being doomed to a certain and ghastly death.
This point was conceded by Major Molloy, who then returned to the
AmRover, in a state of some agitation. I asked Professor Saunders what,
with the wisdom of hindsight, he now felt was the most interesting aspect
about his first-ever First Contact, either from a morphological or an
evolutionary or simply a taxonomic perspective.*

*Professor Saunders declined to respond, and commenced to swear and
yell and, to my amazement, weep, and at this point I was forced to leave
him, in order to join the rest of the expedition.*

Sorcha drove the AmRover fast through the jungle. Plasma blasts
blew a path through the Flesh-Webs. There were tears on her cheek
and she didn't bother to brush them away. The sharp yellow sunlight
brushed her skin and made her flesh shimmer like rippled water at
dawn. She took a deep breath, and drove and drove.

She'd voted in favour of letting Saunders die. He was tied with
unbreakable wire to an Aldiss tree. He had no weapons, just his
body armour. And before they'd left they had fired twelve rockets
high into the sky to allow the Dravens to pinpoint his position.

9 Rhetorical question; the answer is yes!
10 I'm quoting, of course, from my favourite poem, Patrick Spence's *Alien Dawns.*

Sorcha was confident that Saunders would be found and killed within hours. And, finally, the rest of them would be safe.

"A brilliant man, we'll never see his like again," Hugo muttered defiantly, and Ben seethed with rage. He was sick of Baal's so-called witticisms, his pedantry, his sheer annoyingness. The man was impossible, and shouldn't be allowed to blight the lives of others.

Ben resolved to wait a few hours, then find an excuse to go into the jungle with Baal and kill him. Slowly and painfully and horribly. It was no more than the man deserved, for being such a tedious ass.

"Although, in fairness," Hugo added, "and contrariwise, I did find Saunders, as we must now categorise him, to be a little bit on the pompous side. N'est-ce pas, old chum?"

He *has* to die soon! Ben thought to himself, with the mental equivalent of gritted teeth.

Sorcha was studying the virtual map of New Amazon. "The coast," she said at last. "That's where we should go. Away from the jungle, away from the Flesh-Webs."

"It's going to be bitterly hard driving to get there," Tonii counselled. "We'll need to cut through another Jungle-Wall. And there's uncharted terrain most of the way. Gods only know what we'll encounter."

"It's worth it," said Sorcha. "There, we'll be safe. Sea. Surf. Red sand. We can build there. We can make a new world."

And she flashed them all a confident glance, to prove she was still their leader and that nothing scared her, and that she wasn't just a sad and vulnerable woman mourning the inevitable and imminent death of the man she loved.

It took Saunders two hours, two awful and humiliating and painful hours, to get the pencil plasma gun out of his arse.

First he had to get his body armour off, which was difficult enough, since he was both cuffed and shackled. Second, he had to strip off his trousers and underpants. And, then, third, he had to insert his fingers —

Anyway! At one point a host of Rat-Insects swarmed over his half-naked body and he had to use a sonic-scream to get them off. The jungle was generally hot and humid, but it was also blighted by savage cold breezes. Saunders found the pain of the windchill on his unprotected body appalling. It was one thing to savour the breeze on your cheeks, quite another to endure the bizarrely hot–cold New Amazonian temperatures whilst bare-arsed.

Even when he had removed the gun from its sticky niche, he still had to re-dress himself in clothes and body armour. Only then could he set about the task of burning through the connecting cables of his cuffs and shackles. And only *then* could he burn the diamond-hard tether that wrapped around his neck, and held him fast to the Aldiss tree.

It took twenty minutes of burning before the tether snapped. Then Saunders began walking through the jungle.

The plasma gun contained a micro-thin Bostock battery, so though it was a tiny weapon he was confident it would last him some months. The priority now was to get away from this part of the jungle. The flares had ignited in the lower atmosphere, on a faintly sloping trajectory, so Saunders had mentally calculated that the DRs would have to search more than sixty square kilometres of jungle to find him. That was, Saunders guessed, a deliberate strategy on Sorcha's part — the longer it took the DRs to find and kill him, the longer Sorcha and her people had to get away to safety.

Her logic was impeccable, but she was wrong. It was now appall-ingly obvious that Hooperman would have programmed the robots to kill every single person who had ever worked with his enemy and nemesis, Carl Saunders. This wasn't a targeted revenge, it was to be a massacre.

This must explain why Saunders was still alive. He was being taunted and mocked, forced to play a role in a Grand Guignol theatre event. Hooperman wanted his enemy to know that all his friends and colleagues had been horribly and brutally killed, before he would allow the DRs to, horribly and brutally, kill Saunders himself.

But Saunders had a few tricks to play yet. He set his body armour on high hover and soared up into the air and flew just below the level of the Canopy. From time to time poison shit rained down, making his armour sizzle, but he was making good time. He hadn't seen any Dravens. Maybe he would get away from this region without encountering the enemy.

And then he saw them. Six flying DR Humanoids. They spotted him and formed an attack formation.

Saunders tilted his body and flew upwards, then plasma-blasted a hole in the tree canopy and flew through.

Sorcha lurched forward in her seat, as the low-hovering AmRover abruptly halted, froze briefly in mid-air, then crashed to the ground.

"What the hell?"

Sorcha patted herself for broken limbs. Ben was staring at her, puzzled.

"Check the engine," she snapped.

They got out and inspected the vehicle. Ben snapped the bonnet open and peered down into the AmRover's engine. He touched the smooth metal with a finger, and it came out green and sticky.

"Corrosive vegetation," he said.

"Not possible," said Sorcha.

"Microscopic spores," speculated Hugo. "They could have been here months. The heat of the engine is enough to germinate them."

"These are sealed units!"

"Microscopic," explained Hugo, "may mean micromicroscopic. Smaller than air molecules."

"Let's all move into the other vehicle," grumbled Sorcha.

The remaining AmRover was spacious enough to take all ten survivors. But Sorcha hated the fact that they were reduced to one vehicle. There was no margin for error now.

"We drive day and night," she said.

"You're the boss," Ben told her, in tones that implied he thought she damned well shouldn't be.

Saunders exploded through the tree canopy and saw clear blue sky above him for the first time in a year. The sun was bright yellow with a hint of blue corona and three times larger than any sun he had ever lived under. He could see some nearby asteroids, virtually moons.

Saunders carried on flying upwards, then he looped and looked down.

The Humanoid DRs burst through the canopy in pursuit of him. The Roc nest he had crashed into was now a wreck and a hapless Roc chick was circling aimlessly, old enough to fly but not mature enough to defend itself. A flock of Deadbirds appeared as if from nowhere and ripped it to shreds in moments. Then a few seconds later a flock of adult Rocs appeared and turned the Deadbirds into dead birds.

The Humanoid DRs were in the midst of this, and the Rocs plunged at them. A haze of plasma fire lit the sky, turning the canopy an even more lurid green.

But the Rocs had scales that could, miraculously, deflect plasma bolts. They were roused to rage and plunged in on the Humanoid DRs.

Saunders flew on, amused at the sight of the most powerful robots of all time being ripped limb from limb by a flock of birds the size of killer whales.

Ben's head was throbbing. He was sick with desire. He beckoned to Private Clementine McCoy with the time-honoured "Shall we fuck?" finger-flick signal, but she frowned and shook her head.

"I'm important to this mission, you should think of my morale," he pointed out acidly. He knew that Soldiers were hard-wired to be promiscuous — all sex was casual to them — so what was this bitch's problem?

"Oh for heaven's sake," she told him scornfully.

"You've done it with me before," he said sulkily.

"Only when drunk." She replied, lightening her words with a smile.

"Oh don't be such a spoilsport."

"Back the fuck off, Ben. I'm not in the mood, OK?" She wasn't smiling any more.

"Just a quickie?"

"No!" Clementine was baffled at his eerie persistence.

"Go on. You'll hardly notice."

"No!"

"No? No?" Ben was consumed with blinding rage. He could suddenly see himself strangling Clementine to death, and pleasuring himself upon her corpse.

"You don't look well," she told him gently.

"Are you sure that was the right thing to do? Leaving the Professor to die?" Hugo said to Sorcha.

She was angry with him for questioning her judgement. And startled that he had spoken to her about something that wasn't a scientific issue.

"It's the only way to divert the DRs," she said carefully. "Saunders is the one they want, not us."

"We don't know that," said Hugo pedantically.

"Of course we know that! Hooperman is the one who set his dogs on us, and he and Saunders have been enemies for more than two hundred years."

"True," Hugo, conceded, but couldn't resist adding: "But it was all Hooperman's fault, you know—well, that is, apart from the bomb bit. After all, I mean, *he* was the one who told those stupid lies about what happened in the Amazon rainforest. I always knew Saunders would never have—"

"I don't care *why* they hate each other, I just care that they do."

"It was all nonsense! What Hooperman said, after he crawled—"

"Let's not rehash this now."

"In fact," Hugo continued, inexorably, "Saunders honestly believed that—"

Sorcha glared at him.

Hugo subsided, grudgingly.

Sorcha drove on, in blessed silence.

But then a mist covered her eyes, and she blinked swiftly to clear it.

"What's wrong?" asked Hugo.

"Nothing."

"You're upset."

"Something in my eye."

"Of course," Hugo realised, "it must have been hard for you to leave Saunders behind. Considering—"

"That has no bearing on the matter."

"But you were—"

"We had sex. That's all. He was one of my conquests. I didn't even like the odious little shit," Sorcha said, with all the arrogance and emotional disdain of the born and bred Soldier.

"Oh, I see," said Hugo, his theory crushed.

Sorcha drove on.

"Well," said Hugo, thoughtlessly. "If Saunders isn't dead yet, he will be soon."

"Good," said Sorcha. "I'm glad. The useless bastard!"

She drove on, stony-faced.

The sky was black with Gryphons. Saunders knew that if they saw him as prey, and plunged, and attacked him, he stood no chance.

They did not plunge. Saunders flew on.

Sorcha realised with a sense of horror that she couldn't do this.

She slowed the AmRover down, and glided gently to the ground.

"I'm going back."

Hugo stared at her aghast. "What? What are you on about?"

"*Is there a problem?*" asked Private Clementine McCoy, from the AmRover's recreation room.

"Why the fuck have we stopped?" snarled Sergeant Anderson, from the back seat of the cockpit.

"The Professor," Sorcha explained to Hugo. "I have to be with him."

Hugo fought his bewilderment. "But you left him to die."

"And I shouldn't have," Sorcha said, anguished. "I have to go back, before it's too late."

Hugo did his best to follow this bizarre switch from loathing to loving. He failed.

"Um, I don't think I follow," he said.

"Have we stopped?" asked Jim Aura, blinking awake.

"What's your problem, Soldier?" Sergeant Anderson snarled.

"Start the fucking truck!" roared Ben.

"I'll be getting out here," Sorcha said, sadly.

Through his helmet amp, Saunders heard a whirr of wind and suddenly he was ripped out of the air and buffeted and battered.

It took him several seconds to realise what was happening. A Gryphon had attacked, and was gripping him by his head. He flailed helplessly for a moment, then managed to take out his plasma pencil and fired. Feather-scales flew and the Gryphon's head was severed, but its beak had pecked at his hardglass helmet, scratching it, and the power of the whiplash caused Saunders to black out.

DAY 14

It took a day and a night for Sorcha to walk and fly back to where they had abandoned Saunders.

At last, she arrived at the clearing where they had left him. She checked her bearings; this was definitely the right spot. She looked anxiously for him, amazed at the way her heart leaped and skipped, and—

He wasn't there.

His tether was cut. An Aldiss tree was weeping pus from where it had been burned by a plasma blast.

Sorcha subvoced a curse, and raged at her own stupidity. Now she didn't have Saunders, she didn't have an AmRover, and there was a very good chance she was going to end up dead.

What the fuck was *wrong* with her?

Saunders woke, his head pounding, and a Gryphon sat before him, huge and sharp-beaked and terrifying.

He realised he'd been unconscious for some time, nearly a day. His body armour had been sedating him while it healed his injuries. A visor display showed him the X-ray of his fractured skull, now almost knitted back in place.

Saunders calmed his breathing, and tried to meet the Gryphon's eyes, but then he realised it had no eyes. There was a trace of blood on its beak from a recent kill. With his peripheral vision, Saunders tried to piece together where he was. Not in the jungle—because there were clouds above him but also below him. And there was a crack in the centre of his field of vision. The hardglass helmet was cracked. A few savage pecks and the Gryphon might well be able to break it.

Saunders looked closer at the creature before him. It was large, twice the size of an Earth lion. And it was similar to a bird in shape, but it was a far more terrible creature. It had no eyes, a bullet head, and a "beak" that had serrated edges and held several dagger tongues. The "beak" was in fact a manoeuvrable claw, which it used to rip food.

The scales were blue and silver, and finely polished. And the Gryphon had six sets of claws, with bilateral symmetry. Saunders estimated that when its wings were fully expanded it would be nearly twenty feet from tip to tip.

The Gryphon flicked its deadly tongue towards him, and Saunders flinched in fear. Belatedly, he fumbled for his plasma pencil — and found the holster empty. The Gryphon cawed. It raised up one huge talon. It was holding his plasma pencil.

It knew that it was a weapon. Saunders began revising his opinion of the Gryphon. It was smarter than the average avian. He found himself counting the neck scales, and making a mental estimate of the distance between beak and forehead. There was definitely a patch of differently coloured skin on the forehead, maybe that was the retina-skin.

The Gryphon brain, Saunders recalled from his autopsies, was situated in its chest. And inside the skull, there was —

It was putting the plasma pencil down! Its claws were surprisingly delicate, and it laid the thin plasma gun on the ground between them, as an offering. Saunders smiled. "Thank you," he said loudly, "I come in peace!" And he mentally calculated how he would do this; a quick plasma blast to blow the creature's head off, then he would roll sideways, and —

The Gryphon snatched the plasma pencil up, and cawed angrily. It lunged forward and pecked Saunders's helmet savagely. It felt like being hit by a crowbar. It pecked again and again, and Saunders rolled himself up in a ball. Then he screamed, shrilly, and that silenced the bird. It was a peace-screech, they'd recorded the Gryphons using it in flight, and it was his secret weapon.

Saunders screamed shrilly again, and the Gryphon backed off. Saunders's cry was an uncanny impersonation; he'd always had a remarkable knack for imitating bird cries. (His party-piece was a nightingale being eaten alive by a kestrel.)

Saunders then tried out a short trilling noise, another Gryphon sound he had recorded and memorised. He had no idea what it meant, but hoped it would have a lulling effect.

The Gryphon was calmer now. It was shaking its head from side to side, as if considering its options. It raised the plasma pencil up to its forehead and peered...

Oh my God! Saunders was consumed with excitement. This was proof positive that the forehead skin was the creature's retina. It was peering at his plasma gun!

He hoped that it didn't have enough dexterity in its claw to activate the gun's trigger.

And suddenly, strangely, an image was in his mind, of a *Gryphon chick being hatched, and taking flight, and being killed by flying Robots.*

Saunders blinked. What had just happened? Was that a hallucination? Was he still concussed?

Another image filled his mind: *himself, falling from the sky. Hitting the ground, hard. Stirring, groaning, swearing.* Where did this image come from? He hadn't witnessed it, he couldn't have seen himself fall.

He looked at the Gryphon and then he knew. This was the Gryphon's memory of what it had witnessed. The Gryphon was planting images in his mind...!

The Gryphon's forehead stared at him. And an image appeared in his mind: himself, bedraggled, bloodied, mad-looking, staring at the Gryphon.

He was seeing himself through the Gryphon's eyes.

Saunders marvelled, and immediately began wondering how this was possible. An electromagnetic pulse, transmitting brain waves? Was that possible? Especially since the images were being passed between different species?

A gust of wind sent rocks scrabbling past them. They clattered down the mountain crag. Saunders ignored them. He kept his focus on the Gryphon. It occurred to him that the Gryphon's brain was in its chest, and in the skull there was a spongy organ which seemed to serve no function. So perhaps the spongy organ was an organic electro-magnetic amplification device? And maybe, indeed, instead of having one brain that does many things, the Gryphon had two brains. A brain in its chest for doing and thinking, and another in its skull totally devoted to *seeing*?

Saunders thought: *My name is Carl Saunders. I am a human being.* The Gryphon was impassive. No reaction.

Saunders conjured up an image of *a body-armoured Soldier killing Doppelganger Robots by the score.*

The Gryphon cawed, with seeming delight.

Just images, then, not thoughts. Not telepathy, projective vision. And it must involve some kind of resonance effect that allowed neurons or whatever passed for neurons in the Gryphon's brain to spark neurons in *his* brain.

An image appeared in his mind: *a flock of Gryphons flying through the acid rain. Steam was boiling off their scales. The sunlight was creating a vivid moving rainbow out of pillars of falling acid.* It was an uncanny and a beautiful sight. And the image was moving against the backdrop of the sky; it was a POV recollection of what the Gryphon had seen once when it had flown through the rain.

Saunders remembered going on a trip to Niagara Falls, when he was twenty. He was with a girl, pretty, blond, well stacked, who always wore very tight shorts. Jennie? She'd been mesmerised by the sight of the waterfall, the sheer power of nature, the clouds of spume and the roar of water crashing against rock. He remembered it all now, in acute detail. And he tried to send the image.

The Gryphon cawed. It patted him with a talon. The image had been received.

Saunders remembered spacewalking outside the colony ship that had brought him to New Amazon. He saw *the spaceship below him, its squat body, its portholes, its Bridge jutting out from the bow like a bump on a head.* And beyond it, he remembered seeing *space all*

around, stars, a vast panorama of space, with galaxies and nebulae jos-
tling for attention in the black backdrop.

The Gryphon cawed, as if alarmed. Its head tilted upwards, towards the sky, and it cawed and cawed. And Saunders made a "cawing" noise in response, and pointed a finger up at the sky.

Yes, his cawing said: I come from outer space.

After twelve hours of brutal high-hovering in the AmRover, includ-ing two hours once again spent cutting through a Jungle-Wall, they were close to their destination. Ben had his eyes fixed on the com-puter screen, as the dot of the AmRover grew ever closer to the pink part of the electro-map, the bit where jungle ended.

Then, in real life, the AmRover trundled over the hill and the jungle vanished.

"We're through," said Mary Beebe.

"I can see that," Ben told her, still staring at his screen.

Sergeant Anderson grunted.

Tonii opened up the hatch and flew out of the AmRover to get a better view. Behind them was the knotted density of dark jun-gle. In front lay a vast expanse of yellow grass, and clear blue skies above. Six-legged and three-legged and no-legged grazing animals of various unknown genuses grazed. Small shrubs flourished, and some moved around. A stream ran through the grass, and sparkles and splashes in the water indicated the presence of aquatic life. And beyond the grasslands was the sea, tree-haunted and tempestuous, as the New Amazonian winds sent waves crashing high up into the branches of the Ocean-Aldiss-Tree.

They all got out of the AmRover and recced. Mary took some grass samples. Tonii checked their position.

"The grass is toxic if eaten," said Mary.

"Then don't eat it," said Ben.

"There's no cover," Sergeant Anderson pointed out.

"Then whatever is coming, we'll see it," said Ben.

"Who made you the fucking boss?" Sergeant Anderson complained.

"You want to be the boss?"

A beat. "Yeah," Anderson growled.

"Too bad." Ben smiled, with effortless self-confidence, and Anderson stared at him flintily.

"I guess we should have a vote," said Hugo.

"You want to be in charge?" said Ben.

"Well, no, but—"

"How about you?" Ben said to Mary Beebe. She shook her head.

"You?" David Go shook his head.

Ben looked at Mia; she shrugged; no.

Jim Aura shook his head; no way.

"Well, that's a decision," said Ben, smiling like a wolf. "I'm civilian leader, you're the senior ranking Soldier, Sergeant Anderson. And naturally I'll defer to you in any military emergency, but I think you should trust me on this kind of high-level strategic decision-making, don't you? I mean, considering I have four PhDs and I'm Professor Emeritus of World Building at the Galactic University, whereas you, ahem, forgive my candour, are an NCO?"

All eyes were on Sergeant Anderson. He flushed, catching the mocking intellectual arrogance in Ben's tone, as anyone but an imbecile would, but not knowing how to react to it. He scowled. He thought about how to deal with this delicate situation, but no answers came to him.

"Whatever," he said, at length.

"We'll make our home here," said Ben, and they looked across at the grass, and the sea, and the sheer cliffs.

"Good call," said Hugo, snidely.

Sorcha was cautious about using the MI-radio network, because of the danger of the signal being intercepted by DRs. But she had to know which way to go, so she risked a download from the Satellite, which gave her a sighting of the AmRover two hundred kilometres west, by the sea.

Then she ran a maproute program, and was appalled at how treacherous the terrain was going to be for a solo traveller. The other option was to fly *above* the canopy; but then she'd be an easy target for flying predators.

And even then, she realised, once she hit the Jungle-Wall she was fucked. She could fly like a bird with her body-armour jets, supported by the thick atmosphere. But to fly over the top of the wall she'd need to go way up high, at virtually escape velocity, and that was beyond her power limits.

But Sorcha had no choice; if she couldn't find Saunders, she had to rejoin her team.

She flew as high as she could for a few hours over swamp and snakegrass. Twice she was attacked, by creatures she had never seen before—a ball with spikes that crashed into her armour and tried to open her up like a tin, and a jelly-like being that erupted out of the snakegrass, flew upwards fast and enveloped and blinded her. In both cases, a combination of heated body armour and wild plasma blasting as she whirled around in the air saved her.

But then she reached the Jungle-Wall. She tried to plasma-blast her way through, but soon realised that without an AmRover's plasma cannon this might take years.

So she fired her body-armour jets and took off into the air. This was the danger point—she was totally exposed, and any passing Draven or native predator would see her immediately. But she rose as fast as she could until she reached the canopy of trees, which merged with the wall. The branches were thickly tangled, but she could see a narrow gap between canopy and Jungle-Wall, shielded by the branches. So she clawed her way in and crawled painfully through.

Within seconds she was trapped, and could feel the wall and the canopy closing in on her. Above, the branches gripped her body in a predatory fashion; below, the Six-Heads swarmed over her, knitting her into their rotted vegetal palace. Her vision vanished as swarming insects covered her helmet visor. Her sensors indicated she was experiencing severe pressure trauma on her body armour. She took some calming breaths and made a search in her database—"Jungle-Wall, Help, Now!"—that found one of Hugo's diary entries, entitled, *How to scream your way through the Jungle-Wall.*

So she followed Hugo's emergency wall procedure; she switched off her helmet earpieces, and released a loud sonic and ultrasonic blast:

Blast!

And again.

Blast!

And again. And again. And finally the branches of the Aldiss tree recoiled, and the Six-Heads fled. A gap appeared between canopy and wall, and she could squeeze her way through a little further.

She was crawling blind now, relying on her visor to show her the route she was pursuing. Hugo had discovered that the branches of the wall, though vegetal, had certain animal qualities, in that they could react to stimuli swiftly and dramatically; and they reacted badly to high-frequency sound. So every sonic/ultrasound blast allowed her to scare her way a few precious feet further inwards.

Every now and then acidic vomit and shit and piss rained down on her from above, but her body armour self-cleaned it off. Sorcha could vividly imagine herself getting stuck in this ghastly trap, and over a period of weeks becoming part of the jungle substrate, before she died of starvation and thirst. But she kept dragging herself through, hacking a path with raw sound energy, following the red line on her visor that kept her on the straightest of paths.

And finally, after about five hours, she was through the Jungle-Wall. And there was nothing beyond it...She started to tumble from the sky, and so she swiftly turned her body-armour jets on.

But nothing happened. She continued to fall. Faster. And—

She clicked the rocket switch again and again—nothing! So, falling like a stone now, she switched to emergency power.

Jerkily, her fall halted, and she lurched upwards, and badly shaken she began to fly again. And as she flew, she checked the Bostock battery on her body armour. To her horror, she realised it was running on Empty. It must have been damaged earlier, and been slowly leaking power ever since.

Sorcha panicked. She was flying miles above the ground in a spacesuit without batteries. The emergency power wasn't meant to last more than ten or fifteen minutes at a time, before being recharged by the Bostock battery. And it dawned on her—she could tumble from the sky at any moment, to be inevitably killed by the crash-landing.

So should she glide back down to earth? But that way, she'd be trapped on the ground. So instead, she took out her plasma gun and cut a path through the maliciously thick and convoluted branches of the canopy.

When she'd cut a big enough gap, she lunged out and grabbed hold. And she climbed up into the canopy itself.

She had to rip a path through the brambles and vines that snarled around the main Aldiss tree branches. Inch by inch, she crept along the branches until she emerged on to the topside. Then she staggered to her feet, and looked around.

It was a whole other jungle, high up in the air. Trees larger than houses grew on the top branches of the Aldiss tree. Flowers flourished up here, a carpet of blazing colour. Sorcha saw deerlike animals grazing. She saw a horned beast with no head and fire flaming from its arse. She saw Butterfly-birds flying free, swooping and pouncing. She saw a red bird with no beak but a bright blue head and vast wings strutting on a branch, then gliding down, and trilling all the while. She saw insects, a horned creature of some kind, Basilisks, and hundreds, thousands, tens of thousands of Two-Tails and Two-Tails with three tails (Three-Tails?) scampering from branch to branch.

Then she turned her hearing back on; and was awed at the symphony of sounds. Hissings, screaming, squawkings, trills, bells, bassoons, oboes, the howling of arboreals, the lilting melodies of trees, and flowers that could sing. The sounds were varied and overwhelming and intense; and yet they blended into a single rich crescendo and decrescendo and allegro and andante and piano and forte, a brutally savage and unbearably sweet soundscape of evocative disharmony.

Sorcha marvelled, briefly. Then she filmed the panorama, capturing all the sights and sounds, and took a few close-ups of the creatures nearest her. She saw shards of glass nestling in the higher branches of one of the Parasite trees (as she mentally dubbed them) and was puzzled. Looking closer, she saw that the shards were in fact one continuous mass of glass-like material, which sprawled from tree branch to tree branch as far as the eye could see. She ran some tests and confirmed her hypothesis: it was a frozen lake, that spanned the gap between the trees. But what was it made of? It couldn't be frozen water; despite the icy winds it was far too humid up here for water to freeze. It must be—

But Sorcha decided she could wait for another day to discover whatever the hell it must be. For the moment, survival was her priority.

And so Sorcha began to walk as swiftly as she could through the canopy. She used vines and lianas to pull herself along, supplemented with occasional boosts of power from her body-armour jets to keep her airborne between trees. As long as the emergency power lasted, the exoskeleton of her body armour gave her enhanced strength, so after a while she was able to leap and fly from tree to tree like a primate, much faster than walking speed, but using far less power than if she flew.

The sun above dazzled her when it stole through a crack in the tree cover. She marvelled at the strange life-forms growing on the Aldiss tree trunks up here. And on she travelled, leaping and swinging from branch to branch, occasionally attacked by Basilisks or spitting insects or fang-toothed bat-creatures or flailing predator vines or other horrible things she could not name or identify.

Then she saw the head of a Humanoid DR, nestling in the under-growth. She stopped to inspect it, prodded it with her foot. Its eyes opened, and she had a lurch of fear — but the silver lids flapped shut again at once. It was lifeless, severed from its power source.

But what the hell was it doing here? Who or what had killed it?

Sorcha looked closer and saw gouges and scratches on its neck. Bite marks? Or maybe peck marks? Either way, it looked as if the DR had been ripped to pieces by some New Amazonian predator.

Sorcha marvelled. The Doppelganger Robots were built to be super-warriors, but even they were no match for this infernal planet.

She moved on, and after a while she checked her bearings. Another ten hours at least to get to the coast. She decided to gamble that she had enough emergency power to descend on her body-armour jets, so she pointed her plasma gun down and fired and the canopy burned.

Then she leapt through the hoop of burning fire and dived to earth.

Saunders carefully explored the territory to which he had been carried by the Gryphon, on the top of a mountain that soared high above the can-opy of trees. From his vantage point he could see right the way across the jungle to the ocean. In the other direction he could see the vast sweep of the canopy across the continent, interrupted by towering Jungle-Walls that forced through the canopy and extended beyond the clouds, thick vegetable mountains that seemed to almost touch the stars.

It was a stunning panorama. He took photographs with his hel-met camera, and tried to imprint the magic of the moment in his mind and memory, as well as in his brain implants.

All around him were strange white domelike structures. These, Saunders guessed, were the Gryphons' nests. There were tunnels connecting the different domes, forming a kind of mountaintop city. And Saunders could also see holes in the cliff, caves that had either formed naturally or been hewn out by the Gryphons' beaks.

Hundreds of Gryphons strutted on the bare rock. Gryphon chicks played, rolling pebbles between them, hurling them up in the air and catching them in claws. Some of the Gryphons were silver, some a bright rich dark blue. Saunders wondered if that was how the sexes were differentiated. But in their Gryphon autopsies, no one had ever fathomed which bit of the beast was the sexual organ.

Suddenly, to Saunders's utter astonishment, a spaceship appeared. A Kelly Lander, with its octagonal body turning slowly in the air as it descended. On its side, a giant H. H for Helms. It was *his* Kelly Lander. They one they'd used to land on New Amazon, that they'd had to leave behind in—

The Lander vanished. Saunders blinked. The sun was lower in the sky, the clouds were different. It was a different day. He hadn't seen the Lander; he'd seen the *memory* of the Lander.

Behind him, he heard a smug caw. He turned, and saw his Gryphon, the one who'd found him, and grinned. It was messing with his head.

Saunders walked across and stroked the creature's head and it purred like a cat, and once again Saunders marvelled at the wonders of convergent evolution. Then, to verify his forehead-eye hypothesis, he raised a hand in front of the Gryphon's forehead skin and held up two fingers.

Caw! said the Gryphon, excitedly, and raised two talons. It was mimicking his action.

Confirmation of his hypothesis that it could see through its forehead!

But then, on a hunch, he shielded its forehead with one hand, then held his other hand in front of the creature's breast, which was marked with a lurid zigzag pattern. He held up three fingers. The Gryphon cawed.

Caw. Caw. Caw. Three times.

He held up two fingers.

Caw. Caw.

He held up five fingers, twice in in a row.

Caw caw caw caw caw caw caw caw caw caw.

It could count to ten—and it had eyes in its breasts!

Saunders was exhilarated. He said "Saunders. Saunders. Saunders," and the bird did nothing.

He remembered a photograph of himself, looking dapper and handsome, and thought the image at the bird, and said: "Saunders."

"Sawdaw," cawed the Gryphon. Close enough.

Saunders had now discovered that the Gryphon could hear, it could communicate through sound, but it could only say syllables ending in "aw". No wonder the wretched creature had been forced to evolve visual telepathy.

Then an image of a Gryphon, *his* Gryphon, appeared in his mind's eye, wings outspread, and Saunders felt a surge of warmth and love towards it.

"Gryphon," he said, determined to teach the damn bird to speak English.

"Caw," said the Gryphon.

Ben convened a council of war inside the AmRover. They were still parked in the grasslands near the sea, but after a bitter debate, and at Hugo's insistence, they had moved the AmRover across to shelter under the shadow of the escarpment, with exit routes on either side. Sergeant Anderson was outside the AmRover on sentry duty, connected to the discussion via MI-radio link. Tonii Newton was seated in front of the Hostile Alert grid, with half an ear on the conversation. The rest of them were clustered on the armchairs in the AmRover's living area—Mia Nightingale, David Go, Clementine McCoy, Hugo Baal, Ben Kirkham, Mary Beebe and Jim Aura.

David Go, the only surviving microbiologist, raised the first item for the agenda: Hugo Baal's controversial "animalish" and "plantish" expansion of the Kingdom system instituted by Professor Richard Helms, as was.

"I propose," said Go, angrily, "that we take this opportunity to entirely revise the taxonomy of New Amazon on a microbiological basis."

Ben looked at him in astonishment. "We're talking about our fucking survival here!" he pointed out.

"I'm talking about science," Go retorted waspishly.

"I don't think," said Hugo, "that the fact the Professor has brought destruction and death upon us all should affect our work on the classification systems."

"Can you guys cut the crap?" said Sergeant Anderson on the MI-radio.

"We have two options," said Ben firmly. Hugo waited excitedly. "In terms of our survival," Ben added, and Hugo's spirits were dashed. "We can build a new city here, with the resources available in the AmRover. Or we can travel along the coastal region until we reach the Space Elevator."

Jim Aura tilted his head and listened, but felt disengaged from the whole debate. He thought about Sheena, and wondered if she'd loved him.

"Can we have a breakdown of what those resources actually constitute?" asked Tonii.

"Five Bostock batteries," said Mary Beebe. "Giving us enough power to last for almost a century, provided we don't fight any more wars. Two tanks of nanobots, and enough hardglass seeds to build a small Dome. Two spare plasma cannons with projectile-firing capacity, plus the KM45s the Soldiers are carrying, twelve plasma pistols, three lasers and a flashmortar. Two spare sets of body armour. And an intact food-synthesis kit. It's enough to build a civilisation, just about."

"With only nine people?" commented Private Clementine McCoy.

"And only three are women," commented Sergeant Anderson.

"Four," Ben reminded him. *"Sergeant Newton is child-bearing."*

"We're talking in vitro, I hope," said Tonii nervously.

"What about the DRs?" said Mia.

"They should have killed Saunders by now. We're safe."

"We don't know that."

"True," conceded Ben.

"Hooperman must be here, on the planet," said Mary, and the rest of them blinked. "Think about it," she urged. "If he was on Earth, how could he remote-control the DRs? Juno is gone, so is the Quantum Beacon, we're cut off from Earth completely. So Hooperman must be on New Amazon. He's holed up somewhere, controlling the DRs with his virtuality helmet on a long range wireless network."

"Or the Quantum Beacon may still be intact."

"We saw Juno blow up."

"We saw a flash of light in the sky," said Hugo, accurately.

"The second option," said Ben doggedly, "is to risk all by travelling till we reach the Space Elevator, fight the DRs who will be implacably defending it, and then make our way up to the Satellite. Make that our colony ship."

"I like it here," protested Mia.

"I thought you hated it here."

"I hate it everywhere. I hate it less here."

"I vote," said Mary Beebe, "that we stay here. Make New Amazon our home."

"I vote we leave for space," said Tonii.

"Stay here!" Hugo protested. "Our work is barely begun."

"Stay here."

"Space," said Clementine.

"*Stay here,*" said Sergeant Anderson.

"Stay here," said Ben Kirkham.

Jim Aura was silent. They all stared at him.

"Stay here," he murmured, though he didn't really care.

"Seven to two, we stay," Ben summarised.

He hid a grin. This was just the result he had wanted.

"*And I'm gonna be your leader,*" said Sergeant Anderson, and Ben's smile faded.

DAY 15

From the diary of Dr Hugo Baal

June 36th.

Deplorable news: yesterday Sergeant Anderson has appointed himself as our new leader, on the grounds that he is stronger and more dangerous and more skilled at violence than the rest of us; he has scoffed at our calls for a general election.

We are in a state of some confusion and disarray and the group is breaking up into factions — those who hate Anderson and want to defy him, and those who hate Anderson and want to placate him. We are united in one thing only: we all hate Ben Kirkham, and we can't imagine why we ever let him become leader.

However, despite all these problems, our work continues.

Today we went foraging for molecules. We flew the AmRover across the plain and over the red sand and into the heart of the Ocean-Aldiss-Tree.[1] It's a rich habitat, with creatures that resemble rotting corpses[2] growing from the tree barks and a host of previously unknown insects and birds, too numerous to taxonomise just yet.

We saw no other trees; the Ocean-Aldiss-Tree dominates to a terrifying degree, and all life in the ocean is in one form or another, a parasite or symbiote of the Aldiss mare. We connected a gather pipe and began sucking up tons upon tons of the Aldiss mare bark and leaves and all the flying insects and sessile sealife we could encounter. These will be stored in the AmRover's bilge and converted, over the next few weeks, into edible[3] protein.

The ocean is now our garden and our farm. It is a less hazardous habitat than the land; we have yet to encounter any predators and

---

1 *Aldiss mare.*
2 The team have taken to calling them the Horrible Fucking Corpses, but I prefer the less judgemental *Cadaver oceanus.*
3 But utterly disgusting.

there aren't any of those ghastly swamps and quicksands that have killed several of my most esteemed colleagues[4] in our years on New Amazon.

I caught a fish today! It was embedded in an Aldiss tree trunk, with only its head and gills emerging. And it had a mouth that could rapidly engorge and became large enough to swallow a puppy or a kitten, if anyone had been rash enough to bring a puppy or a kitten along on this expedition.

I'm assuming that this creature has de-evolved from ocean animal to sessile excrescence over the course of several eons. We call it Stuck in the Bark. I haven't yet performed a morphological analysis and taxonomy, and I can't for the life of me think of a Latin name for it, but honestly! What a stupid and pathetic creature! Given a choice between being a fish, swimming freely in the ocean, and being a trapped and helpless creature unable to move and at the mercy of any passing predator, which would you rather be?

Though come to think of it, we're pretty well trapped too.

Sorcha woke from one of those awful dreams where you dream you've been buried alive.

And then she realised she couldn't see anything in front of her or around her and her sensors recorded she was submerged in quicksand. She must have slowly sunk into it during the night, but hadn't realised because she was wearing body armour and had no sense of touch.

She turned on her backjets and the quicksand boiled and bubbled but she didn't move.

Then she reached out with her hands, and with a swimming motion, tried to gain some purchase on the quicksand. It was thick,

---

4 For obituaries of the deceased, see *previous diary entry* and *previous diary entry* and *previous diary entry* and *previous diary entry* and *previous diary entry* and *previous diary entry* and *previous diary entry* and *previous diary entry* and follow the links.

like molasses, or molten lava, and it was actually possible to get a hand-grip. She pulled herself up, inch by painful inch, until her head was above the surface. All around her was a suppurating mess of yellow liquid shit. The previous night, this had been a field, with firm ground and luxuriant grass.

Sorcha kept swimming and digging and tugging, until eventually she was close to firmer squelch. She fired her body-armour jets again, and this time she was propelled out of the clammy grasp of the quicksand and ended up in a huddle on purple grass. She rolled over and got her breath back. Then she tried to stand up but couldn't. She turned on her suit's self-clean, but nothing happened. She fired her body-armour jets but they didn't fire.

So she checked her emergency power. All gone. No Bostock battery, no emergency power. The suit was dead.

Sorcha rolled over and slowly managed to get to her feet. Without the exoskeleton motors and the anti-inertia wheel, the body armour was a dead weight on her. She tried to walk and was immediately breathless.

So she stripped off the body armour. Underneath, she was wearing knickers and a jogging vest. Her skin was damp with sweat, but the minute the winds struck her she was icy cold. She slapped her arms to keep herself warm, and realised that she couldn't walk any distance without the suit. But nor could she walk any distance *with* the suit.

Sorcha put the suit back on, clambered on to a rock, called for help on the MI-radio, which fortunately didn't rely on the BB for power, and went back to sleep.

"So how are we going to resolve this?" Sergeant Anderson asked.

Hugo entered the cavern and was startled to find himself in the midst of a showdown between the two rivals for leadership — Ben Kirkham and Sergeant Anderson.

Hugo hesitated, but didn't dare leave, in case something intriguing might occur.

The mood was electric. Ben and Sergeant Anderson were standing close together, face to face, without body armour, both exuding danger.

Ben smiled, eerily. "You're going to back down."

"No fucking way."

"I'm the best choice as team leader. I'm smarter than you are."

"Nah. You're so clever, you're stupid. I'm the smart one." Anderson grinned, nastily.

Ben grinned back, just as nastily.

"Maybe we should all vote on this," said Hugo firmly.

"No," said Anderson, who hated democracy.

"No," said Ben, who knew he would lose.

"OK," said Hugo, phlegmatically. He wondered if violence was about to erupt. He was fascinated by the dominance behaviour, as the two silverbacks vied for supremacy. How come, he wondered, *I* never get to vie for supremacy?

"Look," said Anderson, "there's only one way to decide this—you can *fight* me for the leadership." Anderson was a solid mass of violent brawn; Ben was a lean aesthete.

Ben eyed him. He calculated his chances. "Only if I get to choose the weapons," he said cunningly.

"Fine by me."

"Swords," said Ben, who was a champion fencer, and was stronger than he looked.

Anderson grinned. Ben did a search on his brain-chip, and discovered that Anderson had been galactic sabre champion three years running.

"I'll fight you blindfold," said Anderson, "with the sword in my left hand. I'm right-handed by the way."

Ben searched again; Anderson had won five sword-fighting contests while blindfold and with the sword in his wrong hand, and had killed all five opponents.

Maybe, Ben decided, discretion was the better side of valour.

So Ben smiled a shit-eating smile. "Ah, what the fuck, you can be leader, I don't care," he said humbly.

Anderson punched him in the face. Ben's nose broke and he squealed with pain.

"Any trouble, any conspiring, any double-crossing, I'll break every fucking bone in your body. I'll cut out your intestines. I'll eat them in front of you. I'll shit them back out again. Then I'll make *you* eat them. You got that?"

"That's a highly elaborate—"

"Got that?"

"I'll be dead before—"

"Got that?"

"I got it. You're top dog. You're leader."

"Wasn't so hard, was it?" mused Sergeant Anderson.

Ben stared at him furiously. Then he lowered his eyes. Fear filled him. Anderson could smell it on him; Ben was afraid.

Though what Anderson didn't realise was that Ben Kirkham had been picked on and persecuted all through his childhood, and so he was highly skilled at pretending to give in to bullies. Inwardly, he seethed with rage. But, knowing that rage would get him killed, he forced himself to project abject cowardice.

"You broke my fucking nose," he whined, and Anderson grinned.

Saunders explored the Gryphons' mountaintop eyrie. It was strange to look down over the canopy of trees. The winds were even more bitter up here, and the skies were black with birds and huge insects riding the wind swells. Saunders saw a flock of Rocs slowly gliding past, almost touching wings, with extraordinary balletic precision.

He walked on and saw evidence that this mountain was in fact an extinct volcano. Black magma had frozen into magnificent shapes. In places, the rock was warm. And when he climbed higher he saw an amazing sight—the dead crater of the volcano was home to thousands of vermilion eggs, delicately balanced on the wide rock rim, in perilous proximity to the sheer drop at the crater's centre.

Adult Gryphons were hovering over the eggs, blowing air on to them. Saunders guessed their breath was warm, and that this was the Gryphon way of hatching eggs.

Then as Saunders watched, he realised that the red eggs were cracking. More Gryphons flocked across to watch the sight. Before long the lip of the extinct volcano was soldiered by a thousand and more adult Gryphons.

The army of Gryphons waited, patiently, as the first chick emerged from its egg. Its body was damp, *it had eyes,* and it flapped membranous wings and tried to fly.

Another egg cracked, then another. The scrawny awkward chicks toppled on slender legs, they rolled over, they picked themselves up and finally — oh joy! The tiny birds flapped their wings and hovered a foot or more above the ground. After a while there were thousands of chicks hovering above their cracked eggs. Saunders watched, rapt, curious, puzzled.

Then the Gryphons pounced. They flew into the hollow of the volcano and they gulped up the baby chicks, sometimes two in a single mouthful. Gryphon bumped against Gryphon in their race to eat the squealing desperate chicks. The sound of soft bones crunching merged with the shrill keening of the dying newborns who tried and tried but could not fly any higher.

It was ghastly, heartless carnage, and Saunders was shocked.

His own Gryphon — Saunders had christened it Isaac — flew up to Saunders, cawing with delight. Saunders's face was a picture of horror and disgust, and he hoped the Gryphon would not be able to tell how revolted he was. Then it dawned on him:

These were not Gryphon chicks.

The more he thought about it, the more sure he was. The body shape was different, the wing span proportionately smaller, they had eyes, and they did not have the typical Gryphon bulging forehead. And, of course, it made no sense that the Gryphons would eat their young. But there was nothing to stop them eating the young of some other species...

Saunders tested his hypothesis by visualising a nest full of eggs being looked after by a cartoon bird. Then he visualised Isaac the Gryphon sneaking into the nest and stealing eggs. And he kept visualising this, while staring at Isaac, and tried to will his thoughts across.

Isaac cawed with delight; exactly! And the image in Saunders's mind started to shudder and change, as Isaac took control of his visual cortex. The cartoon bird was replaced by *a real bird, a silver-furred creature with a small head and eyes and six limbs and two sets of wings.* Saunders had never seen such a beast, but he automatically started to analyse and taxonomise it. He called it, just for the moment, the Biplane-Bird.

And suddenly *the Biplane-Bird was being attacked by Gryphons,* and while it was distracted, *other Gryphons were sneaking into the nest and carrying out the eggs.* It was like a military raid; hundreds of eggs were conveyed away. And then, finally, Saunders had a mental image of *the Gryphons carefully placing the eggs on the lip of the volcano.* The rest he had seen for himself.

Thus, his hypothesis was confirmed. This was the Gryphon method of predation; to steal the eggs of other birds, incubate them over a period of months, hatch them, and eat them.

It seemed, even to a seasoned xenobiologist like Saunders, a peculiarly vile thing to do.

Sergeant Anderson drove the AmRover back to camp, feeling satisfied at the way the day had gone. They had tons of animal and plant matter in the bilge. Already, it was being processed and catalysed. This would be their lunch in a month's time, to supplement the declining supply of dried food in the AmRover's galley.

His coup had gone effortlessly. Ben Kirkham was a coward, and it had taken very little effort to establish a humiliatingly hierarchical relationship between them.

The others had capitulated swiftly. The truth was, most people liked to be bossed around, and Anderson was a natural boss. Things were now just as they should be.

However, Anderson was already aware of tensions among his small band. Ben Kirkham might be a coward, but he was also sly, and an egomaniac. Hugo Baal was impractical. Tonii Newton was a good soldier, but a pervert. What decent woman would ever want to fuck a monster like *him*? Clementine, however, was a looker. Sergeant Anderson had resolved to take her as his personal mate.

Mia was a sycophant, always wanting to be loved. Anderson hated the type. Mary Beebe was having some kind of nervous breakdown; if she didn't pull herself together Anderson was going to have her shot. And David Go was taciturn, and boring, and an awkward customer. The kind who was never happy. Anderson knew the type, and hated it.

All flawed, but Anderson had made do with worse in the past. He'd turn them into an army.

It was a shame about Sorcha leaving them, though. She was a fine Soldier and a beautiful woman. He'd never fucked her — she didn't like to fornicate with the lower ranks. But this might have been his opportunity to have sex with her, on a regular basis. After all — look at the useless men they were lumbered with! It wasn't as if the competition was up to much. Nerds, geeks, Scientists, bores, and a man with a fanny.

And this of course — the sexual thing — the man/woman thing — the breeding babies and getting fucked a lot thing — was going to be a major morale issue in the years to come, until they could age-accelerate embryos into new breeding stock.

Still, Sorcha always did have a rod up her arse. And since she outranked him, she would have insisted on being in command, which was not the way Anderson wanted to live the rest of his life.

Anderson liked power. He was good at it.

He was going to enjoy building his new empire.

Isaac hopped along into the cave, and Saunders followed him warily. Then Isaac flapped his wings and vanished through a hole in the cliff. Saunders more laboriously picked his way over the jagged rocks, then clambered head first through the narrow rock opening.

He emerged in a huge cavern with an echoing acoustic. Gryphons perched upside down on the roof of the cavern, like bats. There was a lake of something black and pungent, which Saunders guessed was probably flammable.

Saunders stepped anxiously into the Gryphon lair, trying to radiate peacefulness and trustworthiness. Two Gryphons swooped on him and gripped an arm each in their beaks and lifted him up in the air. They carried him up high and dropped him on a rock shelf. Saunders wasn't anxious, he knew he could use his body armour jets to get down from here. And from his shelf he could see the vast expanse of this cavern. He wondered if the birds could fly through it to an exit elsewhere.

He touched the wall of the cavern and through his touch-sensitive gloves was surprised at how smooth it felt. He realised that the wall was broken up by pillars, carved and gnarled out of rock. And there were shapes in the rock too. *That* was an image of a Juggernaut. The carving over there was a Godzilla. A giant Gryphon was carved on the roof, its wings outstretched vastly, almost beneficently.

It was magnificent—a Gryphon Cathedral, an art gallery, and also a diabolically spooky lair; all in all, a wonderful and complex work of alien art and architecture.

Saunders wondered if the cavern itself was a natural formation, or if the Gryphons had pecked the whole thing out of solid rock with their beaks.

Saunders closed his eyes and visualised *a spaceship flying through the blackness of the galaxy.*

A huge "cawing" echoed through the cavern. The noise deafened him, almost knocked him off his feet.

Message received; they knew he was from space.

Then he visualised an image of *a Doppelganger Robot recklessly firing its plasma gun*. He thought of *a Gryphon being shot to pieces by the DR's plasma gun*. And he imagined *the beast with its body rent in twain, falling to its death*.

The cawing was even more intense. They got the message. And it was clear they hated DRs too. Because every month, since the planet was first discovered, Earth humans had been using DR bodies to hunt the native fauna with bloody excess—and many Gryphons had been killed by the hunters.

Then Saunders visualised *Earth, its beautiful blueness, the richness of its greens, the Moon orbiting around it.*

A powerful cawing. They knew that this was his home planet.

Saunders visualised *himself, riding on the back of a Gryphon.* His way of saying, let's be friends.

A Gryphon flew over to him, on his narrow ledge, grabbed his arm, and pulled him off the ledge.

Saunders fell and for a few seconds he thought about firing his body-armour jets. Then something hit him from below—a flying Gryphon—and he was being carried around the cavern on the Gryphon's back. Then the Gryphon looped the loop and Saunders fell off. He turned on his boot jets and side jets, and righted himself, then hovered in mid-air.

The cawing was even more intense. The Gryphons were impressed.

And so Saunders hovered there, in the cathedral cavern, an armoured speck surrounded by flying psychic behemoths.

And he started to think about the possibilities.

DAY 16

Ben woke up, exhausted, with someone shouting in his ear.

"Come on, you lazy fuck!" said Sergeant Anderson. "Time to get moving!"

"I normally get up, urgghhh! a bit later," Ben grumbled.

"Not any more!" Anderson thrust his face close to Ben's. "Not on my watch."

Ben stumbled out of bed and found there was a queue for the shower. So instead he went to have a shit and there was a queue for the AmRover toilet too. One toilet per vehicle was ample normally; but not when the AmRover was being used as a home.

"You'll find your duties rostered on the following sheets," Sergeant Anderson explained to them all, once they had gathered for their morning briefing in the Rover's living space. "Civilians will now take an equal share of sentry duty. And our priority is to get a dome in place within the next six months."

"What about stealth?" said Mary Beebe, astutely.

"Good point," said Anderson, who had given no thought whatsoever to how they were going to hide their presence from the Doppelgangers. "Suggestions please."

"We were OK when we were hidden under the tree canopy," Tonii pointed out. "But now we're out in the open, it's just a matter of time before a Draven spots us and the DRs come in. Our current location is much too easy to see from the air, even with the cliff overhang."

"Good point," said Anderson, alarmed at their initial folly in setting up camp in such a stupid place. "What the hell are we doing here then?"

"Beats me."

"Maybe Sorcha had a plan."

"Typical fucking Soldier, they never plan ahead."

"If you're so clever, why didn't you —"

"All right, all right!" roared Sergeant Anderson. Silence descended abruptly. "Suggestions, anyone?"

"We move back into the jungle."

"We find a cave."

"We go back to the Depot, see what we can salvage."

"Too dangerous."

"Yeah, but—"

"We—"

Anderson interrupted: "Can we plasma-blast a cave in that cliff?"

There was a moment's silence, as all considered it.

"No problem, Sergeant," said Private Tonii Newton.

"Maybe that's what Sorcha intended?" said Private Clementine McCoy, the one Anderson wanted to hump until she squealed.

"Don't defend that bitch, I'm in charge now," Anderson snarled.

"If we create a cave, maybe we could build a new lab there?" said Hugo, hopefully.

"Forget the science, we don't need it," Anderson told him brutally. "Listen up: this is what we do. We get a roof over our heads. We build a dome so we can breathe air. Then we carve ourselves an ecological niche, we survive, we thrive, then we dominate. And I don't give a shit how many alien fucks die in the process."

The two Gryphons circled high in the air. One of them was Isaac; the other, a larger bird with a black and white pattern on its neck ruff, who Saunders had decided to call Gottfried.

Saunders had been watching the birds play and gambol in the air for quite some time, but it wasn't until they began to lunge and rip and hiss and scream that he realised they were trying to kill each other. Isaac and Gottfried swooped high and dived low and every now and then their beaks engorged and became monstrous spiked shovels that clashed loudly in mid-air, and the two creatures hissed some more and roared at each other.

The other Gryphons were perched on rocks, watching. Saunders tried to think of a way of asking what was going on. He visualised a question mark, but that was meaningless.

So instead he observed, and compared, and hypothesised. He noticed that Isaac and Gottfried were both large and magnificent specimens, with richer colouring than many of the other Gryphons and more complex patterns on their ruffs. He observed that no other Gryphon attempted to intervene, and instead they formed a perfect circle from which to watch, like the audience in an amphitheatre. He realised swiftly that the two fighting birds were sparring, not merely brawling. There was a definite ritual: a clash, a hiss, a hover, then one bird would sink like a stone while the other flapped back-wards. Then the sinking bird would fly back up and battle would recommence. It was like dancing, with danger.

Saunders thought about the most recent and the more ancient theories of flock and swarm behaviour, made some obvious compari-sons with Earth zoology, and developed his working hypotheses:

- Hypothesis 1: Isaac and Gottfried were Dominants, the other Gryphons were Submissives or Followers. In that case, this was a simple case of ritualised aggression to establish a linear domi-nance hierarchy. Isaac and Gottfried were fighting to become the Pack Leader among a herd of passive beasts who wanted to be led by the strongest and most vicious of their kind. It was the equiva-lent of two silverback gorillas vying for power.
- Hypothesis 2: They were bickering about a favourite crag of rock on which to sun-bask, or some other such unfathomable disagreement.
- Hypothesis 3: This wasn't a fight to the death, it was a work of living art, which might end in death, which would mean these creatures were very scary aesthetes.
- Hypothesis 4: This was an elaborate and stylised courtship ritual, which would culminate in sex. (Though Saunders had no notion what genders Gryphons might have.)
- Hypothesis 5: Gottfried wanted to kill Saunders, and Isaac was fighting him in order to save his human friend.

An image came into Saunders's mind, in an eerie moment of psychic violation. It was an image of *himself, stark naked, but without a penis or body hair, with his stomach gashed open, and an improbable blue and green scaly organ being pulled out of it by a Gryphon with a black-and-white ruff,* i.e. Gottfried. Saunders realised two things; first, Gryphons knew fuck all about human anatomy.

And, second, it was

- Hypothesis 5.

Gottfried lunged and Isaac went tumbling backwards. Blood dripped from a wound in his chest, splashing the rock below. Isaac soared low and as he flew past Saunders, *his head fell off and purple blood spouted and Saunders screamed and Gottfried plunged and pecked Saunders in the head, then ripped his stomach open, and pulled out an improbable blue and green scaly organ from his insides.*

Then reality returned. Isaac was still alive, so was Saunders, and the blue and green scaly organ, which he did not possess, had not been ripped out of his bleeding corpse. Saunders gave Isaac a thumbs-up sign. He got it, he really did!

And the battle to the death continued, with Saunders's life at stake.

Saunders was oddly touched by Isaac's heroism. It startled, excited and puzzled him. What did Isaac hope to gain? Was he ruled by selfish genes, or by self-destructive memes? Or was he just, well, *fond* of his human captive?

The two Gryphons fought and cawed and pecked in the bloodied air above him. The volcano crater below the fighting birds was a bloody mess of broken bones of bird chicks, spat out and excreted by the Gryphons. When Saunders retracted his helmet he felt the cold winds on his skin and smelled the stench of death.

Then the circle of watching Gryphons suddenly arose as one, and flew/shuffled over to the crater's edge and watched as Isaac and Gottfried glided and fought above the crater itself, catching updrafts of hot air, effortlessly sliding on layers of atmosphere, still pecking and gashing with talons. Then Isaac pounced, and went for the kill.

But Gottfried kinked in the air and was past him. He arched back his beak and a sharp tongue flew out and burrowed a hole in Isaac's head and Saunders's bird cawed with fear and pain and flew backwards. Gottfried lunged again.

The birds locked beaks, their tongues pecked, their wings thrashed against each other. Neither bird could fly now and they plummeted, but before they crashed on the crater's floor they broke beaks and flapped away.

Rich purple blood was flowing richly over their blue-black scales now. Isaac cawed angrily.

Gottfried lunged again and dug into Isaac's throat and Isaac's claws grew and gripped the other bird's torso and ripped.

They broke again and Isaac was bleeding badly. He could barely hover.

Gottfried went in for the kill, Saunders waved a hand in the air, and unseen by all a thin beam shot out of the pencil plasma gun and bored a hole in Gottfried's neck. Gottfried almost froze in mid-air and Isaac plunged to the attack. His teeth ripped out Gottfried's throat.

Gottfried plummeted and crashed into the crater. His wings flapped but none went to help.

Isaac did a victory roll, and an image appeared in the minds of all those present, the Gryphons and the human being, of *Saunders sitting on Isaac's broad black back with his arms held high in triumph.*

The Gryphons cawed their assent. And suddenly Saunders's mind was jumbled with a thousand separate images, of *himself, on Isaac's back, Isaac flying, and Saunders raising his arms up high, in triumph.* He thought his head would explode, with the bellow of the cawing, and the massive image overload.

Then the cawing stopped. All the Gryphons turned their bodies and stared, with foreheads and breasts, at Saunders. Saunders raised his arms in the air in triumph, and said, rather bathetically: "Caw!"

And this was the way of it: Carl Saunders, Human Being, was now Isaac's ally, and his friend.

After a day and a night in the tree, with no sign of help arriving, Sorcha was so fed up she got out of the tree and began walking.

Sorcha was strong; she could bench-press 200 kilos, and run twenty miles in full military kit including a portable oven and a collapsible six-person tent. But the body armour was punishingly heavy, and each step was laborious agony.

"Ready," said Sergeant Anderson. Tonii checked the mount on the plasma cannon. "Fire," said Sergeant Anderson, and Tonii clicked the switch to turn the gun on to its highest setting.

A pulse of hotter-than-burning plasma ripped out of the cannon and hit the cliff face. The blinding heat burned through rock in seconds. Another pulse followed. And another.

"Stop firing," said Sergeant Anderson, and Tonii turned the cannon off.

"Sweep," said Sergeant Anderson, and the Scientists and Soldiers moved forward and began shovelling and sweeping away the shards of rock. The dust was hoovered up by Mary Beebe, wearing what looked like an old-style spacesuit with a nozzle attachment. Then when the hole was clear of debris, they all moved back and to one side.

"Fire," said Sergeant Anderson, and Tonii turned the plasma cannon on.

It took eight hours to build a cavern they could live in. At the end of it, all of them were exhausted, except for Sergeant Anderson.

Saunders visualised *a naked man and a naked woman having sex.* He focused on the man's large erection and the woman's vulva, and graphically visualised the moment of penetration.

Then he visualised a schematic diagram of *a sperm swimming down the vagina and fertilising an egg.*

Then he visualised *the egg growing, multiplying, developing into a foetus.* He visualised *the baby emerging from the woman's vagina.* He visualised *happy smiling faces, a diaper being put on the boy baby,* and then cut straight to a *grown naked man.* (To visualise all the childhood tantrums and teenage strops went way beyond his reserves of visual stamina.)

Then Saunders paused. And he said: "Sex."

Isaac said: "Caw."

Saunders visualised the man and the woman fucking, missionary style, like an animated version of a sex education film, and visualised the letters: S E X.

The Gryphon cawed. Was it laughing? Then Saunders cleared his mind of all thoughts. And Isaac cawed again.

And then, unbidden, an image appeared in Saunders's mind:

S E K.

Close, thought Saunders, overwhelmed by a familiar sense of awe at the presence of alien sentience. He focused again:

X, Saunders visualised.

S E X, Isaac thought at him.

Saunders raised his arms high in triumph.

Isaac cawed.

Saunders waited.

An image appeared in his mind: *a bird, flying.* It was one of the three-winged birds they'd seen—with a finlike extra wing on its back—but Saunders didn't recognise this particular variation. Was this a caterpillar stage of the Gryphons' lifecycle?

The three-winged bird was in a nest of some kind. It was eating slug-like or wormlike things.

Saunders was now *inside the bird's body. A slug had been swallowed whole and was swimming down the creature's intestine. The slug merged with a cell in the bird's body. A new cell was formed. It grew. It became an embryo.*

It plopped out of the bird as an egg.

The egg was being incubated by the three-winged bird. Then it was joined by *another bird, with two sets of wings.* It was the Biplane-Bird! *The three-wing and the Biplane were nuzzling each other*—Saunders guessed they were the male and female of the species, despite their radically different anatomies.

Then *the Biplane was in the nest, protecting the eggs.* All alone. Three-wing was off, foraging for food no doubt.

Then *a Gryphon pounced and killed the Biplane-Bird and a host of other Gryphons carried away dozens of eggs from the nest in their mouths.*

This was all looking eerily familiar.

Then crash cut to another image: *the volcano crater, full of thousands of such eggs.*

Then *the eggs were hatching, and chicks were emerging, and the Gryphons pounced and ate the chicks.* Just as Saunders had witnessed.

Then Saunders was *inside the body of a Gryphon. Mashed up bits of chick were recombining all around him.* He peered closer, and saw *the bits of chick were forming into an embryonic replica of a Gryphon* inside the body of the adult Gryphon.

Then Saunders saw *an adult Gryphon vomiting.* In its vomit, *a squirming creature squealed. It picked itself up and waddled away.* It was now clearly recognisable as a baby Gryphon.

"Oh my God," said Saunders, trying not to let any negative images drift into his mind as he vented his disgust, "that is *so* absolutely appalling." He took a deep breath, and tried not to be subjective, or judgemental, or inappropriately disapproving. And he failed, and was subjective, and judgemental, and highly disapproving:

"Isaac," he said savagely, "yours is the most obscenely barbaric species I've encountered in the course of my entire career."

"Caw," said Isaac.

Sorcha woke and it was dark. Then she realised she was lying face-down in the dirt.

She tried to get up and couldn't. Eventually she managed to roll over. There was something on top of her. She screwed herself round to see.

A Basilisk.

She clawed and managed to get her plasma gun out. The Basilisk had its coils wrapped around her body armour, and was tightening its grip. It was actually buckling the armour. She could feel her head pulsing, her eyes bulging. She remembered how Margaret had died. She fired the plasma blast high in the air, then waited. Moments later, hot plasma rained down on to her, on to the body armour, and the Basilisk squealed and broke into two separate parts.

Sorcha rolled away and got to her knees. The two parts of the Basilisk were hissing, still alive. She rained plasma on both, until they were ashes and memory. Then she got to her feet, and fell over.

She blacked out again.

Next time she woke up, she could see. She was face up, looking at the canopy. There was nothing on top of her.

Painstakingly, she began to shed her body armour. If it rained, she would die. But she couldn't carry on walking with this mon-strosity on her.

"I'd like to say a few words," Sergeant Anderson said, as Tonii tried to get the Aldiss tree fragments to burn in the fire. The cave was small, but it felt safe. They'd driven the AmRover inside, and posted two sentries. In time, they would be able to carve tunnels all the way through the cliff, with a hardglass biodome nestling up against the rock for extra security. And so long as they were in here, they couldn't be detected by Dravens.

"There are going to be some changes around here," Sergeant Anderson said.

"Now that the military crisis is over, I vote we vote on who should be our democratically elected leader," said David Go, with surprising boldness.

"Fifty press-ups," said Sergeant Anderson, grinning.

"You are kidding me," David Go said, unflustered.

"Now," said Sergeant Anderson. David Go stared at him, stubbornly.

"Private Newton," said Sergeant Anderson. "Beat this man and then rape him." Tonii got up, punched Go in the face, and started pulling his trousers down.

"No!" said Mary Beebe, appalled.

"That'll do, Private," said Sergeant Anderson. Tonii stopped the attempted rape, while David Go wept on the ground. The others sat and watched, aghast, afraid, and secretly relieved that it had been David Go, not any of them, who had incurred Anderson's wrath.

"Military discipline," said Sergeant Anderson, "is a wonderful thing."

There were no midges or mosquitoes or comparable bite-y insect-like creatures on New Amazon, and hence, thankfully, no risk of being bitten. Sorcha used the laser setting on her gun to cut off the body armour's utility belt, containing all her medical supplies, food pills, oxygen pills to supplement her implanted oxygen-release tube, and the holster for her plasma gun. Then she cut the feet off the armour to use as boots, which clung tightly to her calves and protected her from ground-lurking snakes and swamps. Her arms were bare, revealing her holographic tattoos of fire-breathing dragons (right arm) and revolving spirals (left arm). She wondered why they hadn't thought to include a thin mesh armour in the suit's supply kit for just this eventuality.

But the answer, really, was that the suits weren't expected ever to fail; the Bostock battery was meant to last for at least two years, and it was supposed to emit a warning siren when the energy level was running low. Sorcha had been using this battery for less than three months; and there had been, she realised now, no warning siren.

She resumed walking, carrying the helmet in one hand. She was now only a day's march from the sea, according to the satellite display. And the jungle was less dense here. The Aldiss trees were fewer, and there were more of the Bush trees, which had no trunk but expanded from the ground in waves of green round leaves to reach incredible heights.

Sorcha was bored so she began to sing, not well, but loudly. She sang soul songs and roughmetal songs, she even sang a blues song, about a mutilated asteroid miner who had never lost his joie de vivre. The songs of distant Godzillas merged with her tuneless screeching, and she realised she was actually enjoying herself.

When night fell, she climbed up a Spiderweb tree, with its interlocking branches, and slept fitfully.

Saunders stood on the mountaintop, as dark crashed all around, and the distant red glow of the setting sun shone its last beams on the jungle below.

And he felt a pang of pride at the sight of it, the glorious vista, the glowing skies, the beauty and the terror, the wildness and the unpredictability, of this world, *his* world.

DAY 17

From Dr Hugo Baal's diary

June 38th

Sergeant Anderson has decreed that from this point on, no scientific work is to be done. No animals or plants are to be studied. No findings are to be discussed. All conversation should relate to personal matters or rostered duties. Shop talk will be punishable by flogging or beating, or other humiliating things which I do not care to discuss in this journal.

Each of us has a full set of rostered duties, including cooking and cleaning. My own concern the food supply. I am expanding the AmRover's synthesising tanks, and I am also tasked with the job of determining if we will ever be able to eat New Amazonian meat. But even this job cannot be done scientifically, at a microbiological level. I am simply told to thaw out some rat embryos, grow them fast to adulthood, then feed them dead Rat-Insects and Grophers to see if they live or die. This is empiricism verging on the practical; it's no job for a trained Scientist.

Privates Tonii Newton and Clementine McCoy are in charge of security. They have installed motion sensors at key points around our cavern and its environs. Concealed laser and plasma guns have been put in place. Buried mines can be exploded remotely. Sergeant Anderson fears a renewed attack by the Doppelganger Robots, and so we are on a permanent war footing.

Mia Nightingale and Dr Mary Beebe are tasked with ensuring the oxygen supply. They will be seeding catalysts in the ocean which will convert water to oxygen which will then be conveyed to shore via a network of pipes. Each of us has a slow-release oxygen cylinder embedded in our lungs, which can sustain us for weeks without air. But without nanobots the task of removing and replacing the oxygen implants is beyond us; and so from now on we will be using the oxygen tanks on our body armour exclusively. No more taking off our helmets to feel the breeze on our cheeks; we will be breathing bottled air all the time now.

David Go is acting as Sergeant Anderson's liaison, passing on his orders and interpreting his needs. This is a real lickspittle job for which Dr Go is eminently qualified.

I am plunged into total despair. I do not mind danger, I can endure pain, I don't fear death; but the thought of spending the rest of my long life on this planet without ever being able to do proper science fills me with horror.

There is so much, so very much wonderful work to do here. And instead, all we're going to do is survive.

DAY 18

From the diary of Dr Hugo Baal

June 39th

Today I dug a great big hole in the jungle, which is going to be our latrine. Sergeant Anderson had first shit. The Sergeant believes strongly that we have to conserve our supplies of absorbent underwear, and that the queues for the AmRover toilet are becoming untenable. So the Sergeant has decided that the vehicle's toilet will be reserved for senior ranking officers, i.e. himself, and from now on the rest of us will perform all bodily functions outdoors. Some of us have argued that we risk contaminating the New Amazonion ecosphere with our alien (to it) micro-organisms, but Sergeant Anderson responded to that concern with disdain, and imaginative invective.

Hence, the hole.

DAY 19

From the diary of Dr Hugo Baal

June 40th

We cut down many trees, and at the end of the day I had my first Number 2 in the new latrine. It is really quite an elegant construction: a series of hardplastic benches with holes in their middle leading to a central cesspit, viz, the great big hole I dug.

However, the undergrowth is already growing back, and Rat-Insects are poking up through the earth. So I cauterised the soil with sulphuric acid, and put up a big sign: DO NOT STAND NEAR THIS AFTER DEFECATING. Dr Hugo Baal, MSc, PhD, FRS.

I saw many creatures in the course of my work on the latrine—flying insects, mammalian octopods, birds with horns and suchlike—but my mood was so bleak that I made no notes about them. I am so fucking tired. The highlight of my day was having a shit in the new latrine, and not having my arse burned off by acid.

And I—

Octopods?

Did I really see octopods?

Surely not. So far all the terrestrial animals we've seen have been tetrapods.

It's dark, I'm tired, I need to sleep.

I am so fucking tired. I have lost my will to live. My will to—

Octopods? Yes, they were! Yes, I'm definitely right.

Hmm. I wonder if—

No. Forget it. Sleep. Tomorrow is a—

This is puzzling me. Why didn't I take a photograph? Why didn't I look closer? Birds with horns, who gives a damn, but land animals with eight limbs not four means—

I have to know more. But I can't—

Sergeant Anderson won't—

Hold on—he doesn't need to know. I could—

Yes.

That's it. I can—

After all, I have a torch. I have a plasma gun. I have body armour. Perhaps…

I'm back.

It is 5 a.m. I have just returned after four hours in the jungle in the dark. It's a wholly different experience, you know. The jungle is a gentler and more wonderful place, once the sun has set.

And this was a good time to go hunting for eight-limbed things. It turns out that the octopods are mainly nocturnal—there are thousands of them out there!—and they are also bioluminescent. So I played a hunch, and laid a trail of sulphuric acid, which they followed and ate. The acid made them glow more brightly. Sweet, n'est-ce pas?

The octopods are endlessly varied. Some are furry, some have scales, some have pale soft skin like a small baby. Some glide from tree trunk to tree trunk. Some scurry through the undergrowth. I must have seen more than a hundred different species—different species, nay, different genuses! They are playful, and they wholly dominate the night life of the jungle. But you have to be patient. I spent an hour waiting for the first octopod to appear. And then it flipped in front of me, rolling cartwheels, like a hamster in a wheel, glowing scarlet and silver.

This of course represents a wholly different evolutionary line. This planet is no dull Earth, with its relentless catalogue of terrestrial tetrapods—for dinosaurs, humans, birds, dolphins, they are tetrapods all! All descended from the same lobe-finned bony fish that took to the land and miraculously conquered the world.

But here, the octopods and the tetrapods survive side by side, one occupying the daytime, the other the night.

Perhaps the octopods were once arboreal lungfish, clambering along branches into the midst of the jungle for food then retreating to a watery home—until slowly the jungle became their home. While the tetrapods echoed the classic evolutionary line of Earth and so many other planets,[1]

---

1 For a list of such planets, click here—no damnit, I haven't time to do the links, just Search it, or reference Saunders's *Encyclopedia of Alien Life* and type "alien tetrapods".

of being swamp-dwelling fish with adapted fins and lungs that, one day, discovered the joys of the land.

Perhaps too the octopods were once deep-sea dwellers—hence the bioluminescence—and then found that the ability to light up the jungle darkness secured them an evolutionary niche??? (!) ?

We have been two years on this planet and I have just discovered—single-handed!—an entirely new Superclass of animal life.

This has been a ghastly period. Many of my friends are dead. We face, I believe, certain death on this godforsaken planet, pursued by monsters, led by fools. I am fatigued beyond all measure, my arse stings because I just accidentally kicked over a carton of sulphuric acid near the toilet hole just as I was voiding myself, and I am bored and angry and frustrated.

But none of this matters. I am the first to find the New Amazonian octopod.

And I can hardly speak for joy.

DAY 20

From the diary of Dr Hugo Baal

June 41st

Disaster upon disaster! I overslept and had to be woken with a mild taser blast, which has left me with a runny nose. No one is interested in my accounts of and photographs of and theories about the octopods.

And despite the sulphuric acid, the vile undergrowth has grown back over the cesspit, and the soil itself appears to have moved, so we can't find the damn thing any more, and the earth all around where it might be is infested with millions of small furry creatures which vomit some kind of green slime when you go near them. We plasma-blasted the ground to a depth of ten feet, then dismantled one of the cabins in the AmRover and rebuilt it on the purged earth.

However, I cooked lasagne for the whole team and it was generally acclaimed. We each drank a glass of wine fresh from the AmRover's food synthesiser. In the night, I suffered badly from stomach cramps. I woke at 3 a.m. and wrote this diary.

I miss my old life.

DAY 21

When dawn came Sorcha felt a familiar shock—colours leaped out at her, shadows vanished—but she carried on walking, step after painful step. She'd rest later, when the sun was high. It was easier, she had discovered, to travel by night, or in the morning and early evening.

At night the Rat-Insects slept, the Flesh-Webs stopped growing; and the way was lit by flying and crawling bioluminescent creatures of a kind she had never seen before. The large predators that made it so dangerous in the daytime—Godzillas, Juggernauts, Basilisks—all seemed to sleep at night. It was a time for small creatures, grey ghostlike creatures, and vast pillars of the swarming howler insects, which swept like tornadoes through the jungle, but never approached or threatened her.

In the daytime the ground was swampier underfoot. The heat haze induced a kind of visual paranoia. And the myriad tiny-bird-things that looked like gnats were constantly swarming in a haze of coloured feathers in front of her face. She had to use her plasma gun at its lowest setting to fly-swat the wretched things away, but even so they landed on her cheeks and got snarled in the roots of her hair and she had to semi-burn her own face and head to get free of them, leaving her flushed and sweaty and itchy.

But at night, there were no tiny-bird-swarms, and she no longer had to endure the smell of her own scorched hair. And the absence of sun and of visible sky above was no longer oppressive to her, when it was actually dark. Sorcha missed the stars but she loved the way the purple canopy up there shone silver and gold as it was bathed by the rich starlight from above and the bioluminescent glows from below.

"Major Molloy to Professor Saunders, come in please," she muttered, on the Professor's private channel. No response.

As she walked, she kept a mental tally of all the new species she saw, but didn't attempt to name or categorise them. She just used her implant to take photographs to show to the boffins later.

"*Major Molloy to Professor Saunders, come in please,*" she muttered, but there was no reply.

Sorcha was reconciled to the fact that she had lost Saunders for ever. It was no big deal; it caused her no pain.

He'd always annoyed the fuck out of her anyway. With his arrogant sarcasm, and his assumption of superiority.

And his droll humour.

And his twisted smile.

And his brilliance of mind, and his shameless flattery, and his blazing charisma.

And his kindness. And his ability to peer into her soul and know her inmost thoughts.

No, no way, she wouldn't miss him at all!

Sorcha reproached herself for risking her life to rescue Saunders in the first place.

It was an act that ran counter to all her training, and her instincts. She was a killing machine; she didn't do self-sacrifice. And as for love — that was just folly and moonshine.

"*Major Molloy to Professor Saunders, come in please,*" she muttered, as she walked, on a strict twenty-minute rota. But there was still no reply.

Sergeant Anderson believed that hard work was good for the soul.

Other people's souls.

And so he drew up a tough schedule of manual jobs to be done by the other survivors, and spent every day in the AmRover, watching old movies.

And from time to time he employed his unique leadership skills to persuade everyone to give of their utmost.

"Bitch, you know what? You're a fucking imbecile," Sergeant Anderson advised Mia Nightingale.

"You fucking moron!" Sergeant Anderson snorted at Hugo Baal.

"Jesus fucking wept, they should've fuckin' drowned you at birth," Sergeant Anderson explained to David Go.

"Fucking freak," Sergeant Anderson muttered, every time he saw Tonii Newton.

"You're a short-arse fucking frump, but I'd give you one, sweetheart," he reassured Mary Beebe.

"Dyke!" he sneered at Mia.

Clementine was his sexual partner of choice. She fucked him uncomplainingly, as was her duty as a Soldier, though she would have much preferred to be hanged.

"I hate that man," Mary muttered, as Anderson stomped past.

"We all do," Mia said.

"We don't need to do this stupid job," Mary said. "It's make-work."

"I know."

"This stupid hole we keep digging! We don't need it. It's just a way of keeping us busy. It's a power thing."

Mia nodded; she still knew.

"So maybe we should refuse to dig it?" Mary suggested.

Mia shook her head.

"Anderson is the boss. We're his slaves. Get used to it," she said, and began blasting a new hole in the ground.

Jim Aura was hovering high above the red sands when he saw the Rocs flocking towards him.

He called Sergeant Anderson on the MI-radio. *"Permission to descend, sir, I can see hostiles approaching."*

"You're a fucking lookout, Blackeyes. Keep looking."

"*Hostiles approaching. A hundred Rocs. Coming straight at me.*"

"*They'll pass by.*"

"*They look hostile.*"

"*There's no record of any human being attacked by Rocs. Besides, you have body armour, don't you?*"

"*I don't like it, sir.*"

"*Keep your position, Blackeyes.*"

"*I'm coming down.*"

"*Come down and I'll fucking court-martial you. Keep your position.*"

The Rocs struck Jim like a thundercloud. His plasma blasts reflected off their scaled armour and made lightning jags in the air. One Roc grasped him in its beak and shook him and when the armour wouldn't break it dropped him. Jim was mashed internally by the mauling. He was almost dead by the time he hit the ground and made a vast crater in it.

And after that, he was entirely dead.

"Good news," said Sergeant Anderson. "You don't need to dig another latrine today."

From the diary of Dr Hugo Baal

June 42nd

The death of Jim Aura has affected all of us badly.

I didn't know him well, I have to admit. I've never really connected with the Noirs. And there was something about Jim's staring black eyes that repelled me. Though he was a fine Scientist, albeit of a practical bent. And, apparently, so I'm told, he had a wonderful singing voice. A lyric tenor, of professional calibre. Though he never sang for us. In fact, to be honest, we hardly ever spoke to him. Or at least, I hardly ever did. He was such a reserved and distant individual. He never got animated, even when the Fungists were in full rant. He always wore black, and apparently he always knew he was a Noir, though he didn't have his eyes and the tattoos done until we reached Xabar. In fact, I think it was only a few months before the Hooperman attack that he made the final surgical commitments. Though I might be wrong about that, I didn't really notice him to be honest.

And, as I say, he never talked about himself much. Or, indeed, at all. He kept himself to himself, even after our shared trauma at the Depot. Though perhaps by that point he was in mourning, for the rest of the Noirs? I suppose he was, in a sense, the last of his kind?

Even so, we all thought he was rather spooky. Or at least, I did. Although, looking back, I wonder if—

Well, I suppose. Maybe—

But no. No maybe about it! We definitely *should have made more effort to talk to him. After all, we're all in this together aren't we?*

Except he's not. Not any more.

But those black eyes! So alienating. And yet—

Anyway. His death has shocked us. It was an unnecessary death. A foolish death.

The impact of Jim's body hitting the earth created a vast hole in the ground, deeper than any we have dug. We attempted to retrieve the body but a landslide took it away from us. We have analysed soil samples and discovered that at a depth of forty metres and more the soil here is infested with and almost possessed by a complex interlocking micro-organism. The soil in this region is, it seems, alive.

But I have no zest for analysing this in any more detail. Jim was a bright and brilliant spirit, so I'm now told, and had a dark wit and a wonderful sense of humour, though I never experienced it myself, as well as black eyes. I feel his death as though it were my own, well OK, not quite, but I am certainly very moved by it.

Things are not good.

Saunders flew with the Gryphons, way up high, to the very limits of the atmosphere. This was a realm rich in weird jellyfish creatures, which danced on the thermal currents that gusted in the thinning air. The Gryphons never seemed to tire. Saunders's body armour wasn't capable of horizontal flight at this altitude, so he held on to Isaac's back and let the huge bird carry him. And he flew with his helmet retracted, though he knew that sooner or later he'd have to face the issue of oxygen deficit.

He'd been with the Gryphons almost a week now, and had learned so much about them, and yet even now he found them hard creatures to fathom. They were vicious, generous, smart, stupid, and utterly strange.

And now Saunders flew with the Gryphons on a mission whose purpose he did not fathom. They flew far and wide, to a region beyond the tree canopy, to a land where grass grew and lakes meshed. Then they soared down low and Saunders saw creatures he had never seen before. Dancing creatures of shadow and light that seemed to be able to hide in the sunshine. And they flew on further and further, to a strange land of low hills and yellow grass that slithered and moved.

And there they paused and waited. And there, in the yellow fields of living and slithery grass, the battle began.

It took Saunders some time to realise what was happening. The yellow savannah below them was thronged with a variety of Grazers and smaller land animals, which stalked the "grass" with eerie intensity. But then he saw a large ball-like creature the size of an elephant wobble into sight. The creature was like a giant porcupine, with vast quills sticking out of its body. The Grazers skittered away nervously when it approached. The Giant Porcupine stopped. And then another Giant Porcupine appeared. And another.

A Godzilla rumbled past, alarmed at the sight of the Giant Porcupines, and tried to trundle away. But one of the Giant Porcupines turned, and a hail of quills erupted from its body. And the Godzilla was harpooned. Blue flashing lights shot out from its body—clearly, the quills carried a deadly electric charge. Within minutes the Godzilla was dead.

Saunders was awed. It took an entire team of Soldiers with plasma guns almost as long to kill a Godzilla.

More of the eerie Porcupine beasts appeared, forming a semicircle, as Saunders and the Gryphons hovered above.

Saunders glanced around and saw that the Gryphons had also formed themselves into a semicircle in the air, mimicking the Porcupines' positioning.

Then a vast six-armed beast lumbered into view. It was four times as tall as the largest Porcupine, twice as large as a Godzilla, and covered with orange fur rather than scales. Its back legs were huge, its two feet broad, each of the six arms had claws, and the head was crowned with horns. The shape of its jaw gave it a ghastly mock-smile, and in the centre of its forehead was *an eye.*

Saunders mentally christened the creature Cyclops (*Cyclops giganteus)* and took photographs with his helmet camera. There were three of the Cyclopses against a hundred Giant Porcupines, with nearly five hundred Gryphons hovering in the air.

By this point, Saunders did have some inkling of what was going to happen. The Grazers were fleeing now, some at a saunter, some galloping away. Saunders was low enough to see hundreds of grass-hugging creatures burrowing down to safety, or scurrying away. A vast shrub in the centre of the savannah space suddenly erupted and flew into the air and glided off, powered by jets from its branches.

Then the Gryphons swooped.

They moved fast, and the whirring of many wings became a roaring thunder in Saunders's ears. And they plunged down first on one of the Cyclopses, gashing and ripping with their claws and gouging with their beaks, as the vast six-armed orange beast swung with long claw-hands and battered them out of the sky. The other two Cyclopses stood clear as the Gryphons ripped at the head and body of their companion. But the Cyclops was fast and skilful, and its reflexes were uncanny. It crushed Gryphon after Gryphon in its claws and swallowed birds whole, and when it had finished, green blood was pouring from its head but it was still standing and it roared in triumph.

Then the Porcupines charged, in a slithering but rapid fashion, with their spines pointing out. A hail of quills flew through the air and the Cyclops was impaled a hundred times and flashes of light flew from its body as the electric charges pulsed through it. The Cyclops was shaken. It sank to its knees and stared with its huge forehead eye till light erupted from the eye and the lead Porcupines burst into flames. Again light flared, and again Porcupines exploded.

Then the other two Cyclopses joined in, firing light from their eyes. Hails of quills ripped through the air and impaled flesh; triple bursts of light were discharged and each penetrated into Porcupine flesh and exploded the Porcupine bodies from the inside out.

The eye wasn't an eye; it was a receptacle for focusing light, an organic laser. Shrubs burned, grass burned, insects fled the conflagration and the Gryphons attacked again.

Saunders looked at Isaac and tried to think a question at him, but he couldn't think of an image that would carry his meaning. And besides, Isaac was lost in the battle now. He screeched horrifically and his feathers were raised and fierce and there was a gleam in Isaac's eyes as he swooped that appalled Saunders.

Wave after wave of Gryphons plunged to the attack, diving low on the Cyclopses and attacking their central eyes. Now the laser beams flared in the air, and Gryphons exploded. The Porcupines changed the focus of their attack and sent hails of quills into the air and Gryphons were impaled and died. Several quills crashed into Saunders, bruising him badly, but bouncing off his body armour. He was afraid of being caught in a Cyclops's laser beam, he didn't know if the armour could handle it.

Saunders was now hovering on his body-armour jets, and below him he could see Isaac, diving and swooping and gouging. But then suddenly Isaac flew upwards, and all the Gryphons flew up too. And they hovered in a thick cloud in the air between the Porcupines and the Cyclopses. There were still hundreds of Gryphons left alive, though the corpses of their companions littered the ground.

So there they hovered, low above the ground, motionless, easy targets for quills and laser beams. All the Cyclopses roared with angry anticipation, while the Porcupines slithered and snarled, and bowed down ready to loose their deadly quills. Saunders found himself yelling at the Gryphons to "move their fucking arses", but they stayed in position.

Saunders marvelled at the Gryphons' folly. Up until now they had been losing with dignity. But their only weapons were speed and manoeuvrability. If they kept moving and dodging, they stood some chance. Or if they flew up high and let the Cyclopses fight the Porcupines, they stood some chance. But now they had incurred the wrath of both sides and they were patiently waiting to be massacred.

Were they really this dumb?

Saunders flashed an image to Isaac of a battlefield littered with the corpses of dead Gryphons, with a weeping Saunders standing among them.

Saunders got, in return, a scarily vivid image of himself being sexually penetrated by his own penis. The quick translation: *Go Fuck Yourself.* (Saunders briefly marvelled at the anatomical precision of the image; Isaac must, he surmised, have seen him getting undressed.)

The battle recommenced. The Cyclopses fired their laser beams. The Porcupines fired their hails of quills. It was a massacre. Gryphon after Gryphon fell from the sky, burning alive or impaled with electric quills, or both. Some of the Porcupines were now partially denuded of quills, and the sky was turned into raining death and blazing death-giving light. Then the skies were empty, and the ground was littered with dead Gryphons, five hundred or more, the bodies stacked up like a bloodied wall.

Then one of the Cyclopses roared with pain and two of its arms fell off, its eye exploded, its skull opened up, and its brains flew into the air and splashed to the ground. Two Porcupines flew up in the air, turning upside down, discharging quills in blind panic and hailing death down on the other Porcupines before falling and smashing on to the hard ground.

Another Cyclops was whirling round and round, giant eye staring up, as blood gushed from its arse and a long coiling substance was pulled out of its anus — its entrails were being ripped from its body! And then its head fell off and the searing light from its eye ceased.

The third Cyclops tried to run, but blood was gushing from its face and a long rip appeared in its stomach. Its eye exploded and it fell to the ground and roared, and whimpered, and died.

And the Porcupines were milling wildly now, spouts of blood gushing from the naked skin where they had lost their quills. More and more of them flew up in the air squealing with rage, firing quills madly, and were dropped to a ghastly death.

And so the battle continued, as the Porcupines fought and lost to an invisible enemy, and one by one the dead and broken Gryphons on the ground vanished with a magic flourish until only fifty or so corpses remained.

And finally, Saunders got it. He blinked, and his mental image of the scene changed as his eyes finally saw what was actually in front of them: a host of Gryphons goading and biting the Porcupines, lifting them up in the air and dropping them, then biting their flesh open and ripping out their entrails.

When the carnage was over, the savannah was an abattoir, the slithery grass was black with blood, and the corpses of all the Cyclopses and all the Porcupines lay dead upon the ground.

The Gryphons made no attempt to feed upon the creatures they had slaughtered. Instead, they gathered in the sky and performed a ceremonial circuit over the battleground.

And they flew home, with a terrified Saunders in their midst.

"*I haven't done this sort of thing for*" (*puff*) "*years,*" said Mary Beebe, as she clambered up the Ocean-Aldiss-Tree.

"*Try not to fall,*" said Mia.

It was a blessed relief to be away from the camp. After Jim Aura's death, Sergeant Anderson had become even more tyrannical and appalling. Even the Soldiers found it hard to endure his endless petty bullying.

"*I shan't.*"

Mary reached the topmost branch and fastened the pipe tether to the bark with a rivet gun. She threw the water-catalyser box up into the air, and moments later they heard a splash.

"*Fasten here,*" said Mary, and Mia secured the pipe tether in place.

"*And here.*"

The tether pipe was ten centimetres in diameter. Once the catalyser was operative it would send a steady flow of oxygen to shore. But their job was to make sure the pipe wasn't too near the water, because they'd seen Crock-Fish with teeth jagged and sharp enough to rip a hole in the tether's hardplastic cover. There was still a risk that arboreals like the Two-Tails or the Tree-Wolf would take a fancy to the pipe tether, but overall it was felt that the branches were the safest home for it.

Which meant that Mary and Mia had to crawl like monkeys through those branches, securing the pipe tether to the tree trunk or branches all the way from sea to shore.

"*This reminds me,*" said Mary Beebe, and crawled to a new branch. A long pause followed as Mia, dangling upside down, fastened the tether, but finally she spoke:

"*Yes?*"

"*What?*"

"*You said, 'This reminds me.' Of what?*"

"*Of what? Oh. Sorry.*" Long pause. "*Had a brief moment of fugue there. This reminds me, yes indeed it does, of a similar experience on Cloaca. Climbing through dense vegetation, when your body-armour jets had malfunctioned.*"

"*I've never been to Cloaca.*"

"*No, of course you haven't. I meant William. William's jets. William was with me. We were together. His body-armour jets failed. Happened a lot in those days, they used to outsource the technology to a slave planet that liked to sabotage stuff. He told me to fly back to base to get someone to rescue us, but instead—*" Mary laughed. "*Ah.*"

They crawled onwards through the branches, to the next tether point.

"*Instead, what?*" asked Mia.

"*What?*"

"*You said, 'Instead'. Instead, what?*"

"*Instead we ... well, I didn't leave him. Of course not. We clambered through the branches. It took days. The vegetation was mainly comprised of Hex-Trees, they have serrated edges. Quite deadly if you don't have body armour, though of course we did. Although of course—*" Mary laughed, gently.

"*Of course, what?*"

"*What?*"

"*You said, 'Of course'.*"

"*Sorry, yes, of course. I was thinking of that other time. Remember?*"

"*Huh?*"

"*No, of course you don't, you weren't there. That other time. Where was it? Planet beginning with X.*"

"*I don't know, I still wasn't there. Xavier?*"

"*Xerxes.*"

"*What about Xerxes?*"

"*Well, that was the other time.*"

"*What other time?*"

"*I was talking about body armour, the jets failing, technology ... It reminded me of that other time, when that cockroach type creature ate a hole in my body armour, in my groin region ...*"

"*And?*"

"*What?*"

"*I said, 'And,' in pointed tones. You've only told half the story. Cockroach, armour, hole. And?*"

"*Ah yes. I see. 'And' meaning, 'Tell the rest of the story, you old fool.' Well, all right. I shall. You see, the atmosphere was corrosive as well as poisonous. I could have had my clitoris burned off, and that really wouldn't have done. And so you had to keep your hand tightly fastened on my crotch as we flew back to base, snuggling on my back, one arm around my neck to secure you in place, the other hand on my privates, remember? Very sexy, if I may say so. And funny too, wasn't it?*"

"*I don't know, I wasn't there.*"

"*I know you weren't there. I was talking about my husband, William.*"

"*I rather liked William.*"

"*Oh good, he always loved grudging praise.*"

"*I didn't mean to...*"

"*Oh that's all right. Nothing like a bit of understated belittlement, that's what William always used to —*"

"*Oh my God, I'm so sorry. Dr Beebe...I didn't mean to...*"

"*For heaven's sake, Mia, I'm just teasing.*"

"*You're not angry with me?*"

"*I'm furious. I hate you. I'm going to rip your BB out and leave you for dead, you horrid bitch.*"

"*You're teasing me again, aren't you?*"

"*It's a habit. Forgive me.*"

"*Do you...miss him?*"

"*Who?*"

"*William?*"

"*Who's William?*"

"*Your husband?*"

"*Oh that old bastard. I'm well shot of him.*"

"*You're teasing again, aren't you?*"

"*I'm being ironical.*"

"*I can't always tell.*"

"*It's easy. I'm always ironical.*"

"*That's not possible.*"

"*You really are a literalist, aren't you? You should have been a Soldier.*"

"*I can tell you two must have been close. Even though, well.*"

"*Even though, well, what?*"

"*Even though you two were always quarrelling.*"

"*I never quarrelled with William. He* always *quarrelled with* me. *It's a fine distinction.*"

"*I don't think I understand.*"

"*[Sigh].*"

"*I think I do understand. How long were you two married?*"

"*Two hundred years. And never a cross word.*"

"*Never a cross word?*"

"*Foul invective, or total silence. We never went for that halfway stuff.*"

"*I've never had a long-term relationship.*"

"*I thought you said you were married for twenty years?*"

"*Oh yes. But never anything long-term.*"

"*Did he chuck you, or did you chuck him?*"

"*She.*"

"*You're gay?*"

"*Didn't you know?*"

"*No. I always thought——*"

"*What?*"

"*Nothing.*"

"*You thought——she's such a slut, she must be hetero?*"

"*Well you do seem to have an eye for the men.*"

"*I just——well. I don't know. Do I? I guess I just like flirting. And I love being with Tonii, because he's so gorgeous. But I haven't fucked a man in, ooh, well, put it this way, we had democracy then.*"

"*That's quite some time ago.*"

"*Yes, it is.*"

"*So what happened to her? Your wife?*"

"*She was eaten.*"

"*Ah.*"

"*By an* Invidia sordida. *She was a microbiologist. I stopped dating Scientists after that.*"

"*Invidia sordida. That's the major predator on Strangely, isn't it?*"

"*Yes.*"

"*I'm sorry.*"

"*Thank you.*"

"*Did you love her?*"

"*No.*"

"*Well. Still, it's very sad.*"

"*Oh yes.*"

"I'm lucky to have had William as long as I did."

"I think you are, really."

"I thank my lucky stars."

"Do you? Do you really?"

"No, of course not," Mary said. *"Of course I don't 'thank my lucky stars', are you fucking insane? Those bastards Hooperman and Saunders! I blame them both, in equal measure, for killing the man I loved. May they rot in hell!"*

David Go was cutting a tree down with a plasma pistol. It was a slow and tedious job. After several hours' work, the tree toppled and crashed to the ground.

"What now?" David asked.

"Nothing," said Sergeant Anderson.

"You wanted me to cut the tree down?"

"And now you have."

"But —"

Hugo Baal was burning a hole in rock to create a cavern-office for Sergeant Anderson. It took him, also, about five hours.

"There," said Hugo proudly.

"Now fill it in again," said Sergeant Anderson, with zest.

Hugo almost retorted. He remembered what happened the last time he had retorted — and shuddered inwardly.

"Yes, Sergeant," he said, with as much humility as he could fake. "Whatever you say, Sergeant."

Hugo began working out how to create a rock-fall that would close off the new cave.

Tonii and Clementine were cleaning the AmRover, inside and out.

This was not Soldiers' work; nor was it purposeful work. For the AmRover, of course, was made of self-cleaning numetal. They knew that, Anderson knew that, but they still did as they were told.

And so the two warriors scrubbed and mopped gleaming metal that would never, ever get dirty.

The sun was setting over the Ocean-Aldiss-Tree, making it look like a forest fire frozen in time.

On the beach, Mia, Ben, Mary, Clementine, David and Tonii were building a fire out of treebark on the soft red sands. They had filched a raw steak from the galley, together with two bottles of wine. And at the end of a long tiring day they were aiming to get blind drunk.

Sergeant Anderson strolled over to join them.

"Cheers, sir," said Tonii, passing him a glass of wine.

"Nice fire," he said. The flames burned red against the red red sand. Anderson drained the glass of wine.

"It gets so claustrophobic in that cave," Clementine said, with a grin.

Sergeant Anderson poured himself another glass of wine. "You're using up oxygen," he pointed out.

"Well, you can't drink wine with your helmet up." Mary Beebe laughed.

Anderson drained the next glass of wine. "Leave the bottle with me, return to your posts. Sit in the AmRover please, there's oxygen to spare in there. Or sit in the cave, with your helmets up. I think standing orders are pretty clear on that."

"With respect, sir," said Mary Beebe. "We can't spend all our time in the cave, or the AmRover."

Anderson drained another glass of wine.

"Do as you're fucking told," Anderson said affably, "or I'll ask my men to strip you naked, and stake you out on the sand in the noonday sun. You'll peel like a lobster, you old hag."

"Don't threaten me," Mary said, with a dangerous look in her eyes.

"Private Newton, Private McCoy," Anderson said.

Tonii and Clementine drew their plasma pistols.

Mary stared at them disbelievingly. "You wouldn't?"

"They would." Anderson laughed. "Military discipline, you know—"

"Is a wonderful thing," said Mary Beebe, bitterly.

DAY 22

Dawn burned now on the Ocean-Aldiss-Tree. Giant birds flew through pink clouds, and a handful of stars still shone, lingering for a few precious minutes in black-and-blue-and-red sky, before being banished by the sun's glare.

Mary and Mia were back at work on the oxygen-catalyser, laying cables along the beach to their cave.

Hugo was down in the savannah, stalking a No-Brain, so he could kill it, and feed the meat to the rats in his lab.

David Go was hewing a tunnel out of rock, as part of Sergeant Anderson's strategy to make this a city within the rock. David's body armour was splashed grey with dust, and flames surrounded him as the plasma burned through rock. He looked like a troglodyte burrowing hellwards.

And Sergeant Anderson was in his cabin, exploring the porn archives on his virtual computer, when Ben Kirkham arrived, breathless and agitated.

"What's the fucking hurry?" Anderson said, freezeframing the loving couple.

"I've found something, sir," Ben said. "In the edges of the forest. You have to see it." His tone was excited, and oddly cheerful.

"What is it?"

"You have to see for yourself," Ben said.

"I'm busy," Anderson informed him, glancing at the beautiful blonde who was now motionlessly orgasmic in the arms of a Hispanic Adonis, their limbs entangled and their bodies hovering above the floor. It looked, even to Ben's jaded eyes, rather bizarre.

Ben dragged his gaze away. "I think I've found another Depot!" he told Anderson, with barely contained excitement.

A smile lit the Sergeant's face.

"Lead on," he said.

Ben low-hovered away from the cave, and Anderson followed. They flew along the red sands of the beach, then across the yellow savannah, until they reached the swamplands.

"*What does it look like?*" Anderson asked.

"*It's carefully concealed. But I spotted the landscaping. It's buried underground, but there's a trapdoor entrance next to a rock. I think Saunders may have built dozens of these places.*"

Anderson flew on, quietly thrilled. They entered the swamplands, and flew carefully now, wary of the danger of fish and swamp water leaping up to kill them.

"*Land here,*" said Ben, as they reached a ghastly, gloopy fetid swamp lake with bubbling waters.

They landed. Ben pointed at a rock formation. "*Look, there. Hidden in the rock.*"

"*I see nothing.*"

"*Use your scope.*"

Anderson took his microscope out of his belt. He retracted his helmet and put the scope to his eye. It gave phenomenal magnification, ten times better than the helmet scope. He could see every grain on the rock, every insect that flew past it.

"I don't see anything," said Anderson, and Ben fired a controlled taser blast into his temple and Anderson's body danced in wild epilepsy.

"What the fuck?" said Anderson, his limbs twitching and his body jerking, and he reached for his plasma gun.

Ben tasered him again on the temple. Anderson's body spasmed once more, but he still held his plasma gun. Ben moved in close, unclipped Anderson's helmet and threw it aside, then took Anderson by the throat with his two powerful hands and began to choke him. Anderson held the plasma gun to Ben's head but Ben choked and choked and Anderson lost the strength to press the trigger. The gun slipped from his grip and his face grew redder and redder. He clawed with his hands and wriggled his body weight to find a way to throw his adversary. He tried to bite and headbutt, tried to shoulder-charge and karate strike, and most of all he tried to break Ben's grip.

But despite all of the Sergeant's enormous strength and his extensive martial arts training, Ben was a man possessed, and Anderson simply couldn't break free of the stranglehold. Ben exulted at his own raw invincibility. Anderson marvelled that this puny fool was *killing him*.

Then Anderson went floppy, and his eyes rolled back in his head, and he stopped breathing.

Ben ignored the feint, and carried on strangling him. Anderson jerked back into life for the killer punch, but he was still being choked and he had no strength at all now. The strangling continued for some time.

After a long time, when Ben was absolutely sure the other man was dead, he dropped him to the ground.

Anderson fell and slumped down on the New Amazonian earth. His face was bright scarlet, he had bitten off his own tongue, and blood trickled from his mouth.

But then his body-armour jets fired. He flew up into the air and ripped through undergrowth till he crashed into a tree and fell to the ground. He was disorientated, more than half strangled, but the will to live was still strong in him. He stood up, spitting blood, and reached for his reserve plasma pistol.

But Ben shot a taser bolt into Anderson's temple again. Anderson fell, badly, and began to spasm. And Ben strode swiftly over, and smiled at Anderson's tree-battered contorted face. He took out a scoop from his utility belt, forced Anderson's mouth open, then squirted a Rat-Insect into the Sergeant's mouth.

Anderson writhed helplessly. The creature was inside him, eating. He screamed. And screamed again.

Then Sergeant Anderson stopped screaming. He was dead. Ben dropped two other Rat-Insects on to his face, and they gnawed away at the flesh until nothing but skull remained.

Ben put Anderson's helmet back on, but left it retracted. Then the Rat-Insects hopped off and returned to their native habitat.

Sergeant Anderson was dead. And Ben felt a pang of regret.

Regret, because the old thrill was no longer there. The killing had been difficult and bloody, but he had taken no pleasure in it.

For there was a time when Ben had exulted in the killing of another human being, when he had revelled in every last moment of the death throes of his helpless, desperate victims. It had been his special, terrible joy.

But now he felt nothing. The murder had felt mechanical, soulless, almost tedious.

He must be getting old.

Sorcha was so tired she fell asleep as she was walking. That was how she got caught in the Flesh-Web.

She woke, blinded. She shone her flashlight—nothing. The Web was enveloping her, but it wasn't crushing her. So at least this wasn't a reprise of the Basilisk incident. She took a firm grip of her plasma gun and prepared to burn her way out.

But then she realised she was moving. With its velvet-soft touch, the Flesh-Web was gripping her and moving her, passing her from web tendril to web tendril, like a shrub playing handball.

She realised that she was being swallowed up by the Web. Part of the creature's macabre digestion system. Sorcha called up Hugo's briefing notes from her brain-chip:

Carnearenum. *Flesh-Webs. The heart of the interconnected jungle of New Amazon. This is definitely Animalia not Plantae, we've seen these creatures eat a full-size gantelopelle. The visible part of the Flesh-Web is, we believe, the creature's stomach; its brain and other organs may be buried in the complex latticework. It eats by breaking up the component parts of the prey by pressure or via digestive juices of some kind, then conveying the pieces somewhere, we know not where.*

But for some reason, the Flesh-Webs weren't breaking her into her component parts; they were swallowing her whole. And she was moving *fast*. Suckers caught and released, caught and released her, and propelled her deep into its heart—till suddenly she was free of the Web, inside a large oozing sac of some kind, and she was looking at a huge, round, throbbing object that oozed slime. Was this really, as it seemed to be, the pulsating brain of the Flesh-Web entity?

"*Major Molloy to Professor Saunders, come in please, if you can hear this. I need help!*" she said, desperately, into her MI-radio.

"*Sorcha, is that you?*" a voice said back.

"*Shit. Can you hear me?*"

"*Of course I can.*"

"*Sorry, dumb question. I've been trying to—where are you?*"

"*I'm flying below the canopy. Give me your location.*"

She checked her brain implant, and gave him the grid reference of her current location.

"*OK, give me an hour or so, I'll be with you as soon as I can,*" said Saunders.

An hour or so!

She waited, as the slimy "brain" wobbled and oozed. It seemed like an eternity, though it was probably no more than three hours. Then she heard Saunders's voice again:

"*OK. Me again. I'm flying over your coordinates now. But I can't see you.*"

"*I'm in the middle of that thing. The Flesh-Web. The jungle.*"

"*In the middle?*"

"*Well, somewhere inside it. It's a continuous organism. An animal jungle.*"

"*I know.*"

"*Richard...*"

"*Carl. Call me Carl.*"

"*Carl. Whatever the fuck your name is. How do I get out?*"

"*Why don't you use your body-armour jets?*"

"*I have no body armour.*"

"Shit."

"My battery failed."

"Do you have a plasma gun?"

"Of course."

"Treat it like a Jungle-Wall. Full plasma blast. Don't look back."

The "brain" exploded. A thousand tiny skittering sluglike creatures swarmed over her, covering each part of her body.

"It's doing something."

"What?"

"They're all over me. Fucking creepy shiny things. The brain is not a brain, it's an egg."

"It's trying to mate with you. There are fish that do that. They use the sperm of another species to spur them into laying eggs. And the Gryphons—well, let's not get into that."

"It's trying to eat me."

"Maybe it wants your DNA."

"I don't like this anymore."

"See you up top."

Sorcha scrambled to her feet, opened up her plasma gun to tight-beam, and fired. A long high hole appeared in the Flesh-Web above her.

Then she pointed the gun at the ground, set it to high-frequency energy pulse and fired downwards. With a whoosh, the plasma gun rocketed her up high, like a cannon ball, flying into the air, through the hole, past the suckers, ripping through the remaining Flesh-Webs and upwards and into the sky.

Into the sky! She was flying high up in the sky, half a mile from the ground!

Without body armour.

She glided, for four or five whole seconds.

Then she started to fall—

Hugo inspected the corpse of Sergeant Anderson. He took photographs from every angle.

Then he did a battlefield autopsy, splitting the corpse from head to toe with a laser, and photographing all the marks and lesions on the body. The skin on the face had been eaten away by some predator, but Hugo found unmistakable burn marks on the temples. Was there a New Amazonian predator that blew flame into its victim's face? That would indeed be an interesting phenomenon. So maybe Anderson was killed by one flame-breathing predator, then gnawed to death by Rat-Insects?

Hugo looked closer, and pulled the mask back off the face, then cut open the throat. He observed that the hyoid bone in Anderson's neck was broken, a clear indication of manual strangulation. He then stitched the throat back together. He had seen no contusions on the skin of the neck, but Hugo injected an accelerant to speed up the lividity process, and a few minutes later dark red fingermarks appeared.

He opened up the stomach cavity and found a live Rat-Insect, which had eaten most of Anderson's colon. Hugo killed the creature with a laser burst and split it open, and a bloody goo spilled on to the ground, the remnants of Anderson's entrails.

It was obvious to Hugo that Anderson had been manually strangled before he'd swallowed the Rat-Insect. It was also possible, Hugo speculated, that someone had forced the insect down his throat. How else would a trained Soldier come to swallow whole one of the vilest and ugliest creatures on the planet?

The evidence was incontrovertible: Anderson had been murdered. Hugo wrote his notes up carefully. Then he reconsidered.

First he deleted his notes, including his brain-chip memories. Then he opened up his camera, took out the memory card and buckled it in his fingers before burying it in the ground. He inserted a new memory card and photographed Anderson's autopsied corpse from a distance, so that the lividity around the neck wasn't apparent.

He took out his stun gun, rummaged in the undergrowth to capture a dozen or more Rat-Insects and dropped the scurrying creatures inside Anderson's body. He allowed them to feed and filmed the feeding.

According to his new report, Anderson had suffered an armour breach and had been eaten alive by Rat-Insects.

—and still Sorcha fell, fast and awkwardly. She wondered if she would fall back into the Flesh-Web and die a slow lingering death; or alternatively, hit the hard ground at speed and be killed instantly?

Then a flock of birds descended on her. She recognised them as Gryphons, deadly and beautiful black raptors. One of them caught her in its beak.

"Don't shoot, whatever you do," Saunders said in her head, and she narrowly avoided killing the Gryphon with a plasma blast.

"Where are you?"

"Look."

She looked. She was held in a Gryphon's mouth. Beside her flew a second magnificent huge-winged bird with black scales that glittered in the sunlight.

And seated on its back, like a cowboy on a horse, was Saunders.

Hugo returned to camp. "A tragedy," he explained.

"My gods," said Ben Kirkham.

"How did it happen?" said Mia.

"That bastard! If anyone deserved to die, he did," muttered David Go, viciously.

"His armour must have ruptured," said Hugo soberly. "There's a lesson to all of us there."

"Where's the body?" asked Ben.

"It's…well it's out there somewhere. But it will have been eaten by now."

"The body armour?"

"Too heavy to carry. I salvaged the weapons and the Bostock batteries."

"Good man," said Ben. His eyes glittered.

Clementine was visibly elated. Hugo remembered a rumour that Anderson used to sexually harass the subordinate women in the company, treating them as sex slaves. Motive for murder?

And what about Tonii? He had been remorselessly humiliated by Anderson, day after day. He had every reason to resort to murder.

And David Go was untypically quiet. He was a proud man, who had every reason to loathe Anderson, after the near-rape incident.

They all had ample motive to kill him.

In fact, Hugo realised with a sense of relief, he himself was delighted that the bullying shit was dead. And, after all, it didn't really matter who had murdered him. It wasn't up to Hugo to play detective.

The killer had done them all a favour.

The Gryphon flock flew high above the Canopy. Sorcha clung on to the back of her beast and she marvelled at Saunders. He'd been left for dead, tethered and without weapons, in the middle of a deadly jungle with killer Doppelgangers on his trail, and now here he was, alive, unharmed, in cheerful spirits, and commander of a legion of flying monsters.

How the hell did he do it?

As the wake, known by some cynics as the "Thank Fuck the Bastard's Dead Party", began, Mary took Hugo to one side.

"What really happened out there?"

"Like I said. A tragic accident."

"You can't kill a Soldier in full body armour that easily."

"Something did."

"Something, or somebody?"

"Are you suggesting—" said Hugo indignantly, and Mary froze him with a scornful stare.

"Oh all right, you've got me," said Hugo, cheerfully. "The ignorant wanker was manually strangled."

"Lord above," murmured Mary.

"As you say, he was a trained Soldier. Body-enhanced. And yet one of us managed to strangle him to death."

"Who the devil could do a thing like that?"

"I don't know. Maybe Clementine. Or Tonii. Unless it was you?"

"Of course not," Mary protested.

"Well, it was definitely one of us who killed him. Which means, of course, one of us is a killer," Hugo told her.

Mary winced—not at the facts of the case, but at Hugo's use of repetitious, tautologous diction. William would have—

"But who cares? Anderson deserved to die," Hugo continued, sternly.

"True," conceded Mary, "But."

"But?"

"But."

"Articulate your subtext please," said Hugo.

Mary shrugged. "But," she said, "who dies next?"

"You live here?" Sorcha marvelled.

She leaped off the Gryphon's back and stared out at the vast landscape of craggy mountain summits.

"Top of the world," said Saunders.

The sheer drop induced in Sorcha a sense of vertigo akin to blind terror. It was exhilarating.

"What the hell," Saunders asked softly, "are you doing here?"

"I was worried about you."

"You left me to die."

"So I guess I had cause to worry about you."

"You were right to leave me. Your logic was sound."

"I couldn't bear to —"

"What? Couldn't bear to what?"

"Don't make me fucking say it," Sorcha snarled, and Saunders smiled.

"It wouldn't have worked," he told her. "Killing me, it wouldn't have made you safe. Hooperman won't stop till we're all dead. Every last one of us."

"Not Hooperman. Just a bunch of damned robots," Sorcha told him.

"I'm not so sure about that," Saunders confessed.

It was the ultimate space-age urban myth. And for years, Saunders had dismissed it as superstitious nonsense.

But now, after the events at the Depot, he was beginning to wonder.

The story of this myth is always couched as something that "happened to a friend of mine". And sometimes the friend comes from New York, sometimes from London, Hong Kong, Johannesburg, Mumbai or Sidney, sometimes the Moon, or Mars, or the Asteroid Belt. Allegedly this "friend" is murdered by his jealous wife while having virtual sex with a woman on an alien planet. And this "friend" is then carried away in a body bag. And then the Doppelganger Robot marries the woman — and they live happily every after...

In another version the "friend" is a middle-aged man who has foolishly neglected his rejuves, and who likes to spend his spare time killing aliens on an exotic alien planet in a Doppelganger Robot body. Then this idiot suffers a massive heart attack, induced by the stress of all the alien-killing. But his mind lives on, and he is still there now, killing aliens all day and all night, and will be there till the end of time...

Some say there are coma wards in every hospital in every city full of Gamers whose minds never returned from their Doppelganger sojourns. But, it's further alleged, this scandalous truth has been hushed up by the authorities—because the Galactic Corporation has a desperate need for volunteers to keep donning virtual helmets for stints of 10–20 hours a week, in order to maintain its control over the Colony Planets.

There are also stories of rich dying men who upload their minds into Doppelganger Robots made as perfect replicas of their human form, in order to achieve immortality. No one has ever verified any of these accounts, but whenever men and women meet in bars and tell tall tales, the stories of Doppelganger Ghosts are legion.

There is even a theory to explain it—based around the concept of "persistence of consciousness". When the mind of a human inhabits the cybernetic circuits of a robot, it is postulated, something new is created—a free-floating "virtual mind" that dwells in the cybercircuits and that can survive the death of the actual human being.

Saunders was now convinced that this was what had happened to Hooperman. He was still here, on New Amazon, as a mind-without-a-body, parasitically inhabiting a myriad robot bodies, mocking and taunting the human survivors.

But was this Hooperman Ghost really the man Saunders once knew? Or was he just a shadow of the man, a remnant of what used to be Hooperman?

There was no way of telling. But the voice that had spoken to him after the massacre at the Depot was certainly Hooperman's. Arrogant, snide, whiny, contemptuous—*that* was no tape recording. That was Hooperman—or rather, Hooperman-Ghost-in-the-Machine.

And if all this was true, Saunders realised, then Hooperman would never die, so long as there were robot brains for him to inhabit.

It was a terrifying prospect.

Sorcha and Saunders talked for hours, sitting on the mountaintop, as clouds danced below them.

Saunders explained to her his theory about Hooperman's Ghost. He'd expected scepticism, but Sorcha believed it utterly, and at once. She was, after all, a Soldier, and all Soldiers believed in Ghosts. It was part of their conditioning.

"My father and my mother," she told him, confidingly, "are Ghosts in Valhalla. And my brothers too. That is where we go to live, after the body dies, and we cross the river Styx, that river of death that flows below the glorious Rainbow Bridge."

"Yes, of course," Saunders said, drily. He hated all religion, but especially this one. It was a cynically devised invention, a junkyard of mythologies.

"If I thought," Sorcha admitted, "that there was no life after this one, I couldn't endure it."

"So you really believe there is a Valhalla?" Saunders taunted.

"Of course there is a Valhalla." Her scornful tone implied that this was like debating whether there is a sky.

"I hope you're right," said Saunders kindly.

"But there is, I regret to say, no Valhalla for Scientists."

"So I understand."

"That's just the way it is. You don't merit an afterlife."

"Hmm," said Saunders, hiding a smile. "So what happens when we worthless soulless boffins die?"

"Nothing. Kaput. It all ends."

"That's a bleak prospect."

"Yeah. I don't know how you sad fucks deal with it."

Saunders toyed with the idea of explaining to her how Soldiers were originally evolved, and how it was possible to brainwash an entire society of human beings into believing that slavery is empowering. He'd read the major textbooks on mind-melding—all banned books on the Soldier planets—and he knew the theory in detail. It was one of the great accomplishments of the CSO in his two hundred years in office: the quiet supplementation of robots with killer humans who had an inbuilt, conditioned death wish.

These highly trained human warriors proved to be far more effective than either AI robots or Doppelgangers. For fleshware Soldiers were more adaptable, better at battle strategy, more ingenious in devising methods to destroy the enemy: in short, they were the perfect killing machines.

But Saunders said nothing. Sorcha was who she was. A killing machine. A Valhalla-junkie. A slave who thought she was a master.

"How do you cope?" she asked him wonderingly, "with the thought of a death that ends everything?"

"I guess I kind of assume," admitted Saunders, in a rare moment of candour, "that it'll never happen to me."

It was getting cold. Sorcha was starting to shudder. Saunders took out the thermal wraparound from his body armour's storage cavity. She cuddled up against his armoured body.

"You're lucky it didn't rain."

"I guess."

A few moments later, it started to rain. A gentle patter fell down on the grey glorious rocks. Above them the Gryphons cawed and whirled in the air, savouring the soothing drizzle. Their scales protected them from the burning effects of the acid, and because they had no eyes, they could not be blinded.

Another blob of rain landed on Sorcha and Saunders. Sorcha winced in pain.

"Let's get you inside."

Saunders led her into the Gryphons' cavern, and the carvings and paintings on the walls leapt out at her like colours at dawn.

"They did these?" She sounded impressed.

"And more. There are sculptures deep inside the cavern. Giant Gryphons, Godzillas, Juggernauts giving birth. This is a species possessed of true artistic genius."

Sorcha marvelled at the artwork on the rock walls. She saw scenes of Gryphons killing Godzillas, Gryphons killing Two-Tails. She saw Gryphons fighting and killing each other. This was a warrior species, and Sorcha felt a glow of kinship.

"This proves they are sentient, did you realise that?" Saunders told her.

"I did," she said, "for I am sentient too."

He blinked, then took the insult on the chin.

"They're as smart as we are," he clarified.

"Bullshit. We have spaceships and plasma guns. They live in caves and flap their wings."

"They paint, they sculpt, they have culture. They can communicate complex concepts. They can manipulate tools. And they sing. Their songs are wondrous."

The Gryphons dangled upside down, mute.

"When? When do they sing?"

"When they like you."

Sorcha thought about that; it was a weirdly stupid idea.

"You'd better get me my body armour back," she told him. "I can't live long like this."

"Of course." Saunders stood up.

Saunders left the cavern, emerging from darkness into light, and walked to the edge of the cliff. He leapt and fell. When he saw the canopy loom towards him, he fired his jets and he flew.

Four hours had passed.

Sorcha wondered if Saunders had got lost. She'd given him the exact coordinates, but Scientists were notoriously bad at directions.

She sat crosslegged on the rock, in the heart of the Gryphons' Cave, and stared through the narrow crack in the rock at the world outside, and at her only way in and out. The clouds outside darkened.

If she had been a different person, she mused, and not a Soldier, this situation might have frightened her. She was alone, it was dark, she was surrounded by perching avian monsters, and it was pissing down deadly acid outside.

But, as she was a Soldier, and a Warrior, none of this alarmed her in the least. Nor, indeed, was she remotely worried about the fact that Saunders had been gone so long.

Although, in fact, now she came to think of it, perhaps she was just a *little* bit worried.

Saunders had been gone for more than four hours! She had no plasma gun, no armour. She was easy prey for these fucking monsters.

But Soldiers are never afraid. And so, fear was not an option.

She waited—calmly, fearlessly, but checking her watch every fifteen minutes—and watched the Gryphons as they perched like upside-down dragons. Their body scales gleamed like armour in the flickering light. She wondered where the light was coming from. It wasn't just from the entrance—there must be tiny cracks in the rock.

Unless the rock itself was glowing? She looked closer and saw shiny patches of rock that glowed out light. The patches moved. They were alive. Tiny rock-embedded creatures were illuminating the cave; living light bulbs.

The knowledge of this bizarre fact made the cave feel even creepier.

The rocks glowed, the dragon-birds cawed at her, water dripped from the rocks. Sorcha could hear her own heart thumping. As it grew dark, her night-vision implants kicked in, and the world of the cavern seemed even more strangely ethereal and unreal.

And she started hearing things. An ethereal choir. An organ playing. A flute. The sound of a heart, leaping. The sound of joy, flying.

It dawned on her. *The fucking beasts were singing.*

"I like you too, guys," Sorcha said, and felt an unfamiliar emotion, and managed to name it: awe.

She heard a scrabble of rock and reached for her plasma gun, but it was Saunders. He flew into the cavern, followed by her body armour, which he was flying remotely.

He landed on the ledge beside her, and carefully guided the body armour to the ground before he shucked his helmet back.

"You OK?"

"I'm fine," she told him.

"You weren't—?"

"Of course I wasn't."

Saunders listened to the Gryphons' singing. "They're singing," he marvelled.

"It's annoying me."

"You have no soul."

"Give me the suit." She took the suit from him, and touched it, and felt a jolt.

"What's wrong?" he asked.

"Nothing, I'm fine. Come here, baby," said Sorcha, still stroking her body armour. She realised that the jolt was love.

The body armour was soft to the touch, yet stronger than steel, body-morphic, and richly hued—jet-black, but with a warmth that suggested gold and silver lurking in the blackness.

"Guess what?" said Helms.

Sorcha had owned this suit for nearly fifteen years; she had fought eleven wars in it. It was a part of her.

"What?" she said, utterly distracted.

"I said, 'Guess what?'" Saunders repeated. He took out her old BB from his armour pouch and held it in his hand, with that crooked smile on his lips.

"Yeah, I think it must have been damaged when—" Sorcha began.

"It was sabotaged."

"What?"

"Someone sabotaged it. Do you have enemies, Sorcha?"

A burning hate filled Sorcha. She thought about the possible suspects, and realised—

Ben Kirkham! It had to be. She knew from his biog and psych profile that he was a rehabilitated rapist and murderer. And Sorcha was of the old-fashioned school of thought that said once a murdering psycho, always a murdering psycho.

"I guess so," she said lightly, and hid her rage with a smile.

Saunders powered the suit up. Sorcha stood, ready to put it on.

"You're going somewhere?"

"I just want to put the armour on."

"You don't need it on. We're safe in the cave. Just use a breathing tube, you'll be fine."

"I need to wear it."

Saunders shrugged. Sorcha dismantled the armour, then put it on section by section. First, the upper leg and groin armour. Then the boots and greaves. Then the breast and back plate, with the tent and paraglider neatly stashed within. The arms and gauntlets. The utility belt. She tested the systems: plasma cannons, side and back jets. She put the helmet on and breathed air. She engaged the helmet visuals, checked the hologram display, flexed her fingers and tested the slider on the sensitivity settings.

Then Sorcha leaped in the air and hovered. She limbered up her arms, swinging each arm in a circle in turn. She flipped and hovered upside down. She fired a plasma blast at the cave wall, and carved her name with plasma in the rockface.

Finally, she landed on the ledge beside Saunders again, and shucked the helmet back.

"Happy now?"

"Happy."

DAY 23

The sun dawned red and the Canopy glowed. The jungle erupted, once more, into outraged wakefulness.

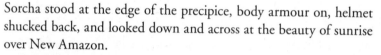

Sorcha stood at the edge of the precipice, body armour on, helmet shucked back, and looked down and across at the beauty of sunrise over New Amazon.

"It's glorious, isn't it?" Saunders said.

"Have you filmed it?"

"Of course."

"It'll make a wonderful documentary."

Saunders marvelled at the view, and at the stupidity of Sorcha.

"They'll never make a movie of this planet, Sorcha," he said gently. "That bridge is burned."

"I guess," she conceded.

"You look gorgeous."

"Do I?"

Sorcha looked like shit: like she'd fallen into a quicksand swamp, and walked for days in the blazing skin-searing heat, and for long nights with her face lashed by icy winds, then been swallowed alive by a monstrous hedge and spat out again; but yes, she also looked gorgeous. "Would I lie about a thing like that?" Saunders said gallantly.

Sorcha remembered a few things about Professor Carl Saunders. He was nearly six hundred years old; he had been divorced sixteen times; he had once been accused of bigamy. And he was famous for his charm, and womanising zeal.

"Hmm," she said.

"He's mad, you know," Saunders told her. "Hooperman. Or rather, he's *become* mad, over the centuries. The Andrew Hooperman

I knew was an angry and vengeful and, let's face it, frankly annoying bastard. But he would never have done all this. He would never have massacred innocent men and women. So Hooperman must have gone mad, it's the only explanation."

Sorcha shrugged. "Whatever."

"Which is tragic if you think about—"

"Skip the fucking philosophy. How do we *kill* him?" Sorcha said bluntly.

"We can't, if he's a Ghost. He's not alive, he's incorporeal, he's beyond our power to hurt him. So all we can do is smash and obliterate every single Doppelganger Robot on the planet. And then we have to rebuild a civilisation without robots, and without AI. Because then, Hooperman will have no way of attacking us. He'll be a spirit, without flesh, without metal, sans everything."

"That sounds like a plan," Sorcha said, and felt the breeze on her cheeks, and exulted in anticipation of war to come.

"It's great, seeing all of you back with your science projects," said Mia with a shy laugh.

"It's what we're here for! We're Scientists, for heaven's sake!" Ben told her. "That's what that idiot Anderson never understood."

"You're right. Absolutely right. I wish I—" She broke off, embarrassed.

"What?" he prompted, gently.

"Well, I envy you, really," Mia said, disarmingly. "I'd love to have been a Scientist. I was always hopeless at that stuff, I flunked my maths degree. So I admire people who can do maths and science without, you know." She grinned. "A brain implant and things."

"Oh there's no shame in getting answers from a brain implant," said Ben, with ostentatious generosity.

"Still, I'm trying to train myself to think more scientifically," said Mia. "So—can I just ask—" She conjured up her virtual screen, and was presented with an endless array of photographs of skeletons of New Amazonian animals.

"—you to explain to me," she said, "about the two sorts of vertebrate?"

He smiled. "Of course," he said. "Well, where shall I begin?" And he began, using the photographs on his virtual screen to illustrate his points.

"This is Type A: creatures with a bonelike vertebra, or double vertebra, or triple vertebra, or those with a latticelike vertebra made, strangely, of copper. This is a good example of Type A," he said, tapping the mid-air image with his finger. "And this is a Juggernaut, with a copper lattice infrastructure. And this is a Basilisk."

"And Type B?"

"Has anyone ever told you," said Ben gently, "that you're a wonderful, warm, special, sexy woman?"

Mia laughed, a lovely bell-like laugh, which she had copied from Mary Beebe because it was so cute. "Not nearly enough people!" she admitted, smiling.

"You like men, don't you?" Ben continued.

"Actually, I'm gay," Mia told him.

"But you like flirting with men."

"I'm not a flirt!" she protested, and laughed another bell-like laugh.

"And you like telling men you're gay, because they immediately have an image of you naked with another woman, and that turns them on."

Mia's smile faltered. She held back on the bell-like laugh.

There was something not right about Ben's tone; was he mocking her?

"But you're not," said Ben, "not really."

"I'm sorry, Ben?" said Mia, baffled.

"People think you are, but you're not," explained Ben. "You're not wonderful at all, or warm, or special. Far from it. You're mediocre. Tediously average. Deplorably *pointless*. And you're not sexy, either," he continued, in the same gentle tones. "You're not even highly sexed.

Sex is something you endure, but it gives you no pleasure. Because you're emotionally frigid," he said, still gently. "Aren't you?"

She blinked. Something had gone badly wrong here.

"You're sad," said Ben. "Sad. Empty. Pathetic. People feel sorry for you, don't they, Mia? Or rather, *sometimes* they do. But usually they just think you're a sluttish, stupid, manipulative bitch."

The walls and floor were collapsing in Mia's world. She'd wanted to win Ben's friendship. Why was he taunting her like this?

"That's not true," she replied, pathetically.

"You act like a whore. You flirt with men and with women, with total lack of shame. You're insincere. And you ingratiate yourself with people," Ben explained. "Don't you? Hmm? You're like a chameleon. But there's no real you, is there? You're just a nothing, a sycophant. But the truth is, when your back is turned, people laugh at you."

Mia flushed, stifling her rage, knowing it was all true.

"But don't take it personally," Ben continued, in calm, reasonable tones. "It's just the way you are. Some people have oodles of charisma and sex appeal. But there's only so much to go around, isn't there?"

"Fuck off, Ben."

"Ah. I've struck a chord."

"No, you haven't!" She didn't know how to counter him: denying what he had said felt like an impossible task. "I was just asking you," she said tensely, "about what passes for bone on this godforsaken—"

"I'd really hate to be you, Mia," Ben crooned at her. "You're so utterly fucking useless. But I am, really, I'm fond of you." Ben stroked her hair, teasing some strands away from her face, sending shivers down her body, but of hate, not desire. "But don't worry your pretty little head about the science," he told her. "You just work on your cooking skills, and keeping yourself pretty and cheerful and being nice company. Because you know what? You're going to be a Mummy soon, aren't you? You're going to have dozens and dozens of little babies, and that will be your role in life from now, until you die."

"I'm—looking forward to that," Mia said coldly, her heart in hiding.

Saunders was on his knees, inspecting some insectoid creatures with his visor magnifier.

"Are we done?" asked Sorcha.

"Not nearly done."

"I'm bored."

"How can you be bored?" he marvelled. He beckoned her to look. "You see that rock?"

"No."

"Look. The rock."

She bent down and looked. She used the magnifier and did an ultrasound scan. "It's alive."

"It's alive."

"So it's not a rock."

"It's not a rock."

"So, who gives a fuck?"

"It's a previously undiscovered life-form," Saunders told her. "A new genus, a new species."

"Does it move?"

"I don't know."

"Can you polish it, and put it on a necklace?"

"It's a living creature, Sorcha."

"It's kind of a nice colour," she admitted. She picked up the rock. It was red, like a ruby the size of a thumb. As she moved it, patterns of light appeared on the rock. "It would look pretty neat on a necklace."

"Put it back."

The rock evaporated. Sparkles tumbled from her fingers. "I killed it."

"Maybe not. Maybe that's part of its life cycle."

"Let's go back, huh, spend some time in the sack? Or do I mean, on the rock? Whatever." She laughed.

"It was so wrong," Saunders said.

"What was wrong?"

"What we were planning to do on New Amazon. It was evil."

The blank look in Sorcha's eyes alarmed Saunders. He persisted.

"Rocks that dissolve into sparkles. The millions of life-forms. The Aldiss trees, the Rat-Insects, the Flesh-Webs, the Juggernauts, the Exploding-Trees, the Gryphons—do you really think I could bear to kill all that?"

The truth hit Sorcha hard. "You always intended to do this. The fake attack on Xabar, blowing up Juno, the Depot."

Saunders nodded, hiding a smug smile. "Hooperman forced my hand. But yes, this was always the plan. I've been preparing for it for the last two years. I built a missile silo, I built the Depot, I bought antimatter, I did all that I did, in order to save New Amazon."

"All those people died!"

"Not my fault. Hooperman killed them. With my original plan, no one would have died. The missile attack was intended to be all sound and fury, killing no one, signifying nothing—that's a quotation by the way. But I needed an excuse to justify destroying Juno."

"That's some elaborate scheme."

"I'm the man who spent forty years devising a way to merge chess and Go. This, by comparison, was simple."

They walked back to their camp. A cloud swirled above them, creating dark and light patterns in the air, then condensing into an oval shape, then sweeping away fast. Without even realising he was doing it, Saunders subvocalised a description of the cloud patterns for his MI, and speculated that it might be some kind of aerial life-form. So much to—

Sorcha interrupted his thoughts: "So the Gryphons are sentient, huh?"

"Yes."

"How—" She screamed.

"What?"

"My father. My father! He's right there." She stopped in her tracks, and pointed madly into space. Saunders smiled. Behind them, Isaac cawed.

"I see nothing."

"He's there!" Sorcha could see him, tall, brooding, angry, just as he always was in life.

"He's not there. It's an illusion. His image is in your memory. The Gryphon plucked it out, made it manifest."

"He was thinner than that, in real life," she said accusingly, staring at the hollow-faced man who was staring accusingly back at her.

"Show me the security perimeter," Ben said frostily to Private Clementine McCoy.

"Yes, sir." She walked him through it. "We have four cameras here, four here. Three sentries on duty at any one time."

"You use the Scientists as sentries, don't you?"

"Yes, Sergeant Anderson told us to do that. It gives us a bit more time to—"

"Don't you realise the Scientists have work to do? Important work."

"I appreciate that, but Sergeant Anderson said—"

"Complex, unfathomable work. Work you could never begin to comprehend. Do you have a PhD, Private?"

"I have a BA. In Military Engineering. I—"

"I said, do you have a PhD? Do you know what that is? Can you do a Fourier Analysis? Do you grasp the topology of N-space? Name the atomic mass of four fundamental particles. You can't, can you?"

"Give me a—"

"Don't do a search, you good for nothing waste of fucking space."

"No, sir."

"You're a good for nothing waste of fucking space, aren't you?"

"Yes, sir." She was comfortable with this level of abuse.

"In future, don't be so fucking useless."

"No, sir."

"And wipe that stupid smile off your face."

"Yes, sir."

"You're like a little automaton, aren't you," said Ben, marvelling. "All I have to do is wind you up."

"Yes, sir."

"Take your armour off."

"Yes, sir."

One, two, three, four—it was a bewilderingly fast kit change. Clementine stood before him in vest and knickers, sweat trickling down her skin, past the goosebumps that sprang up on her flesh in the weirdly chill breeze.

Ben retracted his helmet. He took off his right gauntlet. Clementine stood to attention, semi-naked, utterly composed.

Ben kissed her, and tongued her, and touched her breasts with his one bare hand, then gripped her arse and squeezed. Clementine allowed it all, still standing to attention. She hated it, but this too was fairly standard military protocol.

"We may have rebels in our midst. I want you to kill them."

"Yes, sir."

"Will you do that?"

"Yes, sir. Just name them, sir."

Ben grinned, a slow unfolding grin of delight. "In due course. Dismissed."

"Yes, sir."

Sorcha's father vanished.

"So, what do you say?" Saunders asked her.

"About what?"

"About joining me in my mission to save New Amazon."

"We're marooned, had you forgotten? What's to save, from what?"

"Before Juno exploded, it would have sent out a Mayday signal. Earth will send a rescue party."

"It'll be at least a hundred years before troops arrive," Sorcha pointed out.

"That's not so very long, in the scale of things," Saunders retorted. "And once they arrive, they'll terraform the planet according to the original plan."

Sorcha thought hard. "What are you asking me to do?"

"I'm asking you to join with me," Saunders told her, "to build a garrison planet, and fight the Earth expeditionary force when it arrives. To protect this beautiful planet."

"You want me to take arms against the Galactic Corporation?"

"I want you to build an army that can fight them."

Sorcha was stunned. Then incredulous.

"What army?" she mocked. "There are only eleven survivors. Even if we all start having babies, there won't be—"

"Caw," said Isaac, and Sorcha had another vision of her father, staring at her, accusingly, blood trickling from his eyes, dying. She shuddered, and her father's body ruptured and he turned into a pool of water and the water glistened, and it turned into a floating globe. The planet of New Amazon.

"Ah," said Sorcha, looking at Isaac, and the thousands of Gryphons in flight above her.

"Ah, indeed," said Saunders, and smiled, with faith and hope and rich anticipation of the years to come, as the vast flock of Gryphons above them blackened the sky.

"There," he told her, "is your army."

"You miss him terribly, don't you?" said Ben to Mary Beebe, as she filled the oxygen tanks with air catalysed from seawater.

"I don't like to talk about it," she told him curtly.

Ben didn't take the hint; he lingered, standing rather too close to her.

"I've read William's security file, of course," he told her casually. "In my new capacity as military commander of the expedition."

"I said," repeated Mary, "I don't like to talk about it."

"He was unfaithful to you, apparently. Back on Lima."

"That doesn't bother me."

"You had an open relationship, did you?"

"I don't like to talk about it."

"You know about his children there? The two girls? They must be eleven or twelve by now. Twins. By that allegedly very sexy spaceship trooper."

A flash of pain appeared on Mary's face. She and William had chosen never to have children. This came as a shock.

"I don't," said Mary, hiding a world of anguish, "like to talk about it."

Ben didn't even bother to hide his smile.

"Can I tell you a secret, David?"

David Go liked to work in his cabin, alone, without interruptions. But Ben Kirkham insisted on an open-door policy: he liked nothing better than popping in to chat to his "team".

"I don't want to hear your secrets, Dr Kirkham."

Ben leaned on the doorway, peering in, in a fashion that infuriated David. He liked doors that were closed!

"We're all one big happy family here, David. We all look out for each other," said Ben gently.

"That's good," said David grudgingly, and insincerely.

"Except, that is, for you," Ben added. "That's because everyone hates you, David. And do you know why? Because you're an arse-licking bottom-feeding piece of shit."

"If you're trying to goad me, Kirkham, you need to be a lot more subtle than that."

"Hugo Baal hates you more than anyone. 'Why should *he* be alive?' That's what he said to me the other day. 'Why is David Go still alive, when cleverer and more worthy men and women have died?'"

"Fuck off, Kirkham."

"You're a sad and lonely man, aren't you? And mediocre. And socially embarrassing. And annoying to have around. But you should be nice to me, you know, David. Shall I tell you why? Because I'm the only person here who can actually bear your company."

David gulped, and couldn't speak; and realised, to his horror, that he believed every word of what he had just been told.

Tonii was working out on the punch and kick bags when Ben drifted in to chat.

"Hi there, my goodness, sweat and muscles, a potent combination," Ben chortled. Tonii wiped himself down, and forced a grin.

"Hi there, Ben."

"How are you feeling?"

"I'm fine."

"You're not missing Sergeant Anderson?"

"I'm a Soldier. I don't 'miss' people."

"So sharp! So droll! You really are a marvel," Ben crowed, openly eyeing Tonii's masculine/feminine torso.

"Thank you, sir."

"There's just something I wanted to say."

"Yes, sir."

"Um, there's no tactful way of saying this," Ben admitted, and paused.

"Yes, sir. I mean, no, sir." Tonii waited. "What, sir?"

"Tonii," said Ben, smiling, "you are not normal."

Tonii flinched; then cursed himself. A Soldier never flinches.

Ben continued in the same soft tones: "You are not normal. You are not even human. You are not man, nor are you woman, you are just—a—pathetic—fucking—freak." And this time, Tonii remained stony-faced.

"Yes, sir," he said flatly.

"What are you, Soldier?" Ben asked. "Hmm? What are you? Answer me. That's an order, you piece of shit. What are you?"

"A freak, sir," said Tonii Newton with familiar, awful, numb, unquestioning obedience.

"You've done what?" said Hugo, disbelieving.

Hugo was in the galley, cooking Two-Tail meat to feed to his rats. To his annoyance, it simply wouldn't darken or show any other signs of cookedness.

"I've deleted your diary entries," said Ben, smirking. "By remote computer link. We don't need your silly jottings, man, we have the official log and the download of the *Encyclopedia of Alien Life* to rely upon."

Hugo grinned. "Don't be so—"

"I mean it. I've done it."

Hugo's look of desolation and despair sent a shudder of joy running through Ben's body.

Hugo slept badly that night, and every night, because of the sound that cracked the darkness of the AmRover dorm, a shuddering gasping sound that ate away at his soul.

Mia couldn't sleep either, because of the same, ghastly sound.

Mary Beebe was on sentry duty outside the AmRover, but even she could hear the gasping/shuddering sound through her helmet amp.

Tonii Newton was on sentry duty inside the AmRover; the relentless moaning noise was driving him insane.

Finally Clementine McCoy shook David Go awake. "You're doing it again," she said fiercely, and David looked up at her with panic in his eyes, begging for her forgiveness, and her pity. "Just," she said more kindly, "stop making that fucking noise."

David nodded, and lay back down. And he was silent for a while.

And after a long period of silence, sleep came to Mia and Hugo and Clementine; while Tonii and Mary were able to keep their watch in peace.

But eventually David too fell asleep. And he began to dream dark nightmares. He dreamed of being raped and humiliated, he dreamed of being snubbed and disregarded, and he dreamed, most of all, of being treated like a *nobody*.

And in his dreams, he began to weep, again, and the sound of his anguished, gasping sobs cracked the night, again.

In the morning Ben Kirkham, who now slept in the soundproof and heavily fortified Observation Bubble, woke as fresh as a daisy. He couldn't understand why everyone else looked so tired.

From Dr Hugo Baal's diary (covert)

June 44th
This is a living hell. I don't know who I hate more—Ben Kirkham, for being an evil manipulative blackhearted monster, or David Go, for his incessant fucking <u>nightmares</u>.[1]

I have made a worrying discovery about Dr Ben Kirkham. Well,

---

1 The answer is Ben, of course.

not so much a discovery as a hypothesis, or even a theory, but worrying nonetheless.

I am now convinced that Kirkham is the murderer of Sergeant Anderson. But I'm quite happy to condone and indeed celebrate that. The man[2] deserved it, and it was essential for our survival that someone killed him. So good luck to Kirkham for having the balls to do it.

But Dr Kirkham, as well as being a murderer, appears to be a seriously strange individual, even by the standards of xenobiologists. He's introverted, but sometimes wildly extroverted. He's brilliant, but also slapdash. And there are times when it seems to me he doesn't understand anything, literally, not anything at all, about human psychology.[3]

I've made a detailed analysis of Ben Kirkham's behaviour over the last two years, and I have cross-collated it with the following, the check-list of psychopathy which we used to use to test the sanity of our lecturers back at the University of Pontus:

Key Symptoms of Psychopathy

Emotional/Interpersonal	*Social Deviance*
glib and superficial	impulsive
egocentric and grandiose	poor behaviour controls
lack of remorse or guilt	need for excitement
lack of empathy	lack of responsibility
deceitful and manipulative	early behaviour problems
shallow emotions	adult antisocial behaviour

Like most of us, I'm sure, I score five out of ten on this scale. Eccentric and grandiose, and proud of it! Lacking in remorse and guilt! (Well, I never do anything wrong, do I?) Deceitful and manipulative, c'est

---

2 *Homo motherfucka*, in the common lab argot.
3 Not that I'm the expert on this. My first girlfriend told me I was a sad obsessive who ought to get a life—and she was an avatar prostitute on Third Life!

moi. And an endless need for white-knuckle-ride daredevil excitement, of course,[4] coupled with a dreadful addiction to chocolate, though an addiction to chocolate isn't on the list, I concede.

But Kirkham scores ten out of ten. He is a human being who does not feel emotion, who pretends emotion, who acts emotion. He is acerbic, cruel, unreliable, mocking, his hand gestures are large and elaborate, and he playacts all the time. (I've even seen him wear spectacles when he wants to seem professorial, even though his eyes are less than ten years old.)

He is, in short, a clinical psychopath.

And his behaviour since the death of Sergeant Anderson has been appalling. He has undermined and belittled every member of our small company. He has no respect for our academic authority, he taunts the Soldiers with their inefficiency, he issues impossible orders and berates us for not obeying them. And as for David Go, who of course is still traumatised by his near-rape experience during Anderson's vile regime—Kirkham constantly goads him in a way that is unendurable to witness.

Most unforgivably of all, he tried to use the network Censor system to delete my diary entries, not realising that not only do I wirelessly connect every diary entry with my brain implant, but I do so twice, the second time using a secure imaginary number code of my own devising, on a frequency that, according to the textbooks, does not exist. In the old days, apparently, this was known as the belt and braces strategy.[5]

Kirkham is a danger to all of us. He is a predator in our herd of whatever it is we are a herd of.

He has to die.

Sorcha watched the Gryphon Egg Ritual, and wasn't even remotely shocked.

---

4 *Harumph!* I hear you think.
5 A sartorial reference, pre-dating the invention of "smart" clothing.

"They inseminate themselves," explained Saunders, "by eating the chicks of other birds."

"Yeah, I got that. Cool, huh?"

"Cool?"

"Pretty much."

"It's appalling! Savagery beyond belief!"

Sorcha laughed at his earnestness. "You should see some of the things they did to us in basic training!" she joked.

Saunders chose not to enquire further.

"This is a very difficult moment for all of us," Dr Ben Kirkham explained to his army of two—Privates Clementine McCoy and Tonii Newton.

"Yes, sir."

"Yes, sir."

Private Tonii Newton hated Ben Kirkham with all his soul. But Tonii was trained to obey, and he always did obey. So he stood to attention and waited to hear his new boss out.

"In order to survive, we have to be ruthless."

"Yes, sir," said Tonii.

"Yes, sir," said Clementine.

"I think you know what I mean."

"Yes, sir," said Clementine.

"No, sir," said Tonii.

Ben sighed. "The Scientists have to die," he explained.

"Beg pardon, sir?" Tonii asked, incredulous.

"They're a burden. They don't pull their weight. And they are going to consume all our rations if we let them."

"They're part of our team, sir," said Tonii loyally.

"We don't need them. They're not Soldiers."

"No, sir. Nor are you, sir. Sir."

"Don't be insubordinate, Private."

"No, sir."

"I estimate that we could live for four hundred years or even lon-ger with what we have on the AmRover, if there are just three of us eating. Longer still if we access the supplies and equipment on the Satellite, if we can safely get to it. We have all we need to rebuild a civilisation. We have the gene stock, the gender balance. We could create an entire new human race, between the three of us."

"Yes, sir."

"Yes, sir."

This man's a fucking lunatic, thought Private Clementine McCoy.

This man is totally fucking deranged, thought Private Tonii Newton.

And no way am I fucking him! Clementine resolved.

And if he thinks I'm going to *fuck* him...! Tonii thought, appalled.

"This is the plan," Ben explained.

Mary Beebe and Mia Nightingale were watching the flowers fly. It was a slow, tedious job, but it was a relief to finally be back studying nature.

They were standing, with their body armour in stealth mode and helmet visor magnification on High, next to a flowering shrub that wended its way past the Flesh-Webs. It was essential to remain motionless, but it was an uncomfortable experience, espe-cially since—because of the shortage of waste-absorbent under-wear—both Mary and Mia were using catheters.

"*How did you start going out with him?*" Mia asked over the MI-radio, after a few hours had elapsed.

"*Hmm? With who?*"

"*With William. Your husband.*"

"*Ah.*"

They both savoured a long pause.

"*We were on a xeno mission together,*" Mary replied. "*Sharing a two-person tent. One thing led to—*"

"*Ah, I'm with you.*"

"*Inadvertent frottage led to mutual masturbation, which led to aeons of exquisite love.*"

"*That's often the way of it,*" said Mia.

"*Really?*" said Mary.

"*Not really, I was being ironical.*"

"*Ah,*" said Mary, hugely amused.

"*Yes, indeed, 'Ah,'*" retorted Mia. She was getting the hang of this.

"*Why do you ask?*"

"*What?*"

"*About William?*"

"*He's all you ever think about, and I'm a believer in going with the flow.*"

"*Very astute.*"

"*I think so.*"

"*And this, pray do tell me, is this how gay women chat up other women? By asking about their dead husbands?*"

"*Invariably.*"

"*Smart tactics.*"

"*I think so.*"

"*Do you really?*"

"*No.*"

"*Ah.*"

Mia loved the way her banter with Mary flowed; rarely, indeed, had she ever talked such precisely phrased bollocks.

And it soothed and enlarged her soul—to be liked, to be thought amusing, to be allowed to flirt and brag a little. After all Ben Kirkham's endless psychological undermining, it was only her times with Mary that kept her sane.

"*I've been reading up about him,*" said Mia, tenderly. "*His biog. His published writings. He was a very vivid personality.*"

"For 'vivid' read, 'full of himself'," Mary snorted, lovingly.

"I think I would have liked him. If I'd known him. I mean, if I'd known him better."

"He was a cantankerous old bastard."

"That's what I would have liked about him."

They waited, and watched.

Then Mia continued, with hard-achieved casualness: *"I've read all your joint articles as well, you know. Well, the summaries anyway."*

"William wrote them all. I could never turn a word. Detailed observation was my forte."

"I'm the same. It's why I became a film-maker."

"I look, and look, and see what others miss."

"Like the trembling of that stamen."

"Just like that."

"And that flower. That's not a flower. It's an insect."

"Well spotted."

"See, it has a dozen microcreatures on its tongue. There."

"I saw it."

"The tongue must be all of .5 millimetres."

"I'd agree with that estimate."

"The insects hover around the flowers, but they don't seem to inseminate."

"I count forty-two species of insects."

"I count forty-three."

"One just flew away."

"So it did."

"If the insects don't pollinate the flowers, why are they hovering so near?"

"They like the colours of the flowers?"

"It's a vile colour. Fuchsia. I had a flat painted that colour once."

"I rather like it, as colours go."

"William liked it too."

"We have one thing in common then."

"You have several things in common," Mary conceded.

"Such as what?"

Mary hesitated, then compiled her list: *"Acute intelligence. Dry wit. Attention to detail. Refusal to bullshit and pretend you know more than you actually do know, like some people who I shan't mention—Ben Kirkham! A sense of humour akin to my own, and, last but not least, a kind soul."*

"I—ah. Well. I don't know what to say to all that."

"Sorry, I've embarrassed you, through my excessive fulsomeness."

"I'm just not used to being flattered."

"Well, that serves you right for spending time with unappreciative imbeciles."

"I'll take that as a compliment."

"And so it was intended."

"Look. The flowers are trembling. They're about to fly."

The thirteen-petalled fuchsia-coloured flowers suddenly erupted from the plant and flew into the air and hovered. They danced patterns around the hovering Gadflies and Pinpricks and Spiky Arses and Blue 'n' Reds, making whorls of colour in the air. Then they swept away like a mist and landed in a patch of ground a good sixty metres away.

"Now watch the insects," said Mary.

The insects hovered still above the flowerless plant.

"I'm watching. What am I watching?"

"Measure the mass."

"I'm measuring."

"It's an increase of .002 grams per insect."

"The insects are growing."

"The insects feed on the flowers."

"But they didn't touch the flowers!"

"They feed on something the flowers emanate."

"A gas of some kind? They breathe in nutrients from the flowers' farts?"

"That seems the most tenable hypothesis."

"Farting flowers. Hmm."

"This is the sixteenth time I've encountered such a phenomenon."

"You're kidding me?"

"*Well yes, I am, actually. Though I have come across something a little bit similar. A tree on Romola that exhaled methane.*"

"*But why? What evolutionary advantage is there in flowers feeding insects?*"

At that moment the insects pounced upon the flowerless shrub. Within minutes the shrub had been eaten, and all that was left was shreds of root.

"*Damn!*" Mary marvelled. "*I've not seen that before.*"

"*The flowers feed the insects, the insects kill the plant,*" Mia said.

"*They kill the old plant. And the new plants thrive, because they haven't got to compete with their parents. It's so elegant.*"

"*It's awful, really,*" said Mia.

"*Awful. And stupid. And deliriously and preposterously amusing.*"

Mia laughed out loud at Mary's lugubrious, mock-serious tone. "*You have a lovely turn of phrase,*" she told her.

"*Thank you.*"

"*What do you think to Hugo Baal's notion?*"

"*What? About killing Ben Kirkham?*"

"*Yeah.*"

"*His logic seems irrefutable.*"

"*Dr Kirkham is a prick. He deserves to die,*" said Mia.

"*He, the flowerless shrub, we the insects.*"

"*A lovely metaphor,*" Mia assured her.

"*Rather arch and over-elaborate, I felt.*"

"*Not at all, you are a poet, madam.*"

Mary laughed. Mia glowed with pleasure.

The Gryphon cawed, and Sorcha had a vision of *herself-as-Gryphon flying through the sky, and plunging down, and ripping a hairy tetrapod of some kind limb from limb.* She shuddered, and forced a smile.

"What do I do?" she whispered.

"Think beautiful thoughts."

She thought about *the garden in her military academy, the rich colours, the peonies and hollyhocks and Scarlet Flowers and the roses, and her regiment's mascot, a dog called Ruth*, which Sorcha had adopted as her own.

The Gryphon cawed. And Sorcha's mind was suddenly filled with an image of *her beloved dog, Ruth, being ripped limb from limb by a Gryphon*.

Sorcha gulped.

Then she thought about *their colony ship, squat and grey and leaving a trail of faintly glowing ion particles in its wake as it flew through deep space*. And she tried to recollect the star patterns they would have seen, but she couldn't, and instead was forced to visualise a generalised haze of stars. The colony ship was battered, and deeply shadowed, but every now and then *a burst of flame from the ion drive turned the hull into a sparkling marvel*. Sorcha had tether-flown along with the spaceship from time to time, tugged at speed through deep space. That image too was vivid in her memory, and she focused hard on transmitting it.

And then, once again, her thought-image abruptly changed, as the Gryphon dabbled in her mind. And now she saw *a giant Gryphon flying through black space, and then ripping the colony ship apart, into bloodied pieces*.

"These creatures," said Sorcha.

"Yes?" said Saunders.

"They may be sentient, but they're not what you'd call smart."

"They have a one-track mind," Saunders conceded.

The Gryphon, Isaac, sensed Sorcha's unease. A new image filled Sorcha's mind; it was *herself, her helmet retracted, short blond hair shining in the sun, walking through the New Amazonian jungle. Then, out of nowhere, a Gryphon pounced, and ripped her limb from limb, then pulled out her improbable entrails like stuffing from a toy bear*.

Sorcha shuddered, and raised her middle finger to Isaac. Isaac cawed.

"Did you get that?" Sorcha said bitterly to Saunders.

"Hey," said Saunders, "Isaac has a sense of humour."

Hugo was cooking fish, from concentrate. He arbitrarily blended sea-bass with snapper and fabricated a vast potato rosti to accompany it. It was to be washed down with wine. He added poison to Ben Kirkham's portion, and served the meal with some sense of triumph.

"Hidden talents, Hugo," said Ben snidely.

"Leave the man alone," said Clementine. Her long black Afro-hair was a mess, after being crunched up in her helmet all day long. Hugo was aware that all of them stank, with the cloying odour of people who have been trapped for a long time in a small space with inadequate ventilation. The AmRover's force field was up, and they were stationary.

"A toast," said Hugo, raising his glass.

The alarms began to ring.

"Another time, huh?" said Ben.

They began to suit up.

Sorcha was shy.

"What's wrong?" said Saunders, touching her naked body.

"The birds," she said, as his fingers played with her special spot, and sent spasms of pleasure through her.

"What about the birds?" asked Saunders, touching himself to be sure he was hard.

"Can they…"

"Can they what?"

"See us?"

"We're in a cave. No one can see us."

"I mean, see our minds," said Sorcha. She looked at Saunders, at his skinny but muscular naked body. And Saunders looked at her, the glory of her nudity.

"Surely not," chuckled Saunders, and entered her.

On the clifftop outside, Isaac saw it all, from Saunders's eyes and then he saw it all again, from Sorcha's eyes, and he cawed with delight.

There was a huge crashing sound and the AmRover lifted up in the air and turned over. Hugo was half into his armour and he went flying and smashed face-down on the ceiling. Bodies flew around him. Clementine and Tonii were already in their armour, and their flying bodies were like missiles. Tonii's boot barely missed Mary; a fraction to the side and she would have been killed.

Then they were floating in air again, then rolling around, then upside down, then right way up, then falling again. There was a huge smash and they were sliding and—they stopped.

"What the fuck just happened?" roared Ben.

"Something came into the cavern, and picked us up," explained Mary, "and took us outside, and dropped us."

"I thought we had a fucking force field!" Ben bleated.

"It, ah, only works against guns and bombs."

"What sort of fucking force field is—"

"Let's just deal with this, huh?" said Clementine crisply. She closed her helmet and subvoced a request for visuals. On her helmet visor she saw they were out of the cavern and on the red sands, in view of the ocean. And she could see also that the AmRover was upside down.

THUD. The AmRover was picked up again and dropped again. Bodies went flying. The force field could protect them from a nuclear bomb, but it couldn't stop them being worried at like a dog's bone.

"I'm going outside," said Clementine. "To recce."

"I'll cover you, "said Tonii.

They shucked their helmets into place.

"Nine, ten," said Clementine, and opened the emergency door and rolled out. Tonii followed.

Clementine and Tonii hit the ground and rolled into position and inspected their attacker. It was a land-monster of some kind, vast, looming above them, with golden scales and triple horns on its anvil-shaped head. Clementine put her gun on smart laser and popped a red dot on the forehead of the beast. Then she pressed the trigger.

A shaft of laser light lunged from the gun and hit the creature in its skull, burning through bone and whatever else this creature possessed in its head. But the creature didn't shift. Its brain was therefore, probably, not in its head. But the creature seemed baffled, unsure how to proceed against prey that could not be killed by being dropped from a great height, and puzzled too, perhaps, at the sudden draught that had appeared in the middle of its skull.

The monster picked up the AmRover again, and dropped it again. Tonii winced. Then he and Clementine opened fire with a hail of explosive bullets—which, to their astonishment, bounced harmlessly off the creature's armoured scales.

And so they changed gun settings. Sheets of plasma tore out of their weapons and the beast was engulfed in flame. But the plasma beams were reflected off its tough shiny scales. It didn't ignite, didn't even seem perturbed, but merely peered around, looking for the source of the heat. Fortunately, it hadn't yet noticed the two puny Soldiers standing beneath it.

Clementine looked at Tonii; Tonii looked back.

Fuck.

Then Clementine beckoned, and Tonii moved over to the AmRover. It was an upended turtle now. Its rockets were pointing up at the sky, not down. So she took a firm grip on one side, ignited her boot rockets and fired. She flew up in the air millimetre by painful centimetre, gripping the AmRover, until the power of her exoskeleton combined with the boot-rocket thrust enabled her to flip the AmRover back into position.

As Clementine did this, Tonii waited in position, with his plasma cannon ready to blast. He wasn't at all confident he could kill this creature before it could pick him up and dash his brains out, so he just waited.

The doors of the AmRover were flipping open and the Scientists were getting out to inspect.

"*It's not dead!*" protested Ben Kirkham.

"*Sssh,*" said Clementine, spooking everyone. The monster continued to peer down at them.

"*What shall we call it?*" asked Hugo.

"*A Tricorn,*" hazarded Mary.

"*A Golden-Rhino.*"

"*Move back, get behind those trees,*" said Clementine, and added: "*Oops.*"

The creature pounced. Its jaws picked up the AmRover and hurled it away, and its claws reached for the Scientists.

"*Narrow beam, full power,*" said Clementine, and she and Tonii fired thin plasma beams which locked together at the beast's midpoint. The beast moved forward, but the plasma beams didn't waver. And suddenly, the cumulative energy of the plasma beams caused the creature's hide to catch fire.

But even that didn't perturb the beast and, engulfed in billowing flame, it carried on attacking. It spotted Mary Beebe and gripped her in its claw. Tonii changed to laser setting and managed to saw the foot off, so that Mary fell back to the ground. The Scientists joined in, firing erratically and burning vegetation all around but landing the occasional lick. And Tonii and Clementine kept up their continuous bursts of plasma power, firing bullets of energy that slowly melted the damned creature's almost impermeable hide until it finally realised it was in pain, and started to roar.

The Tricorn ran, and the Soldiers ran after it. They fired an explosive shell over its head, which landed and blew a hole in the ground that the Tricorn fell into. And then they rained blasts of plasma down on the trapped creature as it howled with rage.

And finally, the plasma did its job. The Tricorn fell to pieces, and the pieces turned to ash, drifting in the wind.

"*That was close,*" observed Clementine.

"*We didn't even see it coming,*" marvelled Tonii.

"*From now on,*" said Ben, "*two of us on extra-vehicular sentry duty. We can't risk any further attacks on the AmRover.*"

Hugo thought about his meal—ruined. And about the poison—scattered around the cabin.

Would he ever have a second chance?

Sorcha and Saunders flew above the canopy, in the heart of a vast flock of Gryphons. The sky was jagged with sunset. Rocs hovered far above, eager to pounce, afraid to fight the massed ranks of the Gryphons. But from time to time a Roc plummeted and scales exploded and blood poured from a dying Gryphon and the Roc flew away pursued by angry caws.

Below them, for mile after mile, the canopy swept, a vast purple-floored world above a world. Saunders knew they were flying over the ocean now, but still the canopy held, as the Ocean-Aldiss-Tree loomed high and joined the canopy created by the Earth Aldiss. Saunders always admired the sheer chutzpah of the Aldiss tree in capturing the entire damned planet for its greedy self. Now *that* was a tree he could respect.

But now the canopy was thinning. Below they could see red sands starting to emerge. They flew over the red sands, and past a range of mountains, until the desert began. Here the flock of Gryphons flew down, and Saunders and Sorcha with them.

And they beheld a city. From the air, the white sands shimmered in the heat; but on the surface of the dunes, patterns emerged and solidified. Saunders marvelled at the sight. Huge octagonal buildings had been raised out of the sand. Sand towers soared high, in place of the Aldiss trees. And there was a vast dome, held up by tiny pillars of sand.

"*They live here?*" Sorcha subvoced.

Isaac cawed and hovered before them, and flashed an image into Saunders's mind. It was just the same shimmering city of sand with towers and pillars, but the image was growing larger, they were moving closer to it. And Saunders could now (in his mind's eye) see *Gryphons flying through the city, which was even vaster and more magnificent than it had been in real life, and he was flying past the towers which shone like jewels, and now he was inside the city, and he could see below him on the ground Rocs and Godzillas pulling carriages like horses, and everywhere Gryphons flew and plucked hapless prey from the air and danced patterns of aerial dance in a whirlwind of freedom.*

"*You see it?*" Saunders marvelled, to Sorcha.

"*Yes. But what? What is it?*" Sorcha said, over her MI-radio.

"*It's a dream.*"

"*This is what the Gryphons dream of?*"

"*A dream, and also a blueprint.*"

They landed. Reality returned. The city was impressive, but much less magnificent than the dream of it, and utterly devoid of life. There were no Rocs inside, no jewels on the towers, no dancing Gryphons or fearless prey. And Saunders hunkered down and picked up a handful of sand. He used his helmet magnifier and saw a dozen tiny Rat-Insect-shaped creatures wriggling in his palm, each clutching a grain of sand.

"*See these?*"

"*I've seen them before. Rat-Insects.*"

"*Not so. Twelve legs not six. The thorax is larger. Claws on the back. They don't look at all like Rat-Insects.*"

"*They all look—*"

"*Don't ever say that,*" Saunders rebuked her.

"Don't get huffy."

"*This is as much like a Rat-Insect as a rhino is like a koala bear.*"

"*Can you get over yourself? Why am I looking at this creepy-crawly thing?*"

"*Let's call them,*" said Saunders, mulling, "*Sand-Ants.* Harenaformica Sorchae.*"

"Sorchae. That sounds like Sorcha."

"It does."

"You're naming it after me."

"I am," said Saunders, basking in the warm glow of his own generosity.

"What the fuck for?"

"Huh?"

"It's a creepy-crawly. If you're going to name something after me, make it a scary predator. Not a fucking—"

"Let's keep to the point."

"What point?"

"These creatures. The Harenaformicas. *They built the city. They made this monument. It's the same process as the Jungle-Wall; the city is built out of sand that's been processed and turned into builder's cement by this creature's digestive system."*

Sorcha looked at the city, its vast scale, the grandeur of its architecture, and blinked.

"But why? There's no nourishment in sand. Why eat sand and shit it out as cement? What's the evolutionary purpose of that?"

"They have no purpose. They see an image of the city and they build it, but they don't know why."

"The Gryphons make them do this?" said Sorcha, awed.

"Yes," said Saunders. *"This city, it's the Gryphon vision of a better place. A safe place. This city is the Gryphon Heaven, built for them by Sand Ants."*

Sorcha felt a sudden, cold, overwhelming shudder of fear.

"I have gathered you together," explained Ben Kirkham, "to explain our new and brilliant survival strategy."

Then he beamed, like a dog with two-tails, three cocks, and a brand-new bone.

Clementine was in despair; but it was her duty to obey orders.

Tonii was in despair. He desperately wanted to disobey his orders. But he knew that if he did rebel, Clementine would kill him.

Hugo seethed with rage about the fact that his plan to murder Ben Kirkham had failed.

And David Go was, as always, for every moment of every day, simply in despair.

One hour later, at Ben's orders, they abandoned the cavern and started driving the AmRover through unexplored and treacherous terrain.

The new plan was to travel to the Space Elevator, and thence to the Satellite. This, Ben had abruptly decided, was their best hope of salvation.

It was clearly a plan conceived on a whim, and Ben had allowed no discussion or dissent. Mary Beebe privately thought it was madness to go anywhere near the Elevator, because of the danger of meeting enemy DRs—it was the DRs, remember, who had already killed so many of them! But she didn't say so, because that would have made Ben angry. And Ben angry was not a comfortable experience.

The others were just blindly following, worn out by Ben's boundless optimism and refusal to think about problems.

The AmRover soared above the Flesh-Webs, and wove its way through tree trunks, but suddenly the engine started to stall. And then it cut out entirely.

For a few seconds it continued to hover, out of sheer cussed refusal to believe in what had happened.

Then abruptly, it crashed to earth.

Saunders awoke, trembling.

"What's wrong?" Sorcha said.

"Nothing...a nightmare."

She stared at him blankly. He looked down at his dinner tray, with its half-eaten dried food tablets taken from his body armour's larder. He wasn't in bed, he was sitting in the cavern, with Sorcha, and they were eating dinner. "I'm sorry. Did I fall asleep?"

"As I was talking to you."

"It—happens sometimes. Petit mal. It's a sign of age."

Sorcha looked at him with an expression of pity merged with fury.

"What happened in your nightmare?" she asked, mildly.

"I saw...a world in which I was king of the Gryphons. But all my people—my fellow Gryphons—turned on me and ate me and shat me out as they flew through the sky."

"You dreamed that?"

"Someone dreamed that. Some*thing* dreamed that."

Sorcha was baffled; then she got it. "You were having a Gryphon's nightmare?"

"I must have been. Maybe they transmit images and thoughts without intending to."

"Fuck."

"Indeed, fuck."

Ben finished his inspection of the AmRover's engine. He emerged smiling.

"The AmRover's Bostock battery has been leached of energy," he explained. "It must have been damaged when the AmRover was dropped."

That's impossible, thought Mary, but she said nothing.

"Fortunately, there is a solution to our problems. We can walk to the Space Elevator," said Ben, smugly. "It'll take two or three weeks, but we've got the time to spare. Once we're there, we'll stock up on some batteries, then send the Soldiers back to put a new BB in the AmRover. And then, bingo, we'll hop up into space and colonise the Satellite."

"But you still haven't dealt," explained Mary, "with the problem of what we do if we encounter DRs at the Satellite, and find they want to kill us. I mean, for heaven's sake! If we don't even have the AmRover to—"

"If we find any enemy DRs, we'll destroy them, or reprogram them," said Ben, casually. "Tonii and Clementine are Killing Machines, they're pros, they'll handle it. No worries. Trust me."

"But—"

"Trust me," said Ben, smiling even more now, which made it worse.

"Yes, sir," said Tonii.

"Yes, sir," said Clementine.

He's going to kill us on the journey, thought Hugo.

Isaac picked up the plasma gun in his talons but couldn't work the trigger.

"Don't show him how," said Sorcha.

Saunders was suddenly enveloped in a vivid image of himself being eviscerated (again!) by beak and talons. He paled. He took the plasma gun, slyly put it on Stun, then held the trigger. Isaac studied it.

Then Isaac held the gun in two claws and manipulated the trigger with a talon. A haze of energy flew out, hitting a tree.

Isaac flew off, carrying the plasma gun.

"I shouldn't," said Saunders, "have done that."

The jungle was dense. Moisture rose up in hazy pillars from the earth. Hugo and Mary and David Go and Mia kept close together as they walked.

"How are you doing?" called out Ben, and Hugo threw a grenade and blasted him off his feet.

"*Run!*" screamed Hugo.

The Scientists ran towards the jungle. "*The Soldiers will kill us,*" screamed Mia.

"*Just run!*" And Hugo and Mary and Mia and David Go vanished into the purple and red depths of the jungle.

Ben got to his feet. Blood poured from a cut in his temple, but the body armour had absorbed the blast. Clementine and Tonii ran up to join him.

"What happened?"

"They counterattacked first," said Ben, cheerfully. "But don't worry, they botched it. I'm fine." He retracted his helmet and wiped the blood off his forehead.

Clementine raised her plasma gun and blasted Ben in his unprotected face. His skull exploded and melted, and only the memory of his sneer remained.

There was a long pause.

"What the fuck?" said Tonii, tensely.

"It's done!" Clementine shouted.

Hugo, Mia, Mary, and David Go drifted back.

"Are you with us, or against us?" said Clementine to Tonii.

Tonii was frozen, conflicted, confused. "That was cold-blooded murder," Tonii said.

"Yeah."

"Yes, of course it was," said Hugo.

"Ben told me to kill all the Scientists," Clementine explained. "Every single one of them. To give us a better start. He faked the

AmRover breakdown. The batteries are fine. This whole excursion was just a trap. Are you with us or against us?"

"If I'm against you," asked Tonii cautiously, "do I die?"

"No. But you'll be on your own."

"With," said Tonii decisively. "That man was a prick."

Hugo was elated as they began marching back towards the AmRover. His plan had been brilliantly conceived and audaciously executed. It was hard to kill a man in full body armour, even with a bomb or a plasma blast. But Hugo knew it was human nature to retract your helmet after being blown up. The minute Ben had felt fresh air on his cheeks, he was doomed.

"I'm the new military leader of this expedition," Clementine told Hugo as they walked, their helmets retracted so they could savour the rich aromas of the jungle.

"Fine by me," said Hugo, humbly.

"You don't have a problem with that?"

"No problem," said Hugo.

There was a long pause, as they walked on.

"So, um, what do we do now?" asked Clementine.

"We walk back to the AmRover," said Hugo, patiently. "And after that, we follow Kirkham's plan. It was a good plan, even if he was too stupid to know that. We can't live in a cave for ever, so we have to go to space. Travel to the Space Elevator, destroy or outwit the DRs, if there are any, but there may not be, travel up to the Satellite. Create two bases, one on the land, one in the sky. There'll be a supply Depot near the Space Elevator, we can restock there, and make it our capital city."

"How do you know there'll be another Depot?"

"It's the kind of thing Saunders would do. He's a sly bugger. Also, we need a celebration tonight, to bond us as a team. You need to be a bit less military. Make Tonii your official Number Two. He doesn't like you, you've got to win his love, you can't expect him to just blindly obey any more. Oh, and beware of Mary Beebe. She's still in trauma, she's flaky. Don't forget the Doppelgangers are out there. We're still at war."

"Have you finished?" Clementine said, acidly.

"No. We're running low on fresh water. We need to dig a hole and replenish. That'll take us half a day. We'll start on it tomorrow."

"We're fine for water."

"No, you're wrong. We're running low. We should always have a month's supply of water at any given time. I explained this to Ben but he was too stupid to listen. There's an underwater lake under us now, but it ends a kilometre away. It's on the map."

"I read the map. I didn't notice—"

"Trust me, I'm right."

"We'll dig for water," Clementine said decisively.

"You're the boss," said Hugo, and stopped dead. A few moments later he swore. "Fuck."

Mary Beebe also stopped dead. But she didn't realise that was about to happen, so her body carried on walking and she toppled over, and rolled like a turtle. Then Mia, distracted by her own body armour's malfunction, walked right into Mary and tripped over her. The two of them flailed on the ground, helplessly. Tonii watched it all, awestruck, then he also stopped dead.

Clementine moved her arms and legs. She was fine.

David Go screamed. "I can't move!" he shouted.

"He sabotaged you," said Clementine, realising. "All of you. Just me and him would have survived. He drained your Bostock batteries."

Tonii's face was a portrait of betrayal. Despite his promises, Ben had never intended *him* to live.

"Then you'll have to carry us," said Hugo.

"All of you?" said Clementine, scornfully.

"Then we'll stay here, you go for help."

"I'll go for help," said Clementine.

"We'll stay here," Hugo concurred.

"We can take the armour off and walk," protested Tonii.

"Too dangerous," Hugo decided. "We'll stay here."

Clementine set off into the jungle, at a brisk pace. Hugo shucked his helmet back into place.

And Hugo and the others waited.

And waited.

And waited.

After a few hours, the earth below them began to shake. It felt as if a monster from the depths was going to rip the ground apart. Instead, pillars of steam ripped through the soil in countless fountains. Hugo took a spectrometer reading. It was oxygen. Pure oxygen!

This, Hugo realised with dawning delight, was how life was able to thrive on this planet. Oxygen storms! Ripping through the planet's crust and billowing through the jungle, and replenishing the oxygen sacs of these nitrogen-loving but oxygen-needing organisms.

After twenty minutes the storm abated. The ground returned to normal. Hugo's oxygen meter read High; they could take their helmets off and breathe the atmosphere. Except, Hugo noted, the oxygen was blended with gaseous sulphuric acid and would burn their lungs. So better, perhaps, he concluded, to keep their helmets on.

Night fell. The oxygen level slowly dipped, the acid drifted away, and the atmosphere returned to its normal, non-toxic, unbreathable form.

DAY 24

The sun rose.

Hugo, David, Mia and Mary were still frozen in place, like over-zealous players of Musical Statues who had failed to notice the band's departure.

Clementine's suit warned her there were predators nearby. She stopped hovering and glided to a halt. She hunkered down behind a Flesh-Web and waited.

After an hour a troop of Basilisks slid past. Clementine was silent. Her armour gave off no odour, her camouflage blended perfectly with the Flesh-Webs. She waited patiently for the danger to pass. She could if need be defeat these creatures, but the risk wasn't worth taking.

When the coast was clear she stood up and stretched and took two steps forward and stood on the landmine. The impact threw her six feet in the air, and when she landed she could feel her spine snap.

DAY 25

Another day of ghastly waiting.

Hugo was desperately hungry.

Mia managed to lie down, by falling flat on her back. She found it more comfortable.

David was suffering acute claustrophobia.

"Clementine, come in please, Clementine, come in please," said Mary, in a continuous loop.

Hugo succumbed to a desperate torpor, and was filled with despair.

Motionless.

Tired.

Bored.

Afraid.

Waiting.

DAY 26

Another slow, tedious day of even more ghastly waiting.

Until—

"*That's fucking it,*" said Tonii. "*We're walking!*"

Hugo didn't attempt to argue.

They took their body armour off and spent an hour flexing and stretching. Then they turned the food pouches into makeshift haversacks and loaded up as much of the suits' food and water supply as possible. They were all heavily armed, but they had no protection against armoured predators, or against the acid rain.

They walked. And walked.

The jungle was less dense here; but it was raining leaves from the canopy. A whirlwind of purple leaves blocked their vision and slapped viciously against their faces and bodies, leaving them bruised and bleeding. But they carried on walking.

An Exploding-Tree exploded fifty metres away from them. By this time they were so jaded and fed up they didn't even break step. Hugo noticed, with some interest, that the Exploding-Tree had managed to burst through into the canopy. Did the trees commute between ground and canopy? Was that the reason for the exploding?

And on they walked.

David Go feared the acid rain, even though he knew they were on the second day of a rain-every-ten-days weather cycle. He was fed up, but didn't wish to grumble, because he was always being told he grumbled too much.

Tonii imagined how he would look if the rain fell. His skin would peel, his eyes would fall out, he would die ugly, and in pain. It was not what he wanted for himself. He missed his armour badly.

Mary Beebe wished William was here, so she could criticise him, to take her mind off this godawful fucking walk.

Mia admired Hugo for his resourcefulness in killing Ben Kirkham. Who would have thought that tubby, funny little man had it in him!

And Hugo—Hugo was worried about Clementine.

Worried—and puzzled, and indeed, intrigued by her too. She was a quietly spoken, decisive, courteous warrior. But was that all there was to her? Did she have hidden depths? Hobbies?

Clementine was immensely calm, and capable and competent, in a way that Hugo admired, and had a style and a swagger that he adored. He himself was brilliant, analytical, insightful, arguably a genius. But never capable or competent, except in purely scientific matters. And never calm. And he never ever, except in his academic writings, swaggered.

Yes, he admired her very much indeed.

Hugo wondered if she'd managed to reach the AmRover yet.

He wondered if she was in any peril.

He wondered if a DR had found her and killed her; or if a Godzilla had stomped her; or if she'd been overpowered by Basilisks; or carried off by Rocs; blown up by an Exploding-Tree; or buried alive in a mountain of Wiggly-Worms.

And he also wondered, idly, irresponsibly, and with mischievous glee, if one day, she might ever consider fucking a geek such as himself.

But no! Surely—

It began to drizzle.

Mia felt it first—a scalding pain on her shoulder. Then the drizzle thickened and they were all jumping and hopping, stung by the painful rain.

Hugo looked up at the dark stormclouds abruptly gathering. "Monsoon," he predicted, sadly.

"But the rains aren't due for—"

"It's fucking raining! It's the weather!"

"But—"

"Let's walk back to the suits?"

"No chance."

"Then?"

"We die, in agony, flesh peeling?" suggested David Go.

"Oh fuck," said Mia, and there was panic in her voice.

"What do we do?" Mary asked Tonii.

"I—don't know," he muttered.

"You're a Soldier! You must have some idea!"

"Find shelter? Under a tree?" said Tonii, pathetically.

"I think I may have the glimmerings of a notion," said Hugo.

Mia let out a wail of utter fear.

David Go closed his eyes and counted his blessings. It didn't take long. His eyes flicked open again instantly.

Mary conjured up a memory of William; she wanted that to be the last thing she ever saw.

"I said," Hugo repeated impatiently, "I have an idea."

"What?" said Tonii.

"What?"

"You do?" said Mary, with relief.

"What is it?"

"This," said Hugo. He took out his plasma gun. "Let's dig a hole."

Clementine knew she was close, and the knowledge filled her with a savage exhilaration.

She had crawled, inch by inch, for almost two days, with a broken spine. Her guess was that the landmine had been seeded randomly by a DR, or a Draven. She was a fool not to have considered that possibility. Though it still seemed bizarre to her—it was a big planet, how could she have been so damned unlucky?

After a while she'd stopped crawling, and had given up, and had lain unconscious for some hours, and the Flesh-Webs had attempted to envelop her. But her suit had self-sealed, healing serums were pumped through her veins and arteries, and then she woke up again and through sheer will-power she kept herself conscious. Occasionally, she subvoced a Mayday call, but she was out of radio range now.

But she kept her nerve and carried on dragging herself towards the AmRover. She was crawling face-down, gripping the earth with her gauntleted fingertips, and pulling herself forward in a complex slithering motion that covered the ground with remarkable speed, at a terrible cost to herself.

Only pride and hate and a desire for revenge kept her moving.

"One, two, three, fire." At Hugo's cue, they opened the plasma guns to Full and blasted the ground. The blazing heat incinerated soil and carved a long trench into the ground.

"Now move." They moved and blasted the ground from the other side. The aim was to create a triangular wedge in the ground that could be collapsed from the inside.

A streak of lightning shot across the sky.

"And more."

Hailstones fell. The Flesh-Webs shuddered and closed up into black impermeable balls and steam arose from the ground where the hailstones hit. Hugo took a hail stone in the forehead. His eye stung and he could feel his own flesh burn.

"Fuck!"

"Let's get in."

"Too soon, we . . . !"

"Get in the fucking hole."

Hugo, Mia, Mary and David scrambled into the hole, pulling down earth on to themselves. The ground was hot, it was burning them, but the acid rain was burning them too. Hugo scrabbled desperately at the earth, then suddenly they collapsed downwards deep into the hole and there was an earthslide and the soil closed around them and above them.

They were now trapped under the earth, dozens of feet below the surface, breathing air from their oxygen implants, with no certainty they would ever be able to get out again. But at least they were spared the acid rain.

"Well, that went almost according to plan," said Hugo cheerfully.

"Swim?" said Saunders. Sorcha nodded.

And they each leaped from the escarpment and landed in the icy cold tarn below. Both still wore their body armour, but in the water the suits no longer seemed bulky and inhuman. And the exoskeletons allowed them to swim powerful strokes.

They dived deep under the surface and swam through shoals of Water-Beasts—water molecules in an organic lattice that blobbed like jellyfish from hither to thither. Saunders had seen remote robocam footage of these creatures but he'd never encountered them at first hand before.

Then they swam/clambered a path through the underwater roots of the Freshwater-Aldiss-Tree, and spotted some Digger-Crabs. An Octagon swam lazily passed them. Saunders realised the Aldiss-Tree was flowering underwater and subvoced some notes.

Sorcha spiralled elegantly in her black body armour, which was perfectly contoured around the swells of her body; diamond-hard, yet soft to the touch. The armour made giants of them both. But even though Sorcha was embedded in an exoskeleton nearly five inches thick, Saunders found her wonderfully sensual.

"*Are you OK, Carl?*" she asked.

"*I'm fine.*" He realised he'd stopped swimming, and was just floating free, staring at her. "*Waxing inwardly lyrical again.*"

"*You do that, don't you?*"

"*I do. Can I ask a question?*"

"*Ask away.*"

"*What do you think of the Gryphons?*"

"*They scare me.*"

"Me too."

"Can we enslave them?"

"Huh?"

"I said, can we enslave them?"

"And I say again, Huh? Why would we do that?"

"So they can fight for us. That was your plan, remember, a Gryphon army?"

"I was thinking more in terms of asking nicely."

"How intelligent are they?"

"On a scale of what?"

"Humans are six, flame beasts are ten."

"I'd say four, five. But I might be wrong."

"They're dangerous."

"Yes, I know."

"You saw what they did to the Sand-Rats."

"They did nothing bad. Gave them a purpose in life. No, fuck that, I take your point. Any creature that can do that can—well, who knows what they can do."

"Agreed. And that whole visual telepathy thing is spooky."

"It's worse: they're evolving it."

"Huh?"

"They're evolving it."

"Again, and I'm quoting you here, Professor, Huh?"

"I saw them wage a war. An unnecessary war. No land was at stake. Survival was not an issue. They just picked a fight with the two most dangerous predators on the planet and fucked them over. Just to prove they could. And as a way of honing their killing skills. This is how the visual telepathy evolved. Through war."

"That's cool."

"But even so, they're a gentle species. Generous too. I think of Isaac as a friend."

"He's just a fucking bird."

"He's more than that. He risked his life for me." Saunders found himself strangely moved. *"It's a long time since I had a friend who*

would risk his life for me." As soon as he subvoced it, he knew that was a lie.

He had *never* before had such a friend.

Clementine saw the Rat-Insects swarming over her body and turned her armour heater on. The creatures burned off her back. But they kept swarming and swarming on her, trying to bite off bits of her body armour. Before long, her body was enveloped in biting insects, but she kept crawling, and crawling, and dragging her body across the ground, her lifeless legs trailing.

It was dark. Very dark. Hugo felt as if he was suffocating.

Clementine wept and crawled, and wept, and crawled.

So very dark.

Sorcha and Saunders sat by the shore of the tarn, and retracted their helmets, and felt the breeze.

"I used to love swimming when I was a girl," she said wistfully, "but most of all I would love to be able to fly."

"You could have the surgery done. It's quite safe these days."

"Maybe. When I retire. I could find a high-gravity planet."

"Like this one."

"Maybe like this one. Once we've terraformed it."

"Would you still do that? After all you've seen?"

"Why not?"

"I can't answer that."

"My great-grandmother was born on Mars. Are you saying that shouldn't have been terraformed?"

"I'm not saying that. But—" Saunders hesitated. "Well, those beach resorts, I always felt that was a step too far."

Sorcha snorted; she got his jokes far more often now.

"Things have to change," she said. "Planets have to change."

"People can change too," said Saunders.

"Nah, not so much."

"I've changed," Saunders admitted. "I'm not the same person I was."

"How so?"

Saunders thought very hard. "I used to be a shit?" he said, eventually, and Sorcha laughed.

"Changed how?" she taunted him, and Saunders realised that he loved her, as he had never loved any woman, as he had never before loved any other human being.

He had changed, and *that* was how.

And still Clementine wept and crawled, and wept and crawled.

And still Hugo, and Mia, and Mary, and David, and Tonii lay trapped and desperate beneath the dense choking earth.

Slimy and slithery and venom-oozing burrowing creatures crawled over their bodies. The soil itself coagulated and tried to crush them. Claustrophobia enveloped them and threatened to push them into madness.

And it was dark, so very dark, so very, terribly dark.

DAY 27

A Gryphon swoops and lands with a scrabble on a crag on the mountaintop.

And far above, far far above, a larger bird hovers. It is a Draven, with its black-jewelled hull, and it peers at the Gryphon like a hawk looking down from the clouds, and assessing a sparrow on a tree-branch.

The Draven flies too high to be visible from New Amazon even to the sharpest eyes. It floats at the outer limits of the atmosphere, almost in space. But its cameras and robot eyes can see everything that happens above the Canopy; and its infrared and X-ray vision allows it to see some of what happens below the canopy too.

The Draven's robot eyes can see the Gryphon land. They see the pebbles that are scattered by its claws, the colour of its ruff. They see the two humans who emerge from the cavern to greet the Gryphon, they even see the sweat on their brows.

In the cavern itself, nanobots lurk, they clamber on the rock walls, they perch on the ceiling. These creatures are smaller than a microbe, but large enough to contain a lens and a computer chip that can be controlled by a human mind. So when the humans go back in the cavern, eyes are watching them there too.

Hooperman's eyes.

"How was your day, Isaac?" Saunders asked.

The ground moves below the canopy above is vividly purple the ground approaches fast claws extend a basking creature with soft blue skin is caught up in claws and up and up and the creature is screaming and its head is bitten off in mid-flight then land on the canopy colours all around to eat, and eat, until only bones are left.

Saunders blinked at the overwhelming torrrent of visual information; it was like seeing a movie compressed into a millisecond.

"Great, sounds good, we spent the day exploring," he told Isaac cheerfully.

Isaac didn't move or respond.

So Saunders focused his thoughts, and remembered the events of the day:

Walking on rock, Sorcha in front, her helmet is up, she bounces like a spaceman on the grey rocks, there's the lake, blue and beautiful below, and rocks bouncing, feet scrabbling and then — {a time jump} — they are under the water, fish swimming around them, and {time jump} the bottom of the lake below and on the surface a coral reef with sessile fish with heads sticking out of the coral and the reef starts to move and swims away and it is huge, it is ten miles long but it moves.

"A Coral-Beast," Saunders clarified. "We took some samples from the rock it had been clinging too; it's mainly silicon-based. The largest silicate life-form I've ever encountered."

Isaac shook his head. He could hear noise, but he didn't know what it meant.

Saunders focused and remembered the images of the memory again: *a kind of coral reef inhabited by sessile fish with heads sticking out of the coral and the reef starts to move and it swims away and it is huge, it is ten miles long but it moves.*

Then he visualised, a letter at a time, the words:

CORAL BEAST

And then another mind entered his mind, and dabbled in his visual cortex, and spelled out the letters:

CORALBEAST IN WATER LIVES?

Saunders raised a thumb — spot on.

Isaac cawed.

The cameras watched it all; and Hooperman guessed at what had just happened, and marvelled.

When he was ten years old, Andrew Hooperman built a wooden replica of an ion-drive colony spaceship. It was a work of art, perfect in every detail. It even had pods inside where the colonists would sleep in Hibernation.

Hooperman had a flair for sculpture; he later whittled a life-sized replica of a lion out of mahogany, and kept it in his room. His parents were astonished.

At twelve years of age, Hooperman took a BSc in physics, and at fourteen he took degrees in history and biology and natural science. He was home-schooled, but never had a tutor; he learned everything from the computer.

When he was eighteen, Hooperman went to Oxford University to study under the great Carl Saunders, and found himself entirely deficient in social skills. He was shy, he was gauche, he didn't know how to talk to girls. He had, he was aware, an annoying whiny voice; and people used to go out of their way to avoid him.

So Hooperman applied himself to the study of human nature. By the end of his first year in Oxford he was a master of Western social mores, and had completed a dozen courses in self-improvement and how to make friends and influence people.

And still no one liked him. And still his voice was a whiny drone.

But Saunders had taken a shine to his precocious pupil; and the two men became fairly close. Hooperman never went down to the bar with the other eighteen-year-old students—all of them were struggling with their courses, while Hooperman already had four degrees and was doing an advanced DPhil in microbiological classification. But he also hated mixing with the other DPhil students, who were older than him, and jealous, and used to tell him lies about which pub they were meeting up in.

And so Saunders became Hooperman's only real friend. They talked about science. They talked about poetry (or rather, Saunders talked about poetry, and Hooperman swotted up). They talked about girls (Saunders talked about girls, while Hooperman listened, jealously). And they shared a passion for *life:* all the countless millions of species on Earth already discovered, and all the many thousands of species which had yet to be seen by human eye.

Other students accused Hooperman of having a crush on his mentor. And Hooperman didn't bother to deny it. For him, Saunders was a genius, a father, an inspiration, and a god.

Then they went on the damned Amazon expedition together, and it all went sour. Love turned to hate. Saunders, in the field, proved to be arrogant, dismissive, patronising and vain. He discovered a new species of millipede, and named it after himself, *Archispirostreptus saundersi.* And when Hooperman pointed out that this wasn't a new species at all, it was just a slightly differently coloured example of *Archispirostreptus gigas,* Saunders pathetically denied it, then mocked Hooperman in front of everyone. (Hooperman, of course, was later proved right.)

Looking back, this was the moment when the rot set in. Because, from that day on, perhaps because he knew he was in the wrong, Saunders treated Hooperman with open contempt. He patronised him, he belittled him; and he failed to acknowledge his genius. And then, when they got separated from the rest of the expedition in the depths of the Peruvian rainforest, things went from bad to worse. The two of them bickered and rowed constantly, and on several occasions almost came to blows.

And so, when they discovered the nocturnal hummingbird—which turned out to be the last species of non-microscopic land or sea animal ever discovered on Earth—Hooperman had decided to teach Saunders a lesson. He would abandon Saunders, take the bird, reach civilisation and claim the credit for himself. He didn't of course intend to harm Saunders—he just wanted to establish his priority, and have a chance to register the creature's new name as *Eulidia hoopermani.*

But it all went wrong. Hooperman abandoned Saunders, but then got lost in the rainforest and contracted malaria. He almost died. He was rescued by a search party—sent out by Saunders, on his return to civilisation! And then, to rub salt in the wound, he learned that Saunders had already named the new creature, on the basis of his digital photographs of the tiny bird. And he had called it, with mocking irony, *Eulidia hoopermani*. He'd named it after Hooperman!

Hooperman never forgave him for this act of boundless generosity.

And that was when the feud began in earnest. And it continued, shamefully, and notoriously, for decade after decade — the fist-fight in the Royal Society café, the libel case, and a host of similar disgraceful acts and deeds — until the fateful day when —

Ah! Here they were!

Hooperman's robot eyes saw Sorcha and Saunders emerge from the cave. They were heading back to the lake. There, he knew, they would swim in their body armour for a while, and explore underwater. And, as Hooperman also knew from his past observations, they would eventually succumb to temptation and swim naked, and then make love by the shores of the lake.

And when they did, Dravens would be watching from the edge of space; and nanobots from rocks and tree trunks nearby. And Hooperman would be watching them.

For Hooperman was everywhere.

His mind flitted from robot brain to brain. In his new state of being — this curious state of free-floating-consciousness, which left him able to inhabit robot brains — Hooperman had the powers of a god.

A capricious and a vengeful god.

Sometimes Hooperman wondered: Who was he? What was he?

But not often.

For these days, introspection bored him. These days, Hooperman had eyes, but he had no soul.

He had mind, but he had no flesh.

He had purpose — an obsessive vengeful purpose — but he had no point.

He had memories, but he didn't bother to explore them, unless they were memories of why he so much hated that bastard Saunders.

He was the distilled essence of a human being; he was mind without all the nonsense of humanity. His intellect was undimmed, his curiosity insatiable. He was, he vehemently believed, made up entirely of all the best bits of that thing known as "human".

He was Hooperman.

Hooperman is here, and he is there, and he is everywhere.

He is on the mountaintop eyrie, watching Sorcha and Saunders and the Gryphons.

He is buried in the ground, hearing the sad last words of Hugo and Mia and David and Tonii and Mary through his nanobots' ears.

And he is in the jungle, watching the Soldier Clementine trying to crawl back to the AmRover.

Clementine doesn't realise, although Hooperman does, that a herd of Godzillas is almost upon her. Her body armour is hard but the smell of blood is on her and they will chew and eat her and hurl her body around like a football and she is unlikely to survive the multiple traumas.

Hooperman knows this. He knows she will die soon, and he is beginning to repent.

He can see everything, he can be everywhere. But that doesn't mean he is always right.

He has the powers of a god; but that doesn't mean he *is* a god.

It occurs to him, suddenly, that even to think such a thing is an act of hubris, and self-delusion, and—dare he even think it?—madness.

And then he posits to himself, as a provisional hypothesis, that perhaps the shock of his "death" has made him temporarily deranged.

And that leads him to think about all the terrible things he has done since his mind entered the New Amazon system. And he concludes that, yes, he has indeed been acting like a psychopathic lunatic.

And then, guided by his own inexorable and exceptional powers of logic, he ponders too on all that he has done in the last two hundred years, during his blood-drenched pursuit of Saunders. And he comes to the conclusion that not only is he mad, and a danger to humanity, but he has been thus for centuries.

This insight comes as a devastating blow, for Hooperman has always prided himself on his rationality. He might, perhaps, arguably, be evil. But he has never believed himself to be *irrational*. So perhaps—

And at this moment, haunted by memories too terrible to be denied, the truth of his own guilt falls upon him like a house collapsing. Remorse consumes him. Exceptional, extraordinary, unprecedented remorse.

At this moment, too, conscience dawns in Hooperman. Like a universe coalescing.

How, he wonders, could he have killed so many? What kind of monster is he? And how can he atone for his sins?

Hooperman thinks for a long while, and then he works out what he will do. He decides how his redemption will be achieved.

He sends a Draven swooping down into the jungle where the five survivors are trapped under the ground. The Draven disgorges its cargo of DRscalpels. They swarm and ready themselves, then on his order they use an adapted surgical tool to dig out the earth. They are tiny creatures, but amazingly fast. And after some hours they have dug out a vast hole in the ground, in the midst of which dwell the exhausted and hysterical survivors.

A Humanoid DR swoops in and lifts them out. They are pathetically grateful and hysterical and spit soil into the air and vomit earthslugs and acclaim the DR as their "saviour".

Then the Draven flies with the five survivors in its cargo hold and hurtles through the jungle and lands beside their abandoned AmRover, and opens up its hold to give the five their freedom. They are visibly amazed, and delighted, and actually say: "Thank you." Hooperman feels a glow of triumph at what he has have achieved.

Then he drops a Humanoid DR into the jungle near the sixth survivor, who is still crawling with a broken spine. A pack of Godzillas is almost upon her. And now they *are* upon her. A Godzilla has her in its jaws, it is trying to crunch her. And then it swallows. And now she is inside the Godzilla, she has been eaten alive.

But the DR arrives just in time. It blows open the Godzilla's stomach and the Soldier's armoured body falls out and crashes to the ground. The DR then uses its explosive shells on these giant monsters. The carnage is considerable. When the shooting is over, it picks the unconscious Soldier up in its arms and flies her to the AmRover. And it deposits her outside the AmRover and bangs the sides of the vehicle.

Then the DR walks away, as Hooperman imagines deliciously the scenes of joy that will ensue.

All the survivors have been saved. Hooperman has saved them all.

He is everywhere. He sees everything. And he has done Good.

And now one of Hooperman's Dravens descends and deposits another Humanoid DR on the mountaintop eyrie colonised by the Gryphons. With Hooperman's mind inhabiting its robot brain, it flies to the lakeside, where Saunders and Sorcha are cavorting naked. And it waits, and Hooperman watches, with shameless delight.

And when they are done, Hooperman shows himself in his Humanoid Doppelganger Robot body and walks over to them.

"Hello, Carl," says Hooperman.

Sorcha looked up and saw the robot, and a gasp escaped her lips.

Saunders rolled over and he saw it too. A Doppelganger Robot, with a tall silver body, and a bizarre smile on its lips.

"Hello, Carl," said the DR.

Saunders cursed himself.

"Fuck," said Sorcha, counting the paces to her plasma pistol.

"Don't try it, bitch," said Hooperman DR, and she lunged for the pistol, and he tasered her. Her naked body twitched. She retched but could not spit the vomit from her mouth.

"Dear me," said Hooperman DR, drolly.

"Don't hurt her!" said Saunders. His pulse was racing. How could he have been so careless?

Sorcha sat up, and glared at Hooperman DR. The robot eyes stared at her neutrally, as if deciding whether to finish her off.

"I mean it. Don't hurt the girl. Just kill me and be done with it," Saunders continued, sincerely.

Hooperman DR laughed, but it sounded hollow and false.

"Is that what you really want?"

"No," Saunders conceded, as his courage starting to leach out of him.

"I'm not going to kill you," Hooperman DR said, in flat empty tones. "Not yet, anyway." And Hooperman DR smiled, in what was meant to be a comforting way, but wasn't.

"Then what?"

"I want you to apologise for what you did to me."

The sun was hot on Sorcha's bare shoulders. The mechanical man was tall and formidable, but even so cut a strangely forlorn figure. And Saunders seemed older now, tired. His skin was unwrinkled, but his soul sagged.

"I apologise, unreservedly, for what I did to you, Andrew," said Saunders.

"Not good enough!" roared Hooperman DR, and then the Gryphons flocked above his head.

"Is this your army?" taunted Hooperman DR.

Saunders thought an image: *the Gryphons flying away.* Then: *Hooperman DR firing plasma blasts, killing Gryphons.* The clearest possible warning. The Gryphons flew away.

"How did you do that?" marvelled Hooperman DR.

"What else can I say! I apologise! I bitterly regret what happened, what I did to you," said Saunders, passionately, and truthfully.

The silver DR studied him for a long painful moment.

"In that case," said Hooperman DR, "I forgive you." And he smiled an eerie silver-faced smile.

"You forgive me?"

"I do."

"No revenge?"

"I've had my revenge. All those people who died. Their deaths are on your conscience. That's enough for me."

Saunders laughed, relieved. He was safe! After all those years of running, all that fear, he was—

Guilt struck him, like a physical blow.

He remembered all those who had died. William Beebe, Django, Sheena, the other Noirs. All the hundreds of Scientist colleagues and Soldiers who died on New Amazon, plus the two librarians on Rebus who were caught in the cross-fire in a gunfight between Saunders and two DRs, and the passengers and crew who died in the plane crash on Paxton, and the dozens who died during the torpedo strike at Asgard. And he realised that they would all be alive if it weren't for him. His arrogance. His single-mindedness. His obsession.

How could he have been such a monstrous selfish fool?

"Oh you bastard," he snarled at Hooperman.

"You deserve it."

"They didn't."

"You brought it on them."

"I did. I did." Saunders was consumed with self-hate.

"And these birds. These Gryphons. You're fond of them?"

"They're an amazing species."

"You're uplifting them?"

"I'm giving them a helping hand."

"They could be a threat to humankind."

"I don't think so."

"Well, they might be."

"Yes," conceded Saunders. "They might be. But—"

Hooperman DR fired up his jets. "You've got twenty-four hours, Carl."

"For what?"

"To enjoy your dying days."

Hooperman DR flew off.

Saunders was pale.

"What did he mean?" Sorcha said, tensely.

"His final revenge. He's going to terraform the planet."

From the diary of Dr Hugo Baal

July 1st

An amazing thing has happened. We have been saved from certain death, just in the nick of time. Just as we had all sunk into total heart-wrenching despair. It's a miracle!

I therefore distrust it utterly.

Imagine my chagrin—more than chagrin, my absolute and total humiliation—when I tried to use my plasma gun to blow our way back out of the great big hole we were in. Only to find that the blast was being reflected back by the soil, baking and burning us.

Once we realised the plasma guns were useless, we tried to tunnel our way out of the soft, flaky soil. But that simply packed it even tighter around us. We were still all able to breathe, thanks to our oxygen implants, and talk to each other, via the MI-radio links. But my plan to save us from the acid rain had failed miserably. We were doomed to die of thirst and starvation deep under the ground.

It was claustrophobic too. The earth was packed around my mouth and nostrils, I was breathing in earth, and spitting out Hornbeetles and lord knows what other creatures. The touch of the soil was clammy. I could not see, I could only silently scream; but my silent screams were agony for my companions, since they could hear them via the MI link, and at one point someone threatened to use their stun setting to silence me.

One learns a great deal about oneself, when buried deep in the soil in an alien planet.

Desolation. Despair. Loneliness. I plumbed the depths of each of them.

And also Hope. Optimism. Joy. I explored those too. I am not, and have never been, a despairing kind of person. And hope—hope is important to me. I always hope for the best, it's just the way I am. And I always take joy in what I'm doing—my work, and, and, and—well, my work, and criticising the half-baked efforts of others, these are the things that always bring me joy. And optimism—that is my natural state of being. I always assume there will be an answer, a solution, a way through.

On this occasion, however, I could see none such. Despair was the only sensible course. And so I despaired.

After a while, I and the rest of the Buried Doomed began to talk to each other. We shared stories. We reminisced. And rather to my astonishment, no one reproached me for my error of judgement in burying us alive in such an astonishingly stupid fashion. No one carped, or niggled, or undermined me. And for that I was profoundly grateful.

After a while, we played the game of "Favourite Day".

But that got a bit boring because we all said the same kinds of things. The Scientists talked about their great moments of scientific discovery; the Soldiers talked about the great battles they had won. So then we played, "Favourite Day That Doesn't Involve Anything Scientific Or Any Acts of War and Carnage", and I remembered the day I rode my bike down the hills of Shadalia and the bike actually took flight and I was only seven years old and I thought it was marvellous. And it was a wonderful story to tell, because I'd never told it before, not to my father, not to anyone. It was a solitary joy, half-forgotten, and now I was sharing it.

Others had similar wonderful stories. And for a time there was a mood of camaraderie, a tenderness, a closeness.

After a few more hours, however, all that wore off. We all became very aware of the fact that we were BURIED ALIVE and would stay that way until we choked to death, or starved to death, probably in about four weeks' time, when our food and water implants ran out.

I slept and dreamed and talked in my sleep and they all shouted at me and I woke up.

I had some kind of New Amazonian beetle in my mouth, and I ate the fucking thing. What did I have to lose?

Someone suggested playing "I Spy" and that notion was poorly received, I mean, really, no one saw the funny side of it at all.

I began to hallucinate. I could see nothing, I had my eyes tight shut to stop soil or microbes crawling into my eyes, and after a while the floaters in my eyes began to obsess me, and then I started seeing multicoloured pillars of light. They danced, they whirled, they formed into new patterns. I was becoming hypnotised by my own hallucinations.

I let my mind disengage. I drifted. I thought about all the things I wished I'd done with my life, and most of them involved having friends, and that made me feel a bit pathetic.

Then the earth began to move.

We whispered to each other—was that really happening?

The earth moved again.

I wondered if we were about to be eaten by an earth-burrowing creature of some kind, but I chose not to articulate my fears.

Then the earth moved again—and suddenly we were free! Strong hands were pulling us up, at astonishing speed. We landed in a huddle on the surface, blinking into the light, five soil-baked near-corpses. And a silver-skinned Humanoid DR stood above us, surrounded by a miasma of DR scalpels. We looked at the DR in fear and dread, but he waved at us, cheerfully. This, we realised, was our saviour.

"I'm Dr Hooperman," said the Humanoid DR. "Greetings."

I stammered out some kind of response. Inchoate, incoherent, enraged, and pathetically grateful.

"You probably all hate me," Hooperman DR said, "for what I have done to you and your colleagues. But now, I'm glad to say, the fighting is over. You're safe." Then he threw us into the hull of a Draven and an hour later we were dumped outside the AmRover.

Then he left us. Filthy. Bewildered. Shocked.

We were no longer buried alive. It was a concept that took some getting used to.

And then we crawled inside the AmRover and into the shower and bathed together in a single sodden muddy heap. The alien soil we were covered in was seething with life, I had organisms all over me, and in every orifice. I had to boil them off, and did things to clear the orifices *which really don't bear recounting. But the pain was welcome. It made me feel alive.*

A few hours later Clementine was also deposited outside the AmRover by the Humanoid DR and his army of flying robots. We welcomed her joyfully. She was exhausted, crippled, anguished, but alive.

A miracle indeed.

But as I say, I mistrust miracles. I think this is Hooperman toying with us. No one else agrees, there's now a general mood of elation, and salvation. The consensus is that we should be glad that Hooperman finally came to his senses, and we shouldn't look a gift horse in the mouth.

But I disagree. Hooperman is a bastard; this is a trick.

And my initial instinct is to tell the rest of the party that they are wrong to be celebrating their release. That they are all just gullible, shortsighted fools—because it's obvious to anyone with half a brain that Hooperman is toying with us, like a cat with a mouse!

And I come very close to saying all this; and it is, I must concede, very much the kind of thing I usually say.

But on this occasion, I think twice, and I bite my tongue. For I realise that it would be crass to damage the mood of elation and salvation with my usual sarcastic tirade. Instead, I go with the flow; I drink the champagne; and I hug my fellow survivors, repeatedly, whilst drunk. Because I realise—they need this! And I need it too. We've been through so much, we deserve a moment of relief, a breathing space from all the horrors we have endured, however illusory our salvation.

However, secretly, I begin planning for a variety of worst-case scenarios. I believe it is essential for me to anticipate in detail what might happen next, so that I can plan countermeasures for every possible eventuality.

What, I wonder, could Hooperman have in store for us?

Sorcha got dressed. Her bruises hurt. Saunders was in a sombre mood.

"So that was Hooperman, huh?"

"Yeah."

"As you say, he's fucking nuts."

"Indeed."

"What are we going to do?"

"Sorcha, there's something I want to tell you."

They were clothed now, but not yet in their body armour. Their bodies sang with the cold and baked with the heat. Her arms were brown and muscled. Her eyes blazed with her usual wild energy.

"What?"

Saunders hesitated.

"I — it doesn't matter. Nothing. Forget it."

She glared at him.

He hesitated again. Then he kissed her. "You're a very special woman. That was it, that's what I wanted to say."

"You don't need to flatter me, you've already had your fuck for the day."

He grinned.

And Saunders looked at Sorcha, intently, at her radiance, her beauty, her youth. He exulted in her spirit, her *herness*.

"You do realise, it's the end of the world soon?" he said to her.

"Maybe," she said. "We'll see."

And her eyes sparkled with the anticipation of battles to come.

From the diary of Dr Hugo Baal

June 48th (cont)

I am busy drafting ways to defeat Hooperman, assuming that he is, as I fear and suspect, a duplicitous shit.

But there are many other pressing concerns that I have to deal with.

I'm worried, in particular, about Clementine. She is maimed, perhaps permanently. We don't have the resources to rebuild or replace her spine. I have to keep her confidence high, but some instinct tells me I can't do that by being nice to her. I have a hunch she would find that patronising.

So instead I constantly make rude and sarcastic comments about her pathetic failure to rescue us. I swaggeringly challenge her to a one-armed press-up competition (which she would win, by the way, even with a fractured spine), and she grins, and feels better, because I'm not humouring her, or pitying her.

And, I must concede, I'm fond of Clementine. There's a wonderful quality to her, and she is an undeniably attractive young woman.[1] And to be perfectly honest,[2] I never thought a girl like that would look at a tubby and annoying little geek like me.

But after all the horrors we've been through, I know it's now my job to protect her, to boost her confidence, to keep her strong.

And sometimes I think, though I may be wrong, that she actually rather likes me.

I'm worried, too, about Mary Beebe.[3] Mary is still, even now, grieving for her dead husband. But it seems to me that Mia Nightingale has fallen in love with her, and that Mary is encouraging it. In Mia's mind, she has already replaced William Beebe, and she is the new Mary's soulmate.

But my feeling is that Mary doesn't reciprocate.[4] She doesn't love Mia, she doesn't need her as a friend, she's not even bisexual. She's leading her

---

1 More precisely: tall muscular body, dark Afrocarib skin, lean physique, pert and gorgeous breasts, thick thighs, good posture, long black hair, oval face, grey eyes, a narrow nose, bushy eyebrows, long lashes, a few wrinkles including laughter lines around both eyes, no lobes on her ears, disproportionately large hands, bitten fingernails, and did I mention the gorgeous breasts and her lovely, laughing, soul-melting smile?

2 I'm not in fact being perfectly honest here, I'm just trying to be amusingly self-deprecating. Is it working?

3 If you really want to know Mary Beebe, you need to read her book on Silurian worms, *Silurian Worms, An Introduction,* which contains some of the most hauntingly evocative writing about subsoil life I have ever read. Also her article, "The Flame Beasts: Alien Beyond Belief", in *Solar Neighbourhood Science, vol. 4,555.* She and Dr William Beebe made a formidable team; he is a great loss to science, and to the world. (For an account of his life and work, click here.)

4 I have no evidence for this, of course, and it's possible I'm wrong. However, I've spent a lot of time studying Mary over these last eventful and traumatic days, and I feel sure that her relationship with William was no ordinary thing. I suppose the correct and precise technical term for it would be: "true love".

on, and there's a very good chance that Mia is going to get her heart broken.

It's not that Mary is deliberately deceiving Mia, or using her. She's just being—a little bit selfish, I guess, and thoughtless. And it's understandable: Mary enjoys having someone to talk to, someone who can banter as William did.

I do feel terribly sorry for Mary, and I know that it's my job to protect her.

But I also have to protect Mia. She doesn't deserve to have her heart broken, and I can't afford to have her morale damaged.

I must give more thought to the question of how to handle this delicate issue, without hurting either of these decent, honourable and yet unutterably lonely people.

And Tonii Newton, of course, is also extremely lonely. I increasingly find him to be a delightful man: beautiful, and courteous, and kind. Not like a Soldier at all really. But he's much too self-contained. He sees himself as some kind of new human, Homo omnis, but he's clearly subject to deep depressions and lack of self-esteem, and I honestly think that, unlike every other other Soldier in the galaxy, he actually fears death.

Tonii and I are fast becoming good friends. We play chess together; we are developing a nice line in chit-chat; and I can see his dawning realisation that, regardless of biology, and whatever sexual equipment one carries, everyone needs friends. And I would like to believe that, one day, I might be Tonii's friend.

David Go is one of the most interesting members of the party. To be honest, I never used to like David,[5] mainly because he's such a typical microbiologist and looks like a frightened rabbit; but now I admire him more and more. He's a quiet achiever, one of those people you never notice even when they're in the room, or the conversation, but who are able to make things happen, and who never get the credit for what they do.

All in all, David has a sensible head on his shoulders, and real

---

5 But I absolutely love his amazing reference work, *Cells: How they Work and Why They Need Us* (Walkley Press), which I have read six times, and is one of the greatest microbiological textbooks ever written.

integrity. But deep down, or in fact not all that deep down, he's afraid, and paranoid, and convinced that he doesn't "fit in". I have to find a way to integrate him into the group, and to draw out his better qualities. He has much to offer; he needs to know that he belongs, and that we care for him. So I've started teasing him, and letting him tease me. He enjoys that—I'm an easy target for his mordant sense of humour. And I would rather be mocked and treated as a buffoon, than allow one of my people to slip into depression and despair.

These are difficult times, for all of us; and I am weighed down by the knowledge that I have many challenges ahead of me. But one consolation is that I find I am no longer afraid of things. And that is because I can no longer afford to be afraid of things. I have too many responsibilities for fear to be an option.

For, you see, it's now my job, my role, my duty, to protect everyone.

The sky was black with birds. The Gryphons formed a huge cloud and in their midst flew Saunders and Sorcha.

They flew blind, held aloft by Gryphon claws, wary of using their body armour jets in case the flames burned their protectors. And as they flew, they heard a slow thunder around them. Occasional gaps appeared in their protective escort. Dying Gryphons screamed with pain and fell to earth, their bodies smashed open, blood pouring out of them in torrents.

Hooperman was firing missiles at them, to blow them out of the sky. And the vast Gryphon flock was absorbing the punishment of the plasma blasts and explosive shells intended for Saunders and Sorcha.

Saunders had conveyed to Isaac a vivid image of what would happen to their planet if Hooperman had his way: the death of everything, and all of them. And Isaac had passed on those same images to the rest of the Gryphons. So all of them knew what was at stake.

The Gryphons were fighting for their survival.

From the diary of Dr Hugo Baal

July 1st (cont.)
Where is Hooperman? On Earth? Is the Quantum Beacon still working? Or is he, as Mary Beebe once surmised, holed up somewhere on New Amazon?

I wish I knew.

I have completed my Worst-Case Scenario plans, which are detailed and bloody but rely a great deal on blind luck to save us from Hooperman's tireless robot killers.

I now consider there are three hypotheses which explain our current situation, with varying degrees of plausibility:

1) Hooperman has mellowed, and no longer wants to kill us.

2) Hooperman is dead, and someone else has control of the Doppelganger Robots. Saunders?

3) Hooperman is toying with us, as a prelude to ghastly horror of some kind or other.

After a healthy discussion with the team[6] it was unanimously[7] agreed that we should proceed on the basis of Hypothesis 3. Hooperman is toying with us; that's the proposition. The logical corollaries are:

---

6 I thought I would have trouble getting those idiots to listen to sense! But, in fact, nothing of the sort. Once the celebrations were over, David Go was the first to raise his concerns, pointing out that he didn't trust miracles. Clementine, though she was still in pain, agreed with his impassioned argument that we couldn't trust Hooperman. Mia chipped in with her own analysis of the dangers facing us, and proposed that we should travel to the Space Elevator and do battle with Hooperman's DRs. Tonii Newton agreed, and he pointed out that a leopard doesn't change its spots, which of course isn't true if you're talking about the Barsoomian Land Leopard, which can change its spots, fur colour, and body shape at will, but is a fair enough analogy in the circumstances. And then, to my surprise, Mary Beebe spoke fulsomely about how grateful they should all be to me for attempting to save them from the acid rain. I pointed out I almost got them all killed, through my idiotic idea of burying us alive, but she argued that without me they would have all dithered and panicked and been

i) *He will kill us soon.*

ii) *He will kill us in a way that is even more painful and horrible than dying of starvation and thirst whilst buried under the soil of an alien planet.*

iii) *He will also wreak some kind of havoc on this planet, out of sheer spite.*

iv) *We have to defeat him, or flee; but either way we need to get to the Satellite in order to stand a chance.*

v) *Hence,*

"Stop writing your journal and drive the fucking jeep!" roared Clementine.

Fair enough.
  To be continued.

---

flayed to death by the rain. She persuaded the group that I, Hugo Baal, was a fucking great guy to have by your side in a crisis, which is a comment that astonished me. Clementine kept smiling at me throughout all of this, which I found enchanting. Rather bolstered in my self-confidence by this point, I then showed them my Worst-Case Scenarios for dealing with Hooperman, including plans for using the three spaceships which (I had learned through assiduous searches of the database) were concealed near the Space Elevator, so we could fight Hooperman in space if need be. After hearing this, David Go patted me on the shoulder, and said: "This guy never ceases to amaze me," at which point I found myself getting rather emotional.

7 I was also elected President, I think, but that may just have been a joke, so I'm keeping quiet about it for the moment.

DAY 29

"*Oh fuck*," said Saunders, as they flew towards the Space Elevator. They had been travelling for two gruelling days, flying in their body armour over the jungle with their Gryphon escort without a break.

"*Why? What?*" Sorcha asked.

Saunders was staring down, looking at the Space Elevator Base Camp. He was transfixed by the sight, the awful, terrible sight, of the thing that was not there.

He pointed. And Sorcha couldn't see it either.

Because it wasn't there.

"*It's all over*," Saunders said, with utter weariness. "*Hooperman was smarter than us. We've lost.*" They flew closer and saw the AmRover. "*They're alive!*" said Saunders in delight. "*The others, they're alive.*"

But Sorcha didn't answer. She still was looking down, at the thing that wasn't there.

For the Space Elevator had at its base a small squat building, the Elevator HQ, which connected to the Satellite by a thick and almost unbreakable carbon nanotube cable, balanced many miles away by a counterweight cable that extended out from the Satellite into space. Cargo trucks and lifepods could be sent up and down this cable at will; it was the simplest and cheapest form of space travel ever devised, a simple wire-pulley system linking the ground and outer space.

But the cable snaking through the air like a beam of light reaching to the stars — that was the thing that wasn't there. Instead, there was just a vast pool of wire on the ground. Hooperman had cut the cable. He was already up in the Satellite.

They were too late.

Saunders and Sorcha entered the Elevator HQ. It was a cavernous building, with a glass dome offering views up to the sky above. The

Elevator had been built in one of the largest jungle oases, and above them was clear blue sky and a winking light—the Satellite.

Saunders was in a sombre mood; and he didn't much relish the prospect of a reunion with the last survivors of his scientific expedition. But he felt he owed it to his people to put a brave face on things.

So he fastened on his best, charming, self-deprecating smile, and confidently walked into the spartan HQ building.

Hugo Baal strode towards them, out of his body armour, his stout frame striding fast. "Professor," he exclaimed, and there was a light of joy in his eyes.

"*We're too late*," Saunders told him, through his helmet mike. "*Hooperman*—"

"We know, we know," said Hugo cheerfully. "Come through, we have a lounge. Major Molloy, delighted you survived."

"*We're too late*," Sorcha told him, bitterly. "*That means*—"

"Yes I know, I know," said Hugo, with a trace of impatience. "Doom, destruction, the end of everything. But at least we're out of that fucking hole, pardon my French. David! We have guests!"

David Go, the microbiologist, with his cautious rabbit's face, emerged into the central hall of the HQ, and greeted them. "We have air, you know, you don't need body armour," he said, gently.

"*I'll keep this on.*"

"Helmets off at least," said Hugo, also gently. They were joined by Private Tonii Newton, Dr Mary Beebe, Mia Nightingale and Private Clementine McCoy, in an exoskeleton.

Saunders shucked his helmet back and breathed air. "Where's Dr Kirkham?" he asked.

"Dead," Hugo said.

"Jim Aura?"

"Killed by Rocs."

"*Sergeant Anderson?*" asked Sorcha.

"Dead also," said Hugo mournfully. "You know, you sound like a tin man through that helmet mike. You're with friends now, come, come." Hugo was fussing in that annoying way he had. Saunders bit back a sarcastic comment. Sorcha sighed, and shucked back her helmet.

Hugo promptly raised a plasma gun and pointed it at Sorcha's head. Mary Beebe had a plasma gun pointed at Saunders's head. David Go, Mia and Clementine also had their weapons raised.

"Take your body armour off," said Hugo.

"Hugo," said Saunders wearily.

"Shut up, Professor," said Hugo. "Now, this is the situation, just to be clear about it: You are our prisoners."

From the diary of Dr Hugo Baal

July 3rd

We have arrived at the Space Elevator, and have been reunited with Professor Saunders and Major Molloy. It was really rather nice to see them again alive.

However, as a precautionary measure, we have taken them both prisoner pending a further investigation into the causes of our troubles on this planet.

So many have died, after all, and on the face of it, it does appear to be all Professor Saunders's fault. And if Major Molloy has allied herself with him, she too is suspect.

We would all, I feel, like to know the truth before we die. Because there's little doubt that we will all die, soon. There are no DRs left at the Elevator HQ, the compound was unguarded, and we have encountered no opposition. However, the Space Elevator itself has been sabotaged; the superhard cable which connects the planetary surface with the orbiting Satellite (TFS) has been severed. And we have no other way of reaching the Satellite. All the space shuttles in Xabar were blown up in the blast and subsequent fire. I had hoped to utilise the three other spaceworthy vessels that were hidden in a secret silo near the Elevator HQ, but Hooperman found them and they have been destroyed. I fear we are doomed.

The next stages are inevitable. The Satellite—the Horseman of Death, as some call it—will rain down destruction upon the planet, acting in concert with the three other Satellites which are in orbit around this planet. The oceans will burn, the atmosphere will ignite, poison torrents will drench the soil, and every last trace of life, every animal and plant and spore and seed and bacterium and nucleara cell and soil-based organism, all will be eradicated. Only when life is extinct will the nanonets fall and the process of oxygenating the dead planet begin.

I am familiar with the process; I have allowed it to happen on the many planets I have studied. This time it's different. This time I, too, will be rendered extinct.

Rather than morbidly obsessing about my imminent and terrible and untimely and unfairly soon death—oh my God I'm going to die!!!—I try to focus on more positive matters. I try to keep busy.

And this is one of the reasons we are staging a trial for Saunders. It's a way to keep busy; to spend our last hours in pursuit of the truth about what has happened to us.

Oh, I have asked Clementine McCoy to marry me, and she has said yes. Due to her injuries, however, it will be impossible for us to consummate our marriage before the heavens erupt and all life on New Amazon, including ourselves, is—no, no more of that! Stay positive.

Dr Mary Beebe has agreed to conduct the marriage service[1] and David Go will be my best man, but we don't even know if there will be time to marry, before—

Move on, Baal.

I've been studying the Gryphons.[2] They are remarkable creatures. They are intelligent tool-users, they are beautiful in flight, and they practise an extraordinary form of visual telepathy. I visualised to one creature an image of my mother, cradling me, when I was a baby. It reciprocated

---

1 She is a qualified Atheist Minister and plans to do a reading from *The Book of the Universe*, that wonderful atheist text about the joy and beauty of our universe, which of course argues that we should allow a magnificent wonder at the complexity and ultimate rationality of the real world to infuse our souls on a moment-by-moment basis, without dragging God into it.
2 Henceforth, *Gryphon sapiens*.

with an image of a Baby Gryphon ripping the infant Hugo Baal limb from limb. It was, I surmise, a joke, but it certainly shook me.

I would like to spend longer on this planet. There is so much to learn.

I would like to have a wedding night.

I would like to live.

However, none of these are tenable options; we will die very soon.

"Kiss me, Carl," said Sorcha.

And, still in his handcuffs, he did so, passionately, urgently, sadly.

Saunders was calm as he addressed the makeshift court. They were in the lounge of the Elevator HQ, and a coffee machine bubbled on the kitchen counter behind them. Clementine was stretched out on a sofa. Sorcha had sworn a parole, and had been unshackled. Saunders, also unshackled, was in an armchair, facing Hugo, who sat at a desk surrounded by papers, looking a little confused by his new role as judge.

"Right, let's get started," Hugo snapped. Everyone stared at him; what was the procedure meant to be?

"Don't I get a defence attorney?" Saunders prompted.

"No, that's a waste of time," said Hugo briskly. "Just tell us the truth."

Saunders nodded, hiding his amusement, and wondered if this court had the power to order his execution. And whether, if they did so, they'd be quick enough, and efficient enough, to execute him before they all died.

"I've told you the truth," said Saunders calmly. "Hooperman hates me. That's why he's killing all of you people."

Hugo glanced at David Go, somewhat at a loss. David nodded encouragement. So Hugo stared beadily at Saunders again: "Why?" he barked. "Why, I mean, does he hate you so disproportionately much?"

"Because I tried to kill him."

"Hah! We know that. The question is—why?" Hugo snapped again, abrasively.

Hugo was starting to get his rhythm now. And he rather relished inhabiting the roles of judge, jury, defence and prosecution, all rolled into one.

Saunders sighed. His body language was relaxed, his tone assured, but he was about to take an irrevocable step. He looked at Sorcha, her soft skin, her brimming energy, and marvelled at her beauty and her passion and her potential for rage. And he hoped that he wouldn't lose her. Not now, not after all they had been through.

"It was an accident," Saunders said, at length.

Puzzled looks hurtled around the room.

Hugo snorted. "You expect us to believe that?" he roared. "You put a bomb in Hooperman's book by *accident*?" David Go nodded approvingly at Hugo's lawyerly tone, and deft use of sarcasm. "You'll be saying next that—"

"May I continue?" Saunders interrupted. Hugo screeched to a halt, and nodded.

"The bomb," explained Saunders, "wasn't intended for Hooperman. It—" he hesitated, and then finally, after all this time, after centuries of lying, he told the truth: "It was intended for the Cheo."

There was a shocked silence.

The silence persisted, and evolved into awed silence.

And then—a roar of anger from Sorcha.

The others came to life. Hugo blinked, astonished. David Go instinctively subvocalised, audibly to all of them, "*Fuck.*" Tonii and Clementine braced themselves for what was to come.

"You evil bastard!" screamed Sorcha, more banshee than woman. "You swore to me, you told me—"

"I didn't think you—"

Sorcha leapt at him. Tonii stunned her with the taser setting of his plasma gun but she carried on moving. Tonii braced himself to shoot again.

But then the strength went out of Sorcha's legs. She crawled her way to Saunders. "Private Newton! Private McCoy!" she cried. "He's a traitor, kill him, now!"

Clementine didn't move.

Tonii hesitated.

Both knew, as they knew that air had to be breathed, that treason against the Cheo was instantly punishable by death. It was therefore their sworn duty to execute Saunders. Their every conditioned instinct told them both to draw their plasma guns and start blasting.

But neither did.

Tonii looked at Clementine. She looked back. She met his eyes and shook her head, and a silent vow was exchanged between them: *no more.* No more being a slave to their conditioning. No more being a vassal of the Chief Executive Officer of the Galactic Corporation. Those days were gone.

"Hear the man out," said Tonii. Sorcha was dragged back to her chair and shackled.

And Saunders told the tale.

"I discovered the first sentient species. The Lyra. They weren't beautiful creatures but they were profound. I had many friends among the Lyra, in the Galactic Zoo. I used to visit them often. They used to ask me Why? Why did we do what we did?

"Why did we destroy the Lyra? They were no threat to us. But we took their planet and terraformed it and killed every species that lived there and all but two dozen of the billion Lyrans living there. Then we followed their spaceships and destroyed them. We found their secret colony and blew it up with an antimatter bomb. This was all, you see, to pre-empt retaliation on their part. They might have wanted to take revenge for the destruction of their home world.

"The Lyrans in the Galactic Zoo were wonderful poets. I spent many days there, listening to their songs-made-of-words. I was fluent in Lyran, I caught every nuance. They spoke poems about great heroes and wondrous battles, although the Lyrans were herbivores who had never fought a single battle in the history of their entire civilisation.

"The Lyrans did not blame me for the excesses of humanity. But they did blame humanity. I tried to explain that humans are essentially decent honourable people. It was just one man who was doing all this! One evil dictator! Peter Smith! The Chief Executive Officer of the Galactic Corporation.

"*He* was to blame for everything. The murders, the rapes, the slave planets, the use of DRs to crush and colonise, the enforced whoredom of entire generations of people, the breeding of brainwashed Soldiers. He was to blame for every rancid bit of it.

"But the Lyrans firmly believe that leaders have no power if no one follows. And they observed that almost everyone in the human universe followed and obeyed the edicts and laws of the Cheo, and CSO, and the other members of the Corporation Board. Out of fear, out of duty, out of blind obedience. But follow they did.

"And I began to wonder—who should we blame most? The evil, or the good? For the evil are following their own nature. But the good—the people like us—me, and all of you—we just obey because we don't believe you can "beat the system". We are complicit in genocide, year after year, each of us, every one of you. You all have blood on your hands, not just the Soldiers. *All* of you.

"So I decided to make a difference. I conceived a conspiracy to thwart the CSO by saving an alien planet from genocide, just as I told you earlier. And I confided my plans in Andrew Hooperman. And, as you know, he betrayed me. So I bribed my guards to allow me to escape from Earth. And before I left, I conceived a new plan, a cold-blooded conspiracy to murder Dr Jeremy Marston, the Chief Scientific Officer of the Galactic Corporation, and all the other members of the Board. *Including the Cheo himself.*

"I planted nanobot bombs in the airconditioning of Westminster Abbey, timed to explode during a Board meeting when I knew the Chief Executive of the Corporation would be present. And for backup, I put a bomb in Hooperman's book of the Tree of Life, which he was due to present to the Cheo in person." Saunders stared at his accusers. "And I thought, with all of them dead, Marston, Peter Smith, the whole corrupt gang of them, I thought there'd be some chance to—no matter. I failed.

"You see, the nanobots were disabled by the Board's security systems. And the nuclear missile I launched from a warehouse on the South Bank of the Thames was blown out of the sky by satellite lasers. And Hooperman was snubbed by the CSO and the Cheo, and never got to hand over the fucking book to them. And so he went home and he was blown up by mistake, and you know the rest.

"I wasn't acting alone. I had a dozen co-conspirators, the best and the brightest and the boldest men and women in the world. None of them informed on me. All remained steadfast. Between us, we built the bombs and the nuclear missile and cracked the Cheo's security systems and we almost succeeded. But we didn't succeed. We failed. His empire is too great, his security too perfect, his Doppelganger Robots too powerful, his Soldiers too loyal. No one can ever defeat the Cheo; and so I predict his regime will prevail until the end of time.

"All of my co-conspirators were captured and, I don't doubt, died in agony. I managed to flee, and for centuries I have been fleeing. Pursued by the deranged Hooperman, but also wanted by the Cheo's secret police. I have lied to all of you and I feel no shame for that. I have deceived everyone, and I am proud of it. I am a failure in my life's mission, to make a better universe for humans, but I exult in the fact that at least I fucking tried. And that's my story. That is me."

There was another stunned silence.

"Why didn't you tell us all this earlier?" Mary Beebe said bleakly.

"Because Major Molloy and the other Soldiers would have killed me on the spot," Saunders said. "It's the first principle of the Soldier's Code: to protect the Cheo with their lives, and to kill anyone who threatens the Cheo. It's their conditioning. So I had no choice. I had to lie, to protect my life."

Mary turned to look at Sorcha, still shackled to the chair. Then she looked at Tonii and Clementine. "Is this true?" she asked.

"It's true," said Tonii.

"Yes," said Clementine.

"Yes," said Sorcha. "I'm sorry, but I have to kill you, Carl. The minute you let me go, I will execute you."

There was an extremely awkward pause. Then Mary looked back to Tonii and Clementine, who were both armed and body-armoured. "And what about you?" Mary asked.

"I — must," said Tonii, and wrestled with his conscience. "No! I owe no loyalty to the Cheo. Not any more."

"Clementine?"

"This is my tribe now," said Clementine. "What's done is done."

"Traitors!" Sorcha roared.

"Sorcha — please —" Tonii begged.

"Make a fresh start?" Clementine implored.

But Sorcha wrestled wildly with her bonds, and with her killing rage, and would not heed their words.

"Sorcha, I love you," Saunders said wearily.

Sorcha spat at him and fought to get free. She rocked the chair until blood dripped from her wrists, and still the bonds didn't break and finally she was still. She sat and glared at Saunders, her enemy, *thinking* her hate at him as if communicating with a Gryphon.

"And so *this* is why?" Mary said, in jagged tones, to Professor Carl Saunders.

Saunders was very aware that Mary had a plasma pistol strapped to her waist.

"*This* is why," continued Mary, "why William died? And why so many thousands of my colleagues died? Because of you? Because you tried to assassinate the Cheo?"

"Yes," said Saunders. "And I'm—"

She waved him silent with an imperious gesture.

And then she smiled.

A rare, exhilarating, crazy smile.

"Well, I'd say," said Mary Beebe, and her eyes were moist, "and I'm sure William would agree with me, that certainly is a cause worth dying for."

Hugo was cooking sausages over an open fire made out of laser-beam-severed Aldiss tree. The others were gathered round, sitting on the ground or on camp chairs. Sorcha sat nearby, cross-legged, silent, tethered with unbreakable wire, at what was considered to be a safe distance away from Saunders.

"This is nice," said Saunders.

The jungle was loud. The crackling of sausages merged with the sounds of insects and birds and monsters howling and screeching and cawing.

"Lull before the storm," said Hugo. He seemed calm, adept in his sausage cooking, attentive to the mood of all around him.

"It's going to be grim," Saunders admitted.

"Too fucking right," said Clementine.

"I feel—" Saunders broke off. He had a vision of bloodied bodies and corpses, and his guilt was starting to drown him. "I'm tormented," he said eventually, "by the knowledge that—"

"Have I ever told you," said Hugo, interrupting with panache, seemingly oblivious to Saunders's yearning to expiate himself, "about my first tour on a xenoexpedition?"

Saunders blinked. He had lost his train of remorse. All eyes were on Hugo, waiting for him to tell his story.

Hugo took his sweet time. He started serving up the food. Tonii got up and helped him. Clementine was able to use the exoskeleton of her body armour to move her arms and legs, but it made it hard for her to drink wine elegantly. However, she persevered. She drained her glass and smacked her lips.

"Nice wine," conceded David Go.

"Thank you, David," said Hugo, who had synthesised it himself.

And still they all waited for Hugo to tell his tale. It suddenly dawned on Saunders: this tubby little man had the whole group in the palm of his hand; he had them *captivated*.

They began to eat. There were no vegetables, just plant extract tablets, but the sausages were freshly thawed and delicious. Saunders sipped, and ate, and waited.

And finally Hugo began: "I cried, for six months afterwards," he said, still referring to his first xenoexpedition. And he let the pause linger for a while.

And then he continued: "After, that is, you know, the genocide."

They all nodded, sharing his pain. It was a moment of group catharsis.

"Which planet?" asked Saunders.

"Delphi."

"Swamp planet," Saunders recalled, and Hugo nodded. "The green warthogs," added Saunders. "*Biggus verdus.*"

"I apologise for that. I had some very jejune colleagues," said Hugo.

"Slimesnakes," Saunders continued. "Amphibious birds that could spend half the year in the ocean, half the year in flight."

"*Persephone aves,*" Hugo recalled.

"A beautiful planet?"

"Not especially. An unvarying habitat. Swamp and mud and muddy swampy ocean. Even the air was rich in colloid, it was like oxygenated mud. My body armour turned brown. But even so, I had a month of tears after I destroyed it all."

"Same here," admitted Saunders. "I've done it six times now. I had no choice. I was a fugitive. Science is my only skill. Each time it gets worse."

"I weep every time, too," admitted Mary.

"Such wonderful worlds. Ugly creatures. Beautiful creatures.

Gentle creatures. Savage creatures. Vile biospheres. Visions of paradise. But all different."

"Unique."

"Special."

"We destroy them all."

"And why?"

"We need the planets," said Sorcha stubbornly, from her position of tethered isolation.

"Don't you ever fucking listen to a word I say?" Saunders snapped at her.

"I listen, I usually don't agree."

"There should be a God," said David Go firmly. "For if there was, he would smite us down, as vile and evil murderous sinners."

"We are who we are," protested Clementine.

"Yes! We're animals," pointed out Sorcha. "We do what all animals do. We promote our own survival."

"Animals don't kill for pleasure," retorted Mia.

All the Scientists snorted at her naivety.

"Animals don't lay waste to other planets."

"They would if they could."

"Then we should be better. We should fulfil our destiny," Mia protested.

"We have no destiny," said Sorcha. "Except survival."

"Anyway," said Hugo. "Let's agree this much: it's a tragic waste to kill so much life. A deeply tragic waste," he repeated, with calm insistence. "And stupid. And immoral. And wrong." He stared at Sorcha fiercely, and finally she actually flinched.

"But not this time," Hugo added. "New Amazon must survive."

"Even if we could save the planet," scoffed Clementine, "it won't be for long. They'll send another expedition, they'll conquer us, they'll terraform. What's the fucking point?"

"It's the moral thing to do."

Sorcha and Clementine winced at his use of that word. But Tonii nodded; he agreed.

There was a howl in the distance, of a Screech-Lizard. An eerie song, as two Godzillas mated. Smoke from the fire billowed out towards the canopy of trees beyond the oasis clearing, and Saunders could swear he saw arboreals on the lower levels of the Aldiss tree trunk peering down at them.

"The real point," said Saunders shrewdly, "is do we want Hooper-man to win?"

"Fuck no," said Sorcha, suddenly changing her ground.

"No fucking way," said Clementine.

"Cream that mf," added Tonii.

"So, do you have a plan?" asked Hugo.

"Oh yes," said Saunders, chewing slowly.

They all looked at him. He'd been saving this moment up for some time, and it didn't disappoint.

Saunders milked the pause for as long as he dared. Then: "Yes," he said, "I do know a way to defeat Hooperman."

"Explain," said Hugo.

And Saunders explained. And they listened.

"That could work," Hugo said.

"It's a suicide mission," Saunders pointed out. "We'd need a volunteer." He waited.

"That's not a problem," said Sorcha, proudly. "I'm a Soldier. Tell me where I die, and there I will die."

"If we let you go, you'll kill me," Saunders pointed out.

Sorcha grinned. "Hey, that's a risk you have to take."

"It should be me," Tonii argued.

"No, me. I have less to lose," said Clementine, "because I'm a cripple." And a look of pain flashed over Hugo's face.

"No, it should be me," said Hugo, calmly, and they all stared at him, amused and sceptical. And Hugo stared them down.

"I'm willing to die," he said. "And I'm expendable."

Saunders smiled, and then realised Hugo was serious.

"I'm a zoologist, a taxonomist," Hugo continued. "But so is Mary, so is Professor Saunders, my skills aren't needed. But we desperately need all our Soldiers to defend us in the times ahead. And we need all our women, to create a new generation. So if you need a volunteer to die, then *I volunteer*. I have to, you see. Because it's my job. My duty. My imperative." Hugo blinked fiercely. "To protect my people."

Sorcha couldn't sleep.

All her life she had dreamed of a Glorious death. Her parents had died Gloriously, so had her brothers, and most of her friends from military academy had died Gloriously. She had never wanted anything more out of life than her own death.

But at the moment when Hugo Baal volunteered to die, Sorcha had been overwhelmed with…*relief*. She'd glanced at Tonii and seen the same look in his eyes. She looked at Clementine, and saw it there too.

Hugo was right, he was expendable. And furthermore, *he embraced his death*. Sorcha could smell his raw courage, and was in awe of it.

Because Sorcha herself had lost her faith, her creed, her will to die.

Everything she had believed in now felt worthless. When Saunders had cut her bonds, she'd had a chance to break his scrawny neck and beat him to a pulp; but she couldn't do it. He had kissed her on the temple, and she'd allowed it.

Her killing rage had vanished. Her loyalty to the Cheo now seemed futile. She remembered the wind on her hair, the touch of Saunders' skin on hers, and she didn't want to lose the chance of more moments like that. Traitor or not, she couldn't bring herself to kill him. In fact, quite the opposite.

And so, despite all her instincts, despite her own better judgement, she wanted to live—so very very much.

Mary watched Mia as she slept.

The two of them often shared a bed these days. They didn't have sex, but Mia had said she needed the company, and the comfort of cuddling, at this time of stress and horror. And Mary didn't have the heart to say no.

And in truth, Mary didn't mind having Mia in her bed. Anything to take the curse off her loneliness. She had no desire for Mia—no love—no fondness even. But it helped, a little bit, to have someone sleep beside her.

Mary stroked the hair off Mia's face, gently, so as not to wake her, and thought, as she always thought, about William.

Hugo Baal was eleven years old when he had his first microscope, and from that moment on he was lost in the joys of the insect world. He lived on a terraformed planet called Shadalia with no wasps or bees or scorpions, but a wealth of beetles, ants, millipedes and, most of all, butterflies. Hugo built his own wind chamber with magnifying-glass walls so he could watch the butterflies in flight, magnified to the size of birds.

Hugo's father was a bureaucrat, and they rarely spoke. Hugo's mother divorced her husband and her son when Hugo was five years old, and he never saw her after that. Occasionally she appeared on television, in her capacity as an Ethics professor, lecturing on family life, but Hugo never watched.

Hugo didn't have many friends until he was in his twenties, and even then they were all fellow Scientists, who were also emotionally withdrawn, many of them orphans. He had never married. He had never, in fact, been in love.

But in a century and a half of life, he had never been lonely, never sad, never dejected, never rejected. Because he had his thoughts, and his ideas, and his insects, and that was all he needed.

Until now. For now, he had a *family* . . .

Saunders was remembering Hooperman's first day as a graduate student. A tall, gangling, awkward wild-haired eighteen-year-old with bad skin and blazing energy. Hooperman had been late and had run up the stairs to the lab, and arrived dripping with sweat, and breathless, and the minute he walked through the door he started talking and he didn't stop for ten minutes. Saunders had been awed by his bravura and charisma, and by his absence of social skills.

Hooperman had been *so* annoying back then. And arrogant. And rude. He didn't care about anyone, or anything, except himself and the thought that happened to be in his head. They had all disliked him intensely. And no matter how many hints they dropped, Hooperman was there at every party, always in the pub, always buttonholing Saunders for advice, in his tedious awful way.

But Hooperman was also, it had to be admitted, the finest and most brilliant student Saunders had ever taught.

And once, a very long time ago, they had been friends.

Hooperman, or rather, what remained of Hooperman, was remembering the hummingbird.

The hummingbird was where it all went wrong. *That* was the real cause of the legendary feud that had sprung up between the two men. It wasn't the bitter quarrels they had during the Amazon Expedition, or the endless low-level bickering, or the sniping over food rations, or Saunders's constantly condescending tone. No, it was all because of a tiny creature like a will o' the wisp that haunted the shadows of the dense rainforest. For hundreds of years this creature had eluded all the naturalists who had sought in vain for new species.

And Hooperman was the first to see it.

But to his astonishment, Saunders had shamelessly and outrageously denied Hooperman's claim; he said that *he* was the first to see the bird. It was so tiny it was almost invisible but Saunders—so he claimed—sensed it, and saw it, and captured it.

This meant, of course, that he, Saunders, would go down in history, not Hooperman. Hooperman would become—well, a footnote.

And Hooperman knew full well that the world would believe Saunders's story, not his—because Hooperman was a nobody, and all the world loved and respected the great Professor Saunders. And he knew too that, because Saunders was faster to reach for his camera, the datestamp on his digital image of the bird would clinch and for ever prove his priority.

And that, looking back on it, that was the moment when Hooperman's love had turned to hate. For Saunders had lied! His mentor, his inspiration, his god, had lied to him. His insufferable *vanity* had made him lie.

And Hooperman could never forgive him for it...

That's when the hate was born. And when the bomb blew up in his study and Hooperman was turned into human wreckage, that's when the hate was stoked to a burning flame.

Hooperman wondered sometimes if it was hate that had kept him "alive" when Juno and the QB were destroyed. What else could have allowed his consciousness to exist independently of his body? Sheer blind hate?

It was a thought.

And Hooperman was certainly aware that in his new state of being he had a limited range of emotions. Intellectual curiosity, that was undimmed in him. Rage, and hate, yes, they flowed freely. But love? Could he feel love? He barely knew what it was any more.

Remorse and guilt, however, these were emotions he *had* felt, and was capable of feeling. These were the emotions that had impelled him to rescue those fools who'd buried themselves alive, and that poor Soldier who had been crippled.

But, as it turned out, these were pale, feeble emotions compared to hate. For at the moment when Hooperman had confronted Saunders for the very last time, by the shores of that New Amazonian lake, hate had filled his being once again. And he had felt all-powerful! Remorse, guilt, shame—these weaker emotions all vanished.

One emotion at a time, that was all he could manage most days.

So when that bitch reached for her plasma pistol—well, what else was he going to do? She threatened him, he tasered her, and hate possessed him utterly.

And now, that one emotion, hate, defined him. It made him what he was. It made him possible.

And thus, tragically, but exhilaratingly, all the humans now had to die! To feed the Hooperman hate.

Oh yes—"pride". That emotion still came upon him sometimes.

"Sorrow"…a delightful emotion. But no, sorrow, no, not any more. However—

"Regret"!

That was an emotion he *could* still feel, and now felt, as he primed the Satellite to commence its deadly terraforming process. A delicious, heart-gnawing, soul-searching regret, as he remembered the hummingbird.

Ah—mused Hooperman, with infinite regret—ah, what beauty it had possessed, that glorious hovering bird!

It was a bird designed to break your heart. Sweet, small, fast, mercury-silver in colour, with a haunting and barely audible song. It took them four hours to trap it. But, once inside a cage, its essence was gone. It was mere flesh and blood; it was no longer the will o' the wisp of the rainforest.

Catching it killed something; arguing about what name to give the damned thing killed something else; bickering about who saw it first killed everything.

If only, thought Hooperman, he had seen the bird and not said anything. Saunders would *never* have seen it, for it was as small as a flicker of light. And if Hooperman had kept quiet it might still, all these hundreds of years later, be undiscovered, unnamed.

And free.

"Will this work?" Hugo asked, anxiously.

"I hope so," said Saunders.

Sorcha and Saunders and David Go had jerry-rigged an apparatus that employed all the body-armour jets of the seven survivors, attached to a hardplastic rig that could be a worn by a single astronaut.

"All you need to reach the Satellite is escape velocity," Saunders explained. "This will give it. The jets in one body armour aren't powerful enough to get you here; but this should do it."

"It's a high-gravity planet."

"Yes, but this will give you a hell of a lot of acceleration."

"How long will it stay intact?"

Hugo looked anxious. Saunders shrugged.

"No idea. Hopefully, long enough."

"How long?"

"Twenty minutes?"

"Not enough," said Hugo, "to get me up and out of the atmosphere."

"He's bloody right, of course!" said David Go, exasperated.

"Maybe we—" said Sorcha, then ran out of road.

"I have an idea," Saunders announced.

Stars.

Planets.

Moons.

A flying creature, flying with the stars.

A Two-Leg flying, on fire. Flames coming out of body armour. Flying, flying, falling, smashing, body breaking up.

Then the picture vanishes.

Then:

A Two-Leg, flying, on fire. Flames coming out of body. Flying, flying. But also Gryphons flying. Carrying Two-Leg. Higher. Higher. Clouds. Wings flapping. Fire bursts from armour again. Two-Leg flies up high.

Two-Leg in stars, flying!

Saunders paused. He was exhausted with the act of visualising so precisely.

Isaac was twitching his head. Happy? Unhappy? There was no way to tell.

Then an image came into Saunders's mind that was painful in its immediacy. *Gryphons, a flock of them, flying high. Flying higher still. Flying among the stars.* Until finally, he saw: *Gryphons in flight in space.*

"No," said Saunders. "Not possible. You couldn't breathe. You couldn't survive."

But the image burned his retina: *Gryphons in space.*

"No...Ah!"

The image burned him. *Gryphons in space.* Saunders finally understood.

"Maybe," Saunders conceded. "Maybe, one day?"

And Saunders then did a wicked thing. He visualised a spaceship taking off from the surface of New Amazon. He zoomed up to the window. Inside the spaceship, comically, but credibly, was Isaac, and a score of other Gryphons, flying inside the vast spaceship in perfect formation. A Gryphon spaceship.

One day, maybe. And that day was all the more likely, now that the seed had been planted, now that the idea was in Isaac's mind.

One day?

DAY 30

"Come!" called Hugo. They all gathered and stared up at the sky.

"What?"

"Shooting stars. Twelve of them."

"It's begun."

"*Yes*," said Hooperman, in Saunders's head, "*it's begun.*"

"*Hooperman, don't do this,*" Saunders told him calmly.

"*Why not?*"

"*There's no need. No purpose. Why save my life, just to kill me now?*"

"*Because that's more humiliating?*"

"*OK then. If you want to kill me, then kill me. I've lived long enough, longer than I ever thought possible. But spare the others.*"

"*Don't go heroic on me now.*"

"*And spare the planet.*"

"*The planet! That's what this is about, isn't it?*"

"*This is a beautiful ecosystem. You can't kill all these creatures.*"

"*You mean, your talking birds? It's about your talking birds.*"

"*They deserve a chance.*"

"*They could be the next Bugs. The next threat to humanity. Is it true they are telepathic?*"

"*It's true.*"

"*Then I'm doing the universe a favour by killing them.*"

"*Please. I beg you. I appeal to your humanity.*"

"*I died thirty days ago, Carl. Whatever I am, I'm a long way from being human.*"

Saunders felt a shudder run down his spine.

The earth shook and the Canopy burned. The Four Satellites were in alignment over the globe. The terraforming had begun.

Hugo prepared himself. He stood in a circle with the rest of the team. The various time-honoured rituals were performed. The Soldiers spat at him and touched fists with him, and shouted "Glory!" The Scientists shook his hand, avoided eye contact and muttered platitudes.

"I'm ready," said Hugo.

"Die well," said Sorcha.

"Die well," said Tonii.

"Go fuck Hooperman," said Mary.

"I will," said Hugo. The knowledge of his destiny was exhilarating; Hugo felt more alive than he had ever done before.

Saunders sat down with Isaac, and prepared himself to die.

He wasn't sure when he had made this decision. Last night, as he lay awake, brooding? Or in the morning with the glorious dawn?

But he was sure of what had to happen next. He had to die.

Because he'd seen the man Hugo had become. He'd observed, with astonishment, the way Hugo now inspired and unified the group. The way that tubby little man had given hope to Clementine, with her broken body, and how he energised and motivated Tonii, with all his hidden insecurities, and motivated David, and comforted Mia, and looked out for Mary. Even Sorcha had fallen under Hugo's spell. She had been traumatised at the discovery that Saunders had tried to kill the Cheo. And she'd been even more traumatised at her subsequent inability to kill Saunders for his treachery.

And as a consequence, Sorcha had been on the verge of sinking into a deep and irrevocable depression. Saunders could see it happening, but was powerless to help. For suddenly, Sorcha stopped being Sorcha; instead she was listless, and rambling, and self-pitying. But every word of sympathy Saunders uttered seemed to make her self-loathing worse.

Hugo, however, had totally and cheerfully ignored Sorcha's

melancholic state. He had offered no words of kindness or s thy; instead, he had teased her and mocked her and insulte inventively. He even did an occasional silly little dance. And So ha had been baffled by him at first; then amused by him; and then, well, fond of him. And then she stopped hating herself and was able to laugh at herself, and at her own crazy conditioned obsessions.

And then, once again, she began to embrace the glorious moment of each moment.

Hugo did all this! And Saunders in consequence was in awe of him. And Hugo was also a brilliant scientist, and he was about to be married to Clementine, and they deserved each other.

So Saunders made his decision: this man shouldn't die. And none of the others should die either. Enough innocents had been killed already.

It was time for Saunders to take his turn, to do penance for his sins. And now it began.

First he conjured up a mental image of *himself being carried through the sky by a Gryphon.*

Isaac cawed. He projected the same image back at Saunders; that meant the answer was still yes.

Then Saunders cawed, a low rolling cawing sound that tickled the back of his throat. It was a perfect impersonation of the sound that the Gryphons used to imply urgent temporal imperative; in other words, it was their sound for *Now!!!!!*

"Let's go," said Saunders, and Saunders got up, and he ran.

The mega-exoskeleton with the seven rocket jets was stored inside the AmRover. Saunders let himself in, and strapped himself into the contraption. His own body armour would protect him from the heat. His oxygen implant would allow him to breathe. All he had to do was get up high.

Then he stepped out of the AmRover, bulky and rocket-armed, and looked up. The sky was black with Gryphons. Isaac had done his work well.

Saunders flashed an image at Isaac: *Saunders in flight.* Isaac sent the same image to the other Gryphons. And the Gryphons descended in formation. A half-dozen of the birds took a firm grip of the flying structure. Saunders braced himself. The Gryphons flapped and flew upwards, and Saunders jerkily took off.

And in this fashion, Saunders was carried up into the atmosphere, on his technological chariot.

The birds cawed as they flew, singing brutally in unison. And they shared a vision, an image that appeared in all their minds:

A star, a bright star, burning over the planet.

Hugo looked up and saw a dot.

"What the fuck?"

"Can you hear me, Hugo?"

"I hear you, Professor. Where are you?"

"Look up."

"That's you?"

"That's me. I'm on my way to the Satellite."

"What the—How did you—"

Hugo realised what Saunders had done.

"You can't do this," Hugo screamed subvocally. *"I volunteered. It's my martyrdom."*

"Don't be such a drama queen, Hugo. You're needed down there. I've had five hundred years, I'm all worn out."

"But—"

"Come back, you bastard!" screamed Sorcha, as she realised what was happening.

"Thank you for those kind parting words."

"I mean it! You shouldn't be doing this."

"Humour me, Sorcha. This is the first altruistic thing I've ever done in my entire life."

"Then don't do it. Come back. You can't die!"

"Everyone dies, sometime. Love you, Sorcha. Goodbye."

"Carl! Carl!"

" *'Love you, Sorcha. Goodbye.' That's a hint by the way. You're meant to say—*"

"*You fucking fool.*"

"*Near enough. So—*"

"*I love you, Carl.*"

He cut the MI-radio link.

Isaac and the other Gryphons flew as high as they could, to the upper limits of the atmosphere, carrying their human passenger. By now they were gliding upwards on thermal currents. But the air was getting thinner. Flight was becoming impossible.

Saunders visualised *Isaac releasing him*, and Isaac and the other Gryphons released him. He fired up his seven rocket jets, initially at their lowest setting, then he slid it up to maximum and was crushed by acceleration. He roared up into space, towards the stars.

The thrust ripped and bruised his body and hurled him upwards. If it weren't for the body armour he would have been burned alive. But instead, he shot up high, through the troposphere, into the cold vacuum of space. Then a rocket jet fell off. And other. The sheer power of the acceleration ripped the makeshift contraption into pieces. He hurtled onwards like a car falling to pieces under the pressure of its own speed.

Then the final rocket died. He ripped it off by hand, the heat seared his gauntlet, and he tumbled weightless in space. Stars were all around him. He'd achieved escape velocity, and he was well above the planet's gravity now, in free fall.

He still had one set of rocket jets, the ones on his body armour, and they were enough to nudge him forward towards the Satellite. A tiny puff of power, a tiny puff more, and his velocity grew, and grew. He didn't fly, he fell fast through space, in the direction of the Satellite, a shining dot in the blackness, which grew larger, and larger, and larger.

Hugo revealed the locked and concealed cabinet in the AmRover and passed around the champagne.

"There's nothing to celebrate," said David Go glumly.

"No," said Hugo. "But if the Professor fails, I intend to die drunk."

As Saunders soared towards his destination with effortless speed, he felt at peace. He had waited a lot of years for this moment. The moment of impending, certain, painless death.

Saunders had loved many women, and even a few men, and he had married often. He had made many friends, and shared confidences with them, and he had loved them as friends, and they had loved him back. He had two younger brothers still alive, and parents who had lived into their two hundreds and who had been devoted to him.

It all meant nothing.

Only Hooperman mattered.

For Hooperman held a unique place in his heart. Hooperman was more than a friend, more than a colleague, more than a father, more than a lover, or a wife, more than anything.

Andrew Hooperman had for all these years been his *enemy;* and between men like Hooperman and Saunders, there was no closer bond.

"Carl, nice to see you."

"Fuck you, Hooperman."

"I can see you coming. You're a sitting duck."

Saunders fired his plasma cannon at the Satellite, from far too far away.

"What a joke. How old are your eyes, Carl?"

"Fuck you, Hooperman."

"Fuck you, 'Professor Hooperman', if you please."

"It ends here," said Saunders, flying at full acceleration towards the Satellite. It was a long, slow charge and Saunders was getting bored. But he held to his course, and he thought about the ironies of life, and he found himself drowning in amusement.

Hooperman fired a hail of plasma fire at Saunders. The body armour held. More plasma fire. The body armour held. But it was getting hot. Then the armour started to melt.

A few more minutes and Saunders would be dead.

"Ha!" A feeble last word, but it was all he could manage.

Saunders went nova, and the Satellite exploded.

Isaac cawed, as a new star was born in his sky.

Sorcha stared up at the new star, her heart broken. She looked at the bewildered Gryphon, and she projected an image of *Saunders exploding into fire.*

Isaac cawed. He understood.

Carl Saunders had died to save them all.

For Saunders had been wearing, strapped to his body, the Bostock battery that powered the AmRover. Enough potential energy to power the planet for an entire twelve months, released in tiny degrees via the battery's filter circuit.

But the battery's filter had been disabled, and when the flame from the plasma bursts ignited Saunders's body armour, the power in the battery was released all at once. The vast reserves of energy in the battery erupted in the space of half a second, and Hooperman and the Satellite were engulfed.

Sorcha stared up at the nova, baffled by grief. Saunders had died, and she still lived.

Why? *She* should have died. That was her job, her role, her destiny, to die a Glorious death. Why had she failed to fulfil her own destiny?

Sorcha remembered:

- Saunders happy, smiling. Arrogant. Funny. Marvellous.
- Saunders angry, glaring. Arrogant. Dangerous. Marvellous.
- Saunders fucking her, slowly and carefully, his face alight with delight.

She would miss him. That was her tribute to him. Her special homage.

For she had never before, in her entire life, missed anyone.

Space was ripped and torn by the blast. The wreckage of the Satellite drifted in orbit around New Amazon, with some of the blackened remnants spiralling down as shooting stars.

New Amazon was a dense green globe floating in black darkness, with tiny pinpricks of blue peeping through the branches and leaves of the Ocean-Aldiss-Tree. Tens of millions of species thrived on this planet. It was rich, it was fertile, and it now had a future.

Then, in the deep darkness of black space encircling the verdant planet, came a sound, a voice.

"Can you hear me, Carl?" Hooperman's voice whispered.

And out of the blackness came an echo.

"Yes," Saunders said. *"But—"*

"Where are you, Carl?"

"You know, I've been wondering about that."

"Nowhere, that's where!"

"Not possible."

"Possible."

"Then—"

"When you die, Carl, something remains. Even when there is no human body, even when there is no robot brain to act as the repository

*for the human mind, something remains. Not much. Just this. And I
don't know for how long."*

"Ah."

"Indeed."

"A presence."

"A spirit."

"So what do you think—"

"Wait! I can sense—"

"What?"

"I—I have a feeling that I don't have long. Not long."

"Andrew?"

"Goodbye, Carl."

"Andrew?—" But Hooperman's voice was gone, for ever.

"Andrew!" Saunders screamed. "Andrew! Don't go!"

No one had ever liked Andrew Hooperman.

But at the moment of Hooperman's death, Saunders missed him,
terribly, and mourned him, deeply. And he wished, looking back,
that they could have been better friends.

He wished, too, that they had never fought, or feuded.

And he wished, with all his heart, that so many innocents had not
died.

Then Saunders finished mourning, and he wondered how long he
was going to survive.

But one thing was for sure: he was going to enjoy it while he
could. So he willed himself to move and he moved.

He willed himself to fly through the atmosphere of New Amazon
and he flew.

He willed himself to exist in the trees, in the animals, in the
plants, in the plant-animals and animal-plants, in the semi-sentient
clouds, everywhere, somewhere.

And though he existed in all those places, all at the same time, the
special thing that made him "him" remained intact. A pinprick of
consciousness, enveloped in more than half a millenium's worth of
memories. But for how much longer?

"*I think,*" Saunders thought, "*therefore —*"

He let the thought drift. He expected death to creep up on him. He waited for it, for the creep of death.

But death did not come.

Hope started to twitch.

He let himself drift. He flew through jungle and into Flesh-Webs and down into the soil and back again, then he flew into the air and saw Gryphons flocking and he flew through them but they couldn't see or feel him or in any way acknowledge his existence.

Saunders realised, this could get very boring.

But then it occurred to him, boring was *so* much better than dead.

He wondered: was he immortal?

And he decided to linger on the joy of every moment. For that was all he had, for now, and for ever, or at least until that instant when his consciousness was extinguished.

He could see, but he couldn't feel, he couldn't touch, he couldn't speak, he couldn't communicate. He *was*, but he had no *why*.

And yet, this was a marvel, and a wonder. For Carl Saunders had evolved into a jewel of consciousness in an ocean of moments, surrounded by a planet of extraordinary beauty and varied marvels.

And as the truth of his situation became vivid to him, and as he thought about the implications of his strange state, his curiosity started to stir and twitch, and to nudge up against hope.

What would happen on this planet, in the many years to come? Would the Cheo send more troops from Earth? Would Sorcha defend New Amazon, as he had told her to? Would he live long enough to see the Gryphons evolve? Would he see them becoming tool users? Would he see them become a spacefaring species?

And would he see Sorcha and the other survivors build a new civilisation?

Would he see Sorcha fall in love again, and have children, by some other man? Would he have time for all that? Could such a thing be possible?

And, Saunders wondered, what if —

APPENDIX 1

GALAPEDIA
The Free Encyclopedia

Terraforming

From the *Galapedia*, the free encyclopedia for all sentient species in the Solar Neighbourhood and beyond.

Terraforming ("Earth-shaping", from the Latin *terra* + form) of a planet, moon or other body is the process of making it inhabitable for human beings by altering its atmosphere, temperature, surface topography or ecology to be similar to those of Earth. The word itself was invented by science fiction writer Jack Nicolson in his 1942 story "Collision Orbit" and later in a series of stories published as *Seette Ship* in 1951. SF author Roger Zelazny pioneered the use of the word "worldscaping," though it never caught on; and some scientists prefer to refer to the process as geoengineering or ecopoiesis (the creation of an ecology that did not previously exist, but not necessarily resembling that of Earth).

The terraforming of the Earth Solar System was a slow process, costly in human lives. It took a century to terraform Mars and 150 years to terraform Venus. However, the development of nano-technology and the development of the Bostock battery has made it possible to terraform a planet in less than 20 years.

The standard terraforming technique, known as TFX, involves the use of four terraforming satellites in orbit around the target planet. (These are sometimes colloquially referred to as Horsemen—Horseman 1, Horseman 2, Horseman 3, Horseman 4—for reasons lost in the mists of time.) Each TFS (Terraforming Satellite) will drop Nanonets over every part of the globe which then begin the process of transforming the planet's atmosphere into an 80 per cent nitrogen/20 per cent oxygen blend. The nets are designed to self-replicate, releasing billions of micro-organisms which are bio-engineered to absorb <u>almost any gas</u> and turn it into an Earth atmosphere blend at a prodigious rate until a breathable atmosphere is achieved; at which point a negative feedback loop will deftly kill all these engineered micro-organisms.

As part of this process, each Horseman will rain down upon the target planet poisons and non-radioactive fusion missiles in order to purge the target planet of all indigenous life-forms, even extremophile bacteria. This is in adherence to <u>CSO's Guidelines 40 a (i)</u>, which states that human settlers should never have to face the threat of being attacked by alien life on a terraformed planet, as occurred on <u>Meconium</u>.

In the case of planets that are too hot or too cold or have other geographical defects (such as an excessive tendency towards <u>vulcanism</u>, <u>earthquakes</u>, <u>tidal waves</u> or <u>comet strikes</u>) or that <u>rotate too fast</u> or <u>rotate too slowly</u>, or <u>have too many suns</u> or have <u>annoyingly small suns</u> or <u>outrageously over-active suns</u>, then more radical techniques of <u>planetary and astrophysical engineering</u> will be required. These include:

- <u>Solar Acceleration</u>: throwing fusion bombs into a sun to make it burn more brightly.
- <u>Orbital Adjustment</u>: hurling huge great missiles at a planet in order to change its orbit by small increments, or by a lot. It is generally considered wise not to inhabit a planet that is being orbitally adjusted.
- <u>"Tidying up the backyard"</u>: hurling missiles and bombs and antimatter bombs at moons and asteroids and planetary rings that may be creating undesired tidal forces or which make the region of space around the planet look messy.

In the case of planets that already have a breathable atmosphere, the terraforming process is much simpler, and consists simply of the <u>extermination</u>, <u>extinction</u> and <u>annihilation</u> of all indigenous life, sentient and non-sentient, using all the techniques of planetary genocide available to the Horsemen.

Strict protocols exist (see <u>CSO's Guidelines 457 b (viii)</u>) to ensure that full scientific analysis and studies are performed on any and all alien species which are to be rendered extinct. Key specimens are of course stored in embryo form or allowed to roam free in one of the many excellent Galactic Zoos.

Contents

[edit] History of scholarly study

It has been suggested that *Planetary genocide* and *Mass Extinctions* be merged into this article or section. (Discuss)

APPENDIX 2

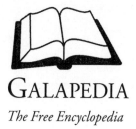

GALAPEDIA

The Free Encyclopedia

Carl Saunders

From Galapedia, the free encyclopedia for all sentient species in the Solar Neighbourhood and beyond.

Carl Saunders

Photograph no longer valid after face transplant	
Born	4 January 2301
	Croydon
	Greater London, England
Died	Not yet
Residence	Unknown due to fugitive status
Nationality	English
Fields	Zoology, taxonomy, geology, mathematics, poker
Institutions	University of Oxford
	Royal Society
	Institute of Zoology
	Croydon Poker School
Alma mater	Jesus College, Oxford
Doctoral adviser	Paul Bostock

Doctoral students	William Whiston
	John Wickins
	Geraldine Pournelle
	Nigel Burt
	Andrew Hooperman
	Jane Shillaker
	Angela Shillaker
	Robert Butler
	Carlo Dusi
	Lisa Neeley
	Emma Adams
	Alliea Nazar
	Felicity Carpenter
	Kurt McLeod
	Elizabeth O'Halloran
	Brian Dunnigan
	Many More
Known for	Encyclopedia of Alien Life
	Theory of accelerated evolution
	Attempted murder of Andrew Hooperman, colleague and former student
	Creation of the first human–dinosaur chimaera (Timothy Blake, see GW entry here.)

Carl Saunders FRS is an English naturalist, explorer, professional poker player and xenobiologist. His *Encyclopedia of Alien Life* is said to be the greatest single work in the history of natural science. In this work, Saunders describes every species and genus of animal and plant and single-cell life on every planet ever explored by humanity. Saunders describes and classifies each species he encounters in meticulous and relentless detail, and yet also magically conjures up a sense of the alien creatures' habitat and lifestyle and psychology in a prose style that is hauntingly evocative, and sinaesthetically vivid, and emotionally overwhelming, and spiritually compelling, and truthful, and sublime, superb, delicious, and witty, and verbose, and prolix, and strangely addictive.

His diligence as a classifier and alien "twitcher" is matched by his phenomenal theoretical expertise. He is the founder of the theory of accelerated evolution which has made possible the creation of the four key subspecies of humanity, namely Lopers, Cat People, Vacuum Dwellers and Computer Brains, and is also a pioneer of the microbiological 22-digit classification system for life, which he later disowned because he felt it lacked "soul".

Saunders's career has been marked by controversy, chiefly relating to his long and bitter feud with fellow naturalist and xenobiologist Andrew Hooperman. Rumours abound that Saunders left Hooperman for dead after a violent drink-fuelled altercation during their legendary Amazon Expedition, though Saunders has always roundly denied this, claiming instead that Hooperman is a "ludicrous fantasist", a "buffoon" and a "fraud".

According to Hooperman, the two scientists became separated from the rest of the party and trapped in the depths of the rainforest. During this time together, the two men jointly discovered a species of nocturnal hummingbird which they named *Eulidia hoopermani*. Elated by this triumph, the two men celebrated by drinking half a litre of 100-year-old malt whisky from Hooperman's flask. Hooperman passed out, and when he recovered Saunders had fled, taking with him the hummingbird and all the supplies.

Hooperman, with rare courage, according to his own vivid accounts, struggled through the rainforest, despite contracting malaria and suffering extreme dehydration and hunger. When he reached civilisation he was nursed back to health by kindly nuns. And on recovering consciousness, he immediately wrote an account on his blog of the whole tawdry betrayal, which was widely reported by the print and internet press and was the basis for a dire TV movie called *Deadly Feud in the Forest*.

Saunders, by contrast, argues that Hooperman's account is bollocks, the product of a crazed mind. According to Saunders, the whisky they drank was 25 years old, not 100, and they drank in moderation. During the night, however, Hooperman crept away carrying the hummingbird. When he finally awoke—after his usual deep and untroubled sleep—Saunders was amused at the joke, and cheerfully strolled fifty or so miles to civilisation. There he was dumbfounded to learn that Hooperman had accused him of attempted murder. Saunders further argued that his subsequent treatment at the hands of the Peruvian police was brutal and unfair; but his allegations that police officers took bribes from Hooperman with an instruction to "give the bastard a walloping" were never substantiated.

Many books have been written about this notorious affair, including *Deadly Feud: How Saunders Betrayed Hooperman* by Robert Hooperman, the scientist's adopted son, and *Nature Red in Tooth and Claw: the Hummingbird, Saunders and Hooperman,* by Arnold Michaelson.

The controversy heightened when, after years of rivalry between the two men, Hooperman published his essay "J'accuse Carl Saunders", in which he accused his former mentor and colleague of falsifying data about alien species and plagiarising the work of others, notably Hooperman himself. Saunders subsequently took out a libel action against Hooperman. In this celebrated legal action Saunders chose to represent himself, and after forty consecutive days in the witness stand, talking eloquently and swiftly and entirely without notes, he succeeded in refuting every allegation made against him and won substantial damages. Hooperman was forced to self-publish a humiliating rebuttal of his wholly fallacious and malicous accusations, entitled And Yet It Moves.

The enmity between these two scientists erupted into violence when Hooperman was nearly killed by a bomb inserted in the cover of an illustrated edition of Hooperman's much-acclaimed Hooperman's Tree of Life. Police quickly identified Carl Saunders as the chief suspect, after discovering an email sent to Hooperman in which Saunders wrote: "Serves you right, you evil bastard! You deserve to die!"

Carl Saunders is currently a fugitive from the law and faces the death penalty. His Encyclopedia of Alien Life, however, continues to be updated online, thanks to the thousands of researchers, many of them former students of Saunders, who have dedicated themselves to continuing his work.

Contents

extras

orbit

meet the author

Credit: Charlie Hopkinson

PHILIP PALMER's first novel was *Debatable Space*, but he has previously written for radio, television, and film. He lives in London. Find out more about Philip Palmer at www.philippalmer.net.

introducing

**If you enjoyed
RED CLAW,
look out for**

BELLADONNA
by Philip Palmer

The Cop was in a cheerful mood. The sky was a rich blue. The twelve moons of Belladonna shone like globes on a Christmas tree in the daytime sky. He could smell orchids.

He was one-day old. He would, his database warned him, grow more jaded with the passage of time. But for the moment, life felt good.

It was a short walk from the spaceport to the crime scene. He was in constant subvocal contact with the Sheriff, Gordon Heath, and the crime scene photos scrolled in front of his eyes as he walked. But the air was fresh, and the orchids were fragrant, and so were the roses, and the hollyhocks, and the grass. The Cop registered felt a faint stirring of remembered regret.

"I'm Sheriff Heath."

"I'm aware of that," said the Cop.

"Pleased to meet you too," the Sheriff chided, and the Cop registered the hint of irony, but decided it would be politic to ignore it.

The Cop and the Sheriff were standing outside a twelve-storey hotel made of black brick with a spire that touched the sky. Police officers had cordoned off the area with holos proclaiming POLICE and MURDER SCENE—KEEP AWAY. Pedestrians on moving walkways were gawping as they swept past, thrilled at the glimpse of a terror that had passed them by.

"Sheriff, feel free to call me Luke," the Cop added, in a belated attempt to build a rapport, though this was not and never had been his name.

"Sure, I'll do that. 'Luke.'"

This time, there was a hint of lurking scorn, but the Cop chose to ignore that too.

Sheriff Heath, the Cop noted, looked shockingly old—too old perhaps for cosmetic rejuve?—though his body was fit and strong. He was bald, heavily wrinkled, with a grey walrus moustache, and peering blue eyes. The Cop had been impressed at his bio: soldier, pirate, artist, scientist and bartender. Now, he was Sheriff of the 4th Canton of Lawless City.

"Through here."

The holograms of the crime scene didn't do justice to its horror. Blood and human flesh spattered the walls and ceilings. A screaming severed head was impaled on the bed; inside the mouth, which gaped unnaturally large, was a human heart, squeezed and squirted.

The Cop adjusted his decontam forcefield and hovered back and forth a centimeter from the ground. He used his finger-tweezers to take samples of blood and flesh, and mentally tried to keep a tally of the corpses. He saw legs and hands and entrails and a set of lungs that had fallen under the bed, and he noted that the carpets were damp with piss and strewn with half-digested food from the shredded stomachs of the victims.

At one point the Cop glanced behind, and was startled to see that the Sheriff was pale, and looked as if he wanted to throw up.

"Murder weapon?"

"We found nothing. We don't know what could have done this."

"Plasma beam? Samurai sword?"

"Look closer."

The Cop looked closer.

VISIT THE ORBIT BLOG AT

www.orbitbooks.net

FEATURING

BREAKING NEWS
FORTHCOMING RELEASES
LINKS TO AUTHOR SITES
EXCLUSIVE INTERVIEWS
EARLY EXTRACTS

AND COMMENTARY FROM OUR EDITORS

WITH REGULAR UPDATES FROM OUR TEAM,
ORBITBOOKS.NET IS YOUR SOURCE
FOR ALL THINGS ORBITAL.

WHILE YOU'RE THERE, JOIN OUR E-MAIL LIST
TO RECEIVE INFORMATION ON SPECIAL OFFERS,
GIVEAWAYS, AND MORE.

imagine. explore. engage.